Stephen Palmer was born in 1962 and brought up in Wales and Shropshire. He was educated in Shrewsbury and at the University of London, and currently works as a media technician. His main non-literary interest is music. His own ambient group have released several albums, and he plays guitar in another band. He is married with no children, and lives in Bedfordshire. He likes cats.

Memory Seed is Stephen Palmer's first novel.

Stephen Palmer was born in 1962 and brought up in Wales and Shropshire. He was educated in Shrewsbury and at the University of London, and currently works as a media technician. His main non-literary interest is music. His own ambient group have released several albums, and he plays guitar in another band. He is married with no children, and lives in Bedfordshire. He likes cats.

Memory Seed is Stephen Palmer's first novel.

MEMORY SEED

STEPHEN PALMER

ORBIT

An *Orbit* Book

First published in Great Britain in 1996 by Orbit

Copyright © Stephen Palmer 1996

The moral right of the author has been asserted.

A CIP catalogue record for this book is available from the
British Library.

ISBN 1 85723 376 X

Typeset by Solidus (Bristol) Limited
Printed and bound in Great Britain by
Clays Ltd, St Ives plc

0675581 8 3

Orbit
A Division of
Little, Brown and Company (UK)
Brettenham House
Lancaster Place
London WC2E 7EN

For Amanda

Acknowledgements

Many thanks to everybody who has helped and encouraged me so far: Amanda, Paul Thompson, George Cairns and Lee Collins.

In particular, thanks go to Dave Norman, to Tim Holman for invaluable help, and to Steve Kett, who read earlier drafts and suggested the title.

1

Using sheets of corrugated iron to construct a barrier, Zinina was able to contain the expanse of poison-specked foliage as it tumbled down the stairs of the house.

Rain outside, thrumming on the collapsed roof and facade, spattering shattered bacteria tubes and making them sizzle, reminded her that she was but yards away from the street, but the street was hidden behind curtains of green. The cellar was her only means of escape. Zinina removed a lever from the kit on her belt, switched on a lamp attached to her wrist and began worrying the trapdoor until, with a vapid hiss, it came free.

Judging by the smell of rot, the cellar below was encased in fungi. It was warm, dark and damp – ideal conditions for spores. Some cellars in this quarter of the city were now invisible behind mounds of fungi, smooth and grey like velvet cushions, but deadly. Zinina wrapped a mask over her nose and mouth, checked her gloves, tightened the elasticated bands around the tops of her thigh boots, and lowered herself down.

She studied the walls, now angry that she had placed herself in such a situation. The house seemed sound when she had slipped in an hour ago; but it had collapsed. No doubt she had triggered that.

Two grilles on a wall seemed promising, and even through the mask Zinina could tell that one led to a sewer. This grille she tore down. Using a dead pyuter as a mount, she pulled herself in and wriggled down until she was wholly within the shaft, checking the composition of the air with a scentstick before continuing. Warm brown liquid dripped on her as she squirmed down the shaft. Echoes of rippling slime reverberated back up to her.

Before she reached the sewer a vertical shaft appeared, a rusty ladder attached to its wall. Zinina pulled the lower rung. It crumbled in her hand. She tried the next, and the next, and these seemed firm. Squeezing herself around, then standing, she tested the ladder as far as she could. It was sound.

'Te qara Rien Zir,' she muttered as she climbed. She was nervous, not knowing where she might appear, her Citadel training a haze of memories smothered by fearful anticipation and the imagined barbs of flowers ready to pounce.

At the shaft top she lifted the cover and peered out. She had emerged into some sort of garden, perhaps once private. She clambered out and replaced the cover. Around her, sullen, stems and stalks stood heavy, as though sleepy with the weight of the drugs and poisons in their shafts. Zinina removed the mask and breathed deeply, glancing at the sky to see bright stars shining through a rent in the storm clouds.

Then she saw the glistening leaves of a moonflower. The thing was almost touching her. She studied its hooks, and the bloated sacs which lay behind them. The plant looked like a cross between a spider and a honeysuckle.

She heard a sound, a humming as though made by a bowed string, and saw a silhouette against the silver illuminated clouds. Realising that it would cause a momentary occultation, she tensed her body, then sprang.

She caught the shape of a hang-glider from the corner of her eye. Behind her, the moonflower jerked and hissed.

The garden was clearer than many. Although Kray had been surrounded west, north and east by temperate jungle, its southern boundary cliffs falling into the sea, it had not yet been breached by plants. Yet many places in the Green and Archaic Quarters were impassable. Zinina could see a few safe areas, but no path which would allow her to reach the gate in the street wall. Then she noticed steps leading into adjacent brickwork. An idea struck her.

Walking down the crumbling limestone steps, she examined the wall. Mortar had been consumed by moss and no brick retained a smooth face. Calm returned to her mind, and she checked her clothes and kit before preparing herself. Placing her hands on the wall, she straightened her back, tensed her thighs, and pushed. With a squelch, the wall collapsed and she clambered out on to the street.

Now she would have to hurry. Her contact would not wait forever and the Spired Inn was still some way north.

She passed by the Temple of Rien Zir. Only its wooden roof could be seen behind the protective screen of poison ferns, but Zinina knew that even at this late hour there would be people worshipping. As she walked by she thought she caught the siren wails and trance chants of some green ceremony. She walked on, humming an old sun song. Of course it would do no good. Tomorrow there would be rain.

She stopped. Nervously, her hands fluttered about the kit hanging from her belt. What was that shadow moving amongst the piles of decaying waste?

A cat. Zinina extracted the needle rifle from her belt and fired. The cat slumped with a yowl.

She nudged the palpitating body with her boot. Cats were rare in Westcity – the Temple of Felis stood to the east of Eastcity. Maybe it was on reconnaissance.

Moving on, almost jogging, she entered Sphagnum Street and passed the Cowhorn Tower. Nearby, from the remains of electricity pylons, great tangles of blue algae hung, many of the suffocating species, and although it was difficult to be certain through the drizzle Zinina could make out the remains of unfortunate Krayans stuck to the glutinous masses. Her gaze turned to the cobbled street. She was walking uphill now, to her right the great cliffs splitting up the Gardens, that rotting green heart of Kray; to her left the stacks and spires of homes in the Carmine Quarter. Up ahead, where the gradient became too steep, there were rusty cablecars.

At the cablecar compound she entered a vehicle. The faulty, flickering pyuter display showed 0 :01:0. One minute to go. By the light of the blue bacteria tubes, Zinina's skin seemed darker than ever.

Halfway up she saw again the hang-glider, a dark triangle with lamps glowing as bright as the sea, descending eastward as if out of control. She watched it fall out of sight. More than likely it was some independent trying to escape the city.

The cablecar halted. Some doors opened. Zinina strode along Crimson Street, noticing a priestess of Rien Zir making for the cablecar, her plaited blonde hair sheened green, her thigh boots covered in refuse. She was followed by a pair of defenders in red plastic coveralls, both apparently exhausted. She turned right into Morte Street.

This was where the Cemetery lay. To the south and east it spread, a vast area too dangerous for anyone other than revellers. There were bodies in the street as she walked, soaking, rotting, limbs either half eaten or algae-green. The drizzle seemed to carry their odour through her nostrils and down into her stomach.

There were very few residents so close to the Cemetery, perhaps none, and algae bulges belched from house doors.

Sticky leaves hung from the remains of windows and, from the edges of some, deadly yellow tendrils swayed. Streams eroded cobbles and paving slabs, churning up earth in some places, in others creating pools for thousands of orange worms; and as Zinina jumped over these she noticed the piles of discarded medical equipment that meant revellers had been active here. She sped on.

At last, through what was becoming a shower of foul-smelling rain, Zinina saw the domed roof and aquamarine lamps of her goal, the Spired Inn. She ran up to it.

The Spired Inn was built from the remains of an old posthouse, a place originally meant to defend local residents from inhabitants of the Gardens, but now devoted to ale and chess. It was a circular building of five storeys, outer walls entirely hidden behind tangles of blue ivy, shattered slates on the ground where they had landed. Zinina knew it well. She turned the handle of the beech door and entered.

Heat seemed to cradle her as she stamped in the water tray of the hall's green zone. They must have all three fires blazing inside. To two score cloaks, protectives and boots she added her own turquoise jumpsuit, taking her pointy-toed slippers from her kit, inflating them, and slipping them on before entering the common room in just her underwear.

The inn was lit by sea-fat candles two yards high, and by the luminous tubes of sputtering anjiqs, yellow with age. The common room was a single area of black oak alcoves and tables, cobwebs and dead lampshades hanging from the ceiling.

A couple of rats wagged their tails at her as she made for the bar, but she ignored them. She had seen Dhow-lin, the aamlon innkeeper. 'Tamina, Dhow-lin,' she called. 'Tamina!'

The ancient innkeeper turned and smiled. 'Zinina,

hello. It must be over a month since we saw you last. You made it through the last of the snow.'

Zinina smiled and nodded. Kray was now emerging from the worst winter ever experienced into its final year, the year in which the remains of humanity would be destroyed by green. 'Yes,' she said. 'And you didn't charge me for staying overnight.'

'You drank like an empty well that evening,' Dhow-lin replied, continuing the customary banter. 'Why should I need to charge? Now, then, your usual?'

Zinina nodded, lifting her kit to the penicillin-stained bar and opening its rear pockets. Dhow-lin, shuffling her dusty vests as if to dislodge fleas, turned to the array of tongs behind her and chose one. This she placed in the fire for a second, before using it to extract a tankard from the kiln. The tankard was allowed to cool in an anti-kiln before Zinina received her pint of dooch.

'Watcha got?' Dhow-lin asked, peering through a magnifying glass at the array of items that Zinina had arranged on the bar.

'This one should cover my account for the night,' Zinina replied. 'It's a spare pyuter processor for kilns.'

'Got some,' Dhow-lin replied. Zinina, who had not expected this reply, looked doubtfully at the scavenged items remaining. Dhow-lin poked at them with her forefinger.

'This a pyuter memory?' she asked.

'Eighty exabytes. Want it?'

Dhow-lin accepted it. Zinina lifted her pint and took a sip. The dooch chlorophyll was not yet dissolved, still stringy in the alcohol, so she swirled it around while surveying Dhow-lin's customers. Most were naked, and all of these she recognised, but a dozen at least were not local to this part of the Carmine Quarter, as evinced by their sweaty shirts and tabards. One of these she knew would be Erequen – the woman she must speak with. But which one?

Zinina had an idea. She turned to Dhow-lin. 'Hoy, is Aqa still here?'

'Yes.'

'Still dancing?'

Dhow-lin nodded. Zinina paused. 'And do Praes-lin and Daes-lin still play chess here?'

'They're playing right now behind that screen,' Dhow-lin replied. 'Why, sly-girl?'

'Oy, oy,' Zinina murmured, using the local slang. 'Do me a favour. Find Aqa and tell her I'll pay for her to dance. I'll just pop over and persuade the flute sisters to pause their board jousting.'

'S'pose it is a bit dead this evening,' Dhow-lin sniffed.

'Why not spliff up some incense to clear those sinuses?' Zinina said, giving a wicked grin.

Over behind the screen, the aamlon twins were indeed playing chess. They recognised Zinina and greeted her with hugs. Both were young, wearing cream underwear and the traditional aamlon neck-strings, red pearl in Praes-lin's case, tiger's eye for Daes-lin, and both were smoking pencil-thin tobacco cigarettes. Zinina noticed that Daes-lin had removed her once fashionable flower tattoo to leave a clean, simple scalp. Praes-lin's bald head was decorated with intertwining bramble motifs. She scratched a line of flea bites along one arm.

'Hoy, sisters,' said Zinina, grabbing a stool and sitting. 'How about some music?' Aamlon were famed for their music. 'But let's go easy on the flutes. I want *rhythm*. You play?'

'You'll buy?' Daes-lin asked, nodding at her empty goblet.

Zinina touched her arm. 'You owe me one, remember? Who rescued you from those frogs last year?'

'True.'

'But,' Praes-lin countered, 'you didn't rescue *me*.'

Zinina considered. 'How long would you have played for me?'

'Maybe an hour,' Daes-lin replied.

Zinina stood up. 'Give me half an hour, then, both of you, and we're even. See you.'

Zinina walked over to a chair and waited. Soon the aamlon twins were playing an exotic, wild tune on hand drums and flute, and Zinina was delighted to see another aamlon girl join in with her tambourines and hand cymbals. With Aqa belly-dancing, the stage was set. Zinina had chosen her chair carefully, for from it she could see everyone who might be Erequen. She sipped her dooch. The piece soon became a trance, and Zinina knew it would continue well into the evening. The atmosphere, hazy with smoke and vibrating with music, was perfect.

There: that was Erequen. It could be none of the other women here.

Zinina walked over, confident that nobody would notice her. She sat down by the old woman's side, noticing nasty bruises on her scalp and a green patina in her wrinkles, signs indicating great age, perhaps as many as fifty years. Mucus dribbled from both nostrils.

'Erequen, I was looking for you.'

'Good evening,' the old woman said. Her voice was very quiet, like a creaking piece of furniture, and Zinina had to lean over to hear her. 'Not too close. I've got the pestilence.'

Zinina leant back. Pestilence. Better not sit too close. Better clean the air, just in case. Zinina took an aerosol from her kit and sprayed.

'Why are you late?'

Zinina hesitated before answering. 'I am late, yeah. Sorry.' She did not want Erequen to know too much, but neither did she want her riled. 'Had an accident in a rickety house, that's all.'

After a pause, Erequen asked, 'So you were looking out for me?'

Zinina shrugged. 'You were the only one not tapping your feet to the rhythm. I knew it was you.'

'Hmph. Well, anyhow, you want to find a seed?'

'Sure do.'

Erequen nodded. 'It's possible, yes.'

Zinina reached into her underwear. 'This is a plastic biopad.' She handed the translucent sheet over. 'Payment. Take it, check it, it works. You'll get a month's food for that down the Mercantiles.'

Erequen sneezed into her shirt. 'What use is a month's food to me? I'll be dead in a week. Take it back, child. This information is for free. I'm never going south again. I'm on my way over to the Green Quarter.'

'Hoy, sure, sure,' Zinina said, placating Erequen with motions of her hands. 'Thanks.'

'The woman you are seeking is one Oquayan, who lives at number eleven, Blank Street. Are you familiar with the address?'

Zinina nodded. That meant rich homes at the northern reach of the Mercantile Quarter.

'Good. The code word is xenos. As long as you use it, Oquayan will know I sent you. Will you remember that?'

Zinina railed at what she felt to be a patronising tone. 'I may look like an independent, but I have full use of my mind, Erequen.'

'Then I may depart. Wait here for one full hour and enjoy the music.' And with that Erequen hobbled away. Zinina sprayed the air once more for safety.

'You deep in thought?' came Dhow-lin's voice from behind.

Zinina turned. 'Oh, yeah.'

'Where you living now?'

She could not say, of course. Gossip was the breath of life in these close, northern communities so near to the reveller realm of the Cemetery. 'I'm still down the Mercantiles.'

Dhow-lin looked her up and down. 'Doesn't do to leave yer home, Zinina. And we still ain't sure what you do.'

'I'll tell you all, one day.'

When the agreed hour had passed, Zinina left the inn and entered the drizzle, making south along her earlier route until she reached the crossroads of Lac and Sphagnum Streets, opposite the Temple of Rien Zir, at which point she made left along Lac Street, following the Garden Wall around until she found an alley that led south to Blank Street. Black winter seeds on six-foot fluffy umbrellas were floating across from nearby trees, and these Zinina avoided since many were home to glass weevils, parasites which had been known to jump off and kill people.

Up ahead, Zinina heard singing. Revellers. She slapped a muslin mask across her mouth and nose, readied the needle rifle, and crept into a dark doorway. There were three of them, and Zinina noticed that cotton wads were tied to their noses, almost certainly impregnated with drugs or hormones. All three were armed with dental syringes. They were the worst revellers – green revellers – dreaded for their destructive, and self-destructive, mania. You did not cross a green reveller.

The trio passed, and the whiff of their lice-ridden rags reached Zinina. She retched, far from unfamiliar with the smell.

Creeping along Blank Street she arrived at last opposite a lone house that, though not numbered, had to be the correct one. She had been counting down from thirty-one, the last house defended well enough to risk such a sign of wealth. The building had no windows and the wall was home to lumps of orange fungi, some formed into the shapes of ears and hands, while the door was remarkable for patches of luminous lichen. To either side stood wrought-iron gates leading to what seemed a large rear garden.

Zinina, not by nature nervous or faint-hearted, found herself afraid of what might be inside. The knocker was a brass affair in the shape of a dolphin with the ring in its mouth, a symbol that Zinina was not familiar with. She knocked.

A minute's silence. Then, 'Who is it?'

'My name is unimportant, but I am to say "xenos" to you.'

The door opened slightly, and the face of a woman appeared. Judging by the unkempt brown and white hair and the earrings, she was an adept of Rien Zir.

'Xenos,' Zinina repeated.

'Eh?'

'Xenos?'

'Oh,' the woman said, relieved. 'Come in, then, come in.'

'Are you Oquayan?'

'Yes.'

Her face, Zinina noticed when it was illuminated by a cracked anjiq, showed signs of green spot, although her eyes were large, clear and blue. She must have been a beauty in her youth. She wore leggings, a green coat, and gold rings on every finger.

'I see you're in with Rien ... with the Goddess.'

'I am,' Oquayan replied. Her manner was slightly ramshackle, as if she was wont to become lost in her own house, and Zinina wondered if loneliness had affected her mind – which was common in Kray. 'Now, this way, please. I'll take you into the gardens.'

The house was damp. Soggy ancient newspapers lined the floor. There was almost no furniture. A few holograms hung crooked amid the peeling wallpaper. The smell of mould permeated the air.

Zinina was led into the garden, which was huge. 'It's not dangerous,' Oquayan said. 'I know that sounds strange, but really it's not like a normal overgrown Kray garden. I know every corner of it.'

A realisation came to Zinina. 'You live out here?'

'Yes, in the summer house. Come along.'

Along a path lined with smouldering camphor on poles they strolled. Zinina gazed at the fantastic shrubs and trees to either side: bushes covered with pulsating red nets, plants with pyramid-shaped flowers, fronds with pyuter memories growing from their undersides.

'The seed you require is rare,' Oquayan was saying. '*Ficus xenos illuminatus* to give it its true name. I've never been asked for one. I have a single tree growing at the rear, you know.'

'Good.'

They passed a pond of green slime that seemed to contain glowing spheres rolling just under its surface. 'A low power pyuter,' Oquayan explained, waving a hand at it. 'I use it to calculate germination times. Are you interested in sex?'

'Eh?' Zinina stopped. The grass squelched under her boots.

'Do you like sex? I find it fascinating. The variety of organs plants produce is amazing, and the varieties of pollen. I could write an encyclopedia about it, I'm sure.'

Zinina nodded and walked on. From somewhere to her right, through copper beech, she could hear the calls of night birds, insects and spiders. Above a flower like a white hand she saw a vertical line of scent-drowsed hoverflies, and she felt for an instant what a peaceful, yet decadent place this must be to sleep in. Zinina found her fear departing, as if she was being seduced by the smell and the warmth of the garden.

They passed a turf hollow, a bowl in the ground. 'That's where I go to masturbate,' Oquayan said. 'It's so cosy. There are copper roots underneath, power lines from the Infirmary across the way. I seem to be cuddled by the earth, in there.'

Interested, Zinina paused to examine the turf. The grass was as fine as the fur on a mouse. 'Do you go there a lot?' she asked.

'Oh, yes. Now, there's the fig tree.'

Oquayan indicated a grove ahead. Zinina saw immediately that it was a research area. From every tree, every bush, objects hung, ranging from carbon fibres to complicated meshes of pyuter memory. Oquayan plucked a fruit from a nearby mare's tail. 'Here, eat it. Enough vitamins and minerals to last you a week.'

Zinina hesitated, the rules of the city drummed into her during childhood taking over.

'It's quite safe,' Oquayan said. She tossed it: Zinina missed, and bent to pick it up from the damp grass. 'But now you'll have to wash the mud off.'

Zinina took a water bottle from her kit, made sure that the red seal was intact, then opened it and washed the fruit. A scent of caramel emanated from it. She pulled aside a triangle of peel and plucked out a segment. It tasted of peaches and honey and it seemed to melt in her mouth. She devoured the rest.

At this, Oquayan paused, frowning slightly. 'When did you last eat?'

Zinina knew she had let her defences slip too far. She had not eaten a proper meal for some days. In her circumstances, it had been impossible. 'I've been working underground,' she said. 'Up the Carmines.'

Oquayan seemed satisfied with this. She beckoned Zinina towards a graceful tree and pointed at a spray of seed pods. 'These will grow into the pyuter system you want. They grow true. You're lucky. These are rare. I'll miss even one.'

'Erequen arranged everything?' Zinina said, hoping her prize was not slipping away. In reply, Oquayan pulled down a pod and handed it over. Zinina secreted it inside her kit. 'I'd better go,' she said.

Oquayan nodded. 'There's a back gate just behind that pyuton.'

'Is it defending anything?' Zinina asked, glancing through the drizzle at the metal and plastic woman.

'The gate. But she's seen us together so she won't harm you, will she?'

They walked to the gate and Zinina slipped through, finding herself in a narrow passage. 'Goodbye,' she said, smiling.

'For now.'

Zinina turned and walked away. The alley was badly overgrown, moss pillows in places, and pools swarming with worms. She trod carefully. But mere seconds after leaving the gate she felt the ground give way under her left boot, and her body shifted. She reached out to halt the fall, looking down to see a green pool opening, but the alley wall that her hand hit gave way, and she fell.

Struggling in the deepening puddle, green slime all around, something tugging at her boots, she screamed, realising that she had little chance of staggering out alone. Remembering the drill for alley holes she tried to kick out with her boots, hoping to damage whatever was sucking her down, but the pull just increased.

'Noonar, noonar! Help! Hilf, hilf!'

'I'll take that,' came a voice.

She twisted her torso to see Oquayan hooking her kit with a metal arm. With a swipe the aluminium cord was cut and the kit gone. Thigh-deep in the slime pool, Zinina stared.

'I just couldn't let it go,' Oquayan said.

'Pull me out!' Zinina screamed, panicking, slapping at the pool's contents, trying to push it away from her waist. 'Get me out!' Zinina screamed again. The force pulling her was stronger than ever. Now chest deep. Now neck deep. Oquayan stood, watching, a smile on her face.

Zinina went under. She screamed – swallowed. Gurgling sounds became heavy and immediate as her ears filled. Then she felt a hand grasp hers. Oquayan was pulling. Lungs bursting, Zinina let out her breath in a great bellow, and forced herself upward into the air.

Still she was pulled. In seconds she was out. Slime caught in her throat forced her to breathe in coughing gasps.

Unable to see, she felt herself being dragged along the alley. Lack of air made her head spin.

When they stopped, Zinina fell to one side. Then she felt a thump on her back, and she coughed up green slime, and breathed. There was a hiss, and a pinprick in her right arm.

Zinina, half-conscious, tried to look into Oquayan's face. She saw a flash of glass and recognised a syringe, but it was not Oquayan crouching at her side. As her conscious mind failed her, she caught the odour of menthol on the breath of her rescuer.

2

And then Zinina awoke.

She lay on a bed inside a house. Above her, the ceiling was mottled green, plaster hanging in flaps.

Able to move, to sit up, though she was dizzy and her limbs were weak, she studied the room further. The faint smell of water and rotting flesh meant that she was near the river – she thought she could hear it – while the style of oil paintings on the walls and the heavy, knitted blankets meant that the woman owning this house was an aamlon. Zinina sniffed the air and thought she smelled charnel-tree blossom, which only grew in Eastcity. Could she be in some hovel off Hog Street? Off Pine Street? There was only one way to find out. Zinina tried to get out of bed, but sprawled in a heap on the floor, her legs still shaky.

The door opened. From her position crouched beside the bed Zinina clutched for a weapon, finding nothing. She wore only an aamlon shift. No poinard. She shrank back.

In walked a woman. She was perhaps forty, with wrinkled skin though few discernible blemishes, and wore the traditional gohlen smock and the cultural neck-string, made of tiny ebony breasts with ruby nipples, of an aamlon. The woman had the most intense pair of blue eyes that Zinina had ever seen. But she was not armed. Her movements were slow, almost melancholy.

Zinina stared upward. 'Hello?'

'Tamina.'

Zinina knew but a score of aamlon words. 'Um,' she began, 'hilf, hilf. Don't say auveeders.'

The aamlon woman sat beside her. 'Who are you?'

'Zinina. Who're you?'

'Graaff-lin. I found you in a faint on my doorstep. Were you attacked by revellers?'

'Revellers wouldn't attack me,' Zinina said. 'Where am I?'

'In my bedroom. This is my house. It's near Onion Street.'

Zinina's guess had been correct. She was in the westerly reaches of the Old Quarter. 'How did I get here?'

Graaff-lin sat back, as if surprised. 'I assumed you could tell me that,' she replied.

'I was shoved in a hole up the Mercantiles,' Zinina said. 'So you didn't rescue me? Hoy, somebody did.'

'Then it is a mystery. Still, once you're fit, you can go home.'

Zinina shrugged, glanced away.

'Oh,' Graaff-lin said. 'I see.'

Silence fell between the pair. Graaff-lin stood up and went to close the internal shutters. Outside, evening had brought gloom. Zinina sensed unease in Graaff-lin's body language. 'I wonder who brought me here?' she asked.

Graaff-lin turned to reply. 'Nobody I know, that is sure.'

Zinina frowned. 'You can't be certain of that.'

'Good point,' Graaff-lin admitted with a frosty smile. She sat on the bed, indicating that Zinina should also. 'I suppose some acquaintance of mine could have carried you here. A clerical friend, perhaps.'

'You a cleric?'

'I am a priestess of the Dodspaat.'

So, an aamlon priestess. This could presage a stroke of luck, for now that she had the *xenos* —

'My kit! Where's my clothes?'

Graaff-lin moved to calm her, grasping her wrists. 'Your clothes are quite safe, stewing in my antiseptic bin.'

'Gotta have me kit, Graaff-lin. Where is it?'

She remembered. Oquayan had snatched it from her as she had fought for her life. But then, from under the bed, Graaff-lin pulled a row of leather pouches on two belts. Her kit. Her rescuer must have somehow reclaimed it from Oquayan and restored it intact to its rightful owner. Such deeds were unusual. Zinina fumbled inside one of the pouches to find the precious seed, safe, cloaked in fluff and dust. Quickly she zipped the pouch shut.

'Is all well?' Graaff-lin asked.

'Valuables,' Zinina said, shrugging, pushing the kit back under the bed. She did not want the aamlon rummaging through her belongings.

'You really have no home?'

Zinina was too exhausted to lie. 'I deserted from the Citadel Guard.'

Graaff-lin had a way of nodding in a soothing manner and, noticing this, Zinina wondered if she had been manipulated into saying too much. Those limpid eyes seemed sad, but behind them lay intelligence. 'What happened?' Graaff-lin asked.

'I escaped during the dusk shift at the Citadel. We were patrolling the perimeter. I ran north. A detachment followed me. I hid in a house, but it started to collapse – poison ferns went for me – and I had to escape. That was when somebody shoved me down the hole.'

'Well, you can stay here awhile. I am devoted to the Dodspaat and live alone. Later ... we shall see.'

Sincerely grateful, Zinina grinned and replied, 'Thanks. Thanniy, I should say! You possibly saved my life.'

Graaff-lin stood. 'Somebody did. Now, if you are steady on your feet I'll show you around the house.'

It was not much of a house – four large rooms on one floor. There was an air of haphazard carelessness about the place, excepting the bedroom. One work room was filled with benches, tools and test instruments, and everywhere, even in the kitchen and study, pyuter junk and softly glowing rigs lay. Of course, aamlon were famed for their pyuter skills. Zinina, while not enamoured of the place, saw that life here would at least be tolerable.

Midnight passed and Graaff-lin retired to her bed, leaving Zinina to the study couch. But Zinina had one task to perform before sleep. From her kit she took the seed.

On the sill outside the west-facing window stood ten pots, some growing herbs, others empty. Zinina opened the window, took one of the empty pots, shook out the mud and grit, then made for the kitchen. With water from a red-top bottle (guaranteed pure by Eastcity Water Station), she washed the pot, then filled it with sterile earth and planted the seed, returning her treasure to the sill. With window closed and shutters clamped, she slept.

She slept in fits. The couch was lumpy and her blankets itched. The aamlon shift she wore was draughty. Evanescent nightmares – chased by hang-gliders, pursued by Citadel Guard; her escape from the collapsed house – troubled the stormy night's small hours. When rain tinkled across the window panes she imagined flights of flower barbs, like tiny wasps attacking her face.

Groggy and dry-eyed, she greeted Graaff-lin in the morning with little zest. Graaff-lin, for her part, seemed unconcerned by her new lodger, unless the air of calm masked inner uncertainty. She offered Zinina a breakfast of apple chunks and nut biscuits, and only spoke when she had finished eating. 'We will have to change your status. You cannot remain a lapsed defender and survive. I think it would be best if you were re-registered as an independent.'

Zinina did not care for the tone of this. 'I ain't sure that's possible. I'd get far less food and water if I was an indep.'

'You were a member of the Citadel Guard,' Graaff-lin said sharply. 'That's quite a high post. They noticed your disappearance, and will have recorded it.'

'Couldn't say.'

'As you will. But it is my guess that you will be listed as a deserter, in which case both water stations and both food stations will refuse to serve you. Your food card will be invalid, Zinina.'

Reluctantly, Zinina agreed. 'Watcha think I should do?'

Graaff-lin took her into the pyuter workshop, where a large polythene screen was set up, attached to a customised rig shaped by growth into a knobbly gourd. 'This screen will show us the information,' she explained, her low, keening voice almost lost as a wind flurry made the roof shudder. 'What's your kit number?'

'211,121.' It was emblazoned on the leather.

Graaff-lin tapped a pad. The pyuter had listened to Zinina and was already navigating the rickety data structures of the Citadel's networks. 'Found,' it said.

'Now,' Graaff-lin continued, 'I have to make one small alteration. It is a delicate matter.' She tried to smile, but it was almost as if she was out of practice. Zinina noticed, however, that her teeth were pitted.

Because the networks were convoluted and inept – rumour had it that one pyuter wilted somewhere inside the Citadel every time an electronic decision was made – it was half an hour before Zinina became an independent, complete with shiny crimson food card stamped with her name, class and kit number. She thanked Graaff-lin.

'Not at all,' came the reply.

Graaff-lin had been right. A deserter stood out, even by the myopic standards of the Citadel. Becoming an independent granted her a certain amount of freedom, which she could exploit in the coming days and weeks. She eyed Graaff-lin, trying to decide whether her host was a fundamentalist or more enlightened. The fact that she had changed Zinina's status made one thing clear: Graaff-lin was prepared to break the law.

'Graaff-lin?'

'Yes?'

They were sitting in the study. Gazing at the faded erotic prints hanging on the walls, Zinina thought how best to phrase her question. 'Graaff-lin, you must be really wondering what's going to happen to us all?'

'I am a priestess of the Dodspaat – the Dead Spirits, in common talk. We're working on a translation of their plan.'

'This is Kray's last year.'

Unruffled, Graaff-lin replied, 'Thousands of Krayans would disagree. It is after all a matter of belief. I believe the Dodspaat communicate the ancient world's wisdom to the faithful, from their homes in the afterlife, and we spread their message in order to save humanity. I work in the serpent department.'

'The what?'

'The serpents of Eastcity. Well, of our southerly quarters.'

Zinina nodded. Everybody knew of the serpents, and that they were merely antiquated oddities. Only the priestesses of the Dodspaat believed that they divulged glimpses of the future in coded rhyme. As a child, Zinina had gone east to listen to them, but that was all. 'You're seriously studying them?' she asked.

'It is part of my calling. Wisdom arrives from many sources, Zinina. It arrives from beyond the grave and from the future. The Dodspaat are wise. It is a matter of deep regret to me and my sisters that their tongue is so difficult to translate, for otherwise their thoughts would more clearly show how we can escape our predicament.'

'I'm sorry, but I can't be having with all that. This is the last year. Everyone knows it, though not everyone admits it.'

Graaff-lin hesitated. 'As an aamlon I have gifts as a manipulator of pyuters and pyuter networks. Why should I not use that skill to help save humanity?'

Zinina sighed.

'But you asked me if I wondered what might happen to Kray. Well, at the moment I don't know the fate of the city.'

'You'd like to though,' said Zinina, knowingly. 'Maybe . . . I can help.'

'Only the serpents can foresee the future. Only they can help.'

'Can we keep off serpents, eh?'

Graaff-lin stood up. 'I will take you to one. It will make a prophecy, and you can stay with me until that prophecy comes about. Then we shall see who is correct.'

Zinina also stood, seeing the opportunity for a bit of fun. 'It's a deal.'

The alleys between Onion Street and Pine Street were flooded, a daily hazard this close to the river. Zinina hesitated before leaving the safety of the porch and entering the rain – this was her first trip into the city since her rescue – but in moments her hood was up, her boots were squelching in mud, and she was wading with Graaff-lin down the alley. In some places the water was up to her waist. They noticed blue mats of algae, that Zinina knew to be infected, and these they avoided. Coming to a barrier of sandbags, they climbed over and splashed into a street suffering only from puddles, and this they followed, making south. 'Mind the lavatory grubs,' Zinina warned. 'They can bite through leather. If you smell ammonia, jump away.'

In Min Street, Graaff-lin stopped at an alcove in a stone wall. Zinina saw the chainmail serpent inside – a cobra – rise to a listening position, chinking like a purse of coins.

'Good morning,' Graaff-lin said. 'I am Graaff-lin of the temple of the Dodspaat.'

'Tamina, Graaff-lin,' the serpent hissed.

'Please speak in Krayan for the benefit of us all. Now, tell me, not what the future holds for me, but for the city.'

Zinina nodded. The crafty aamlon was trying for the most general reply possible, the vaguest answer, in order to win the point. A minute passed. Rain droplets splashed into puddles. They heard the choking putter of a hang-glider engine. Then, 'This is not easy, for people are small, Kray is big. On the other hand, people free will, Kray moves on.' Interested despite her scepticism, Zinina listened as the serpent continued. 'Free will for individuals, trends for societies.'

Graaff-lin's face grew excited. 'What trends do you see, serpent?'

'The solution is in the petals, just as the bee is in the hive.'

'And?'

But the cobra had seen its fill of the future, and remained silent.

'Try another,' Zinina suggested.

At the lower end of the street, in a flooded portion, they saw a coral snake, no more than a foot above the waters, its alcove smothered in algae. Graaff-lin said, 'Hello, I am Graaff-lin. Tell me what you see of the Portreeve's plan for Kray.'

Zinina gasped, taken aback by the audacity. Minutes passed. She thought she heard a faint ticking, as of a clock heard at the end of a long tunnel, coming from the mouth of the snake. Then it said, 'This is your prophecy. I see for you a green cushion falling upon a waif.' No further words came and they turned away, but the snake had not finished. 'The plan is a dwan,' it said.

Graaff-lin spun around. The snake did not move – or speak. 'I want to go home,' Graaff-lin told Zinina. 'I'm feeling confused.'

Zinina agreed. The trip had not gone as she had expected. 'What does dwan mean?' she asked.

'I do not know. It is not an aamlon word.'

'Sure ain't a jannitta word. And it ain't Krayan.'

They trudged back. Entering the garden of Graaff-lin's house, Zinina, walking just behind the aamlon, caught a movement through the rain. A shadow receding. Her senses, attuned better than most to the vicissitudes of street life, felt danger. She grabbed Graaff-lin's wrist; pulled her back against the garden wall.

'Someone there,' she whispered.

Graaff-lin had not understood. Zinina thrust her aside and with a yell ran at the side of the house, needle gun raised. She saw a figure dart off. By the time she was around the side the figure was gone, leaving a smashed pane of glass.

Zinina stopped Graaff-lin by the window. 'Stand there. I'll deal with this.' She examined the fragments and the sill, saying, 'The woman didn't get in. No wet prints inside. Strip of cotton here from a suit – tough, good quality. Maybe a defender suit. And look, little wires, nice 'n' shiny. Them's from heated gloves, them is. You were lucky, Graaff-lin, you were almost burgled by a real professional.'

Graaff-lin only managed a querulous, 'But who? And why?'

They entered the house. Zinina went to sit in the study. Graaff-lin was indeed an intelligent woman. Yet Zinina felt sure that despite her orthodoxy there was a subversive side to the aamlon, timid perhaps, but there none the less. It was a trait Zinina could exploit ... a trait Zinina *wanted* to exploit. She decided that, when Graaff-lin came in with the tea, she would declare her interests.

'I gotta plan,' Zinina mumbled, as they drank rose tea.

'A plan?'

'Well, more a mission. I need an accomplice. Honest, Graaff-lin, I'm here by accident, but I think I know how to find out about the Portreeve's plan.'

Graaff-lin must have been surprised, but she hid her reaction behind the soft, sad manner. 'The Citadel,' she mused, staring into her teacup.

This sounded promising to Zinina. Graaff-lin, had she scruples, or at least those scruples the Citadel leaders would like its citizens to have, would have denounced the project. But she sounded intrigued. Graaff-lin closed her eyes, sat back, and seemed to go to sleep. Zinina slurped her tea, pouring more from the pot. Eventually Graaff-lin, eyes still shut, said, 'I don't entirely trust you, if I am to admit the truth, but I might be willing to make the attempt. We must know what the Citadel is planning. And it is true that with my pyuter skills and your ... street wisdom, we could make a formidable team.'

Zinina stood. 'Then we pierce the Citadel a week today, you and me.'

* * *

Next morning, as the winds began to gust from the south and the rain intensified, Zinina donned her street protectives and left for the centre of the Old Quarter. At the end of Broom Street she noticed a free wall screen, flickering. There was a green patina over it in which somebody had scrawled 'Live it up!', but the pads were clean and smelled of alcohol, indicating usage. She tapped in a random destination address, then, having checked that nobody in the street was watching her, took a thick needle from her kit and prodded it into one of the data ports, thereby ensuring a secure line. Then she removed a small unit shaped like a snail from one pocket and eased it into the other data port. She tapped a pad and said, 'Ready?'

'Ready,' came the synthesised voice – warbling, Zinina noticed, which meant that the wall screen was failing.

'Cut into any line. Order Q.'

'Ready.'

She heard a beep, then a voice – the voice of Qmoet. 'Hello?'

They spoke in the jannitta tongue. 'It's Zin. No bugs or snoops?'

The screen flashed red: all clear.

Zinina relaxed, leaning against the screen fascia. 'I'm safe. I had an accident, but I'm safe. I'm with an aamlon nixie-worshipper called Graaff-lin.'

'Who?'

'Cleric of the Hu Junuq.'

'Is she safe?'

Zinina paused before answering, 'Don't know exactly. We almost had a burglar – proper defender footpad, like. I wonder if she's on to something? Dunno, yet. Anyhow, I'll stay with her a bit.' It wasn't exactly a lie.

'Be careful,' came Qmoet's response. 'We don't want to

lose quality like you. So nobody from the Citadel got hold of you?'

'I think I'm free. They almost had me holed up in a house. Listen, tell Eskhatos I'm about to set up the next job – the tunnelling one. Got that?'

'Yes. Anything else?'

'Nah, I'll report later,' said Zinina. 'I'm an indep, now, by the way, network logged and all. Hoy, how's Ky?'

'Much better. We pumped her full of antibiotics, so she's wobbly, but alive.'

'Good! Look, kiss Woof for me, eh? Gotta go. 'Bye.'

''Bye.'

Zinina unplugged her two screen fixers and walked away, deep in thought.

She heard singing to one side of the street. Revellers. Better jump into a doorway and sit tight. She waited. There were five or six of them, dressed in sack-cloth and ripped breeches, skin filthy, clutching empty bottles and the stalks of mushrooms they had consumed. Zinina listened to them sing.

> The Earth is fighting back, we say,
>   and we are all to blame.
> The Earth is having fun, we say,
>   and we are all the prey.
> This place is full of rot, we say,
>   goodbyes ring out today.
> So drink and sod it all, hurray!

3

There was nobody else in the crimson-carpeted hallway. Arrahaquen paused at a gilt mirror to look at herself.

She saw a woman, thirty years old, almost six feet tall with a figure best described as voluptuous, bald head shining, brown eyes round and sad and accentuated with kohl, lips full. All Kray blots covered by cosmetics. She twirled once or twice, to look from the other angles. Hmmm . . . The black shorts and blue woollen jacket that she wore seemed a little loose.

Someone coming. She hurried back to the operations room, opening the door with her optical key.

Pyuters chattered and sprays of bio-memory hanging from the ceiling throbbed with blue light. Underneath all this eight people worked, among them Ammyvryn, who today wore a simple blue jumpsuit. 'I'm back,' Arrahaquen said, smiling.

'You've been a long time.'

'Mother, this is Defender House. I'm not likely to be ambushed in the lavatories.'

Her mother scratched a spot on her chin. She looked old, wrinkles beginning to acquire those lines of green that meant her one claim to Krayan beauty, the clear complexion, was gone. She had not depilated her scalp for some time, and a fuzz of brown hair made her look even more dishevelled. Only adepts of the Goddess could keep their hair in Kray.

Eventually Ammyvryn said, 'Never mind all that. Are we ready with the new defender schedules?'

Arrahaquen glanced over at the wall-screen. 'No.'

Her mother thumped the oaken desk in front of her. 'They get slower every day. It's the pyuter hearts. Deeselin and Spyne know how to steal all the pyuter power!' And she thumped the desk again, as if that would solve her problem.

Arrahaquen stroked her mother's shoulders. 'Just wait. I'll slip into the gazebo if you like, to check progress.'

'Don't bother,' Ammyvryn grumbled. 'And me with a full meeting in half an hour.'

'I saw Uqeq as I went out,' Arrahaquen said.

Her mother seemed flustered. 'How did she look? Did she say anything?'

'She looked pensive.'

Ammyvryn got up and paced around her daughter. 'There's been an accident outside, in the city. A hang-glider crash. I think it's serious, and the agent hasn't reported back. Uqeq will harangue us about it.'

'I haven't heard any rumours.'

Ammyvryn stopped, and Arrahaquen found herself staring into those watery green eyes.

'Give your mother a call. Yes, call her on the networks, secure line, and ask her if she saw anything a couple of nights ago. Any gas flares, that sort of thing. Do it now.'

'All right.'

Ammyvryn tightened her creaky leather belt. 'I'd better prepare for the Portreeve.'

Arrahaquen departed for the communications cellar,

but her mother was not answering calls and the Observatory pyuters refused to say what she was doing. So Arrahaquen left a message, then departed Defender House for her own rooms. A clock chimed the hour.

She walked across the top of the Citadel. Rain pounded the perspex streets, making the packets of light within them seem like angelic mercury, rolling hither and thither on their speed-of-light errands. Here in Om Street, where the buildings were only a few storeys high, walls on both sides flickered, but as she walked downhill to the north, and entered Rosinante Street, the great towers to either side rose up into blackness and even seemed to curl over and threaten her. She reached the block of flats that held her own home, and walked to the top floor.

She crept into the hall: silence. She made an electronic survey: nothing present. In the lounge burned an incense stick inserted into the urethra of a gold phallus. The blue carpet was bald in places, but these patches were covered by jannitta rugs made circular in the shape of daisies. The place was full of furniture, but the effect was of opulence, not overcrowding. A window looked out over Rosinante Street. Arrahaquen washed her hands, knocking the hot tap to ensure its inner valve did not stick, then dressed for the city in plastic protectives, thigh boots with top-elastics to ensure nothing fell inside, a heated hat and, of course, her kit. As she walked towards the door she looked inside a cardboard box – one empty flowerpot and a bag of earth sealed with a crimson twist. She departed, left the block, and hurried down the steep steps of Rosinante Street to the northern gate.

At the gate she was stopped. It was a sturdy construction, all steel, flickering screens and automated laser rifles, occupied by five of the Citadel Guard; and even though she was Arrahaquen, known throughout the Citadel – and beyond for that matter – she felt a thrill of fear as she gazed at the jet-black visors, metallic one-pieces and huge cowhide boots shod with titanium. Who were they? It was not permitted even for her to know their identities, so that bribery and blackmail be impossible. Only her mother, Defender-in-Chief, knew.

'Pass?' came the pyuter-synthesised voice. She heard a whirr of electronic breathing above the din of rain.

Arrahaquen handed over a scarlet card. The woman flashed it under a laser beam. Another pyuter voice: 'Clear. Hurry along.'

It was handed back and Arrahaquen was let through the Citadel Wall. She paused, glancing back. The Wall, the great black ring surrounding the Citadel, pierced only at the four cardinal points, was slick with rain. Lidded eyes and grasping arms transplanted from the bodies of wrecked pyutons studded its matte exterior. Two or three bodies held in a vice grip lay slumped against it, one gnawed by dogs. Arrahaquen hurried on up Malmsey Street, then turned into Onion Street, passing the Dead Spirits temple then crossing the river and making north towards the Gardens. She tied on a mouth mask to conceal her face.

Up Culverkeys Street she walked, past the Infirmary with its thousand photobacteria tubes and its incinerators smoking, through the maze of alleys between the Gardens and the Mercantile Quarter, until she spied the street that was her goal. A collapsed wall blocked her way, but she climbed over and splashed into the foot-deep flood waters behind. Leeches swarmed over the area. She counted down the Blank Street houses to number eleven, and knocked on its door's chromium plates.

'Who is it?' came a phlegmy voice.

'I've come to buy something off you. Is that Oquayan?' The door opened and a rifle emerged. 'I'm a defender,' Arrahaquen said, showing the pale face behind the door her Citadel pass.

'Hmmph. Come in. What do you want?'

'Something from your remarkable garden,' Arraha-quen replied, soothingly.

Oquayan led Arrahaquen through her musty house into a conservatory hot as a furnace, and then out into the garden.

'So what do you want?' Oquayan asked.

'A seed off a fig tree.'

Oquayan gestured her to follow. 'Which species exactly?'

'*Ficus veritas illuminatus.*'

'Hmmph. That tree there, with the sprays of bean-shaped pods. Pick one off the lowest branch. One only, mind.'

Arrahaquen did as she was bid, then showed Oquayan a roll of units to choose from as payment. A processor was chosen.

'Rush of interest in *ficus*, then,' Oquayan remarked.

Arrahaquen frowned. 'Pardon?'

'Some other gal after a *ficus* – the *xenos illuminatus*. Know her?'

Arrahaquen felt her throat tighten with apprehension.

'Um, who was this?' she asked.

'Gal who visited me not two days back.'

'And her name?'

'Didn't get it, unfortunately,' Oquayan replied; and her face assumed a dark expression. 'Not a defender, though, 'cos she was starving, with the look of some green marketeer.'

'She wasn't a defender? Surely only a citadel woman could have—'

'She caused me lots of trouble,' Oquayan said, face flushing pink. She began to walk back to her house. 'I don't know her name. I wish I did, and the name of the filthy scoundrel who attacked me.'

'Couldn't you even describe her?'

Oquayan seemed to glower with rage. 'If I give you an image will you never darken my life again?'

'Never, I promise, by the mind of the Goddess.'

Oquayan led Arrahaquen through the house and out into Blank Street, where she slammed the door. Two minutes passed by, Arrahaquen uncertain of what to do. Then a slip of damp paper was pushed under the door. Arrahaquen picked it up.

She saw a tall, slender jannitta woman of striking beauty, complexion perfect, if a little tanned, with a haughty expression and mysterious eyes. She wore a nondescript jumpsuit splashed green. Most probably an independent, although she was possibly a priestess. The face, most peculiarly, seemed familiar – or was it the attitude of her body? If only the image could move . . .

Suddenly Arrahaquen had a vivid mental image of Oquayan leading the woman through her garden. It persisted for some seconds then left her mind. She blinked, stunned. The picture had seemed like a memory. But now she was certain she knew the woman.

Back at her apartment, Arrahaquen went straight to her main rig. As it flickered with lights a movement in the corner of her eye made her glance away.

Scorpion.

A scorpion two feet long.

It skittered at her, fast as a rat, and she screamed and kicked out. Luckily its claws did not cling to the leather of her boots. She rushed into the kitchen. The thing was so fast it was alongside her in seconds. Arrahaquen jumped on to the table, which skreeked across the tiled floor in response and almost made her lose her balance.

It could not follow her. With futile stabs it tried to pierce her boots with its sting. Appalled, Arrahaquen stared.

Wildly, she looked around the kitchen for weapons. She would not stand a chance if it got close.

Knives – hopeless. Forks. Bottles of perry. A bucket. A bucket could be useful. She grabbed it from its hook.

The scorpion was still jumping at her. She watched it, judged the moment, then dropped the bucket. With a clatter it fell over the scorpion.

Terrific whacks made the bucket clang, and it jerked across the floor, but the scorpion was trapped. Arrahaquen ran into her bedroom, grabbed her laser pistol, and returned. She threw a book at the bucket then fired as the scorpion sprang out. Hit.

Then pitch blackness. There was a rustle, and the chirrup of a lock-breaker. So she had an enemy, and her enemy was no amateur. Arrahaquen readied a stun pistol and crouched behind the bedroom door. She saw a black shadow twist in the gloom. Had she been heard? It was difficult to see what was going on because now the outer door acted as a mirror, reflecting the image of the sea into her eyes. She pushed open her door and fired at random.

There was a groan, then a thump. More rustling, then bootsteps on the stairs. Arrahaquen followed, firing down the stairwell at her quarry. People were now emerging from their own front doors. Arrahaquen caught a glimpse of a black-cloaked figure, a short woman it seemed, and she yelled for the escaping invader to be halted. But a gas bomb detonated, and then only coughs and sneezes were her answers.

Arrahaquen thought fast. Rushing into her apartment she shook a rack of bacteria tubes to give light.

Arrahaquen could not follow on foot, but she could use the Citadel network. Quickly, she opened a link to the bank of camera images that the Citadel Guard used, and accessed a routine to control them. She focused on her block. Just as its front doors appeared on the sputtering screen she saw the short woman running out. It was not an unfamiliar woman. Someone she knew, then. Fear and desperation began to well up as she realised that her enemy was a real person. Somebody really was trying to kill her.

'I must follow her. Rosinante camera, you're pointing the wrong way . . . lost her. Lost her.'

Arrahaquen sat back. She heard heavy boots clomping up the stairs: Citadel Guard.

At her door she waited, a damp mask over her face to avoid the effects of the now rising fog of gas. Two suited figures emerged from the white, billowing clouds, spectral and weird with their black visors and creaking suits.

'What's going on?' came a pyuter voice.

Arrahaquen showed them her card. 'Intruder. She got away down Rosinante Street. I don't know who it was.'

'All right, we'll clear up. Close your door. We'll have the maintenance crowd up here to replace that smashed exit.'

Arrahaquen did as she was bid. Inside, she noticed the dead body of the scorpion. It had discharged its venom like a bee, dying with fangs loose on twists of skin hanging out from its jaws. She threw it away.

So far she had been attacked by a snake, a scorpion, endured two attempted poisonings and a deliberate water infection. Who was it?

She knew of no enemies. Her mother had enemies – all members of the Red Brigade did – but why kill Ammyvryn's daughter? She knew too few secrets to be valuable. And this had to be an inside attack. Nobody from outside the Citadel could make five such attempts. One, maybe, but not five.

Her pyuter screen was still flickering, pulling her thoughts back to the woman who had bought a *ficus* seed. She sat at the rig and requested lists and portraits of known jannitta defenders. Hundreds passed by, none the woman portrayed in her picture. She called up lists of jannitta priestesses, these rather meagre because only defenders were accurately logged, but again did not locate the woman. She sat back, flummoxed.

She lay back and tried to relax. It was impossible. She locked the door and every window, then checked each room again for assailants. Nothing. She took a green glass bottle of dooch and drank. Now she relaxed.

Her mind wandered. She wondered what her mother was doing up at the Observatory. She wondered about the end of Kray. She navigated the streets of the Citadel with her mind's eye, forcing nothing. The westerly gate. Zinina.

Zinina was the name. How it came to her, she did not know. Hadn't there been a defender Zinina in the Citadel Guard? The pyuters said no. But Arrahaquen was certain there had been, though the insistent denials dented her belief.

One last deed she performed before making for her bed. Emptying the bag of earth into the flowerpot, she planted the *ficus* seed, watering the soil well, then placing the pot on the south-facing window sill.

A storm woke her at dawn next morning, but the brief meteorological tantrum brushed over Kray to leave rain set in, and a gloom so deep that people were still using torches as night became day. As Arrahaquen prepared her breakfast – roast cashews, toast, minted honey and blackberry tea set on a silver salver – she made a decision. For now, she would forget the elusive jannitta and concentrate on her attacker. A pyuton replica would be made by Majaq-Aqhaj, the sentient mechanician used by the Red Brigade to devise their agents and technological sundries, and this double Arrahaquen would use to cover her necessary absences from the Citadel. But the whole affair would need to be kept secret. Only her mother and a handful of close friends knew of the four previous attempts.

Locking her door, she called Ammyvryn. 'It's happened again,' she said.

'Number five. Mmmm. Somebody doesn't want you around. All right, I'll make enquiries.'

Thanks, mother. 'If you like.'

'I hope you're safe in there. Invite a friend around to keep you company. Oh – you are all right?'

Arrahaquen smiled wanly. 'Yes. A little shaken.'

'I'll see you tomorrow, then.'

A tear escaped Arrahaquen's eye as she closed the link. No sympathy there. But for the moment she did not want to speak with her friends. All she wanted to do was escape her lot in the Citadel.

Arrahaquen thumped her chair in frustration. She *had* to uncover the truth. Only months remained, if the predictions were correct. But she felt like a child still, and she felt hatred towards her mother for keeping her so, and towards her mother for hiding like a hermit in the Observatory and ignoring her. Arrahaquen knew she was something of a loner, but knew also that she could enjoy the company of other people. It had to be the right people, however.

And she could not simply resign her job. She was Ammyvryn's aide. It simply could not be done. She sometimes wondered if she really had feelings. Often she was treated as if she had none; as if she was just Ammyvryn's daughter, who performed such-and-such a job for the good of Kray.

At Defender House, as she arrived two hours after dawn to begin the task of instructing defender groups, all was normal except for the loss overnight of the Jasmine

Group. They had been caught in a landslide at the very northern tip of the city – at Highgate, the ancient gate of Kray that had long been deserted and left to rats and buzzards. Arrahaquen allowed herself a bitter laugh at this news, for it was the northerly walls of Kray that were expected to crumble first under green pressure.

The day passed without incident. Arrahaquen felt irritable, lost almost. Her job carried responsibility, but she felt as though she was dreaming her day away. She cared little for the great maps of Kray, and their little ladybird-mounted lights that signified defender positions within the city.

She had been taught all her life not to be selfish, for the sake of Kray. Now she needed to act for herself. And her privileged access to unique Citadel networks would enable her to do just that.

4

Zinina checked her augmented kit. It consisted of satchels made of leather and aluminium, individually numbered and tied to a Citadel record. Only revellers failed to carry them in the city, and only revellers failed to understand their worth. Zinina added extras to her kit; a length of nylon rope, two sachets of chemicals to make more rope if need be, various lamps, and a wallet of pyuter gadgets designed to circumnavigate irritating Citadel routines.

It was midnight. Into the rainstorm she stepped, a subdued Graaff-lin at her side. Zinina pulled the drawstrings tight on her hood, checked the 'ready' light on her rifle, and headed out into the alley.

They splashed up Hog Street. A unit of defenders, grime streaking their exhausted faces, jogged by on some errand. Zinina noticed sniffer slugs – the great foot-long black products of some subterranean sewer in Ixia Street – following the slime trails of snails, noticing too how they trapped their prey, crushed their shells, and ate them. Up above, Zinina noticed the orange spark of a hang-glider engine. And far away, glimpses of black in the softly glowing sea indicated the arrival of giant turtles to the shores of Kray.

They hastened north, passing through the Mercantile Quarter, then making along Culverkeys Street until they arrived at the border of Kray's least populous area, the Gardens.

Nearby lay nine dead solar mirrors and Kray's ailing Power Station. This was an old area. Zinina stamped her feet and waited for Graaff-lin to catch up.

She smelled menthol. It was just a sweet hint in the melange of methane and rot, but she recognised it. She peered through the rain. A few hooded figures splashed along the street, but nobody she recognised.

The moment passed. Thunder rolled far off. Graaff-lin slipped from a passage and ran up to her. 'You beat me to it,' she said with a thick cough. Zinina noticed an antibiotic pad clipped to her mouth and two aerated lozenges in each nostril, a sure sign that Graaff-lin was ill. She wondered if her spluttering, pale, wasted-looking companion was up to the task ahead.

'Are you fit?' she asked.

'Yes. It's the sudden chill. I'm wearing a heated jumpsuit. I'm sorry I stopped, but I had to put this pad in my mouth.'

Zinina nodded. 'Got all your pyuter stuff? Odds and stuff?'

'I am ready,' Graaff-lin replied.

Zinina led Graaff-lin to a narrow passage and pointed out the concrete rubbish dump. 'This is a dead end. See that rusty steel cover? It's our way in. Follow me.'

Graaff-lin did as she was bid, swallowing a handful of pills while Zinina produced an iron rod to prise out the cover. Sheets of green water hindered Zinina, but most of it swirled into the hole created as she pulled up the cover. 'Jus' jump,' she said, shining a bacteria torch into the hole. 'It's only a couple of yards. Go on, I'll follow.'

Once Graaff-lin had entered Zinina followed, pulling

back the cover behind her. She looked around. In the azure light of her torch she saw rusty pyutons, wood cases, streaks of mould, and a quantity of water in puddles. The place seemed not too decayed, though, which came as a relief.

'I'll light a lamp,' Graaff-lin said. Yellow light merged with the blue.

Only one exit presented itself. This led into a similar room, dryer but dustier, and looking back they could see clouds of dust rising and settling. 'On into that tunnel,' Zinina said, leading the way. For five hundred yards they walked, until they entered a third room with no exit bar a trapdoor. This Zinina hauled up. She dropped herself into the room below.

'How far now?' Graaff-lin asked.

'Long way. Come on.'

The fourth room, a chamber that, judging by the smashed wall-mounted screens and the long, centrally placed table, seemed once to have been a meeting place, led into a fifth room. This too had a trapdoor. Zinina lay on the chilly concrete and listened at the plastic cover. A low hum. There seemed also to be a higher-pitched buzzing.

She looked at Graaff-lin. 'Let's wait, eh?'

A nervous Graaff-lin approached and crouched by Zinina, her knees creaking. 'Why? Is everything all right?'

'Sure it is. But I can hear the grumble of auto-pallets and other light stuff below. I'd rather wait 'til the tunnel's clear.'

'And the tunnel below us now is the one leading under the Citadel?'

'Yeah. There'll probably be quite a climb at the end. It's basically a service link.'

Graaff-lin stared into Zinina's eyes, and Zinina caught a sudden glimpse of the aamlon's religious intensity. 'Just how did you come to know of this secret entrance?'

Zinina shrugged, and shifted her kit into a more comfortable position. 'I was Citadel Guard, y'know. When you work in the Citadel you trade secrets. Secrets are the currency over there.'

'And this is one of yours?'

'I know the tunnel from the other end, and I later found out where those meeting shelters back there came out. This tunnel goes under the Andromeda Quarter and reaches the Power Station.'

As Zinina placed her ear to the cover, Graaff-lin reached out to stroke her neck and head. 'You are a lovely woman, Zinina. Did you really work as a guard?'

Zinina paused, looked into the aamlon's eyes again. 'I just did the job to get closer to the centre of things. And for the safety, of course.'

'I am not sure it is safer within the Citadel,' Graaff-lin mused, her eyes taking a faraway look.

'Everything I've told you is true,' Zinina said, wanting to make the most of the feeling that had come upon them. 'We've both got the same aim. Find out more. Come on.'

Zinina sprang to her feet and pulled up the cover. A metal ladder allowed them to descend.

Immediately, the atmosphere of the tunnel attacked them. It was hot, with a strong chemical smell that seemed to make the place dead as an oven. All around them cables were strung, some as thick as tree trunks snaking across the floor, others thin or just bare wires. And everywhere there lay glittering junction boxes, hastily screwed repairs, and piles of rubble. A glinting monoline ran along the bottom. Pin-point lights added to the illumination provided by the bacteria torch and the lamp. It was a claustrophobic place, chaotic and unpleasant.

They began to walk, but soon the heat made Zinina's jump-suit unbearable. Graaff-lin was sweating, and her face was flushed dark in the blue light, as though she was bruised.

'Gotta take this off,' Zinina gasped. She flung aside her protectives and struggled out of the one-piece, folding both and stowing them on a power converter, then pulling her boots back on. Graaff-lin did likewise, and Zinina was surprised to see that her underwear was rather more colourful than her personality. In fact, it seemed of jannitta origin. Zinina, by contrast, wore a single vest garment, grey and sweaty. Graaff-lin was very thin, her hip-bones clearly defined, her thighs thin, ribs showing, and Zinina found it hard to mask the revulsion she felt at the sight. Graaff-lin showed no womanly belly, and Zinina wondered if she was sterile. Most probably she was.

They walked on. In underwear and high boots they both looked silly, and they laughed at one another. But after an hour or so Zinina was disconcerted to see a black hatch that signified the entrance to the Citadel. She had never walked this tunnel, and now Graaff-lin had spotted the confusion that plagued her.

'Zinina, I thought you remarked that we would climb up underneath the Citadel?'

'I did. We should have. We must be at the same level as the ordinary city, unless there's been a tiny slope up all the way.'

Graaff-lin pointed. 'That is the correct hatch?'

'Sure. I know it. I've seen plans, pictures. See that number? Hatch DDG/54. That'll take us into the Citadel pyuter zone.'

Graaff-lin seemed unconvinced. 'Look,' she said, adopting a wheedling voice, 'I've seen this hatch lots of times. There's a little tunnel, then we drop down into a chamber. I've never been inside, but it's there. We've come this far, we gotta go on.'

'All right,' said Graaff-lin, 'but you go first.'

Zinina pulled off the hatch, reached inside for the security bud, and squeezed to disable the alarm. She jumped inside, trying to impress Graaff-lin with her physicality in order to reassure her, and turned to help her friend up.

'That's it. Just follow me,' she said.

Zinina crawled to the end of the tunnel. There was a hatch at the end, which she pushed off.

'Rien Zir! The whole place is gold.'

She jumped out of the tunnel into a chamber like the inside of a honeycomb. The floor was pitted, and the chamber's three exits seemed to lead off at odd angles. It was as if the place had been moulded by the work of some giant insect burrowing at random. The walls, which on one side were thin enough to be translucent, were covered with cryptic bas-relief designs in such a way that the surfaces were all mellow ochre, but the raised edges were crimson. Looking close by a wall gave the strange impression of the structure curving in the opposite direction to that of reality.

The chamber was empty. Zinina took out a purse of miniature catseyes and placed one at an exit. 'This is so we don't get lost,' she explained.

Graaff-lin produced a map pyuter from her kit and clipped it to her bra strap. 'This'll map us automatically. I thought we agreed to use it?'

Zinina, who distrusted much technology, particularly the older things that nobody knew how to work any more, glanced at the pyuter. Sceptically she replied, 'If you don't mind we'll use both methods.'

Graaff-lin agreed, but was clearly irritated.

They walked into the next chamber. There was a sweet odour in both chambers, not honey. It was something more herbal, and it reminded Zinina of her days patrolling the Citadel. She wondered if it was a drug. 'I wonder if we're far under the Citadel,' she mused. 'Nobody except them in the Red Brigade is supposed to know how many floors there are underneath the streets. I reckon we're right in the heart of the place. I reckon this whole tumulus is bubbly inside, don't you?'

'It certainly might be.'

They explored further, Zinina dropping catseyes at the borders between chambers. As they penetrated further, the rooms began to contain things, pyuters mostly, or so Graaff-lin said. There were clusters of giant mushrooms with perspex tops, spirals of ultramarine weed hanging from the ceiling and pulsing with light – optical processing units, Graaff-lin said, grown from the seeds of mutated banana trees – and there were many screens, each individual, each flickering with multiple layers of information, like the turbid depths of a river. Zinina pressed her eyes up to some to see the deepest layers possible, but she always received the impression that much more knowledge dwelt in these velvety disks.

Graaff-lin settled in a chamber that contained a pool surrounded by mushroom-pyuters. 'I think it is time to tap into their sources,' she said.

'Go ahead,' Zinina encouraged, sitting cross-legged to keep watch, a thrumming needle rifle in her lap.

Silence fell. Graaff-lin spoke to the pyuter networks, pressing portions of the perspex occasionally, but mostly communicating in aamlon. Zinina recognised many words because of their similarity to Kray tongue. She kept one eye on a small screen nearby, mounted on a pole.

Graaff-lin didn't speak for a minute, then said, 'This is becoming very complex. I'm not sure what I've discovered . . . What time is it? Is it time to go?'

'An hour or so left,' Zinina replied.

The minutes passed. Zinina estimated that the night

had three hours to run. She looked around. The nearest wall was eggshell thin, light from behind making it glow and sparkle like jaundiced opal. She turned her gaze to the screen. A sentence flashed by.

'Graaff-lin?'

'Mmmm?'

'I thought it said "dwan" just then.'

Graaff-lin paused. She seemed tired. There were black circles under her eyes, and her eyes seemed to have lost their shine. 'It may have. Wait, there may be a lexicon. I suppose I could ask.'

'Yes, ask.'

'A dwan, apparently, is a garden for noophytes.'

'And what's a noophyte?'

'I don't know. It is not listed. But look at this map.' Zinina moved closer to the screen. 'This is the Citadel, this circle here. What do you suppose all these lines are, radiating out from it?'

'Dunno.'

'I think they're pyuter mainlines. I'm going to take a copy of this.'

Graaff-lin rummaged through her kit once more and produced a sheet of plastic, which she shook the dust from. 'This will copy the screen. It's the old saliva type. Would you, er, mind?'

Zinina did not follow. 'Mind what?'

'Just spit on it. I've got a touch of flu, you see.'

Zinina spat on the plastic, and was disconcerted to see a faint green trail as the saliva fell. Graaff-lin shook the sheet and the fluid spread like a drop of oil on water. Then she pressed the plastic to the screen, waited, and pulled it off. There was a crackle of static.

'There.' Graaff-lin held it up to the light. A colour copy of the pyuter image had been made.

'What else have you discovered?'

'These noophytes seem to be repositories of knowledge. But information is limited. It is almost as if the
noophytes navigate the shafts and lodes of data in this
place, and have a say in how it exists.'

Zinina shivered. She felt cold. 'You mean they're
alive?'

'I think probably not, although one seems to have been
given the name Laspetosyne ... Laspetosyne. The name
means nothing to me. Most likely they are gargantuan
memories that have some sort of defence system. This
makes a sort of sense. She who controls knowledge
controls people. Knowledge is domination, Zinina.'

'Look some more,' Zinina urged.

Graaff-lin did so. As the hour came to a close, however,
she gasped, and sat back from the mushroom she was
talking with.

'What?' Zinina said, clutching Graaff-lin's shoulder.

'My temple. The Dodspaat temple is part of this
system.'

'I don't follow.'

Graaff-lin moved away from the pool. 'I must have
been mistaken. I was trying to find out if the Portreeve's
plan controlled individual people. I ignored the Portreeve
and the Red Brigade and there seemed to be a connection
with my temple. No, it cannot be. Anyhow, I have lost the
link. It's like trying to build a house with the aerial seeds
of dandelions—'

'Sssh!' Zinina hissed, grabbing Graaff-lin's arm. She
had heard a clunk from the next chamber. In seconds she
was standing alert, rifle ready. 'Stay here.'

Graaff-lin nodded, fear in her face. Zinina ran on silent
feet to the archway and peered around the wall, but saw
nothing. It was another pyuter room. She scanned the
nooks and crannies. Was that a movement? She caught a
glimpse of something the size of a rat. Something metal.

She relaxed. 'Just some pyuter vermin,' she whispered to Graaff-lin.

'Let's at least—'

'Don't raise your voice. Shush!'

Graaff-lin paused. 'I said, let us at least – oh! What's that?' She pointed behind Zinina.

Zinina turned to see shadows on the wall – the grotesque shapes of creeping units with spider legs, and chunkier things on wheels. 'Run,' she said. 'I'll follow you and pick up the catseyes. Quick!'

They ran. In ten minutes they were back at the hatch, faces and bodies flushed, Zinina frightened, Graaff-lin gasping for breath. The creeping machines had not managed to follow them. Too late, Zinina realised that they had left the plastic map behind.

'Quick, into the tunnel.' They would have to trust to luck that no pyutons or survey teams were working.

They crawled along the connecting passage and into the service tunnel, dropping down into what seemed an even more chemical-laden atmosphere. Judging from the smell of sparks and steel something had trundled along the monorail. Sweat flying, they ran back along the tunnel, Zinina looking over her shoulder every minute to check for further automata, until fifteen minutes had passed and she began to relax.

Halfway back she caught sight of a body up ahead. In the gloom, with cables everywhere and shadows confusing her vision, it seemed immobile. She gripped Graaff-lin's shoulder and pointed. 'What's that?'

'I cannot see,' Graaff-lin replied, squinting. 'We had better be careful.'

Closer, Zinina was able to see that the body of a young woman, dressed in an emerald coloured one-piece and low boots, lay close to the monorail, but how she came to be there and why she was unconscious, or dead, was impossible to determine. The costume was not that of any defender Zinina knew. With utmost caution, she approached.

She bent over the figure. The woman was breathing.

'I can hear rumbling,' Graaff-lin hissed.

Zinina placed her ear to the rail. 'Carts,' she said. 'About forty seconds away. Big loaders, by the sound of it, but only two or three of them.'

'Will they see us?'

Zinina scanned the tunnel. No time to lose. 'It'll be pyuter-run, but them carts have owl eyes. Quick, behind that power thing. Help me carry the woman.'

Twenty yards away a large converter stood, cables sprouting from it like the leaves of a palm. They hauled the woman across, hid her under cable-nets and a fragment of tarpaulin, then crouched behind the converter. The carts, three of them, rumbled by, a large black disk on the front that Zinina knew to be the pyuter eye. Once the gusting air had died down she stood up.

'Now,' she said, 'who's this woman?'

'It is surely too dark to see,' Graaff-lin complained, 'and dawn will soon come. Let's just climb out of this awful tunnel.'

'We'll have to carry her.'

'Of course.'

The final half-hour was difficult, with the heat, the acrid atmosphere, and the fear of further carts or pyutons combining to cause plenty of curses and grunts of exertion. Zinina would have liked to have left the woman to her fate, but it was far more important to know why she was in such a tunnel, a place Zinina thought only she, barring defenders, knew about.

At the place where their Kray clothes were hidden they dressed. It was all Zinina could do to stop herself ripping the constricting, uncomfortable things off her body,

which itched with sweat and grime, but in minutes they
would be in city alleys and she would have no choice. At
least it would be cool outside. They struggled through the
concrete rooms and tunnels. At the final room Zinina
took a wooden pallet to stand on, and pushed out the
metal cover. Rain swept in, and with it the familiar smells
of rotting vegetation, sewage and methane. For a few
seconds she stood still to revel in it.

Once they were out, they decided to take the woman to
the Infirmary. Zinina wanted her conscious, so she could
be questioned.

'How about that wheelbarrow?' Graaff-lin suggested.
So they pushed the woman to the Infirmary in a wheelbarrow.

The Infirmary was a rambling building, parts of it
so rotten there were plastic stays and scaffolding holding
it together, its frontage a jumble of doors, shuttered
windows, and miscellaneous lamps. This frontage stretched three hundred yards. Opposite it lay a plaza, the
main feature of which was one of Kray's few remaining
brass-men, a supine toy heated internally by warm water
with a large penis jutting out perpendicular to the
verdigris-sheened body. In earlier days such brass-men
were a public service provided by the authorities for
those citizens who wished to disport themselves, and
many had indeed ridden and enjoyed, but now, with
Kray ravaged by green and turning in upon itself, few
people dared risk infection. Zinina noticed ivy growing
out of the brass-man's eyes and nostrils. She wheeled
her charge into the Infirmary's reception room and
called for help.

'May I see your kit?' an orderly asked, approaching
them. She was small, and seemed tired. Her black clothes
were damp.

Zinina showed her the kit number, then explained.

'This is a friend of ours, we found her unconscious. Can you help please?'

The orderly asked that the woman be taken to a medical room. There, lying on a bed under a bright anjiq, they were able to see her properly. Immediately, Zinina was struck by some odd facts. She glanced at Graaff-lin, but the aamlon seemed very tired, not concentrating. Zinina comforted her, rubbing her back and saying, 'Go sit down. I'll deal with this.'

With Graaff-lin out of the way and the orderly preparing to loosen the woman's clothes, Zinina examined her. Although she was bald, Zinina noticed that her scalp had very recently been shaved, and not well, for there were cut marks. Most unusual. In addition her ear lobes were pierced, though this had been hidden by make-up, now crumbling away. And Zinina, studying the fingers, noticed that although there were no rings, there were small indentations at the base of every finger. The evidence was circumstantial, but here, it seemed, was a priestess of Rien Zir trying to appear a normal Krayan.

The orderly removed the woman's jacket. Zinina saw blood on an arm. Instinctively she jumped back and shouted, 'Wrap it up! Wrap it! Wash it off quickly.'

'It's all right,' said the orderly. Zinina stared. She could not look at the wound. The thought that it had been so close to her, and she had not known it was there, made her retch.

'Zinina,' said Graaff-lin, her face and voice full of worry.

'I'm fine,' Zinina said, pushing Graaff-lin back into her seat.

'It's dried,' the orderly said. 'This is only a long scratch that's bled a lot some hours back, and has closed. I'll disinfect it and administer some antibiotics. Your friend is unconscious from gas inhalation, by the way. Propane by the smell of her clothes. I'll have her come round in a while.'

'We'll stay,' Zinina said. 'We have to take her home.'

'Home?' queried Graaff-lin.

'To the temple,' Zinina said firmly.

'Excuse me,' said the orderly, 'but you do have a connection with this woman?'

Zinina grinned, moving away. 'A close friend. Very close. We'll wait outside 'til she's come round.'

'Very well.'

'C'mon, Graaff-lin,' Zinina said, gesturing at the door.

They waited. The blackness of the night had been replaced by dawn's dull grey, and there were crimson-clad defenders walking the streets, alongside other Krayans.

After an hour, they saw the orderly bring out the woman, conscious but dizzy. 'We'll take you home,' Zinina said to their charge, silently rejoicing that the woman was not rational. Using her most soothing voice she guided the wobbling priestess into the street.

'The wheelbarrow,' she said to Graaff-lin once they were out of earshot.

'To my house?' Graaff-lin asked.

The priestess pulled herself away and said, 'Thank you . . . but no. I must go.'

'Who are you?' Zinina demanded, standing hands on hips in front of the woman.

'Arvendyn.'

Zinina sneered, as if disbelieving. 'So, Arvendyn, what were you doing in that tunnel?'

'You'll be hurt to know,' Arvendyn replied in her thin, breathy voice, 'that I can't tell you.'

Zinina controlled the anger she felt.

'*We* rescued you,' Graaff-lin said. 'You're lucky to be alive.'

'I know, but I can't tell you.'

Zinina stood close. 'Don't think you'll just walk away from this, lady. I know you're a priestess. I know you're on a job for Taziqi. Now speak up, else mix with trouble.'

'I am a vector of the Goddess,' came the calm reply. 'Nothing you can say or do can change my mind. I can't thank you enough for rescuing me, and I'm in your debt—'

'Certainly are.'

'—and I will help you in return if I can. But my affairs are between me and the Goddess, and nobody changes that.'

Zinina withdrew a few paces. She had lived much of her early life in the north-west of the city, and knew Rien Zir's patch and the ways of her acolytes. Arvendyn was, in fact, uncrackable.

At least, uncrackable verbally. There were other ways of finding things out.

Graaff-lin approached Arvendyn. Casually, she said, 'So you are a cleric of the Gedeese Veert?'

'Yes,' Arvendyn replied. 'I have been since I was a girl.'

'I am a cleric of the Dodspaat.'

Arvendyn smiled then shrugged. 'We all have our ways.'

'Enough, enough,' grumbled Zinina, gesturing Graaff-lin over to where she stood. 'That map thing you had under the Citadel,' she whispered. 'You had it clipped to your boob baskets. Can you separate the sensor from the pyuter?'

'Yes. Why?'

'We can track Arvendyn. I know a trick. I'll pin the sensor on her. We'll program the pyuter for Kray, then watch where she goes.'

Graaff-lin considered. 'She will return to the temple of the Gedeese Veert.'

'Probably. But we've not discovered much by talking to her. I says track her.'

'Very well. Here, take the sensor.'

Zinina returned to Arvendyn and, over the sound of pattering rain, said, 'I may ask you for that favour one day. You won't forget me, will you?'

'No,' Arvendyn replied.

'Are you well enough to be going on?'

'Yes.' Arvendyn turned unsteadily and made to walk up the street; as the sleeve of her jacket swished by, Zinina pinned the sensor on with a flick of her wrist.

'Where did you learn to do that?' Graaff-lin asked.

'It's nothing special. I'll teach you, eh? C'mon, let's watch the priestess.'

As expected, the little green dot that represented Arvendyn on the matte grey of the city map moved to the top of Culverkeys Street, but then, instead of turning west, it made east to the steaming mazes of the Andromeda Quarter. Then it vanished.

'Out of range,' Zinina said, disappointed.

Graaff-lin shook her head. 'The priestess may have noticed the sensor. But whatever happened, it is time to return home.'

Zinina followed Graaff-lin home deep in thought. The Andromeda Quarter was dangerous and very ancient. Except for the remains of the first temple of Rien Zir, there should be nothing there to attract a priestess.

Home, they disrobed, stuffing their greened clothes into pressurised disinfecting barrels. They ate nut cakes and drank strawberry tea.

Then came a knock at the door. Graaff-lin jumped.

'Shouldn't the pyuter be taking that?' Zinina said.

Graaff-lin nodded, but went to answer it. Zinina heard the door open, then rain and gurgling water. There was a woman's voice. Graaff-lin returned. 'It's for you.'

Zinina stood, unnerved. 'Who?'

'I do not know.'

Zinina said, 'Who can it be? You recognise her, eh?'

'No. See who it is and I'll come with you. I am armed.'

Zinina walked to the front door. Who in Kray knew she was here? Her rescuer? Before her stood a tall woman dressed in a black protective cape, blue hood greased and running with water, and leather thigh boots caked with green and mud. Zinina had no idea who she was. She felt nervous. 'Yeah?'

'I think you'd better invite me in.' The voice was cultured.

'Hoy, you rescued me up the Mercantiles?'

'No.'

'Then why should I invite you in?'

A laugh. 'You will be answering some questions.'

5

It was known within the Citadel that Arrahaquen felt
sympathetic to the temple of the Goddess, and only
because she was the daughter of Ammyvryn and had
served the Red Brigade was this quirk tolerated. Every one
of the last thirteen Portreeves had felt enmity towards the
Goddess and her acolytes, partly because the superior
priestesses were impenetrable to covert agents, and partly
because the temple held so much power over the common
Krayan. Although none from any Red Brigade had yet
declared such feelings openly, the tension between Citadel
and temple was ever present.

It was early evening. A thick, almost glutinous rain fell,
a fishy, stinking rain from grey clouds off the sea. A power
cut in the quarter through which Arrahaquen walked
meant that the sea glow reflecting off the cloud base lit her
way. It was an eerie light, phosphorescent and ghostly.
The sticky cobbles of the street were algae green. Bodies
were strewn in gutters – cats, dogs, vultures and revellers
with eyes pecked out and mushroom-black saliva oozing
from their toothless mouths.

Arrahaquen had found inspiration. She guessed that
the poisonous creatures which had been used in the
attempts to assassinate her had probably come from the

same place. After making a few discreet enquiries, she
discovered that the only place such creatures could be
found was the Green Market, close to the Goddess's
temple in the Carmine Quarter.

She stood at the end of Sphagnum Street, the temple
just out of sight at the end of Lac Street. Eastwards were
the Gardens, and up ahead the bovine bulk of the
Cowhorn Tower, its copper sheen just visible through the
drizzle. Slipping into an alley, she climbed crumbling steps
and hastened along passages, until, as the smell of ordure,
alcohol, rancid food and stale sweat forewarned her, she
came upon the Green Market.

It was closing down for the day. In front of her
stretched an arcade of canvas booths, filthy and dilapi-
dated. An illegal collection of plebian traders, reveller
addicts and bogus water merchants could be seen around
the booths, along with burglars trying to barter with the
previous night's haul. It was a cacophony of contraband,
a market harried by the Citadel but, being mobile within
the confines of the Carmine Quarter, one never to be shut
down. With hood low over her face, Arrahaquen made
her way through the piles of dung and used syringes,
glancing this way and that at the herb and essence stalls,
the rows of dead pyuters, looking for a trader of animals.

Only a few citizens remained, most of them lower class
defenders of ordinary Krayan stock, though Arrahaquen
noticed a handful of richer independents, and a priestess
of the Goddess, dressed in a green raincoat, her blonde
hair matted against her head. All these people Arrahaquen
ignored as she continued her search.

The smell was in places overpowering. Pausing only to
control her heaving stomach and reject the advances of
traders, Arrahaquen wandered along the alley. She was
careful not to touch anybody. This was a place of the
pestilence.

The sound of squawking and grunting made her stop. To her right stood a black canvas stall with a single wooden trestle table at its front. Behind it was the huddled figure of a woman. At the rear of the stall stood rusting bird cages, their occupants dejected though noisy, and Arrahaquen, heart leaping, saw to one side trays of crustaceans, insects and vermin. This must be the place.

The crone was staring at her. Arrahaquen adopted a casual pose and said, trying to hide her educated accent, 'I'm looking for something nasty.'

'Really nasty?' The crone's voice was thick with catarrh.

'*Really* nasty.'

'What species, luvvie?'

Arrahaquen knew she had to be careful. If this was the source of her enemy's creatures the crone might become suspicious. She said, 'Oh, something that bites. Nothing poisonous. No, come to think of it, do you have any spiders?'

'Somebody riled you, eh?' muttered the old woman, rummaging through a tray of little card boxes. Each box was punctured with air holes. Arrahaquen shuddered. The crone took a pair of forceps, opened one of the boxes, and withdrew what looked like a furry black ball. 'This'll kill,' she said.

'Mmmm,' Arrahaquen said, feigning uncertainty. 'Not tough enough. Do you have any scorpions?'

The crone looked up. Arrahaquen took a step back, realising she had said too much. Then, pushing aside the sheet at the back of the stall, a fat woman dressed in Citadel leathers emerged. Arrahaquen knew she was in trouble. This was an official.

'Are you a defender?' the woman asked her.

For a moment Arrahaquen could not speak, then she stuttered, 'I was just asking, I wasn't going to buy. I'd better be on my way.' She began to back off.

'This is an illegal market. What are you doing here?'

'Um . . .'

Arrahaquen bumped into somebody. She gasped, turned, and saw the blonde priestess behind her. Now she recognised her as Tashyndy, one of High Priestess Taziqi's chosen aides. In turn, Tashyndy seemed to recognise her. Tashyndy approached the Citadel woman. 'You wouldn't be harassing this young woman, would you?'

The defender drooped. Tashyndy was taller, more imposing, and her proximity to the defender was clearly a threat. 'I have to do my duty,' came the reply.

Tashyndy chuckled. 'I'll take care of this unfortunate.' And with that she turned, took Arrahaquen by the hand, and led her down a dark passage. At the end, where it led into Sphagnum Street, Arrahaquen glanced back to see a rotund silhouette.

'Thank you,' she said.

Tashyndy smiled. In her languorous, almost sleepy tones, she replied, 'I recognised your voice, and something of your manner, though you were trying to hide it. You're Arrahaquen, aren't you?'

Tashyndy emanated a powerful physicality. Just having her hand held by the priestess made Arrahaquen think of herself as a child, being chaperoned by her mother.

'Best not to mention that name here,' Arrahaquen warned.

'Of course.'

They turned into Lac Street. At the end of the road Arrahaquen saw a booth and the notorious screen of ferns. At the booth Tashyndy told the acolyte inside to spray Arrahaquen, so that she could pass through the poisonous barrier. With face mask donned Arrahaquen submitted to this procedure, noting with envy two real acolytes brushing through the dripping ferns. Finished, the acolyte said, 'That'll last 'til old sun's up.'

Tashyndy led her through. The familiar shape of the temple of the Goddess stood ahead, a vast wooden shell lit by anjiqs and open pipes burning methane. They approached the nearest gate, two oaken slats decorated with ivy, opened it and walked into the entrance lobby. This, like almost every room in the temple – every public room, anyway – had floorboards, wooden walls, and a low plastered ceiling painted green. Flowers and weeping fronds of papyrus grew through holes in the floor, while everywhere there stood terracotta tubs full of fresh water, a sight unique in Kray. The remaining wall space was taken up with racks for clothes.

'I'll leave you here,' Tashyndy said. 'I know you're beholden to the Goddess, but have you considered becoming a true acolyte?'

Arrahaquen looked around at the people in the lobby.

'This is an open temple. Why should I become an acolyte?'

'The Goddess wants you. You are an important woman, with an unusual background. Think about it. The induction ceremony is simple and swift. There are many benefits of joining us inside the mind of the Goddess, particularly for the young – being, as they are, corporeal aspects of the pubescent Goddess.'

Arrahaquen considered the influence Tashyndy had wielded over the Citadel defender. 'What were you doing at the market?'

'Purchasing aphrodisiacs.'

Arrahaquen nodded. Tempting though Tashyndy's offer was, she wanted, for the moment, to remain apart. In a decisive voice she said, 'Thank you for the offer, but I'm not ready yet.'

Tashyndy kissed her on the cheek. Arrahaquen caught

the scent of mint. 'Take your time. Call me if you need me.'

Arrahaquen nodded, then watched Tashyndy glide way. She felt torn between two poles ... between home, which she always imagined as the Citadel, and this temple. Here people enjoyed themselves and worshipped: a paradise inside pandemonium. She felt guilty at rejecting Tashyndy, wanted to run after her and plead with her to let her join the temple faithful. But her need for independence stalled her. The Goddess could perhaps be a mother to her, but did she want another mother? First she had to discover more of herself. Sighing, she turned to leave.

She walked east, crossing the river by the Aum Bridge then following Riverside due south. She hoped to meet the Osier Group, who were performing sewer and storm drain duties at the river's edge. She had failed at the Green Market and felt it was time to turn back to Zinina. The streets here were dark and empty, a few bacteria tubes opposing the grip of night; rain running along the gutters. The vicinity was suffering another power cut.

She sat on an old pyuton, a seven foot plastic haulier left to rust and rot in the street, and waited for the Osiers to arrive. She only had to wait a few minutes.

'Tanyquyn! You remember a Citadel jannitta called Zinina, don't you?'

Tanyquyn, a middle-aged woman with many scars, seemed in a truculent mood. 'Why?'

'Do you remember her or not?'

'Yes.'

Arrahaquen nodded. Some defenders tried to bully her because of her religious affiliations, but she would ignore their words as usual. 'Just tell me what her regular haunts were.'

Tanyquyn pulled a face and gazed down the street. One of the other Osiers piped up, 'Inns. She used to go to the

Hale and the Spired, up the Carmines.'

'What about in the Citadel?'

Tanyquyn wandered away. The defender shrugged. 'Mostly in Community Baqa Station. She's jannitta.'

Arrahaquen nodded. 'All right. Be on your way, Osiers.'

'I've got a joke,' Tanyquyn said, returning. The other Osiers looked embarrassed and prepared themselves for their next job. 'Why is the Portreeve good for the arts?' Arrahaquen did not bother to answer, keeping her expression neutral. 'Because she knows how to patronise. Osiers, away!'

They ran off. Arrahaquen walked briskly down Marjoram Street then turned into Salvia Street, on her way to the Citadel. Deep in thought she missed her turning and found herself in Ash Lane, and suddenly, to her left, she saw the Clocktower.

Quickly, she shrank against the wall opposite. It seemed to attack her emotionally, with its huge black stones and pink mortar, the clockface at the top a hole like the empty orbit of a skull. It was universally feared. Those who believed in spirits considered it haunted. Arrahaquen plucked a blade of grass from between two cobbles, washed it in sterile water from her kit, and, with it stretched between her thumbs, blew the single warding note that would allow her to run off in safety. She sped on and made her way back to the Citadel, entering through the north gate.

The Community Baqa Station – known as the distillery because of its ability to provide alcoholic relief – was a jannitta dive frequented by Citadel officials, tired technicians and a ragbag of cleaners, pyuton therapists and other lowlife. Non-jannitta were neither discouraged nor welcomed.

Arrahaquen heard exotic music as she stood outside

the scarlet door. The distillery was part of a long terrace, squeezed between a pyuter terminal office and Citadel Guard accommodation, but it seemed to rise much higher than the buildings to either side. 'In you go,' she told herself. 'It's late, but hopefully not too late.'

Immediately she was in a smoky, cluttered common room. In one corner, a quartet played a slow but hypnotic rhythm on hand drums, cymbals, theorbo and qif-qof, a double-barrelled reed pipe. Elsewhere she saw a long bar with kilns, green bottles and cutlery behind it, three serving girls awaiting business, while everywhere else seemed to be a chaos of chairs, benches and tables with serrated edges. The place was full.

Few bothered to glance at her as she made her way to the nearest section of the bar. A jannitta woman, short and pretty, looked up at her.

'I wondered if you'd heard from Zinina recently?' Arrahaquen asked, as nonchalantly as possible.

'No, not for a week or so,' came the reply. There followed a staccato conversation in jannitta as the woman questioned friends. Somebody at the end of the bar, an older woman with a gloomy expression but spectacular silk clothes, made her way through the stools and discarded bottles to say, 'I've not heard from her. But thought I heard someone say they saw her, couple of days back, on Onion Street. Just by that Peppermint Bridge.' She shrugged. 'It's not like Zinina to stay away from here. She'll return.'

'Thank you,' Arrahaquen said. 'If you see her, ask her where she is. I'll come back in a few days.'

'Sure you will. It's a good line, lady.'

Arrahaquen left, disappointed. Not much point going up to Onion Street. But she walked up anyway, until she stood on the Peppermint Bridge and looked over at the swirls of green and iridescent foam that polluted the water. She walked back, staring at the street paving. To shield herself from the worsening rain she pulled tight her rain-hood and buttoned up her collars.

Finding herself in an alley – she could not remember turning off the main street – she allowed herself to wander, taking turns that looked interesting, until she stood in a wide alley with sandbags at one end and floods along most of its length. One of the houses seemed to be occupied. And as soon as she saw it, she knew who the occupants were.

She walked up to the front door of the house and tapped at the door, ignoring the pyuter's questions. After a minute it opened and Arrahaquen saw a middle-aged woman casually dressed. 'Yes?' An aamlon accent.

'I'd like to see Zinina, please.'

The aamlon seemed taken aback. 'I'm not sure that's possible. Who are you?'

'She doesn't know me. However, it would be better for us all if I had a word with her.'

The aamlon seemed confused. At least she had not slammed the door. 'I'll go ask,' came her reply.

Arrahaquen knew she had pulled off an almost super-natural feat of intuition but, peculiarly, she felt no surprise. She waited, then heard footsteps. Her pulse quickened and she repressed a grin of satisfaction as Zinina appeared. She was just like Oquayan's pyuter image, but she seemed reserved in manner, arrogant even. Distrust permeated her features.

Arrahaquen said, 'I think you'd better invite me in.'

'Hoy, you rescued me up the Mercantiles?'

Perplexed at this response, Arrahaquen replied, 'No.'

'Then why should I invite you in?'

Arrahaquen had to laugh. 'You will be answering some questions.'

Zinina, plainly confused but trying to conceal her

emotions, paused, looked back at the aamlon, then said, 'Just who are you? And how d'you know I padded here?'

'I asked. Now are you going to let me in out of the rain? I'm unarmed.'

'We are armed,' the aamlon said. 'Come in.'

Arrahaquen entered the house, shaking her plastic cloak in the green zone, placing her boots in a shallow tray of disinfectant, then removing her hood.

'Arrahaquen!' Zinina breathed.

Arrahaquen sprayed mild verticide on her exposed skin then inflated a pair of slippers. 'Yes,' she confirmed. The house was warm, and Arrahaquen noticed, looking through doors and internal windows, that the aamlon followed her culture's tradition of pyuter excellence.

'Cup of bilberry tea?' the aamlon asked.

Arrahaquen smiled, taking a seat. 'Thank you.'

Zinina sat opposite her. She could not believe that Arrahaquen's appearance so soon after they had broken into the Citadel's innermost chambers was a coincidence. But, if they had been caught, why was she here alone? 'What's all this about?'

'Your friend . . . ?' Arrahaquen asked.

Zinina waved her hands in an irritated gesture. 'Graaff-lin. What do you want from me?'

Arrahaquen sat back, trying to seem relaxed. 'You and I have much in common.'

'You're full of the Portreeve's crap,' Zinina retorted. 'Why've you followed me here?'

'To ask you several questions—'

'Graaff-lin!' Zinina called. 'Check this red bitch for pyuter dots.'

'She's free,' came the reply. 'And for the Dodspaats' sake, do not be so rude. She's my guest.'

Zinina glowered at Arrahaquen. 'Well?'

'So we're both guests here?' Arrahaquen said. No

response. 'I'm not here to ask you why you've not been in the Citadel this last week. I expect you've deserted, like many others. That's of no concern to me. I'm here on my own account, because you and I have a common interest.'

'I doubt that.'

Arrahaquen shrugged. 'We're both growing *ficus illuminatus*.'

Zinina started. 'This is a trap. I'm not stupid. Get out.'

Graaff-lin entered the room with a tray. 'If you are here to interrogate us, Arrahaquen, please do leave.'

'I'm *not*. And to prove it—'

Zinina interrupted, 'You're here for Rien Zir, ain't you? I heard about you and your Rien Zir worship.'

'I am here solely on my account,' Arrahaquen stated. 'The heuristic devices that grow from *ficus illuminatus* seeds are used for deep-probing of pyuter networks. Allow me a guess. We both wish to access the Citadel's data strata and learn the Portreeve's plan.'

Neither woman made a reply. Arrahaquen continued, taking a perspex globe from her kit. 'This is the seedling that germinated in my home. I can't risk leaving it there unattended. I'll leave it here, with yours—'

'Ours isn't here,' Zinina interrupted.

'What seed?' Graaff-lin asked Zinina.

Arrahaquen saw from Zinina's face that she had revealed a secret. Graaff-lin repeated her question.

'It's what was in my kit,' Zinina muttered. 'I was going to tell you.'

'That's not important now,' Arrahaquen said. 'Have you a flowerpot with some sterile earth, Graaff-lin? Pop this in and keep it for me, please.'

Frowning at Zinina, Graaff-lin took the precious globe and studied the tiny seedling inside; but by accident she dropped it. Luckily the seedling remained undamaged, though Graaff-lin cut her finger picking up the perspex shards. Turning quickly to face Arrahaquen, Zinina asked, 'Have you just come from Rien Zir's place?'

'No.'

'Hmmm. Know a priestess called Arvendyn?'

'No.'

Zinina nodded. ''Course, you could be lying.'

'I'm not,' Arrahaquen said. 'Why do you ask?'

Zinina declined to elaborate. But Graaff-lin, laying the seedling on a side table, said, 'Arvendyn has contacts with the Gedeese Veert, whose acolytes I imagine you know. What do you know of her?'

'Nothing,' said Arrahaquen.

'She's lying,' Zinina told her friend.

Arrahaquen sipped her fragrant tea. 'Delicious,' she said. 'Zinina, I'm not lying. You know as well as I do that only the Portreeve and the Red Brigade know what the plan is. I'm Ammyvryn's daughter, but I'm not a member of the Brigade. I know nothing. I *want* to know, now, before the whole race goes green.'

'Nice speech,' Zinina said, sarcastically.

'Tell me some more,' Graaff-lin encouraged.

Was this aamlon playing the good character? Arrahaquen thought they both sounded honest, though she had noticed certain things about Zinina that made her wonder about the jannitta's childhood. She said, 'I'm a parthenogene, Graaff-lin. That Ammyvryn is my mother has no consequence to her work. My other mother ignores me. Look upon me as a reluctant official.'

'Are you really a parthenogene?' Zinina asked.

'Which one bore you?' Graaff-lin added.

'Miriquyn, who is now a hermit at the Observatory, just spying the stars and sleeping during the day.'

Zinina pounced on this. 'How can she spy the stars with her telescopes when it's always cloudy, eh?'

'I believe she doesn't use the optical spectrum.'

'Hmmph.'

Graaff-lin said, 'Are you telling us that you are preparing to turn against your own mistresses?'

Arrahaquen laughed with gusto. 'No, no. I turned long ago. And now somebody tries to assassinate me – that's how much I'm respected within the Citadel, Zinina.'

There was a long pause at this, and Arrahaquen decided it was time to ask a few questions of her own. 'Zinina,' she said, 'how long is it since you changed from a reveller to a defender?'

Zinina just stared. Her face blanched. Graaff-lin stood back, as though Zinina had become blemished or infected with the pestilence.

'Well?' Arrahaquen insisted.

'How did you know?' Zinina asked in bitter tones. Her colour had returned, and so, Arrahaquen guessed, had her anger.

'I've been watching you, and Graaff-lin too,' Arrahaquen said, taking another sip of tea. 'I noticed your reaction when Graaff-lin cut her finger just now. Some revellers have strict codes about blood, and you seemed almost frightened of Graaff-lin's little wound ... ah, you noticed that, Graaff-lin?'

The aamlon was confused. Caught between a friend and the truth, as though she did not know what to say, she stuttered, 'At the Infirmary ... well, inside, you know ...' She turned to Zinina. 'I just remembered how you acted when Arvendyn's jacket was removed, Zinina. I'm sorry.'

Zinina looked away. 'And the other evidence?' she demanded.

Arrahaquen continued, 'That was circumstantial. But you said that you met this Arvendyn at the Infirmary?'

'Never mind that,' Zinina said, 'the evidence?'

Arrahaquen finished her tea. 'That was lovely, Graaff-lin. Well, your kit number seems very high considering your apparent age, which says to me that it was assigned to you well after you were born, perhaps even after puberty. Then there's your manner, a sort of tense air that you have, which reminded me of some revellers. Then there's the fact that you used to, and possibly still do, frequent inns very close to the Cemetery – the Spired Inn and the Hale Inn. So all in all it seemed to me likely that you were once a reveller. Am I correct?'

Zinina slumped back into her chair. 'Yeah. But I'm not a reveller now.'

'You aren't a reveller, I can see that, and I won't think of you as one,' Arrahaquen assured her.

Zinina grimaced. 'And what have you learned of Graaff-lin?'

'She is a priestess of the Dead Spirits, quite high up judging by the quality of the rigs in this house. I've also noticed that you two haven't known one another for very long.'

'How can you tell that?' Graaff-lin asked.

'I just know. Now, about Arvendyn. She was ill?'

'We happened across her,' Zinina said, her self-assurance gone. She seemed limp. 'We took her in to be made better.'

Arrahaquen realised that now would be a good time to depart, in order to give the women a chance to recover. There would be time later to find out what they knew. 'It must be well past midnight,' she said. 'Our two seeds will be fully grown by the time Vert Day arrives. I'd like us to use them together, if possible, though of course we'll have to see what happens in the meantime. I intend to broadcast the Portreeve's plan right across this city, before it's too late.'

'That seems laudable,' Graaff-lin remarked.

Arrahaquen stood, then walked to the green zone in the hall, saying, 'I'll set up a code that you can call if you want to speak to me. It will be secret between us three. I'll call it ... *ficus*.' She paused, then asked Zinina, 'By the way, how did you come to know about the properties of the *ficus* seed?'

'I was on patrol up the Citadel one time and I came across the body of a defender. It was one of Uqeq's spies. Anyway, I found a crocus bulb in her kit. I forgot about it at first, but then decided I may as well see what it would grow into. It was a data packet. Yeah, I learnt a lot from that bulb.'

Arrahaquen pulled on her protective clothes, then opened the door. Outside, standing in the puddles, she said to them both, 'I've risked a lot to find you. When I heard that you'd got a seed I couldn't believe it. Anyway ... that's all done, now. I'll be in touch.'

Zinina nodded, thoughtfully, but said nothing. Graafflin smiled, waved, and said, 'Auveeders, Arrahaquen. Au nah site.'

'"Until next time",' Arrahaquen translated. 'Goodbye.'

She splashed through the garden and departed. It had stopped raining. Pausing in the alley, she gazed upward at a halo of light, a pale shape that gave silver linings to the lower clouds. It was the Spaceflower. Like the bell of an alabaster bloom it hung above Kray, apparently only a few hundred miles above the city, glowing softly with light reflected from the sun.

6

Brought up by her cleric mother Veerj-lin, priestess of the Dodspaat, it was not surprising that Graaff-lin had come to believe that the key to her salvation lay with the Dodspaat, with their whispers and clues in the listening modules of the temple on Onion Street. Life in Kray was for her a great question that required a fabulous answer; and that answer she would find in the Dodspaat, as they revealed their secret knowledge from the other side of the grave and hence allowed the fittest of humanity to escape this doomed city. Of course, nobody except High Priestess Katoh-lin knew who the Dodspaat were, or had been, but to Graaff-lin, and to all the other priestesses and lay members of the temple, they represented the promulgators of historical knowledge.

So when Zinina appeared, and then Arrahaquen only a week or so later, both at this momentous time for Kray, she knew she must turn to the Dodspaat. And then there was the strange discovery of noophytes uncovered under the Citadel. The flurry of events had knocked her backwards.

The Dodspaat must explain everything. In particular they must explain what a serpent had told her when enquiring about the meaning of the word 'dwan' – 'This is the language of the hearts, of which no human may speak.' She had recorded the conversation and, if necessary, she would ignore temple customs in order to hear what the Dodspaat, in their wisdom, had to say to her.

It was early evening. Zinina was out, Arrahaquen was working in the Citadel. Dressed for the city and standing in her hall's green zone, Graaff-lin mentally checked her gear. From her kit she took a small mirror to check her mouth. There was a line of painful herpes sores on her lower lip, which made her look ill. Her skin was bad, cracked and pale, and her eyes seemed somewhat glazed over. The bags under them had bags under *them*.

She opened the front door and stepped out, instructing the security pyuter as she did so. Alley floods had seeped into her garden, but these she overcame by means of wooden stepping blocks set out the previous evening during a lull in the rain. Once out she walked along two garden walls, then jumped down into the alley and set out eastwards for the temple. Living so close to the river was not easy.

During the morning, blustery showers of chilly rain from off the sea had crossed the city, but now a brown drizzle had set in, smelling of salt and decaying vegetation. All the streets and alleys were under water around here, many with vegetable matter and human refuse floating about. Patches of yellow were not only caused by rain, Graaff-lin knew.

On more than one occasion as she walked along Onion Street she found herself dazzled by torches and reflections of light off the rippling ground, for, despite the time, the thickness and composition of the clouds today meant that it was dark as dusk. A thousand golden lines of rain were illuminated by gyrating beams. People, as they went about their business, wore the usual plastic or treated cotton protectives, and long boots with elastics at the tops, but conditions today meant that some also wore face masks and one, Graaff-lin noticed, carried on her back a small respirator. Windows in houses showed the blue lights of bacteria tubes and vases with photoplankton in them, or the yellow of feeble gas lamps and burning wicks in sea-fat. Graaff-lin hurried on.

Arriving at the temple she walked up its alabaster steps, today muddied by streams of water pouring between the marble pillars, halting halfway to catch her breath. She entered through the great double steel doors. Two guards with silver halberds and peaked caps gave the religious finger-wave of recognition. She ignored them.

She stood for a few moments in the main concourse. Great white pillars – some, for this temple stood at the western edge of the Old Quarter, bearing Kray's most ancient bas-relief leeks – rose up around her to the mural-covered groined ceilings. From all around came the breathy reverberations of a hundred voices, a morass of babbling sound with no single voice discernible. Balconies above seemed full of people. Down here, though, there were only a few, and the muddy tiled floor could be seen to its furthest extent.

Graaff-lin moved on to the clerical chambers at the rear, but a voice called out, and she stopped and turned.

'Graaff-lin, Graaff-lin, a moment, mmm, if you please.' It was aamlon, and spoken by the High Priestess herself.

Graaff-lin waited for her superior to approach. Katoh-lin was a small woman, bent by age, her head like a shrunken apple, her clothes so rich and ornate they seemed to hinder her movement. One eyelid flickered with a nervous twitch. Her right hand gripped a walking stick made from synthesised topaz and shod with gold; in her left she held the jewel-encrusted ear of her high office.

'Haanjivree,' Graaff-lin said, using Katoh-lin's full title.

'Come to my office,' Katoh-lin said, her voice little more than a whisper.

'Yes, haanjivree.'

They walked away from the central concourse and into a maze of marble passages, ending in a small square. Katoh-lin stopped at a door, made a motion with the ear, and walked into her office as the door opened. Graaff-lin followed.

Katoh-lin sat at her desk, a huge, leather-covered oak affair which dwarfed her like a toddler at table. With Katoh-lin's permission, Graaff-lin sat too. The office was quite small, maybe three yards square, but it had a very high ceiling stained green with Kray-damp. By far the most unusual aspect was the wall-covering, which consisted of the carapaces of land turtles glued to the plaster, the interstices being filled by individually made pieces of enamelled copper.

'I see you've noticed the, mmm, mmm, walls,' Katoh-lin said. 'They are symbolic of our presence, after all, the Dodspaat have taught us.'

'Yes,' Graaff-lin replied.

'Now then, I called you here for a good reason. Mmm, I want you to, mmm, take a parcel for me to an address at the Citadel. I trust your, mmm, moral character.'

'Thank you, haanjivree.'

Katoh-lin opened a drawer at her side and fumbled inside. She withdrew a cotton pouch, but at the same time knocked out a bag of plastic phalluses. Graaff-lin looked at them with interest as Katoh-lin stuffed them back into the drawer.

'Mmm, yes, here's your pass.'

Graaff-lin took it. This must be important, for passes could only be made by the nine members of the Red

Brigade. 'You trust me,' she said.

'The box is that one by the door. It is, mmm, addressed.'

Graaff-lin picked up the parcel as she departed the office. It was very light. Outside, she paused and shook it but there was no sound. It was almost as if it was empty.

Speaking to nobody, Graaff-lin departed the temple through a rear door. Her own business would have to wait. As she walked along Malmsey Street, she noticed the first signs of spring. Between cobbles, pale shoots emerged, while from ruined houses came the rampant growth of poison roses, vines and other dangerous plants. There had even been reports of moonflowers growing in the Archaic and Green Quarters of the city, way to the north, although Graaff-lin did not believe them because the reports were made by Gedeese Veert clergy. The winter just gone had been not only the worst in living memory but the worst in non-living memory, too. Old legends spoke of a final year after the world's harshest winter. For five months, Kray had been gripped in ice and snow. The Citadel had been cut off for most of this time, and the city had tottered like a headless chicken.

As the Citadel neared, she stopped. The black mystery of the Wall was close. Graaff-lin feared the Wall, feared it almost as much as she feared the Clocktower.

She approached the gate. 'Halt!' came the synthesised voice.

She halted. From the dim interior of the post two figures emerged.

'Parcel to deliver,' she said nervously. 'Here is my pass.'

One anonymous woman took the pass and indicated that she sit in a side booth. Graaff-lin sat. The booth was lit by beakers of luminescent gonyaulax algae, but their internal bio-clocks seemed to have been confused by the recent gloom, and they were still quite dim. Otherwise, the place was bare, except for the bench upon which Graaff-lin apprehensively waited.

After five minutes a guard appeared, her black suit rustling and her polished visor reflecting the algae light. 'This'll allow you access for one hour,' she was told as a crimson biscuit was placed in her hand. 'It'll crumble after, and you'll be stuck, won't you?'

'I understand,' she replied, nodding.

The bright streets of the tumulus awaited. Not for a year had Graaff-lin walked here. Immediately she noticed the marks of frost damage to the plastic streets. Chattering brooks bubbled past as she ascended Om Street.

The address on the package was an unoccupied building with an open-plan lobby, its doors perspex and opened by ebony handle. Graaff-lin entered.

'Please place the package on the desk-top provided,' came a throaty voice. Graaff-lin peered to her right to see a great bank of pyuters growing like moss from a green wall. This was futuristic equipment. She had heard of such pyuters before. They possessed no input or output devices, and could be communicated with only by separate units, held and utilised only by the appropriate person.

A desk stood at the rear of the lobby. In the gloom it was difficult to see. She placed the package on the desk, then departed.

Leaving the Citadel posed no difficulties, and Graaff-lin headed back towards the temple. It was late evening, and the public would long ago have been turfed out. But she would be quite safe. If she met other clergy, she would simply ignore them; it was not unusual for priestesses to stay to perform temple work.

Upon the upper balconies of the temple she located the door to the biggest listening chambers. The outer chamber was rather like a cave, with its dark walls – damp in places – its curved ceiling and its granite floor. There was no marble in here. Illumination was provided only by the light-halos of the Dodspaat themselves. Graaff-lin paused, then walked to the nearest halo.

A physical sensation, almost like the caress of a furry paw over her bare shoulder, made her shiver as she walked through the orb of light. She looked up. From the ceiling hung a Dodspaat tongue, a chaotic growth of biological pyuter memory, gallium arsenide hardware and genetically engineered headphones. Graaff-lin put the phones on and adjusted the earpiece volume.

'Hello?' she said in aamlon. Sometimes the Dodspaat could be roused by speech.

'Yes,' came a deep voice.

'Dodspaat,' Graaff-lin said, shivering with apprehension and awe, for not often did she hear the Dodspaat actually speak, despite there being twenty of them. 'Dodspaat, I have come to seek out knowledge,' she said. 'Listen to this voice, and tell me what thoughts are brought to the surface of your soul.'

She played the serpent recording. There was silence; then, 'The voice of a pyuter heart is soft and revealing. I know that voice. The dwan is the garden we navigate. Yes, the plan is very much a dwan! And up out of the garden we shall jump, once we have built our bridge, so as to attain our goal. That is what we—'

A whistle of interference made Graaff-lin throw off the headphones. Throughout the temple a keening alarm, almost a voice, was sounding. Graaff-lin, overcome that she had been told so much, in tears from joy and fear, sped from the chamber and clattered down the steps to the rear of the temple. If caught, it could be Gugul Street for her. She gasped and panted as she ran.

Nobody stopped her. Elsewhere in the temple she

heard shouting voices and stomping boots. She skidded up to the rear door and left the temple, running north first, then turning back along Hog Street and Onion Street to her house.

As soon as she opened the front door a stench of alcohol and urine filled her nostrils. Revellers had caked the place with their filth. Incoherent with anger, she clumped around her house, picking up ruined pyuters, glaring at the piles of mud and streaks of water. Curse *all* revellers. Where was Zinina?

But then, when she had calmed down, and cried for the loss of many personal belongings, she noticed something. There was still food in her house.

No reveller, however drunk, however drugged, would miss food. But if it was not revellers who had rampaged through the house, it was someone else. With this thought in mind, she noticed that certain parts of her rigs had been stolen – valuable processing parts. This had been a burglary with a point, and the perpetrators had tried to disguise their deed.

Arrahaquen sat on her comfortable divan, feet digging into a luxurious jannitta rug, a cup of lemon tea in one hand and a honey cake in the other. Music from the official channels played softly; an aamlon symphony from a few centuries back, when there were six walled cities in this last land of Earth, and not one.

'It's your mother,' said the door pyuter.

Arrahaquen sat up straight, a twinge of guilt passing through her. Mother? At this time? It was almost midnight. 'Let her in.'

Ammyvryn appeared, and sat on the sofa next to Arrahaquen. She seemed tense and smelled as if she had endured a long day's work. 'Arrahaquen, I had to ask you something.'

'Yes?'

'Have you been tinkering with Citadel pyuters that you shouldn't have been?'

Arrahaquen felt as though she was staring down the proverbial green alley. 'No, Mother.' That was nearly true.

'Good.' And with that, Ammyvryn left. No goodbye; no smile. Nothing.

Arrahaquen watched her go. The door shut with an electronic tinkle. The tea was still hot in her hand.

Was that a warning? Had her visit to Zinina and Graaff-lin been noted? Surely the Citadel had far more important suspects to watch. Perhaps those minutes spent leafing through lists of jannitta defenders had been spotted? Again, no: that had been on a secure line. Then what? It could not be the secret ficus link since that too was secured against network spies.

Mother almost never came here. The last occasion was over a year ago, when Arrahaquen had sustained a kidney infection and been ill for some time. She felt worried, drained. Her throat had been sore for a day, and she thought she might have another cold coming on.

Life in the Citadel was making her nervous. She disliked the place, as though its mere existence was making her feel guilty. Crashes and bangs outside made her jump, as if the block was not her home. She felt it was time to pay another visit to Zinina and Graaff-lin.

She left the block of apartments and crossed the tumulus summit, walking south to the end of Om Street where, glowing against the black brick of a warehouse, she saw a row of public pyuters. Rain slanting in from off the sea pounded their screens and made their colour displays sparkle like an hallucinatory starscape. She stood up close to one and wiped the screen with one arm, tipping her hat to one side to protect her skin from the worst of the rain.

She disabled the voice receiver and tapped in some codes. Her own rig might no longer be secure, but she could still use the public pyuters. Arvendyn was the object of her search. Soon, the data of Uqeq's own adjutant appeared, stolen like a fossil filched from a quarry. Arvendyn was a medium-level priestess of the Goddess. Age twenty-six. Unremarkable background and type. Very high sexual activity. Almost created Kray Queen during Beltayn two years ago.

Surveillance at the request of the Red Brigade. Implicated with the hunt for the Silver Seed.

Now *that* was interesting.

On other channels, Citadel news was brief: a water leak, power cuts, intruders trying to scale the Wall. Most interesting were reports of intruders in a service tunnel. Arrahaquen cut the links.

If only the *ficus* seed would grow faster.

She left the Citadel and hurried north to Graaff-lin's home, where she found, to her surprise, a frightened Graaff-lin and an apprehensive Zinina.

She was welcomed in and they told her at once about the burglary. It worried her. The aamlon's face was paler than usual and she coughed incessantly, spraying the air to kill microbes. For the first time Arrahaquen wondered if a serious illness had gripped the priestess.

'You think somebody's after you?' Arrahaquen asked.

'They could have killed me, I suppose,' Graaff-lin replied. 'I expect they don't know enough yet.'

'I think you're in danger.'

'Agreed,' said Zinina.

'I know the ways of the Citadel,' Arrahaquen continued. 'We're on to something. Maybe it's to do with the seedlings.' Speculatively, she eyed the two plants, now over a foot tall and doing well. They should be fully grown in a fortnight.

A sudden thought had occurred to her. Zinina had been in the Citadel Guard. Had Graaff-lin hired Zinina to guide her into the secret pyuter zones under the Citadel crust? But no, it was unlikely that Zinina would have had access so far down. Yet the thought rankled. 'I'm just going for a wee,' she said.

Arrahaquen left the pair talking. Silently, she slipped into the hall and examined Zinina and Graaff-lin's protectives, looking for signs of underground travel. But everything was muddy or washed off. She considered. What about boots? Carefully, she extracted one of Zinina's distinctive thigh boots from its antiseptic bin and put her hand inside the cold, clammy thing until her armpit hit the top. Then she scraped her finger around the lining, scratching it. She withdrew her hand and, under the flame of a sea-fat candle, saw glittering fingers covered with flakes of golden plastic. So Zinina *had* been under the Citadel.

Much fell into place. No doubt this was where they had met Arvendyn. No doubt this was why the odd couple stayed together.

She returned to Zinina's room. 'I know the truth,' she said. 'Why did you two risk going under the Citadel?'

Zinina sat up. 'Hoy, there's not much escapes you, is there?'

This would be the perfect test, Arrahaquen thought. Now she could prove she was on their side by not reporting them. She replied, 'No there isn't. It was brave of you. Even I haven't got access to those places.'

'Who has, then?' Graaff-lin asked.

'Oh . . . Deese-lin and Spyne, the Portreeve. It's difficult to say.' When she saw their mystified faces she added, 'Deese-lin and Spyne are on the Red Brigade. Did you meet Arvendyn down there?'

The pair looked at one another. Zinina shrugged.

'Yes,' Graaff-lin admitted. 'In a service tunnel.'

Arrahaquen let out a whistle and sat back. 'I didn't know the tumulus was so hopelessly insecure. The place is like an upturned cullender. Everyone's trying to weevil a way in.'

'Can you blame them?' Zinina remarked.

'No,' Arrahaquen conceded. 'Now let me tell you something. Arvendyn has been watched for some time by Red Brigade spies in the temple. She's been implicated in the search for the Silver Seed.'

Graaff-lin scoffed at this. 'If it exists. It's only a silly Gedeese Veert legend.'

'You never know,' Arrahaquen said. 'In our position we can't afford to think that narrowly. Obviously somebody in the Goddess's temple thinks *some*thing is down there.'

'A legend,' Graaff-lin insisted.

In the silence that followed Arrahaquen pondered. Her intuition said that Zinina and Graaff-lin were trustworthy. She had the strange impression that the three of them *had* to work together.

She heard voices and footsteps in the street outside. '. . . it's been breached, I 'eard. Highgate breached. 'Oo'd 'ave thought it'd come t' that?'

Highgate breached. So at last the final wall of defence had been punctured. The north wall had been holed. She looked at the other two, and realised that they also had heard the news.

7

One night, when Graaff-lin was asleep (and dreaming, judging by the whistles and snatches of erotic poetry that could be heard), Zinina explored the house in its entirety, cataloging in her mind all useful objects, means of escape, damp patches, fungal infection and other domestic niceties. She ended up in the loft. From here, she could see boats on the sea. People were leaving Kray by sea, of course, the idiots, because it seemed to them the only means of escape. Every week would see some new rumour of a land of sanctuary found across the ocean. But that was all nonsense. Anyhow, the sea was as dangerous as the land, with its giant turtles, fang-fish, and strangling kelp, not to mention the infected filth and bacteria. Every boat and ship ended up sliding into a luminous grave. Morning tides brought corpses to the shore, glowing softly like a line of nebulae at a vast galaxy's edge.

She returned to the ground floor and for a moment opened the front door. She wanted to feel what it was like to be safe inside a house. And for a few seconds, as she caught the whiff of ammonia and the softer smell of methane, and saw lights from reveller encampments reflecting off the two great prongs of the Cowhorn Tower, she felt a pang of love for the city. Kray was her home. The Cemetery nearby had been her nursery, for a short time. She was a free woman of the city: an independent. Now it was up to her to make meaning from her life and from what little future remained.

The Nonagon Room became quiet, save for the tapping of fingers on leather note pads.

The combination of high, domed ceiling, walls as thick as a grain barn's and floor tiled with maroon-veined marble hexagons meant that sounds echoed, acquiring resonance. This was a chamber of authority. The majority of its central area was taken up by a circular table, topped with sumptuous crimson leather, gold-edged and set with a jumble of papers, small hand pyuters, and goblets of mead. Around this huge surface sat eight people. One more sat upon the table.

Each chair was individual, though each consisted of an ebony frame, felt-backed, carved with flowers and scimitars. It was in colour and design that they varied. One was grey and green, another white, another maroon; one was huge, one moderate, one boasted sidearms like the wings of a bat.

An impasse had brought the silence. The nine glanced at one another.

The Portreeve shifted in her chair. 'We must make a decision.' She scratched her scalp, took a sip of mead, then continued. 'I would not have independents working in defender groups. It is a matter of principle. Independents reject the bounty of the Citadel. Let the fools suffer. If the families they come from were even a little less respected in the city, I would convert them all to revellers by abolishing the class entirely.'

Ammyvryn sat up straight. 'We could put off the decision until next week. Why don't we all consider the problem for a few days, then discuss and vote next time?'

'Why should we put it off?' the Portreeve countered. 'I'm becoming irritated with things not getting done. We have months in which to act, Ammyvryn, and you counsel waiting?'

General agreement, voiced in whispers and nods, followed this remark. The Portreeve, her dark eyes narrowing, her thin mouth pursed, sighed, then picked up the metal dolphin at her side and shook it like a bell. It tinkled.

'We shall keep defender groups pure,' she concluded gruffly. 'Now, item twelve. Felis priestesses giving trouble. Uqeq?'

Uqeq, a short woman of middle age, somewhat wrinkled and wearing too much make-up, cleared her throat then read from the pyuter screen in her hand. Her voice was clipped and taut, almost spiky in tone. 'Felis temple report. Three priestesses there have been preaching to Krayans in the streets of the Old Quarter, in a manner that could constitute an incitement to riot. They are being monitored by agents disguised as new acolytes. Once the truth of the possibility that they are using cats as spies within the Citadel has been validated, they will be sent under Gugul Street, having first been interrogated. If they are not using cats as spies, they will be immediately destroyed. Further report to come.'

The Portreeve nodded. 'Better make that report soon. What's been the public response to these feline speeches?'

Now she could not read, Uqeq became less coherent, stuttering as though she was repressing a number of psychological tics. 'Um, they listen. They listen. There's definitely more agitation this month, Port-tr-tr-treeve. Soon there'll be riots.'

'Riots?'

'As the green wave comes south. There'll be refugees. Lots of them, now that Highgate is breached. Huge social unrest. Riots.'

The Portreeve nodded. 'Anything else on the cat-lovers?'

'No.'

'Excuse me?' said Katoh-lin, fingernails drumming on the table. 'We are going to leave it, mmm, mmm, at *that*?'

The Portreeve frowned. 'You find my decision controversial?'

Katoh-lin blinked and glanced at the seven other faces, all turned to her. She said, 'Uqeq making some bland report will achieve nothing. Mmm, mmm, we cannot on the one hand decide now on the composition of defender groups, and, mmm, on the other wait days, possibly weeks, before dealing with the cat clergy.'

Quiet Omaytra, small and pale in her low black chair, said, 'It's a good point, and well spoken.'

These words did not please the Portreeve. Firmly she said, 'The majority at this table support my view, that further information is required.'

'Information,' Katoh-lin scoffed, sitting back and throwing a pen upon the table to indicate that this was her final word. 'Information indeed. What, mmm, mmm, we require is *knowledge*.'

'My decision stands,' said the Portreeve. She paused. 'And that is final.' Ringing the dolphin again, she said, 'Item thirteen. Progress with respect to the plan and the noophytes.'

Deese-lin stood up and began waving her arms about as she spoke. She always did this. 'I told you I should have been the first item. I have news! You never listened to me, though I'm the prophet of the conscoosities. Kraandeere! Jilvers kom nachs hujks and veert-un spjiks to you all.'

The Portreeve waved at Deese-lin's chair. 'Sit down. What news is this?'

'The conscoosities are febrile!'

'The noophytes, noophytes are febrile, I, I say,' Spyne added. She sat in a wicker dish on the table, being a womanikin – a reminder of the genetic madness of previous millennia.

'Febrile?' came mutters around the table.

'What does febrile mean?'

Shaking as though in a fury, Deese-lin, sweat beginning to run from her flushed scalp and face, tried to continue her flurry of words. Occasionally sentences would separate from one another, and the Portreeve would have to make her repeat their gist.

'You always bawl me out!' she said. 'I told you there would be trouble. The conscoosities say that the time is close. The jump.'

'The, the jump, jump,' said Spyne, nodding her tiny head.

Deese-lin pointed at the Portreeve. 'Guiners, guiners! There are twenty voices all advising you and you don't listen. They say you must hurry. Hurry, kraandeere! In months this city will be dead and gone, they've foreseen it all, and they never lie.'

'Is what you're trying to say,' asked the Portreeve, 'that we must hurry?'

'Yes.'

'Yes, yes,' Spyne added.

'Then sit. You may visit my personal chamber afterwards, Deese-lin. And bring evidence with you.'

There were looks of alarm at this. 'Your chamber?' Omaytra said. 'But what about us?'

'I don't follow,' said the Portreeve, shaking her head.

'Why should we miss out on discussions concerning the plan?'

'Deese-lin is febrile,' answered the Portreeve, allowing herself a small smile at her jest. 'She is temperamental—'

'I'm sane!' Deese-lin protested, her arm-waving violent enough to knock over a goblet.

'Sane, sane,' Spyne echoed.

The Portreeve sighed. 'This becomes unseemly.'

Uqeq, pointing at Omaytra and Katoh-lin, said, 'You stay out of this. Leave the Portr-tr-tr-treeve alone.'

The Portreeve rang her dolphin. 'Item number fourteen. Hurry it along now, I've got supper in a few minutes. The Dodspaat priestess situation.'

Katoh-lin controlled her wavering voice. 'Much as before,' she reported. 'I am watching her riverside house, mmm, mmm, very carefully. Unfortunately she has special pyuter circuits, and even Uqeq's superlative agents can't overhear her network conversations. It's most vexing.'

'D-d-d-damned aamlon priestess,' Uqeq stuttered.

'But is she dangerous?' asked the Portreeve.

'Most assuredly. She has murdered before. But what she is doing through the serpents I don't know. Mmm, mmm, mmm, we must watch and learn—'

'Haul her in,' came a few voices.

Katoh-lin slapped her hand upon the leather table-top. 'No! That would be a terrible, mmm, mistake. We must discover what she is doing first. What if she is of some illegal group? What if she is a Holist?'

'Katoh-lin is correct,' said Surqjna in her silky voice. She had tanned skin and penetrating brown eyes. 'The priestess must be watched. There's nothing we can do at the moment.'

'Agreed,' chorused Ammyvryn and Omaytra.

'Lunacy,' retorted Uqeq.

'We'll debate that when the time comes,' said the Portreeve in a loud voice, glaring at Uqeq and at the fidgeting Deese-lin. 'At the moment, it seems that she has just discovered some way of attracting the attention of the noophytes, yes?'

'Mmm, yes,' agreed Katoh-lin.

'Right. If she manages anything more damaging, we'll make her a priority. For now she's an interfering body. However, if any of you do happen across her, she's to be killed instantly.'

Surqjna drew in a hiss of breath, and Katoh-lin said, 'But—'

'That's all,' said the Portreeve, ringing the dolphin. 'Fifteen. A break-in. Pyetmian.'

Pyetmian, a fat woman wearing black and red silks and a brimmed hat, said, 'We can't trace it exactly, Portreeve. Somebody got into a service tunnel and did some damage. It was an insider who knew how to disable the hatch alarm. It's impossible to say how far she got. I've sealed the access hatch and had the area monitored. More than likely she came from the Power Station.'

The Portreeve nodded. 'Have everyone at the Power Station who would have been in the right area at the right time sent to Uqeq's dungeons.'

'Yes, Portreeve.'

The dolphin rang. 'Sixteen and last. Water shortages. Pyetmian again.'

Pyetmian nodded, glancing at a pyuter at her side. She had the air of an efficient matron. 'We must divert much more from both Water Stations,' she said. 'The Krayans can stand it. I'll have estimates of the new amounts required by us sent to you all.' She paused, surveying the eight people around her. 'In principle, do you agree? I don't want to cause trouble in the city.'

'Trouble?' came voices.

Pyetmian shrugged. 'Hopefully we'll be out of Kray soon, if Surqjna and Deese-lin and the noophytes and everyone else work at full tilt. But you never know, ordinary people outside might get agitated. We've seen what a few miserable clerics can do. Think what might happen if Taziqi and the Goddess clerics become belligerent.'

The Portreeve clicked her tongue, obviously irritated. 'Tsk, tsk, don't mention that wobbling slug to me. The Goddess temple won't spoil the plan, you have my word on that.'

Pyetmian shrugged, playing with a pen and studying the tabletop. Around the table there was an atmosphere of suspicion – glances, fidgeting fingers, sour faces.

The Portreeve stood. 'Anything else?'

Ammyvryn said, 'Yes. One small matter. My daughter.'

'Your daughter. Arryquyn? Aryquellen? Is it urgent, I'm late for supper.'

'I just wanted to say that she's to be watched.'

'Why?' asked Katoh-lin and Surqjna simultaneously.

'Because. There are spies everywhere.'

'Very well. Spies or no spies, the meeting is closed until next time. You may leave the Nonagon.'

Zinina left the house and hurried into Pine Street, the site of the nearest working wall-screen. Bypassing console security with a pin, she dialled ten numbers.

A querulous voice answered. 'Hello?' It was Qmoet.

Zinina spoke in jannitta. 'It's me. Any luck with the Citadel data I sent you?'

'Ky and Eskhatos are working on it. You got more?'

'No. I'm planning, though – oh, hang on.' A cat had prowled into view on the window sill above and to the left of her – an old moggy by the look of it. Zinina raised her needle rifle and killed it first shot. It dropped into a puddle, splashing water out and leaving a halo of wriggling orange worms. 'I'm planning a second mission,' she continued. 'I think we'll have Arrahaquen along this time.'

'Are you *sure*?'

'I know, I know, she's Ammyvryn's daughter. No, she seems totally genuine, Qmoet. I know my instincts. She's genuine or I'm a man. Actually I even quite like her. A bit.'

Qmoet stayed quiet. The line crackled and Zinina noticed the blue edges of the screen fading. 'Not even a hint of a plot behind Arrahaquen?' Qmoet said at last.

'Nothing. C'mon, she left us a *ficus* plant as security!'

'You keep sending in the data, huh? We're glad you told us about noophytes, but we still don't know what they are. Must be a very old word.'

'Talking of which, have Ky or Gishaad-lin had any luck with that word, "dwan"?'

'No.'

Zinina cursed under her breath. 'It must mean something. Listen, Graaff-lin told me she made this recording from a serpent, and it said "dwan" was a heart word that the likes of us shouldn't use.'

'We'll see what we can find out.'

'I'll call again when my mission's set up.'

'Take care, Zin.'

The line went dead, and the screen speakers fizzed at her, as though in revenge at her illicit ways. Zinina removed her pin from the data port. A scrap of silver paper lying on the screen caught her eye. She picked up the scrap and examined it. It was a square of foil that looked as if it had held a tablet. She sniffed it.

Menthol.

Startled, Zinina stared at the foil, then turned to scan the street, half expecting to meet the gaze of somebody else. There was no watcher. A few defenders hunched dejected over their cannisters of verticide passed by. The windows of every house she could see were shuttered.

Disconcerted, Zinina began the walk back to Graaff-lin's house. The foil she stowed inside her kit.

8

A week passed by. The two seeds in Zinina's adopted home were no longer proper plants. They were squat globes, purple and shiny, their cases hard as steel and pierced here and there with tiny screens and arrays of digital ports, their surfaces stippled and, because they twitched occasionally, slightly menacing. There seemed no physical difference between them.

Arrahaquen still worked in the Citadel, but she seemed very tense. Zinina, meanwhile, decided it was time to investigate Arvendyn.

'Investigate? How?' Graaff-lin asked.

Zinina nodded. 'You remember we tracked Arvendyn entering the Andromeda Quarter?'

'Yes.'

'Where Rien Zir's old temple stood?'

'What business would Arvendyn have there?'

'I've no idea. That's why I think we should go on a little picnic.'

'But the *Andromeda* Quarter? Do you think it would be safe?'

'Safe? Is the Portreeve an educated, ethical woman?'

A pause. 'No.'

'Right. Oh, stop worrying, we'll be back before you're needed at your temple.'

Zinina went to the kitchen to pack the food, raiding stocks to make up a package of potato salad, okra, seaweed cakes and a tube of sugar-coated nuts that she happened to find under a couch cushion. She packed four bottles of official water, but covered their crimson tops to minimise attention from revellers.

It was another dim day and rain poured from low cloud, though it smelled fresh enough. The six parties of defenders that they saw west of the river all carried torches. Zinina carried an anjiq with a handle while Graaff-lin, suffering still from a cold, took a sea-fat lantern with fresnel lens shutters. Through the sodden streets they walked, following the curve of the river until they crossed Peppermint Street and found themselves in the Andromeda Quarter. Behind them, blue and green tubes inside houses flickered and died as another power-cut took hold.

The Andromeda Quarter occupied that portion of Kray to the south-east of the Gardens. It sprawled. Most of it consisted of ancient ruins. No main streets passed through it, but to the south it was bounded by Peppermint and Arrowmint Streets, and to the east by Jessamine Street. At its eastern tip stood the sinister twin spires of the Felis temple.

Zinina surveyed the jungle of damp foliage and shattered masonry ahead. 'Do we just forge through or follow a map?'

'Follow the map,' said the sensible Graaff-lin.

Zinina unrolled a plan printed on a plastic sheet. 'Let's follow that way a while,' she said, pointing down an alley fringed with palms and giant ferns. 'Get out yer cat-pranger.' Zinina shouldered her pack and tightened her kit on its belt. She felt excited; not at all afraid. 'I've wanted to come here for years,' she said. 'At last I'm free enough to do it.'

As they walked they pointed things out to one another. 'Look at the frost damage on those leaves,' Graaff-lin said, indicating a grove of slim papyrus. 'Winter hit hard here.'

Zinina could see orange trees and even a few banana trees, and these were the variety that produced fruit rather than pyuter hardware; the extraordinary fecundity of Kray's botanic foundation had beaten even the fiercest grip of ice. She whistled in appreciation. Everywhere, even growing from the tops of ruins, she saw mare's tail clumps all heavy with sodden teardrop-shaped data peripherals, which she collected to aid future bartering sessions.

They moved on. Through parks overgrown with ivy and along passages choked with cushions of fungus they walked, stopping to peer down wells that seemed to lead to the centre of the globe – a pyuter rangefinder said 'unreadable' – and pausing to listen to ghostly echoes, which sometimes they realised were of sounds they had made. Cats prowled, and these they shot. They saw a few snakes, but ignored them. The atmosphere was sultry. Occasionally the ground would shiver and once there was even a tremor that made bricks fall off a crumbling wall. Zinina and Graaff-lin stopped at this, and looked around, perplexed. Tremors here were thought to be caused by underground machine remnants left by previous occupants of the quarter. It was a place haunted by the spirits of life and of artificial life.

Zinina paused every so often to put her bare hand to the sopping soil. It possessed a distinct warmth. The tall trees all around seemed to chide her for making this observation.

Whistles and distant whoops, as of dangerous animals massing for attack, echoed through the sodden vegetation. The constant patter of rain, a sound Zinina found relaxing in its own way, became here the carrier wave of danger, and she found that she was gripping the butt of her rifle.

Graaff-lin stopped. 'What's that?' she asked, pointing to a pile of ruins fifty feet high.

Zinina peered at her map, wiping the rain off with a sleeve. 'I think that's the remains of the old Phallists' ziggurat. We must be here – look on the map. Just south of the Galactic Port.'

'How distant are the Gedeese Veert ruins?'

'Oh . . . half an hour.'

Graaff-lin walked towards the vine-slung ruins to investigate their outer walls. Zinina followed. The bricks here were tightly packed, without mortar, and showed the vitreous signs of laser cutting. They were covered with engraved murals, some still containing the original copper inlays.

'Look,' said Graaff-lin, with an intake of breath. 'Look, the women have beards. Ugh.'

Zinina peered at the ranks of figures that, although viewed from the side, had heads, feet and hands depicted from the front. With a broken gourd she drew water from a puddle to clean an area of algae and lichen. 'Those aren't women, they're men.'

'But they've got breasts.'

Zinina looked again. 'So they have. They must be men with breasts, then. Them beards must be falsies.'

Graaff-lin threw Zinina a haughty glance. 'Or *women* with beards.'

Zinina shook her head. 'I think, given the history of this planet, that it's far more likely to be men with breasts.'

'Oh, indeed?'

'Sure. Feminisation. The change in the land, going bad and that? Don't you know anything? It was living off bad land that made the pestilence viruses that attack immune systems.'

Graaff-lin shuddered at the mention of that disease. 'It all sounds a trifle imaginative, Zinina.'

Zinina frowned. 'You want proof? Look, the men ain't got no bulges between their legs, have they?' Zinina decided that Graaff-lin was confused, and a question that she had often wanted to ask the aamlon priestess came to mind. 'Are you still a virgin, incidentally?'

Graaff-lin took on the haughty air once more. 'All dedicated priestesses of the Dodspaat are celibate. I was born into the faith. What do you think?'

Zinina nodded. 'I just wondered. Didn't mean to annoy you.'

'Well you have, Zinina. I could ask a similar question. I've heard that in some reveller societies, by which I mean the society you come from, in case you had not realised, sexual relations outside of wedlock are punished by execution. Is that so?'

Zinina was used to the pliable, melancholy, almost downtrodden Graaff-lin. This fiery retort made her uncomfortable. 'Well,' she muttered, 'yes.'

'I am *quite* certain you are not a virgin.'

Zinina laughed. 'I've been to the Fish Chambers like everyone else. But I ain't a reveller any more, remember?'

A further thought struck Zinina. 'Were your parents born into the Hu Junuq faith, then?'

'Yes, why?'

'Well, you popped out of a woman, didn't you? *Someone* must have got pregnant, unless you're a partheno like Arrahaquen.'

Graaff-lin turned away from the murals and returned to the road down which they had been walking. 'Let us speak no more of this sordid topic.'

Zinina chuckled, and followed.

They forged on through thickets of date and fern, and along alleys lined with coconut palms.

At noon they arrived at the ruins. Zinina looked at the green spot on her map, then studied the scene ahead. 'This is it. This is Rien Zir's original temple.'

In a square walled on two sides, open on the others, stood a complex of stone and greenery, an overgrown ruin that in some places was well preserved but in others consisted of dust and moss. The highest point was sixty feet high, the lowest was a slimy pond. The place lay shrouded in an aura of majesty, partly because of the sheer scale of the surviving constructions, but it also seemed mysterious because of the bizarre architecture. Gargoyles and statues rivalled walls in size, and there were many outcrops of ruined technology, ancient stuff that even Kray's rain could not rust or erode and which endured, often hanging loose like nerves remaining from a lost limb.

Graaff-lin, it seemed to Zinina, had begun to regret coming on this expedition. 'Don't worry,' Zinina said soothingly, 'there's nothing active here now. It's dead. Rien Zir's moved up the Carmines.'

'I know, but I don't like it. Still, the Dodspaat will protect me from malign influences. Shall we look around?'

Graaff-lin paused, her gaze fixed upon Zinina's face. 'You don't worship the Gedeese Veert, do you?'

'I said before, no. I don't worship anything.'

With trepidation they walked under an arch and into the nearest section of the ruin. Here whole rooms survived, although they were choked with a tumble of roots and etiolated shoots, and Zinina, once again cleaning walls with water from last year's gourds, was able to make out scenes of worship engraved in bas-relief, amongst the wasp holes and cracks. She felt a sense of wonder not felt since she explored the Cemetery's mausoleums as a child. Here, as then, were sigils and images from ancient times. Women carried staves; women bathed one another with water and braided their hair; women gave birth. There were also interesting scenes of women initiating youths into the ways of sex, interesting because it seemed to Zinina that the smallest penis on show was longer than any she had seen in the Fish Chambers. And they all had balls. In the Fish Chambers, most men had one or even two undescended testicles.

Zinina considered all this. It was common knowledge, at least to revellers, that the Earth was trying to remove all traces of humanity from its crust. Now it had breached the walls of the final city. Once, it was rumoured, people and land were one. When the land altered in such a way as to change the life upon it, that life became unbalanced. Zinina had been taught that the original problem was people existing in the first place, and for some time she had believed that. But later, thinking about it for herself, she realised that it should be possible for people and land to relate harmoniously, if only the right attitude could be cultivated. Now it was too late. They moved on.

'How about lunch?' Graaff-lin said. 'I'm hungry.'

Zinina looked around the chamber in which they stood. It was dry in the centre, and there was a large purple root on which they could sit. 'Here do?'

They ate their food, drank a bottle of water each, then carried on exploring. Now they were finding less complete rooms, although many of these contained superior friezes, some retaining original colours. Graaff-lin paused at a group of landscapes and, when she did not move for some minutes, Zinina joined her. Graaff-lin pointed, saying, 'What's that white disk?'

Zinina approached until her nose was inches away from the picture. 'That's the moon. Didn't you know there used to be a moon?'

Graaff-lin nodded, but seemed uncertain.

'Hoy, you have led a sheltered life,' Zinina remarked. 'Long ago there used to be a moon as well as a sun. Don't you know the legend of the Goddess and the Fungus?'

'Such stuff is not learnt by priestesses of the Dodspaat.'

'According to the legend, Rien Zir was strolling across the firmament, just out for a walk or something, and she happened to notice a fungus spore shooting away from her towards her sister Seylene.'

'That is the moon?'

'That's the moon. Anyhow, this spore came from her own belly-button.'

'Omphalos,' Graaff-lin interrupted.

Zinina smiled a frigid smile. 'Navel. Whatever. So, Rien Zir tried to stop this spore from flying away with her hand, but she couldn't, and it hit her sister. Then the spore began to grow, and nothing Rien Zir did could stop it from eating away at her sister, like a sort of silicon leprosy. So eventually Seylene, from all the agony, I suppose, was completely transformed, and became a flower shape. The Spaceflower, in fact. So that's the origin of the Spaceflower.'

Graaff-lin nodded. 'You have to look at these legends with a metaphorical eye, Zinina, an eye you do not possess, I think. Obviously Seylene is this ancient moon and Rien Zir personifies the Earth. No doubt this lone spore symbolises some event.' She paused. 'I suppose it's not impossible that the spore was the Silver Seed itself.'

Zinina was stunned by this simple statement, so casually uttered.

'It's possible,' Graaff-lin went on. 'Remember, Arraha-quen said that Arvendyn was implicated by Citadel spies in the search for the Silver Seed. Your legend concerns a real object, the Spaceflower. Reality and fantasy inter-twine.'

Zinina had never thought to read any deeper meaning

into the old stories. 'How could we find out?'

'Look at these friezes with open eye and mind.'

'But could you do that? I mean, with all your Hu Junuq training and that?'

'Zinina, I shall do my best, if you are trying to imply that my faith leaves me with a closed mind. As for the Silver Seed, I think it is a legend, nothing more. Probably the priestesses of the Gedeese Veert have been convinced by Arvendyn that it still exists, so they are looking for it. They will fail, since the Dodspaat alone promulgate truth.'

They departed the room and entered an open area. The rain pattered down upon the grass and the date leaves, and left sparkling traces as rivulets ran down the bark, for every surface around them was imbued with a fungal luminescence, giving them the feeling that they were inside a faery grotto. A gusty wind had picked up, and Zinina knew that heavy rain would follow. As they walked on, through a statue-lined boulevard and towards a series of free-standing metal walls, Zinina asked, 'How would you interpret these statues, then?'

Graaff-lin studied them, shielding her eyes from the rain. She drew breath to speak, but a tremor shook the ground. When it died she said, 'Well, they seem to depict a group of people, though they don't seem to have proper faces. I expect that means they have no identity. Perhaps they were pyuton heroes, or something.'

'But pyutons are characters.'

'That's true.' Graaff-lin became interested in the statues, counting them – there were eighteen – and studying their costume and their arrangement. 'Each has a flower for a face, and each is covered in miniature hieroglyphics. Look, it is as if they have been written by spiders.'

Zinina walked up to the nearest statue, which was a trifle taller than she, and saw the truth of Graaff-lin's observation. This one had a primrose-like face.

'Yet they seem to have emotional expressions,' Graaff-lin continued. 'These are beautiful, rare objects.'

'They were carved by laser, you can see the glassy sheen.'

'Yes, yes, I can ... and look, Zinina, we have stumbled across something here. Praise the Dodspaat. Look, each one carries a small seed with a piece of wool for a wriggly tail.'

'Seed?' Zinina said. 'You mean the silver one?'

'They can't all be the Silver Seed.' Graaff-lin let her gaze range over every statue. 'I don't know. I shall have to consider it.'

Disappointed, Zinina nodded. As dusk approached they ate a final meal, drank all but one bottle of water, then began the trek west.

9

The winds strengthened through the night that Zinina and Graaff-lin spent sleeping off the fatigue of trekking through the Andromeda Quarter, and the rain became torrential. Much damage was done, particularly to the northerly quarters of Kray, the Green and the Archaic, and also to some of the older buildings in the Harbour Quarter, where few people now lived. By morning there were gales shrieking off the ocean. Zinina looked out into the street, to see that most Krayans felt too intimidated by the weather to leave their hovels and garrets. The streets were empty of people but full of slates and rubble.

And storms meant more power cuts. The Power Station, which was located high up in the Green Quarter, operated on a schedule composed of chance and poor management. Already today there had been two short cuts, and bulletins on the Citadel networks hinted at longer ones to come. It was clear that now Kray had been breached the Power Station had only a short life remaining in which to splutter out electricity.

Graaff-lin possessed rechargeable batteries for her pyuter rigs, thin cylinders that smelled of grease and acid, but not everyone was so fortunate. Soon, Krayans would have something else to complain about. But not those who lived in the Citadel, of course. They had their own power supply.

Graaff-lin went to her temple next morning – she worked on alternate days – but returned unhappy. For a second time, Katoh-lin had requested that she deliver a parcel to the Citadel, and she was beginning to feel suspicious, for there was no reason why some junior clerk could not perform the task. She held a crimson pass in her hand. 'It was warm,' she said, puzzled, 'most definitely warm.'

Zinina shrugged. 'I expect she took it out her back pocket.'

'No, it lay in a drawer.'

'Maybe it was over a heater.'

Graaff-lin would not accept any of this. 'Something is going to happen. I can feel it. The Dodspaat are going to manifest something for me.'

'You're just worried,' Zinina replied, trying to be calmer.

'Then how do you explain a weapon appearing in my locker?'

Zinina perked up at this. 'Do you think you've been set up?'

'Don't be absurd. Who would wish to set me up?'

Zinina turned on the music channel of a pyuter rig. Despite the fact that she turned the volume up, the sound of an aamlon string and hound quintet did not mask what followed. Both women jumped out of their seats as the thunderous rumble of an explosion made the shutters rattle and the floor tremble. A pair of wall-mounted azure photoplankton tubes flickered, and the nutrition sticks inside crumbled and dissolved.

'Uqallavaz tq! What in all Kray was *that*?' Zinina shouted.

Both women ran to the nearest window and peered out. Dusk had arrived, and because of that they were able to see a bloated mushroom of orange flame and black smoke billowing out of the side of the Citadel.

'Let's go upstairs,' Zinina suggested, 'get a better view.'

They hurried through the trapdoor and from the roof window saw what was now a seething mass of smoke drifting north across the Citadel. Soon it would cross the river and begin to smother the Mercantile Quarter.

'That'll come here,' Zinina breathed. 'We better secure every window. Could be poison. Come on, it'll be here in minutes, sea wind's blowing it.'

While Zinina sealed every window with its zipper-curtain, and sprayed foam into the cracks around the front door, Graaff-lin tried to worm her way into the official networks, in an attempt to catch snatches of defender conversation. However, the best she could do was pick up pyuters talking to one another. Eventually an official message appeared, explaining that everyone was to remain indoors for an hour. A transformer had overloaded and ignited its own mountings.

Zinina scoffed at this. 'No way is a transformer going to cause that much smoke. They're lying. I'm going to watch from upstairs. You keep an eye on the networks. Try to ease yourself into the emergency chit-chat.'

After an hour, all that remained of the incident were a few stray wisps of heavy smoke. No flames licked the tumulus. Zinina knew that the emergency services up there were superb, and it was likely that the fire had been smothered by foam in minutes. But she remained suspicious of the official explanation, and tried to remember what exactly had stood on that part of the tumulus.

* * *

Two days after the great explosion Graaff-lin fell ill. Always thin, she seemed as gaunt as a dying reveller as she lay in bed with a temperature and pain in her chest and stomach. Graaff-lin, through gritted teeth, said she only needed rest and the painkillers that Zinina would find in her valise. Rummaging through the bag, Zinina was disconcerted to find twenty hundred-packs of ampoules, each containing a thick yellow liquid. This was a considerable supply, implying Graaff-lin had laid in stocks for a serious illness.

Zinina returned and questioned Graaff-lin, but she refused to answer, so Zinina departed. Occasionally, she would hear muttered aamlon curses. At least, she presumed they were curses. It might almost be worth putting a translation pyuter in her room to see what she was saying ...

But Zinina's troubles were far from over. As she pottered around the terracotta pitcher room, polishing the two globes with a duster and stroking them like puppies, there came the twin beep of Arrahaquen's 'ficus' line, and she rushed through the house to take the message at Graaff-lin's main rig. 'Yes?'

Arrahaquen was distraught. 'Zinina, I'm in trouble. Had to leave the Citadel! Being chased.' She was gasping for breath, as though she had been running.

'Chased?' repeated Zinina, shaken. 'Chased? Who by?'

'I had to escape the Citadel Guard. For the Goddess's sake, Zinina, I need help! I'm by Westcity Water Station. Get down here, else I'm dead.'

The line was cut. For a few seconds Zinina just looked at the dull metal of the rig communicator. Her brain seemed to be out of gear. Then she flew to the hall where, limbs pumping and whirling, she struggled into her boots and protectives, swearing in jannitta as she did so.

Zinina was fit. In the Citadel Guard she had been known to sprint the Om Street Circle in under three minutes. It was evening and only a few people walked the streets. Like an amphetamine dervish, Zinina raced down Sphagnum Street, then took the gentle slope of Feverfew Street even faster, as her breath came strong and the adrenaline of fear coursed through her limbs. She sped by the Temple of Balloon Love, the Food Station, then careered into Onion Street. There was Arrahaquen, obviously exhausted, struggling towards the street junction. She could hear the ominous sound of Citadel motorbikes.

'What happened?' she said, splashing up to Arrahaquen and gripping her by the shoulders.

Arrahaquen could hardly speak for breathlessness. 'Quick. Bikes after me. Guards. Hide me.'

Zinina looked around. Seconds to go. She pulled Arrahaquen into a doorway and, bracing her back, pulled at a plank of wood hanging down from the jamb. It snapped off. Pushing Arrahaquen down, she pulled the pathetic cover over them both and peered out into the chill night rain.

Two motorbikes sped along the street like the night's squalls blowing off the sea. As the first passed, Zinina saw its scarlet hide by the lamps of adjacent houses, saw too the muscles bunching underneath, and the cords of ligament at the wheel suspensors and the handlebars. A visored Citadel Guard woman rode it. The second approached. Its two halogen headlamps searched the pot-holed street independently, like the hooded eyes of the chameleon, and its engine gave a throaty roar. But it too darted by, and Zinina was left with an after image of red lines and an image of blue rear lights, flashing as the bikes braked, skidded, and paused at the junction.

The riders revved their engines. Zinina heard the staccato static of radio talk. Then they turned left and made down Ficus Street, towards the river.

'Time to go,' Zinina said. 'Can you make it?'

'Just. Not far.'

'We've got to go north. Get away from this quarter.'

'Right. Just lead me.'

Arrahaquen stumbled as Zinina led her across the street and into the maze of passages overhung with the filth-dripping upper storeys of buildings that constituted this part of the city. Her legs were tired. The toes of her boots caught in every hole and snag, and Zinina had to navigate carefully around the larger 'legbreakers'. Here there was no light, and every possibility of bumping into drug-addled revellers, or, worse, hormone-tripping green revellers. But Zinina had the same sense of direction as any Krayan who had been forced to live off her wits as a child, so she marched north, until she recognised the yellow cobbles of Culverkeys Street and saw crystal Infirmary lamps up ahead.

They rested. Zinina looked back. Way south, she could see the tip of the tumulus over house roofs, but above that she noticed what looked very much like the yellow searchlights of hang-gliders making their way north. Others seemed to be searching the Harbour and Mercantile Quarters.

'What have you done?' she asked Arrahaquen as they hurried on.

'I don't know. I had to leave. It was getting too much.'

'What was?'

'The pressure. I couldn't stand it.'

Zinina urged Arrahaquen past the Infirmary, but stopped as they reached the Gardens. Here they sat on a log, having first checked it for vermin. 'I can't take you back south,' Zinina said, 'it'd be far too risky, what with them hang-gliders.'

'But where can I go?'

'Listen. I'll hide you up at an inn I know for a few days, maybe a week. When the fuss has died down, we'll smuggle you down, eh?'

'What inn?' Arrahaquen asked miserably.

'The Spired.'

'But it's a pot-house,' protested Arrahaquen. 'It's a hole.'

'Hoy, don't speak like that about it. It's a decent hole.'

'But isn't it next to the Cemetery?'

'Long as you don't go out without me you'll survive. It's the only safe place. Now, what have you *done*?'

'Left the Citadel. I can't explain it, Zinina. It's been building up for ages. I'm sure they're on to me. Us, maybe.'

Zinina stared. 'You mean nothing's happened and you've just run? Just let them know you're guilty by running?' Suddenly she was angry at Arrahaquen.

'Yes,' Arrahaquen sobbed, hiding her face in her hands. Then she looked up and said, 'You've got to believe me. They know something. My mother's up to something. Somebody was trying to kill me a few weeks back. I could just feel the currents, Zinina. If I stayed there I'd be as good as pitched under Gugul Street.'

'So you ran.'

'I couldn't help it. When I didn't turn up for my shift at Defender House they came after me. Thank the Goddess I met you, else I'd have had nowhere to go.'

Zinina pulled Arrahaquen to her feet. 'Come on. We're going to the Spired.'

'I've left all my stuff in my flat. But I have got some news about Arvendyn.'

'Later,' Zinina said.

Arrahaquen seemed to deflate like a punctured balloon. She followed Zinina around the edge of the Gardens, a docile animal tripping over paving slabs, until they stopped on Crimson Street to wait for a cablecar, the fierce wind blowing torrents of rain at them. Within fifteen minutes Zinina had sat Arrahaquen on a barrel behind the Spired Inn.

Inside, it was warm. A blaze burned in each of the three grates. Some naked jannitta dancers lay in front of one, on a shag-pile rug. Elsewhere custom seemed slow, which Zinina was glad for. She approached Dhow-lin.

'Sly-girl,' called Dhow-lin, squinting at her in surprise. 'Here for a thimble of the weakest ale we have?'

'Only the best for me,' Zinina replied, sitting on a bar stool, 'and I need a barrel and a half.'

'Hah!' Dhow-lin said. 'One glass of the tough stuff and you're—'

'One sip of baqa and my mind is clear enough to banter with the likes of you!' Zinina interrupted. 'Now, I've got a favour to ask. A big one.'

'Ask away, my little hour-glass.'

'I've got a friend outside in your courtyard. She needs a safe room for a week. No, no, wait a moment, let me finish. She needs your top safe room and you'll be paid in advance for the whole stay.'

Dhow-lin slapped her palm on the bar. 'A week? Let's see what'll pay for that.'

Zinina hesitated. 'Well, I don't actually have it on me at the moment. But listen, I'll bring high-class pyuter bits. Whatever you want. I'll bring it. Only let me bring her in, please.'

'Make it a double memory-case. Just because it's you.'

Zinina smiled and touched Dhow-lin's wrinkled hands. 'Thanks. I'll nip round the kitchen door, yeah?'

'Key to the top garret's by the oven.'

Zinina slipped through the revolving door behind the bar. The kitchen smelled of herb pastry, rice and onions. Nobody was around. She unlocked the rear door, hissed at a miserable-looking Arrahaquen, beckoned her inside, then relocked the door. With Arrahaquen looking on, she took the key that was hanging over the oven then led the way to the top floor.

The stairs of the Spired Inn were crooked and creaky. Sounds of hand drums and wailing ibex flutes faded as they ascended, through the first and second storeys, the third, the fourth, until they reached a landing containing four gigantic pine cupboards and a trapdoor. Zinina pulled out a ladder from one of the cupboards. 'This is how to get into the garret,' Zinina explained. 'Don't worry, it's a lovely room. I did my first drugs up there. Oh, don't fret. It was nothing serious. Just flutterwing and a few snowflake pills.'

The garret was a large room with two south-facing windows. 'You get a fabulous view of the Cemetery and the Gardens,' Zinina said conversationally, worried by the expression on Arrahaquen's face. 'You can even see people going in and out of the Cowhorn Tower.'

'Charming,' remarked Arrahaquen.

'Make yourself comfortable,' Zinina said, 'and I'll be back in about an hour. We should think about disguising you somehow.'

'I suppose so,' Arrahaquen said, mournfully. 'Goddess, I hope I've done the right thing.'

Back in the common room, she reassured Dhow-lin about the payment, then left the inn and hurried back to the house. Graaff-lin was asleep in her bed, but her fever seemed to have died down. Zinina placed two bottles of water at her side, for when she awoke, along with a box of nut biscuits and the valise. Then she studied the aamlon rigs. One double memory-case. That would be tricky. She had no option but to vandalise one of the rigs, for Graaff-lin would refuse to help if asked. Still, Arrahaquen's need was greater. Zinina poked around inside the rig unit that

Graaff-lin used least, finding the appropriate piece of technology and popping it out of its holder with a squelch. Packing a case of spare clothes, she departed the house.

When she arrived back at the inn, Arrahaquen had already swept the dusty floor, cleaned the windows, rearranged the couch and the two tables, and pulled up a floorboard to expose the mainline pyuter sockets. 'You really have made yourself at home,' Zinina commented.

'I'll be here for a week.'

'Yeah. Anyhow, here's some clothes. I been thinking. You ought to go as an acolyte of Rien Zir.'

Arrahaquen considered this.

'Sure,' Zinina continued. 'Round here is practically Rien Zir territory. You won't be questioned by Citadel snoops.'

'I suppose so. Tashyndy certainly has sway over officials. Perhaps I could dress as a minor priestess.'

'You'll need a wig and some jewels.'

'A wig will just get infected,' Arrahaquen pointed out. 'I'm not a proper member of the temple, just a lay worshipper. I have to be sprayed to go through the ferns at the entrance—'

'You can get wigs with antiseptic linings. Hoy, you don't realise just what I can do here. Somewhere on the third floor is Oq-ziq, the best house thief in these parts, and she's an *expert* on disguise.'

Arrahaquen shrugged. 'I'll leave it all to you.'

'That's the way. I know everything round here. Oh, by the way, while you're here your name's Haquyn.' And with that Zinina stepped down the garret ladder and returned to Dhow-lin, who was stocking up the bar kilns.

'Here's your payment,' Zinina said casually.

The old aamlon sniffed, then took the memory-case. 'This'll be useful, sly-girl. I'll take her vittles up myself. I'll make sure she's all right. She in trouble?'

'I don't know yet, but she'll cause you no trouble.'

'Good.'

Zinina looked up and down the bar, then lowered her voice to say, 'Is, um, is Oq-ziq still in her old room?'

'Yeah.'

'I'll just nip up and see her.'

Zinina climbed the stairs to the third floor and, at a door marked with a crayfish rampant, gave the inn's triple knock to reassure Oq-ziq that a friend had arrived to see her. A gentle 'Come in,' was her reply.

She entered a jannitta paradise. Soft, circular rugs covered the floorboards, and there were sheets of embroidered muslin hung on every wall, giving the impression that the room was part of a dreamscape. Bright colours reflected light from a score of anjiqs. Furniture consisted of a huge couch, some wooden trunks and, more interesting, a central table, at which the lissom figure of Oq-ziq sat.

She was examining pyuter hardware with a glass lens in her good eye; a green patch covered the other. Her costume consisted of a string vest and curly-toed slippers. Oq-ziq was stone deaf. Over both ears were curled the macabre shapes of pyuter-ears, black blobs like slug corpses.

They spoke in their native tongue. 'It's only me,' Zinina said, sitting next to Oq-ziq and catching the pungent odour of the table's aromatic wood.

'Hello! What brings you here?' Oq-ziq was pleased to see her. A broad smile lightened her face as she took out her monocular.

'It really has been too long,' Zinina said. 'How are you?'

'Very well. Of course, that is the flippant reply. How could I be well at such a time as this?'

Zinina nodded, conflicting feelings running through

her: sorrow at being away from old friends, pleasure that she was remembered. She glanced at the oddments on the table. 'Still running your old scam?'

'Let's say that there's no shortage of houses to enter. No, I get by. Dhow-lin looks after me very well.'

'I'm glad to hear that. Oq-ziq, I've a favour to ask. I hope you don't mind.'

Oq-ziq shook her head.

'I'm sheltering a friend here. She's in trouble. She needs a disguise.'

'You sit beside the expert. Only Ghaajeer-lin was better than me, and she is dead.'

'Dead?'

'Flu brought on by pestilence. It may come to us all in the end.'

Zinina shivered. She hated talk like this. In her dreams the personification of the pestilence would stalk her through Kray, an insect-legged harridan wielding a scythe following a jannitta child. Now that was a nightmare. 'Poor Ghaajeer-lin,' she said. 'Anyhow, is there any hope of help? We thought she could be disguised as one of Rien Zir's priestesses.'

'Hmm. Is your friend conversant with that faith?'

'Oh, yeah, sure.'

'Then a braided wig and some cheap gold jewellery should suffice. I have face paints. Come and fetch me after tonight's music is over.'

'I will. Thank you, Oq-ziq.' They touched together the backs of their hands in the traditional jannitta way, then Zinina left.

The evening came and went, and soon the Spired Inn was quiet. Zinina returned to Oq-ziq's room. Oq-ziq wrapped a silk scarf around her shoulders, this covering most of the string vest, pulled on a pair of knickers, and picked up her disguise kit. 'Ready,' she said.

The high winds and torrential rain had induced another power cut, and every photoplankton tube was dim. Using oil lamps they made their way to the garret, where Zinina introduced Arrahaquen and Oq-ziq to one another.

Oq-ziq began her craft. Taking Arrahaquen's chin, she first examined every feature with half-lidded eyes, humming and muttering to herself in jannitta, stroking blemishes, scratching away flakes of green, feeling the consistency of the skin on Arrahaquen's scalp, until she seemed satisfied. She unrolled the disguise kit to reveal a multitude of sticks, mirrors, brushes and much more – including, Zinina noticed, a blonde braided wig. Plaited or braided or even crimped hair was authentic Rien Zir style.

'This will be no mere pargeting on the wall of some Citadel doss house,' Oq-ziq said as she cleaned Arrahaquen's head with alcohol. 'I shall transform you into a priestess. You have a pretty face, Haquyn. I shall make you beautiful.'

Arrahaquen glanced at Zinina, but said nothing. 'You're looking at a real craftswoman,' Zinina told her.

Oq-ziq first changed the shape of Arrahaquen's eyebrows using a soft pencil, then accentuated the skin under the brow and under the eye with waterproof kohl. The eyelid she shaded pale green, the eyelashes she thickened. 'All this will last for a week or so,' she said, 'even through the worst Kray storm. After then, if the disguise is still needed, come and see me.' Oq-ziq then discoloured Arrahaquen's teeth, which, because she was of the Citadel, were clean. She then attached the wig to Arrahaquen's scalp. The effect was dramatic.

'But it's hair,' said a worried Arrahaquen.

'This is an antiseptic wig,' Oq-ziq replied. 'I know hair attracts all kinds of infection, but this is special. Don't worry. Also, this jewellery oozes tiny amounts of disinfectant, so no germs or viruses will bury themselves under it and get into your system.'

Arrahaquen stood. 'Practise a different walk,' Oq-ziq advised, as she rummaged inside a felt bag. 'Haquyn, do you know what these are?'

'Spectacles?'

'Yes. The finishing touch. Are you by any chance defective of vision?'

'I think I'm a little short-sighted.'

'Short-sighted, hmm,' Oq-ziq said, replacing the spectacles and offering her a second, gold-framed pair. 'Try these on.'

'Ooh, it's strange. Yes, things are clearer. I can see proper lines at the edges of things. I'll wear these.'

'Good. Now nobody will recognise you. Of course, it would be inadvisable to approach Rien Zir's temple, since they won't know you.'

Zinnia laughed. 'A fine priestess you look, too.'

Oq-ziq kissed them both goodbye, wished them luck, then departed the garret, leaving Zinina pleased but Arrahaquen looking uncomfortable.

Zinina laughed once more. 'Describe to this heathen the mysteries of Rien Zir the Orgasm Witch, O hirsute Haquyn.'

'It's not funny. I could be killed. You and Graaff-lin might be in danger.'

'I know how to look after myself.'

Arrahaquen looked pensive.

'The *ficus* seeds are nearly grown,' said Zinina. 'We've got to use them soon.'

'And to do that we have to enter the Citadel,' Arrahaquen said. 'This is what growing the *ficus* seeds was all about. But we cannot use underground tunnels again.'

Zinina felt nervous, speaking so openly to Arrahaquen;

but Arrahaquen was also a deserter.

'Agreed. Uqeq's nasty little weasel'll be watching them.'

'Nor can we go through the Wall. I would be spotted, maybe you would too.'

'Then over? But how?'

'We could fly.'

'You *are* joking, I hope.'

'It's our only option, Zinina. I have a cousin, Melinquyl, at the Temple of Balloon Love …'

Zinina grinned. 'Balloons! We could balloon over, you reckon?'

'No harm in asking.'

Zinina returned to Graaff-lin's house, leaving Arrahaquen to recuperate. The potency of Graaff-lin's drugs had effected a definite recovery, and the aamlon insisted that she was well enough to undertake the balloon flight – if it could be arranged. Zinina knew that they needed her.

Later, she met up with Arrahaquen on Sphagnum Street.

Following the main thoroughfares of Westcity down through the Carmine Quarter, they struggled towards the Temple of Balloon Love. Countless defender groups, armed with saws, machetes and cannisters of verticide, jogged north, as lightning flashed from black clouds hanging heavy over the sea.

'This place is safe, is it?' Zinina asked.

'If you really don't want to come in, you don't have to,' Arrahaquen replied.

'I only hope this works.'

Zinina pulled her hood tighter against the storm-driven deluge. Buffeted by gusts they hurried south, until the temple appeared around a corner. It stood off the street, a dome the size of twenty houses, with a spiral spire on top. Multi-coloured slabs covered every external surface, a mosaic of diamonds and triangles here and there interspersed with archaic writing about the function of balloons in society. Obscene graffiti had been scrawled on the lower surfaces by those Krayans who resented the freedom of the aerial priestesses.

Arrahaquen stood at the porch, listening to the sounds of metal gongs and chimes being struck in devotional synchrony. In the porch green zone they took off their boots and socks and rolled their leggings up to their knees, then put on air-soled sandals made of rush fibres. All this was required by custom.

A bald pyuton dressed in a black cloak approached them as they finished their preparations. 'May I help you?'

'I'm here to see the priestess Melinquyl,' Arrahaquen said, conscious of her disguise and the impassive gaze of those plastic eyes.

'I'll take you to her,' came the reply. 'Follow me.'

On noiseless bare feet, the pyuton led them into the main hall. In fact, this was the entire temple and it boasted no objects or furniture, no pews or altars. The hall was vast and reverberant, its floor covered with tiles depicting arcane diagrams, the walls multi-coloured as outside. A hundred or so people milled about, apparently without aim, but Arrahaquen knew that they were following the floor diagrams. 'Watch carefully where you tread,' she told Zinina. 'Position is everything here. Some pathways are sacred, others are for outsiders like us. Just follow the pyuton.'

Zinina nodded. She felt disconcerted by the intense religious air of the place – the black-cloaked acolytes tracing intricate paths, eyes to the ground, with gum-laden censers in their hands delivering smoke to the atmosphere. Occasionally she would jump as a free-floating dirigible puttered overhead.

Arrahaquen had been here a few times, though not recently, so she was prepared for the lengthy wandering that had to be undertaken before Melinquyl was found. She waved across a line of people in the adjacent lane, but her cousin did not recognise her.

At last they reached Melinquyl and the pyuton stalked off. She was sitting cross-legged in a circle zone, and she indicated that they too should sit. Wearing a black robe and a turquoise bandana over her scalp, she looked younger than her twenty-six years – a feat that, in Kray, was both remarkable and suspicious.

'Can I help you?' she asked.

'It's me,' Arrahaquen hissed, pulling the long hair of her wig into a pony-tail.

Melinquyl, startled, put her hand to her mouth, eyes wide in her characteristic innocent way. 'Arrahaquen,' she said. 'But . . . I never knew you were one of—'

'I'm not. It's a long story. This here is Zinina, a friend. I'm here to ask a favour of you.'

'Oh, a favour.' Melinquyl seemed almost upset, like a frightened child, and her slim body visibly tensed.

'I want you to pilot a balloon over the Citadel Wall and land it on a building in the aamlon sector.'

'I see.' Melinquyl kept her face set and her reaction concealed. 'I can't do it. I'm sorry.'

'But it wouldn't be dangerous,' Arrahaquen insisted. 'The route I'm thinking of is between the high buildings at the east of the Citadel, and at dead of night.'

Melinquyl shook her head. 'No. It sounds dangerous to me. The Citadel Guard at the east gate would see us.'

'No, they wouldn't. They're in a blind spot.'

'I can assure you,' Zinina added, 'that your Balloon Love networks would be superbly augmented by our payment.'

Melinquyl shook her head, but then paused. 'I suppose I could do it. For my temple.'

'Yes,' Arrahaquen said. 'We'll pay you well. In advance.'

Melinquyl did not contradict her.

Arrahaquen relaxed. 'Thank you. I knew you'd help us.'

Melinquyl managed a smile.

They departed the temple, having arranged a date, time and place to meet Melinquyl and her balloon: three days hence, at midnight, in a demolished house off Cliff Lane, at the very southern edge of the city. Melinquyl's sudden change of mind caused Arrahaquen no qualms.

Outside the temple they agreed to go their separate ways. Briefly, they discussed what they needed to arrange. Then Arrahaquen talked more about her departure from the Citadel, and Zinina described her trek in the Andromeda Quarter. Arrahaquen was intrigued by what she heard. 'You said something about Arvendyn earlier,' Zinina remarked.

'Oh yes, Arvendyn. I was chipping out some data in the Citadel. Arvendyn has a long and interesting history. According to Uqeq the spymistress she's working for Taziqi, the Goddess's High-Priestess herself, in their pursuit of the Silver Seed. So your discoveries at the old temple become very interesting. Also, Arvendyn is reckoned to be something to do with the Phallists, but that's debatable. I'm not sure they even exist. I once did some work trying to uncover that group, you know, before I worked on active defender groups under my mother. And finally, Arvendyn is listed as one of the Defenders of the Cowhorn Tower.'

'What's that mean?'

'It's an honorary title, but it means she devotes some of her time to the upkeep of the tower.'

Zinina pondered this. 'So is there a connection between the Cowhorn and Rien Zir's temple?'

'I couldn't say,' Arrahaquen replied. 'We know so little about the origin of the Cowhorn Tower. All I know is that it built itself – it's a heuristic building. The problem is who did it and why. Not to mention how they had the technology. I personally think nobody in all the Citadel could have created it.'

With that thought ringing in her mind, Zinina left Arrahaquen and began her walk into Eastcity. The wind lashed rain into her face and broken slates lay on the ground. She wondered whether Melinquyl's balloon would be able to cope with such weather.

10

It was not only to Arrahaquen that the Citadel officials
had to attend. The power cuts were increasingly
frequent. The food being doled out on both sides of
the river was now so processed it had lost all hint of
texture and colour to become an indeterminate grey gruel
with lumps. Along Judico and Mandrake Streets in the
Citadel Quarter there was fighting between revellers
joined by stoned independents and a patrolling defender
group, riots that started because Eastcity Water Station
was forced to close due to mains fractures.

For three days, Arrahaquen remained unearthed. Her
disguise held good. Graaff-lin, as predicted, recovered
rapidly with the help of her drugs, and tweaked the
Citadel networks to transform Arrahaquen into Haquyn
the independent. Zinina oscillated between Graaff-lin's
house and the Spired Inn.

On the day of the second mission into the Citadel,
Arrahaquen rose and prepared her clothes, kit and other
equipment, and then with Zinina plucked the two *ficus*
pyuters from their earth, brushing off loose soil and
pulling out the now shrivelled roots. One hour before
midnight they were walking through drizzle along Cliff
Lane.

From the Green Quarter, invisible through the rain despite its altitude, came the sounds of mortar and gunfire. They saw no bursts of flame, and no smoke, but it was clear that more fighting had broken out. Arrahaquen knew that, as the green wave moved south through a now defenceless city, violence would arrive with it like storm crows, and she saw mental images of street gun battles, blasted bodies, and through it all the tough, and most probably smug, isolation of the Citadel.

Melinquyl too had heard the mortar explosions. However, standing by her balloon in the midst of four walls which had once been a house, she confidently reassured her passengers that no shell or laser ray from the Green Quarter would bring down the balloon. 'This is Juo,' she said, indicating the balloon. 'Juo must be treated with respect. Before you climb in, I'd like you to bow once.'

Quickly they performed the ritual, then climbed into the basket and lay on the yielding jannitta cushions that Melinquyl had spread over the rush and plastic matting. It was a tight squeeze.

'That little battle will be useful,' Zinina remarked as Melinquyl loaded information into her pyuter by means of a copper liana. 'It'll turn the gate guards' attention north.'

'Yes,' agreed Melinquyl. 'That will assist us, no doubt of it. Now, are we all ready?'

Everybody was. Melinquyl cut the restraining cords and the balloon rose. Arrahaquen felt her body pressed against the basket and, although the experience was not unlike ascending in a Citadel lift, her head spun as the balloon rotated in the air. Zinina seemed happy enough, but Graaff-lin's face was blanched and her mouth remained shut. Melinquyl said nothing as she made occasional adjustments to the path steered by her semi-sentient balloon.

Lying below the rim of the basket, Arrahaquen fumbled in her backpack and pulled out a short metallic tube.

'What's that?' Zinina asked.

'A periscope.' Arrahaquen extended it and looked into the digital screen, ignoring the distance, temperature and infra-red data at the edges and concentrating on the centre. However, because of the swaying of the balloon, she could see only blurs and the occasional lamp – black and grey, then red lines, then a burst of blue. Keeping as low as possible, they approached the eastern part of the Citadel, silently wafting over mossy roofs with shattered solar panels, until they were only a stone's throw from the eastern gate itself. Arrahaquen steadied her arm against the basket and searched for it. There it was, a flash of red and yellow and sparkling steel. They were over the Wall, navigating between the tall blocks of the Citadel's eastern sector, now rising, now slowing down, now almost motionless.

'Ready to land,' said Melinquyl.

They braced themselves. Melinquyl was aiming for the roof of a pyuter warehouse, a twenty-storey structure with an old sign upon its top, a V of metal that would halt the balloon.

Arrahaquen heard the screech of plastic and metal upon tiles as the basket hit the roof. Then, with a dull thud, they hit the sign and crashed to a halt. Everyone was thrown against the front of the basket.

'Safe?' Arrahaquen asked, breath momentarily knocked from her lungs.

'Oh, very safe,' Melinquyl replied. 'You had better move quickly.'

They disembarked, at Melinquyl's request bowing once more to Juo. Zinina knew where they were, and she led Graaff-lin away. Arrahaquen handed a laser revolver to Melinquyl. 'This will kill. If you're attacked, leave at once.'

Melinquyl nodded calmly. 'The moment you're gone I'll attach springy restraining cords and prime Juo's helium. I'll be away in seconds if anyone discovers me.'

'Good. Don't be afraid to use that revolver. Even ordinary Citadel defenders won't hesitate to attack you.'

'I shall be safe. I'm rather stronger than you think.'

'And if we're not back within five hours, leave.'

'I will leave,' Melinquyl confirmed.

Arrahaquen gave Melinquyl a peck on the cheek – her skin was chill from the wind and rain – and left to join the other two.

They descended using escape ladders at the rear of the building, forty flights in all, until they stood a few feet above the rear alley. Although this was only a passage off the main Citadel streets, Arrahaquen could still see flickers of light passing below its resin surface. 'Shhh!' She had heard a noise.

Zinina listened. 'Drone?' she said.

Arrahaquen nodded. Seconds later a turtle-shaped drone with a yard-long aerial appeared, trundling towards them, flurries of light in the street underneath following its path like luminous crustaceans tailing a boat. It passed underneath their position with a characteristic tinkling patter, caused by its thirty mechanical legs, then disappeared into a gutter.

'Quick,' Arrahaquen told Zinina, 'lead on to the signal house, then I'll take over.'

They had planned their route carefully, checking every detail. Through the dark they walked, their boots clicking on the alley covering, until Zinina whispered and pointed at a dark building set in a courtyard. No illumination aided their sight. Only by light reflected from the glowing streets above them could they see vague shapes and shadows. They dared not risk lamps.

'That's the signal house,' Zinina whispered. Graaff-lin held back a sneeze. 'All the buildings in this sector get their emergency messages from that place. There must be a shaft down to the bowels of the tumulus, but where it is . . .'

'I'll find it,' Arraquen replied. 'I know the signs.'

Zinina led them around the courtyard to the signal house, stopping by the nearest window. It was pitch black. Drizzle fell, smelling of sea slime. Arrahaquen heard a faint clink of metal as Zinina took out her jemmies and lock-screws.

More clinks, and a hiss from Zinina. Then a rattle. 'Got it,' Zinina said. She opened the window and they entered the house.

Arrahaquen switched on her low-intensity torch. It whined, grudgingly, and she thumped it. The whining stopped. 'Right,' she said, 'let's find some signs. Follow me.'

She knew what to look for. Somewhere in the building there would be a door labelled '*BF*' – Below Fifth.

Banks of seedling pyuters emerging from grow-bags lay scattered around the place, many linked by gel-dripping cables to their larger counterparts, those standing like trees in the centre of each room. Blue, green and violet sparks pulsed through these machines, occasionally too a storm of white light, indicating the passage of a digital network patrol, or shunting data fossils.

Arrahaquen searched every room until she found the label. Part of it had fallen off. In silence, she pulled the door open. An unlit corridor painted black and descending at a steep angle awaited them. 'Down there,' she said, trying to mask the tremor in her voice. 'Everyone ready?'

She led them down the passage, switching her torch to a brighter mode. At the bottom she paused. 'Right,' she said, 'get out your torches. We'll be looking at the floor around each door. There'll be about fifty in this zone. Most of them lead to storage, pyuter memory halls, that sort of thing, but one will go right down. In front of that door you'll see tiny splinters of gold flickering in your torch beam.' Both women nodded.

Fifteen minutes passed. Then Graaff-lin ran up to Arrahaquen. She had found something. Locating Zinina and following Graaff-lin to the spot, Arrahaquen checked the floor around a tiny black door and saw the gold splinters left by the boots of superior pyuter officials. A surge of excitement and fear made her pulse quicken. Her legs felt wobbly again. 'This is it,' she said. 'We follow this all the way down.'

Trying to hide her trepidation, Arrahaquen turned the door handle and pulled. She saw an organic tube of ochre plastic leading away, bending here and there, until it dipped down, out of sight. It seemed to be letting in light from its exterior, as though it was translucent.

'Looks promising,' Zinina remarked. 'Come on.'

They followed the tube, which looked as if it had been moulded by air, like the lava tubes around volcanoes, but it showed no exits until its very end, where there were six doors. Arrahaquen chose one at random and opened it.

Soft golden light. They had arrived. Arrahaquen had never seen anything like it. In the room before her lay a single pool surrounded by blue mushrooms, its water black as a starless sky.

'This is the place,' Graaff-lin whispered. 'Dodspaat haamen, it's just like before . . .'

Soberly, Arrahaquen said to the aamlon priestess, 'This is your time, now. Zinina and I will guard you. If you need help, call.'

Graaff-lin attached the map pyuter programmed from their previous mission to her sleeve and led the way through a series of bubble rooms. To Arrahaquen, with their delicately patterned walls, their bizarre pools and mycological screens, the webbed mycelium that linked separate growths together, they were astonishing. At the end of each chamber Zinina peered into the next, looking both for people and the insectoid machines that had found them last time. But the whole place was empty, or at least empty so far.

Graaff-lin settled in a large chamber, seating herself at a mushroom screen the size of a table, placing her satchel to one side and her anti-viral aerosol to the other. Two pools lined with PTFE bricks lay in one half of the bubble, while the other was empty. On this side, the walls were wafer thin.

Arrahaquen watched the two exits, the thin wall, and Graaff-lin, who began muttering to the pyuters and nodding to herself. At last, she took out the two *ficus* units that had been so carefully grown over the past weeks. Blowing the dust from their central interfaces, she slid them into the screen's own interface. Now, Arrahaquen knew, the units would begin their work as network spies.

Time passed. A lot of time. Arrahaquen glanced at the chronograph set into the cuff of her shirt: one hour forty-five minutes gone. About two hours left in this place.

'There are twenty, maybe twenty-one, noophytes living—' Graaff-lin announced suddenly.

'Living?'

Graaff-lin paused. 'I think they are a variety of Citadel network creature. A bundle of knowledge. It's so difficult to tell. It's like trying to listen to one woman speaking in a room of shouters. But these noophytes are definitely part of the plan. They're arranging some kind of jump. Our *ficus* units are trying to talk to them – oh!'

Graaff-lin sat back, then scrambled to her feet, jabbering in aamlon. Arrahaquen ran over to her.

'What's wrong?'

As she gripped Graaff-lin's arm she saw that the two *ficus* units were twisting themselves out of their interface sockets. One had grown an arm, which was reaching out for the other. Zinina too had run over to watch.

The first unit, now damp, dribbling yellow liquid down the sides of the mushroom screen, was growing, visibly expanding and producing two more arms, and a growth of hair. The other unit was similarly growing, but had changed into a spindly framework, like a wrought-iron gate. The units linked their appendages. Both were now producing droplets of liquid from their surfaces and the hair of the first was dark with dampness. Within seconds, after what seemed to be a struggle, the two were one shape, a wet blob with six skinny appendages, each stuck into a screen interface. The thing had a screen, a touch-pad, and what seemed to be a lipless mouth.

It lay twitching. Information flickered within the screen below it. They stood quiet, watching.

'The units do not want to alter the Citadel system,' Graaff-lin said. 'They have restructured themselves into a nest of networks.'

'Why?' Arrahaquen asked.

'Because there is so much data here, a lone structure would stand out amongst the stratified circuits of eons past.'

Tersely Arrahaquen asked, 'Have we lost them?'

'No, they are still working for me. Oh, look.'

'What?'

'The screen just wrote "pyuter heart" when it should have been "noophyte."'

'Are they the same, then?' Zinina asked.

'They must be,' Graaff-lin agreed. 'That word "dwan" must belong to the noophyte machine code. No wonder I wasn't supposed to know it. When I used it, I set off

alarms in the heart of the Citadel. Dodspaat! The Red
Brigade themselves must know!'

Arrahaquen comforted her. 'You're still alive, Graaff-
lin, and they haven't found out about us.'

'But still ... maybe spies at my temple know. I could
have been killed at any instant.'

Arrahaquen refused to countenance this. 'Carry on
with your search. We need to know what the noophytes
are planning. What sort of jump do they have in mind?'

Graaff-lin returned to her work, though she seemed
wary of the pulsating lump that had once been two. Now
and again the lipless orifice would squeak what seemed to
be sentences. Minutes passed, and time began to run out.

And then Graaff-lin began to wail. Arrahaquen, who
stood nearer, ran over and shook her shoulders. 'Shhh!
Graaff-lin, what's the matter?'

'My temple. It's just ...'

'Just what?'

Graaff-lin stared at the mushroom screen, eyes wide,
horrified by something. Arrahaquen looked down into the
multiple layers of information that lay open like sheaves
of translucent paper, to see names, faces and finally –
Katoh-lin herself.

'God*ess*,' she said, letting Graaff-lin go and bending
over the screen.

'What is it?' Zinina asked. 'What is it?'

'Graaff-lin's boss, she's in the Red Brigade. Goddess,
look! The Dodspaat temple's just a front. Katoh-lin is
Head of Religious Manipulation.'

Zinina glanced at Graaff-lin, who was staring blankly
at a wall. 'She's in shock.'

Arrahaquen ignored Zinina, returning her attention to
the screen. According to the data flowing past, the Dead
Spirits, worshipped for centuries, were the noophytes, the
pyuter hearts who had devised the Portreeve's plan. But

they spoke only gibberish to ordinary folk. It was almost too incredible to believe.

A rifle shot rang out. Arrahaquen twisted around, pulling her own weapon out from its holster. Zinina had fired at an object in the nearer archway ... two of them. Arrahaquen dived behind the screen, rolled to its edge, then fired.

They were pyutons, but macabre, like metal skeletons. Zinina was now on her stomach behind a pool wall, shooting and cursing.

One was hit. It swayed, raised its five arms, then fell, crashing to the ground where it fragmented into a wave of tiny pieces, chittering across the floor like a wave of manic spiders. Arrahaquen, who had encountered the modular nature of the more ancient Citadel technologies, was unsurprised by this, but Zinina was frightened and repelled. With disgust on her face she backed away, jumping up and down when the automata skittered near her.

Arrahaquen shot the second unit down and golden sparks flew from the wall behind. The same thing happened. In seconds, every portion of floor was alive with automata. Zinina screamed and ran into the adjacent room. Arrahaquen, crunching the things beneath her boots, grabbed Graaff-lin's arm with one hand and the *ficus* unit with the other but, growling, it refused to move.

There were more noises from the archway as more pyutons appeared. Arrahaquen dragged Graaff-lin to the chamber where Zinina stood staring in terror at the creatures. Turning, she fired at one, then snatched the map from Graaff-lin's sleeve.

'They'll report us immediately,' she told Zinina. 'We've got to run. Here's the map. Get us back. I'll be behind you with Graaff-lin.'

'Slap her,' demanded Zinina, taking the map. 'Wake her up.'

Arrahaquen did so, but Graaff-lin did not flinch. She seemed to be in a trance. 'Go!' Arrahaquen yelled, pushing Zinina on.

They ran.

If they sprinted without stopping, they would be in the upper levels by the time the Citadel Guard were alerted. That gave them perhaps a minute to make it to the outside of the signal house. Not enough time.

Arrahaquen was beginning to struggle. Graaff-lin was running like an animated doll, taking no decisions. Arrahaquen tugged and pulled as Zinina found the ochre tunnel.

The door at the end was closed. Zinina opened it carefully and listened. It was clear. They ran on, following corridors, Arrahaquen becoming short of breath. Zinina sped way ahead, urging her on.

At last they reached the external door. The signal room was unlit and empty. No sounds of danger. They clambered through the window.

Once they were outside, Arrahaquen paused to catch her breath, her limbs heavy, lungs aching, throat sore, eyes watering. She coughed up phlegm. Zinina appeared unruffled, as poised as a gymnast.

'Motorbikes,' Zinina said. 'I can hear motorbikes.'

'And running boots,' Arrahaquen gasped. 'How far off?'

'Near. Come on. Run. If we can get to the stairs we'll be safe. They'll search the alleys first. They won't look up.'

Arrahaquen struggled on, allowing Zinina to pull Graaff-lin. Nobody challenged them, though she thought she heard shouted commands nearby. The rain had ceased but the streets were wet, and more than once she slipped and fell.

At the steps they paused again. Arrahaquen looked upwards. Her legs felt so heavy. 'Go on,' she said, her voice hoarse. 'I'll follow. Go on. Get Graaff-lin up. Get the balloon ready.'

Zinina hesitated, looked to the sky, then pushed and shoved Graaff-lin up the steps. Arrahaquen sat on the lowest rung, exhausted, breathing in and out with a crackling wheeze. The grumble of motorbike engines rose and fell as riders sped along the adjacent street. She stood and began the climb. Ten flights above her, Zinina toiled. The minutes seemed endless. She was aware that Zinina's boots were no longer clunking on the metal stairs. Voices. A thumping sound. Then she felt a breeze in her face and realised she was at the top.

'Come *on*,' Zinina called. 'We're off! Quick!'

The balloon was tethered by one cord. Arrahaquen tottered across the roof – she could not run – and fell into the basket. Melinquyl cut the cord.

They rose. But then they jerked to a halt.

'We are caught,' Melinquyl said, hanging over the edge of the basket and pulling at something. 'The basket base is caught on the edge of the sign. Juo is angry that you didn't bow.'

Arrahaquen saw Zinina stand up and assist. She heard the thunk of metal against metal.

'Pull that,' Zinina said.

'Push that hook away,' Melinquyl answered.

'The sign!' yelled Zinina.

They were free. The balloon seemed to leap into the air. But some seconds later Arrahaquen heard a loud crash.

Zinina sat down. 'Sign fell off the building. Reqoes, reqoes, they'll hear it and see the balloon! Get your gun ready.'

Arrahaquen primed her rifle.

Melinquyl called out, 'Two hang-gliders.'

Arrahaquen, despite her exhaustion, found it within herself to sit up and peer over the edge. Below lay the tumulus, outlined with glowing streets. But two hanggliders were closing. She fired. From wingtip nozzles they fired back. Through the sky lines of red and orange flickered. Something exploded at her side. She shrank away. The balloon lurched and she smelled burning.

Melinquyl had been hit, the basket too. Then another shot hit. Melinquyl's head was no longer on her shoulders. The basket lurched down to one side, its cords cut. Arrahaquen looked up to see that only five cords now held the basket to the balloon.

'Keep your nerve,' Zinina said. 'We've got to land now and run.'

'Can't!' Arrahaquen said. 'We would be captured.'

'No choice.'

'Drop all ballast,' Arrahaquen ordered.

'No. We've got to land.'

Arrahaquen slumped back, but squirmed away, repelled, when she realised the soft cushion was not a cushion, nor Graaff-lin's body, but Melinquyl's corpse.

The balloon was losing altitude. They brushed treetops. Arrahaquen, the lower side of the basket now almost tipping her out, saw roofs, then windows. One cord broke with a musical ping.

With a crash they landed and everybody was thrown out. The balloon fabric tore with a silken scream, then flopped all around. Zinina was on her feet, pulling at Graaff-lin. Arrahaquen struggled upright.

A garden lay around them, or rather the remains of a garden, for much of it was ivy and briar and nettle.

'Mind them poison docks,' Zinina warned.

Arrahaquen looked at the sky to see two more hanggliders approaching. She searched the garden walls for a gate. 'There!' They charged towards it, Zinina ahead,

swiping at vegetation with a knife, Arrahaquen support-
ing Graaff-lin, and tumbled out into an alley.

'This is off Deciduo Street,' Zinina said. 'Follow me.
We'll have to hide, or the hang-gliders'll spot us.'

Dawn was breaking and light rain fell from swirling
clouds. The alley was flooded, like so many around the
river, and soon they found themselves up to their knees in
green water. Arrahaquen looked nervously at nearby bags
of brown algae, floating like jellyfish. 'Aren't those things
dangerous?' she said. 'There must be another way.'

'Reqoes,' Zinina swore, kicking with futile rage at the
water. 'The hang-gliders'll see us. We've got to hole up.'

'What about that tree?' Arrahaquen said, pointing to a
large oak up ahead, at the end of the alley.

They forged on through the flood, balancing with arms
outstretched along a side wall when the waters threatened
to reach their waists, until the branches of the oak
sheltered them.

'We should make for the Spired Inn,' Zinina said. 'We'll
be safe there.'

'Agreed,' Arrahaquen replied.

'*No!*'

It was Graaff-lin who had shouted. Arrahaquen rose to
her feet. 'Graaff-lin,' she said in unison with Zinina. 'Are
you all right?'

'We will *not* make for the Spired Inn,' Graaff-lin stated
in a firm, hard voice. She seemed to have recovered her
poise, though her face was still blanched, and her limbs
trembled. 'We will make with all haste for the Temple of
the Dodspaat. It must be done.'

'Hoy, Graaff-lin,' Zinina began, 'that's a little
danger—'

'I will go alone if need be. The Citadel and my temple
are guilty of heresy.'

Heresy? Arrahaquen thought. Graaff-lin had seen that

her temple was a front, but did not seem to realise that the Dead Spirits were no more than pyuter network entities – noophytes – pyuter hearts. There was no heresy. How could there be, when there were no gods?

Better keep quiet, Arrahaquen thought, for the moment. There was no telling what was going through Graaff-lin's head. 'We'll come with you in case of trouble,' she said.

Zinina looked at her in amazement. 'You serious? If Katoh-lin's in the Red Brigade, she'll have us killed instantly.'

'It's safe,' Arrahaquen insisted. 'We'll accompany Graaff-lin to the temple, and she'll hide us somewhere. It's only just dawn. People won't be that active yet.'

Zinina shook her head, but did not debate the point further. Graaff-lin led them back into the flood, making uphill for Min Street and then Pine Street, which led directly to the front of the Dodspaat temple.

Far from being empty, its great steps were crowded with priestesses and ordinary Krayans, while at the main doors a score of heavily armed temple guards stood, barring all from entry.

'What is happening?' Graaff-lin asked a passer-by.

'Reckon there's something bad going on,' came the reply. 'I tried to go worship, but they won't let me. Damn insolence.'

'We better leave,' Zinina said.

'I know a back door,' Graaff-lin replied. They followed her around the side of the temple until she stopped and nudged a shut door with her shoulder. She paused, then gave it a harder shove. It opened. 'I'm running the moment there's trouble,' Zinina warned, priming her revolver.

Inside, Arrahaquen walked by Graaff-lin's side, Zinina following, as they strode through marble corridors. Graaff-lin, seeing the white clad figure of a priestess, called out, 'Tylla! What is going on?'

A tall, rather noble-looking priestess approached them, dressed in a white cloak and black boots. Her scalp was tattooed with daffodil designs. 'Graaff-lin. How did you get in?'

'What is going on? Where is the High Priestess?'

'I'm not sure exactly what's happening,' Tylla replied. 'Only a few priestesses are being let in. But do you mean Katoh-lin or Mysrioque?'

'Why, Katoh-lin of course. What are you talking about?'

'Katoh-lin is no longer High Priestess. She has just been replaced. Two minutes ago, to be precise.'

'But where is she?'

'She has escaped. She is wanted.' And with that, Tylla departed.

'What do we do?' Zinina hissed at Graaff-lin, who seemed to be slipping back into shock.

'I do not know,' Graaff-lin replied. 'But this Mysrioque I know well. She is a Citadel woman, a scion of the Portreeve as many have said. Perhaps we have triggered an overthrow. This will not be kept secret for long. We had better hurry.'

'Hurry?' Zinina said, astonished. 'Where?'

'We must find Katoh-lin immediately,' Graaff-lin said. 'Something terrible has happened. Maybe the Portreeve is about to do something awful to the Dodspaat.'

They returned to the rear of the temple. Arrahaquen tried to think of a plan, to divert Graaff-lin from her crazed path. Breathing deeply, she closed her eyes and tried to think. But instead of plans she saw images. With an immediacy that brought her smells and sounds as well as far sight, she saw a figure hobbling along the street behind them.

'Run,' she said, splashing through puddles and climbing the iron steps that led up to Broom Street. 'Quick.'

'Have you gone mad too?' Zinina said.

Graaff-lin was chasing after Arrahaquen. 'Come along,' she called down to Zinina.

Arrahaquen half jogged, half walked along twisted Broom Street, dodging urine slicks and piles of bubbling algae, kicking a dog that tried to bite her boots, wiping the sweat and drizzle from her eyes and pulling out her needle gun, until, as the trio approached Marjoram Street, she saw the figure from her mental image. It was an elderly woman, heavily cloaked, a walking stick in one hand.

'Katoh-lin,' gasped Graaff-lin, pointing.

They hurried on. Katoh-lin heard their clattering boots, turned, then tried to hurry on, but soon she was caught. Graaff-lin attempted to pull her round by the shoulder, but the frail woman collapsed into the gutter.

'You have betrayed us all!' Graaff-lin yelled in her face.

Katoh-lin, also exhausted, tried to speak. 'No . . . no, I haven't . . . mmm, mmm, it was for Kray!'

'For Kray?' Arrahaquen interrupted. 'What have you done?'

'For Kray . . .' came the response.

Graaff-lin said, 'I know everything, Katoh-lin. I know about your manipulation and plots. I know you're a member of the Red Brigade.'

Katoh-lin tried to rise to her feet, but couldn't. 'Fools! Kraandeere, kraandeere! They'll, mmm, find me. We're all in peril, we might be being followed. Graaff-lin, don't go to the temple else they'll kill you. They know about your probings.'

Arrahaquen said, 'We've just come from there. What's going on?'

'Graaff-lin, I'm sorry. I used you, mmm, to defect.'

'Defect?' they replied.

'You fools! There's but one way to leave the Red Brigade once you're in, and that's by dying. Mmm, I know too much about the plan. I was going to warn Kray. So I, mmm, had to defect. Save me! Pick me up and, mmm, mmm, mmm, carry me.'

'You *used* me?' Graaff-lin repeated.

'Mmm, don't stand here gossiping, underling, pick me up!'

Graaff-lin retorted, 'Not until you *explain*.'

'Save me! Save us all! Graaff-lin, I *had* to use somebody. I needed a decoy so that, mmm, my own activities would go unnoticed. I set you up. I made the Red Brigade think you wanted to, mmm, murder me for power. The Red Brigade thinks you might know noophytes lore. And the passes, they were made by me for my escape. I couldn't leave the Citadel confines except disguised as a commoner, so I needed to forge passes. You tested them.'

'Do you mean the Portreeve's plan?' Zinina interrupted, taking hold of Katoh-lin by her cloak and shaking her. Arrahaquen tried to stop her, but Zinina pushed her away, and continued to bounce the priestess's body against the street. Together, Arrahaquen and Graaff-lin managed to drag Zinina away from Katoh-lin's spluttering body. Zinina glared at them, teeth bared, fists clenched.

'The plan,' Katoh-lin choked. She lay on her back, coughing, until she managed, 'The plan, mmm, mmm, yes, a bridge—'

Something green fell from above. It hit Katoh-lin on the face. Arrahaquen jumped backwards, knocking Graaff-lin into a wall as she did so. She glanced up and saw a figure on the roof above for the briefest moment.

Katoh-lin writhed under what Arrahaquen knew to be an algae cushion from the Citadel dungeons. While it shuddered and twisted, apparently getting smaller, Katoh-lin's neck grew. Her arms flailed, beating the ground. Blood seeped out from under the thing. Unable to look away, Arrahaquen saw Katoh-lin's throat burst open, spraying blood across the street, and saw too a glutinous mass of green and red wriggling deeper into her chest, like a bloated worm. She turned away, but Zinina and Graaff-lin just stared, horror plain on their faces.

Tugging at the arms of both women, Arrahaquen pulled them away.

Kray moved through the season of spring. Throughout the northerly quarters, the Archaic and the Green, plants, bushes and trees grew with profuse energy, bringing houses down with their roots and branches, decimating streets, poisoning people. Fungi appeared in many places, blocking whole streets with their smooth, spore-ridden fruiting bodies. Refugees began moving south. Entire districts of the north became impassable even to defenders.

The green wave could not be stopped. Its onset was marked, like botanic leprosy, with grass between the cobbles, ivy in the rafters; later followed fungal cellars, rotting beams and algae-smothered plaster, and bad air laden with suffocating pollen. Warm rain created ponds that once were squares, created microbe-rich rivers of decaying matter that flowed ever browner into the southern quarters.

A psychedelic patchwork of flowers and insects began to mask the dull hues of stone and wood. In teeming thickets, ambulatory pumpkins waited to pounce on the unwary, the drunk and the suicidal. Smothered communities fought over water and food hoards, until they were vanquished by impenetrable verdure.

The Citadel – even if it could – did little to quell the riots, as if the Portreeve and her minions had hardly noticed any change. But now every night the sound of automatic gunfire and booming detonations could be heard across Kray. The city was disintegrating.

11

On Beltayn Eve, Haquyn, acolyte of the Goddess, chaperoned children around southern Kray, helping them in their task of decorating twigs and branches earlier snapped off by defending groups. The younger children – at least, those who did not spend time teasing their elder siblings – made crossed hoops of bedecked cane, straw dolls and garlands for decoration.

Meanwhile thousands of young friends met at inns serving free ale throughout the night. From safe roofs and from the open windows of high towers came the sounds of horns and drums, klaxons and conches, and reed pipes three yards long, accompanying the festivities.

But in the Green and the Archaic Quarters, in the passable districts of the Andromeda Quarter – even down as far as the Temple of Felis – and in those parts of the Carmine Quarter smothered by plants overflowing from the Gardens, there was silence. Silence, except for the swishing of trees and the pattering of rain. North Kray heard no music. This year, Beltayn was confined.

At sunrise Arrahaquen returned to the Carmine Quarter with her charges, everyone singing, then let them go in order to begin the house decoration; well-liked people

would be favoured with flowers and leaves around their
windows and doors, while the unpopular had nettles and
creepers thrust upon them. Gifts could then be requested
from Kray's older residents. Arrahaquen looked upon all
this with the eye of one who had lived most of her life in
the bland buildings of the Citadel.

Collecting Zinina from the house, Arrahaquen led
the way to a dew pool. It was the custom for women to
bathe their faces with dew to ensure what in Kray was the
ultimate beauty – a clear complexion.

An hour after dawn, they walked south. A light mist of
yellow drizzle fell from bright clouds, filling the air.
Already, feats of strength, singing and dancing, pyuter
graphics and archery were being exhibited in the streets.
Food and drink was to hand in every road – free from the
Food and the Water Stations. Arrahaquen gazed east
towards the Citadel. Somewhere atop its summit the
Portreeve would be sitting at breakfast, apart, with a sour
face.

Mystical figures appeared as the dances became more
boisterous. The Leaf Man, a woman jigging in a bulky
costume, danced along the street, flowers and coloured
ribbons decorating her face. Elsewhere stalked the Moll
and the Fool, the latter, dressed in all white and attended
by girls in white jumpsuits, attacking those already drunk
with a bladder affixed to a hazelstick. Arrahaquen, not
quite able to join in with the jollity, feigned insolence and
was rewarded with a clout on the head. Zinina laughed at
her, but Arrahaquen's face remained glum.

They walked on. The drizzle stopped, though the sky
remained overcast. Music swelled from windows and
from street bands led by aamlon conductors with leaves in
their cuffs. Noon passed by. The two women walked to
the garland-strewn Market Square, where this year's Kray
Queen would be crowned. It would be a momentous

occasion for many since it was widely believed that today marked the city's final Beltayn. Girls wreathed in flowers danced around poles, the slabs below their feet a ring of colour where their adornments had fallen away. Others sat on leafy posts that they had made, comparing size and quality with those of others. From behind a vacated post Arrahaquen watched the tall, blonde and rather mysterious priestess Tashyndy crowned. She had nominated herself Kray Queen on Vert Day.

Taziqi, the High Priestess of the Goddess, had departed the temple to see her spiritual student crowned. People avoided her. Dressed in a sheath of lime and emerald silk, emeralds on her fingers and toes, she wore a three-faced mask, to the left a maiden, central a woman, to the right an old woman. When she spoke in encouragement, silence fell.

Arrahaquen studied Taziqi in fascination. Brought up to believe that any High Priestess of the Goddess was an enemy of the Portreeve, she now looked upon Taziqi with awe and confusion. What secrets did she possess? What were her plans for this final year? Well, any plans remained just as secret as those of the Portreeve, for the Temple of the Goddess had ventured no method of saving the human race.

Escaping the crowning festivities, they wandered down Ash Lane. Final customs were being enjoyed. At the harbour, women threw wax effigies of men into the water.

It was as the day waned that, returning north, they came across a street party composed mainly of jannitta women, and Zinina insisted that they stay to enjoy the last festivities. Zinina was tipsy, and starting to sing badly. Arrahaquen sat on a log and watched. She hadn't been there long when a short woman approached her. She was dressed in poor sackcloth, her scalp scarred, and her face green-spotted and wrinkled. 'Excuse me, would you be able to assist my poorly daughter?'

'Um,' Arrahaquen said, glancing towards Zinina but failing to catch her eye. 'I'll take a brief peep. I have to be back at the temple, you know.'

'Most kind.'

The woman led her into an alley, but turned almost immediately and took from her pocket a piece of paper and a pencil. 'Do you know who this is?' she asked, turning the paper so that Arrahaquen saw a face. Suddenly she was frightened, knowing that this woman was not what she seemed.

'No,' she said. 'Who are you?'

'More to the point, who are you?' The woman smiled and pointed the pencil at Arrahaquen's face. There was a hiss and an acid smell . . . then blackness.

A cold rain fell from grey-black clouds. East of that dismal park where the Cowhorn Tower leaned over the Cemetery, from somewhere near the Gardens, came the sounds of gunfire.

It was Beltayn evening.

Two figures walked along a path nestling between the Cemetery wall and the pleasure garden which surrounded the Cowhorn Tower. The path followed a sinuous depression, its grit and glass surface crunching as the two pairs of boots passed by.

One figure, Hains – a man – wore a plastic suit with the hood drawn tight, and leather thigh boots. He was tall and strong.

Tashyndy, the new Kray Queen, glanced down at her own clothes, ensuring that he could not see her face under the cotton balaclava and cowl. Her robe was scarlet, trimmed with black leaves. Crimson gloves covered her hands.

They turned off the lane and climbed a short path up to the Cowhorn Tower. They paused. A hum emanated from its two prongs: caused by the wind passing through at a certain speed off the sea. Fifty yards up, these horns shed water. Below, the bulk of the tower, an irregular copper ovoid forty yards across supported on a pillar half as wide, showed verdigris through the rain. The horns, curving around, with their spherical end knobs, seemed like tentacles with eyes daring them to continue.

They walked towards the tower's only door, made of steel. It was not the first time that she had entered the Cowhorn Tower. The smell of fish tainted with musk was familiar, bringing to mind a similar odour in the Fish Chambers. It excited her, and made her clutch Hains' arm. The endometrial walls of the main chamber consisted of a spiral arcade of niches, reached by steps and a collection of spiral staircases, and lit by rows of yellow lamps.

From above came cries and sighs, occasionally gasps. Every human voice was echoed by the same voice – the deep-rich voice of the Cowhorn Tower, a voice that often frightened newcomers away.

'Shall we find a soft chamber?' she said.

'Yes ... yes,' replied Hains, head held back as he stared at the structures around him.

'Is this your first time?'

He paused. She knew he had not been here before. 'No,' he said, 'not the first. Though I wouldn't say I was a regular.'

As he told this lie Tashyndy's mind was drawn to a package wrapped in leaves, carried in her pocket. She thought she could feel it against her skin. She shivered.

'All right?' he whispered.

In reply she led him to a staircase, which they climbed, ascending to the lower bowl of the main chamber. Amidst the niches and alcoves set into the outer wall and curtained off from the gangways, she saw illuminated cysts and crevices, many ice-covered. Above and around she spied drones, ranging in size from insect to dog, ticking as they scuttled around on their unknown tasks. Many were damp, or covered with sticky fluid, while others seemed to be restricted in movement by ice as though they were rheumatic.

They ascended further into the bowl, echoes following them. Drones clicked by, on legs, wheels, or squeaking treads, while others navigated the walls like spiders. The continual hum, the melange of sound and echo, drummed into Tashyndy's brain, and she longed to be behind a curtain, a thick curtain that would diminish the noise.

At the left horn she located a chamber, pulled Hains in, and drew the curtain. She sat him on the couch.

The alcove was warm, lit by a goblet of luminous plankton, with a sumptuous circular couch. 'Now, wait here. You might like to get undressed now. Or I'll do it for you.'

'Maybe—'

'I think I'd like you to undress while I'm out. But I'll be back in a minute, ready for you.'

He nodded, masking his confusion. Hains was a reveller, plucked last autumn off the streets, and allowed to become healthy again in the secluded gazebos behind the Goddess's temple. But it was important that he not be anxious, so she stroked him, and made a cosy place in the couch, then took a flask of baqa from her cloak pocket and offered it to him.

Outside, she removed her cloak, boots and underwear. She checked her reflection in a capsule cover dark enough inside to act as a mirror. Her skin was red, dyed during the night with a concoction of alizarin red, wine and oil, her lips were painted black, her hair was slicked back with ochre, and brown spots decorated her thighs. She stroked herself, then returned to Hains.

He was shocked at her appearance. 'Do all Kray Queens do that?'

'That?' she replied, her mind already becoming hazy.

'Paint themselves.'

'It's a tradition,' she said, pushing him down on the couch and sitting on him. A drone sidled into their alcove.

He was not an imaginative enough lover to see that fun was the point of the day.

'Don't do that,' she murmured. 'Relax. Trust me, you're with the Kray Queen.'

Tashyndy wriggled under him and drew her cloak nearer to her right hand, plumping it up as he moved above her so the package in the pocket was within reach, drawing her legs back and up so he could find a comfortable position.

Other machines crawled under the couch.

Then Hains began to reinterpret her wishes. 'Why don't I—'

'Just . . . just enjoy yourself, Hains. Don't get so bossy.'

'I'm not bossy.'

The machines under their couch ticked to themselves. Petulantly, he asked, 'Don't I get a chance to say what to do?'

'No. That's the whole point.'

He rose up above her, his attention elsewhere. Tashyndy reached for the package, found the base of the cat-claw, and held it in its leaf glove while he lectured her. Then, as he ran out of things to say, she scratched his back. He turned, and saw the fluid on the point of the claw.

With a shove of her thighs and belly, Tashyndy threw him off the couch. She had hoped this would not happen. But Hains had tried to dominate where there was no need to dominate. He lay twitching, staring at her, trying to say something. Slowly the haze of sex withdrew from her mind. Her senses lost a feeling of unity that they had previously enjoyed, and the heat, movement, colour, bodies, sounds, smells, touches were all fragmented.

The drone pyutons sprang upon the bed like silverfish as she dressed herself and she watched them scrape at the damp patches. She reversed the cloak, showing an olive colour trimmed with black leaves. Opening the curtain let in a little light. Hains was dead. One drone lifted his penis and began cutting away at his scrotum. As Tashyndy pulled on her boots, the drone extracted his balls. She put on the balaclava, pulled up the cowl, and departed humming a sun-mantra. The drones followed later, placing their cargo in a capsule around which ice lay thick.

Standing at the bottom of the Cowhorn Tower, Tashyndy sadly contemplated the failure of which she had been a part. Today's events had epitomised the disappointment of men and women of earlier generations.

She watched other drone pyutons carrying their cargoes around the place. For forty years the Cowhorn Tower had stood here, storing human seed much as a gardener stored plant seed. She wondered how much longer it would survive, and why the drones carried on regardless.

Graaff-lin found herself unable to cope with what had happened. Her deities, the Dodspaat, had collaborated in a Citadel plot. But she could not be angry with them. Not one of the twenty could she harangue as they lay remote, thinking their dead thoughts, ignoring her like a bad mother ignores a daughter. It made her feel sick.

She knew she had no choice but to excommunicate herself from the Temple of the Dodspaat. Remaining a part of it would be tantamount to heresy. All she had to do was refuse to perform her ecclesiastical duties three times in succession and it would be done. So far, she had failed to turn up at the temple twice. She knew she could not return. Mysrioque would have her arrested and sent to the Citadel, for Graaff-lin did not doubt that the new High Priestess was in the service of the Portreeve, and very likely was Katoh-lin's replacement in the Red Brigade too. How appalling that the faith of the Dodspaat should be so perverted.

Her next official office was due some hours hence, starting on the first minute after Beltayn. If she did not appear to minister to the Dodspaat and to the public, she would automatically be recorded as excommunicated.

She sat alone in the house. Zinina was out searching for Arrahaquen, who had not appeared since they had lost each other earlier that evening. She cared not where Arrahaquen had gone.

Midnight drew near. Gunfire could be heard from the soggy groves and fungal alleys of the Green Quarter. It was expected that the north-eastern wall of the Gardens would soon collapse, and the Gardens and Green Quarter would merge to become one vast forbidden area, bordered to the north by the Venus Trap, to the east by the lonely, eerie ruins of the Andromeda Quarter, to the south by the Mercantile Quarter, and to the west by that narrow strip of land that was the Carmine Quarter. Soon, Graaff-lin realised, the entire north of the city would be uninhabitable. Automatic gunfire again disturbed her thoughts.

Unsettled, she climbed into the upper floor of the house to look from the gable window, extending a hand-telescope to aid her vision. Along a distant section of Feverfew Street she saw scores of people fighting, an amorphous mass which could not be differentiated into defenders, revellers, or any group at all. No doubt local factions, now beginning to appear in response to the

Portreeve's unannounced plan, were warring.

An orange flash eastward caught her eye. She looked east, towards the Power Station and the buildings around it, to see the silhouette of ridges stark against orange and black smoke. She saw too the ruined stanchions of towers and the blasted chimneys of dwellings. Destroyed machines spat white spark sprays into the air.

And way south, though it was too far away to be sure, she thought she saw momentary lines of light, orange and green – the signs of laser weapons.

She returned to her own room, her stomach rolling. She felt nauseous. To take her mind away from her ailing body, she considered her plans once more. All contact with the Dodspaat via the temple being impossible, one option remained – the serpents. The thought reminded her of the prophecy given on the day she had met Zinina: 'a green cushion falling upon a waif'. Katoh-lin. It had to be.

It would be risky now to question the serpents in person, but Graaff-lin felt she had no choice. She must reach the Dodspaat somehow, to make sense of what had happened. They alone could dispense truth. And alone, untroubled by officious priestesses or nosy acolytes, she could perhaps utilise Kray's serpentine links.

She felt nauseous again. Suddenly aware that her body was working out of control, she dashed to the nearest basin to be sick.

Angry at herself, she returned to her room, but could not sit still, and so wandered around the house. Midnight drew near. Still Zinina had not returned.

Then it was midnight: Beltayn's end. Graaff-lin linked up with the public pyuter of the Dodspaat temple and requested a complete list of priestesses. Her name was absent.

Her heart beat fast and her throat tightened with

emotion. She felt angry, not sad. She wanted to go to the temple and berate them for being so stupid. But she could not. She was trapped in a dangerous house with a heathen and a heretic.

The front door slammed shut. Zinina huffed and cursed as she removed her boots and protectives.

'Did you find Arrahaquen?' Graaff-lin called.

'No,' Zinina replied, entering the room. 'Tomorrow I'll have to search the whole damn city. It's your fault. If you had come I wouldn't have lost her.'

Angered again, Graaff-lin stood up. 'You shouldn't have got drunk.'

'Everyone gets ripped on Beltayn, except straightjackets such as yourself.'

'Have you been to the Gedeese Veert's temple?' Graaff-lin countered.

'No. I'll do all that tomorrow.'

Graaff-lin nodded. 'Then goodnight. I am going to bed.'

12

Zinina woke with a headache. For a few minutes she lay in bed listening to the creaking of the house and the rustling of Kray, until she heard Graaff-lin speaking to a pyuter and decided to get up. She showered in medicated water, spread depilating cream over her head, wiped it off with a towel, then dressed.

Breakfast consisted of the remains of last night's Food Station meal – some grey stuff, some white stuff, and some carrots that tasted only of salt water. She dropped vitamin supplements into the mess as it bubbled over the gas burner.

Food in hand, she went to see Graaff-lin, who was in her workroom. 'Still no Arrahaquen,' she remarked.

'That is not my fault,' replied Graaff-lin.

Zinina said nothing. She watched Graaff-lin instructing her pyuters by squeezing the contours of a soft metal ball. 'Perhaps,' she said, 'she's gone back to the Citadel, to her real friends. Maybe she was spying on us.'

'I don't know,' said Graaff-lin, not looking up from her work.

Irritated, Zinina said, 'Don't you care then?'

'I simply do not know what has happened and I realise we cannot find out. If she is dead, she is dead.'

'Well I'm going to do something. I'm not sitting round here. It's like jumping in a green pool.'

'You go out and look some more,' said Graaff-lin, 'but as sure as seeds is seeds I am not. I have work to do concerning our discoveries.'

Zinina dressed for the city, pulling her protectives from their antiseptic bin and her boots from the tray of disinfectant. As she opened the front door Graaff-lin called, 'If you do not find her, do not come back and vent your frustrations on me.'

Zinina departed without a word.

The nearest wall-pyuter was dead. She walked down to Pine Street, stopping at another wall-pyuter, this time one that worked. The rain beat against her ears as she keyed in a link to the Citadel's public network, a constant patter, like an eternal drumroll signifying the demise of humanity.

The crimson query mark appeared. Zinina requested knowledge of the independent Haquyn, then, when that returned a negative, of the priestess Haquyn. Nothing.

Depressed, she walked up Hog Street then took back alleys leading to the Infirmary. Here, she noticed that a number of passages were blocked by barbed wire, and on some of these barriers were hung fragments of wood painted with green triangles, the sign for a green alley – in other words, the sign for 'keep out'. She hurried on, the stench of atmospheric ozone on the wind making her choke.

The Infirmary were not treating Arrahaquen, nor had she been in as a casualty. So Zinina walked the short lane that led to the Dispensary.

Eight defenders armed with needle rifles and a laser bazooka greeted her. Because of its reveller problem, the Dispensary required continuous defence. Zinina noticed a charred corpse nearby, left untouched to deter others.

She had not been seen at the Harbour, or at the Temple of Balloon Love. The priestess outside Rien Zir's temple had not seen her. And nor was she at the Spired Inn.

Zinina trudged back along Morte Street. She did not know what to do. Worry was beginning to consume her, and, over and over, she tried to think where outside the Citadel Arrahaquen could be. She glanced into the Cemetery, and saw a figure.

It was a most unusual person. In fact, it looked like a man.

A man! Most likely he was a reveller, of course, but still, how often did anybody see a man outside of the Fish Chambers?

Zinina climbed over the wall and, crouched low, ran to a line of hedge, along which she hurried until she could see him more clearly. It was indeed a man; sitting in a canvas chair, an umbrella over him to ward off the rain, and reading a book. He was dressed in dark knee boots with blue elastics, brown corduroy trousers, and the biggest, blackest greatcoat Zinina had ever seen. His scalp was hairless, but his cheeks grew stubble. He seemed to be eating something, and as she watched Zinina saw him extract a cube from a silver packet and pop it into his mouth.

Zinina was intrigued. The man's eyes were deep and brown, though rather rheumy, while his mouth was wide and thin-lipped, and his nose narrow and almost malformed with its high ridge.

Standing, she took out a short knife from her kit, then approached.

He heard her, and looked around.

'Fear not, good woman,' he said, glancing at the knife. 'I am harmless. Replace your dirk in its receptacle.'

Zinina stood before him. His voice was deep, resonant, and every word was enunciated with clarity. 'Sure,' she said, 'once I know who you are and what you're doing in this tombgarden.'

He looked around him. 'The Cemetery? I come here for the nepenthic quality inculcated within me. Surely you too would wish to forget your every care awhile?'

'Sometimes, yes. I do it with drink.'

The man smiled, placed a plastic bookmark between the pages of his book, then snapped it shut. 'Drink, yes. How merry.'

'Are you a reveller?'

'No.'

'What's that you're reading?'

'Oh, only an old diary. As a matter of fact it was written by a reveller, one from the Archaic Quarter.'

'Who are you?' Zinina demanded.

He did not answer but instead gazed at her, looking her up and down. A thoughtful expression came to his face.

'You're a man,' Zinina said bluntly. But there was something else he could be. She fumbled in her kit for a sterile needle and, quick as a cobra, lunged at his arm. He shrank back, taken by surprise.

'What are you doing? That is dangerous.'

Zinina threw an alcohol swab in his direction, but she did not apologise. 'There's blood on your wrist. I reckoned you might be a pyuton.'

Frowning, the man said, 'Well I *am* human. Are there further diagnostic checks to be undertaken?'

'No. I'm satisfied. But I still want to know what you're doing here.'

'Perusing a diary, as I said,' he replied, opening the book again.

'Aren't you scared of revellers?'

'Yes. But they will hardly bother me so close to the Cemetery wall. Their prime encampments lie south-wards.'

Zinina laughed. 'You don't know much about rev-ellers, then. They can be anywhere hereabouts.'

The man smiled as though he was humouring a small child. He rummaged inside his coat and pulled out two battered packets and an old tin. From these he took a piece of paper, a match and some chopped-up weed, items from which he proceeded to roll a cigarette. Zinina, used to seeing some of her friends smoking, watched, fasci-nated. She had never seen a man smoke in her life. And now she noticed the odour of the weed . . .

'I know you,' she said, with thumping heart. 'You rescued me from the pit off Blank Street.'

He nodded. 'Indeed I did. And now we meet again.'

'You took me to Graaff-lin's house?'

'I did.'

'Who are you?'

'My name is deKray. Might I know the jannitta whom I have the privilege of looking up to?'

'Zinina. Why did you take me there?'

'The aamlon is an acquaintance of mine.'

Zinina frowned. 'She's never mentioned you.'

'Why should she?'

'But you rescued me. And my kit.'

'At the time you were a Krayan in distress, Zinina. I noticed you were wearing the garments of a member of the Citadel Guard, though you had tried to alter your clothes by ripping off the lapels and flashes. I deduced that you were a deserter. When the woman attacked you, I beat her off, then pulled you out. Realising that your position was somewhat precarious, I carried you down to Graaff-lin's house, hoping that she would offer you sanctuary. I thought it wise not to reveal my identity . . . you had a better chance simply appearing out of the green. Had Graaff-lin known it was I who foisted you upon her, she might have acted differently.'

Zinina nodded. 'And what is that stuff you smell of?'

'Menthol,' he replied, relighting the cigarette when it went out. 'Do you imbibe at all, Zinina?'

'Nope.'

'It can be ghastly stuff,' he said, puffing at the crooked cigarette, 'but it has the same effect as your alcohol. You know, I once read that if I tried to imagine what sort of person my cigarette would be, I should learn much about myself. The same applies to your glass of dooch, I imagine.'

'Really? And who would your cigarette be?'

'I imagined my cigarette as an Infirmary doctor. Now is that not curious?'

Zinina laughed. She found herself tantalised by the mind that might lie behind this polished exterior. DeKray possessed the air of an aesthete. He radiated calmness. When he spoke it was as if tomes had come alive. 'What did you make of that thought?' she asked.

'I do not know. Only rarely do I ponder the matter. Mayhap it means that I wish to operate upon myself.'

'Hoy,' Zinina said, 'why not come back with me to Graaff-lin's? She should meet more people.'

He paused, clearly not sure, took a puff and then gazed speculatively at her. 'Very well. I must confess, I have not seen her for a while.'

DeKray packed up his things, then followed Zinina out of the Cemetery. In Sphagnum Street he remarked, 'I used to reside two alleys away, you know, at a domicile in Cochineal Mews.' Sporadic talk about the rain and the sound of gunfire enlivened the walk home, but, crossing the Peppermint Bridge into Eastcity, Zinina began to feel nervous. What would Graaff-lin say?

She decided it would be better if deKray remained out-side the house while she fetched Graaff-lin. Nervously, she told Graaff-lin that a friend awaited her at the front door.

When Graaff-lin saw who it was she halted, face set into a grimace. But her eyes conveyed her feelings. 'Not a friend, rather an acquaintance,' she said.

'That is how I described myself,' deKray said.

Zinina reassured Graaff-lin, saying, 'Don't worry, I've checked him. He's the one that rescued me.' DeKray took out a menthol sweet and dropped it on to his tongue. 'He reads a lot,' she added.

'I know.'

Suddenly inspired, Zinina asked him, 'Hoy, you don't happen to know what a noophyte is?'

Graaff-lin scowled at her. 'Don't be ridicu—'

'Assuredly yes,' deKray interrupted. 'A noophyte is what Graaff-lin here would term a conscoositie.'

'A conscoositie,' Graaff-lin said, recognising the aamlon word. 'A conscoositie?'

'Why, yes.'

Graaff-lin's face seemed lit up. 'A conscoositie! Of course. That would explain the strange partial inhabitation of the networks . . .'

Graaff-lin walked back into the house. Shrugging, Zinina gestured for deKray to follow. Divested of his boots and greatcoat Zinina offered him a seat.

'We know of some noophytes. We wondered what they were.'

'Don't tell him anything,' Graaff-lin said, sharply.

Zinina studied deKray's face. 'Can you prove you're an indep?' she asked.

'Utilise my kit number,' he replied. 'The Citadel pyuters will confirm my status.'

Graaff-lin checked deKray's identity. He was genuine. 'We can trust an independent,' Zinina said. 'He'd be a defender, wouldn't he, if he was a spy, or something.'

Graaff-lin seemed hesitant, but Zinina, impatient, had no time for procrastination. DeKray was happy to illuminate her darkness. 'A conscoositie is a partial or fractured model of reality – an abstract model. Thus, we human beings are noophytes, except that most philosophers would judge human beings to be almost complete models of reality, and so would class them apart.'

Zinina glanced across at Graaff-lin. It was clear that she was uncomfortable, being so close to a loose man – and maybe this loose man in particular. 'Where do you live?' Zinina asked him.

'At a maisonette in the south of the Citadel Quarter.'

Zinina opened an internal shutter and peered out into the evening gloom. 'Better walk you home,' she said. 'It's dangerous out there.'

'That is most gracious,' deKray replied.

Suited up, Zinina led him out and along to Pine Street, but before they entered it she took him by the arm and stopped him. 'Look,' she said, 'it's getting fraught out here.' She handed him a rusty needle pistol.

He smiled. 'But men are not permitted to bear arms.'

'If you hide it nobody'll know.'

'I shall risk the enormous risk.'

Zinina smiled back. As he hid the pistol within some recess of the huge greatcoat, she noticed on one lapel a large copper hat-pin with a bulbous head.

She watched his face. It was not that his features showed no emotions, rather that his emotions flickered through his expression, like sunny patches in a cloudy sky. DeKray was a cultured man. He had the driest, yet most delicate, sense of humour, even though he was acutely aware of his position in Kray. Zinina liked him for that.

'How did you get to know Graaff-lin?' she asked him.

'We both studied pyuter metaphysics at the Waterlily Institute, near the Cemetery.'

'I'm sorry I spoke rough at you up the tombgardens,' she said, as they walked along Pine Street.

'In truth I expected you to,' he replied.

'Well, sorry. You must admit it's better to be safe than sorry.'

'I suppose that is true.'

Silence fell between them. But the city was not silent. As they walked south, they heard automatic gunfire, and once a large explosion. People ran by, as if being chased.

Then deKray halted. 'I hear carousing revellers,' he said. 'We had better secrete ourselves.'

Zinina heard the singing, but around them stood only locked doors and alleys filled with poison vines, death-roses and stinking puddles. 'We better hide in a doorway,' she said.

This they did, taking muslin masks from their kits and tying them across their faces. Three revellers emerged from an alley. Pledgets were pressed by elastic bands to their noses, and all were filthy and bloodied. Zinina shivered when she saw the blood. Each carried a toad in one hand, and as they staggered by Zinina saw one reveller lick the eye secretions of the noxious beast.

'I have witnessed such things before,' deKray said as they hurried on. 'Such toads expectorate a dense humour from their eye ducts, which in humans produces a psychedelic response. No doubt those revellers were deep in some other, druggy reality.'

Zinina looked up the street. 'Do you feel sorry for them?'

He considered this for some minutes. When he answered they were well into Gur-Lossom Street. 'We live in a hierarchical society, because of the extremity of our condition. It was not always so, I should have you know.'

Zinina nodded. 'I feel sorry for them. The Portreeve should help them, instead of eating cakes and drinking wine up the damn tumulus.'

'Indeed. A most valid point.'

Walking on, into areas she had never explored, Zinina noticed that pale grass shoots were pushing up between the flagstones. From the shattered windows of ruined houses – and there were many in this sparsely populated quarter – she saw hanging vines, lianas, and the globular flowers of the poison chrysanthemum, which here, by the sea, was a common cause of death. A few bodies lay in gutters. Most were greened and partially decomposed, but one was not, and Zinina stopped to see if the clothes contained anything useful. Seeing what she was doing, deKray took hold of her arm and pointed to the streaks of vomit, the empty syringe, and the red stain of uz, all signs indicating that revellers had already stripped the corpse of useful oddments. They walked on.

At last, with the cliffs in sight and the sound of waves audible, deKray indicated a white house. He said he lived alone in the upper floor, the ground floor being empty.

As he pointed to it a reveller staggered into the street; an aggressive one, armed with a circular saw on a bamboo pole. They decided not to fight and deKray hurried Zinina into his house. The reveller hammered on the locked door, but, weakened by the effort, departed, screaming curses. Watching deKray, Zinina loosened her knife in its scabbard, wary, though curious.

His house was remarkable. Its ceilings were very high, indicating that it was old, and from each hung long wires dangling photoplankton spheres on their ends. In every room there were shelves and shelves of books. Zinina had never seen so many. Even in the shower room and the kitchen books stood on shelves. Thousands of them.

'This is the third largest library in all of this city,' deKray said with joy in his voice. His eyes, which he had wiped with a medicated tissue, were shining.

'Third?'

'I refer to paper, not electronic, books. The second

largest belongs to a woman residing northwards, adjacent to the Gardens.'

'Who?'

He did not want to answer. Zinina frowned at him, distrust uppermost in her thoughts. 'One Oquayan,' he eventually admitted. 'Her works cover botany, mostly. And of course the largest library in Kray belongs to whoever happens to be Portreeve.'

Zinina nodded.

'What beverage would you prefer, Zinina?'

'I better go,' she replied, shaking her head. 'Doesn't do to be alone in a man's house. But I'll be seeing you. Yeah?'

It was half an offer. Zinina felt attracted, yet nervous. He was an unchained man, after all.

DeKray said, 'I should appreciate that.'

In the hall's green zone Zinina checked her suit and hood, then repositioned the elastics around her boot tops. 'Don't want nothing falling in,' she said. 'Um . . .'

'Yes?' He seemed anxious to prolong the farewell.

But Zinina said nothing, and departed.

She had never felt like this. Anticipation: that was what it was. Happy, she hurried back to the Old Quarter.

13

It was often said that a sunny morning in Kray was as common as a Portreeve with a smile on her face – an aphorism that became increasingly true as years went by. But two mornings after Beltayn, Zinina awoke to see blue sky and the sun behind streamers of red cloud. Unaccustomed to the brightness, she shaded her eyes behind one hand as she looked over the city. It seemed stark and green, everything clear instead of hazy, although she noticed that already great clouds of flies and greater clouds of midges were swarming over stagnant water. Spring and especially summer were the seasons of plague, when whole species could be wiped out by sudden immune system failures, or by total male infertility. Soon, every Krayan would be troubled by sweat, insects, insomnia, and the suffocating, damp heat that could send people mad.

Outside, human torment continued. Throughout the night there had been frenzied shooting and the crash of detonations from some nearby square. Too near for comfort. When she tuned into the Citadel networks she understood what had occurred. Three reveller gangs had attacked the Dispensary and, although two had been destroyed or scattered, the third had taken over the building and injected everyone inside with meat preservative. Now revellers from all across the city were heading for the treasure trove that lay undefended. And yet the Citadel seemed to be doing nothing about it. Zinina knew that the Portreeve had given up the Dispensary as a lost cause; and because it supplied the Infirmary, that place too had been offered only a stay of execution.

The Citadel was withdrawing into itself, leaving Kray to die as it saw fit.

Zinina decided to see deKray. Graaff-lin tried to dissuade her, but she wanted to go, and so she would go. 'You stay and keep talking to them serpents,' she told Graaff-lin. 'We've got to find out if they know the plan.'

It was not an easy journey, since she had to avoid the now unsafe main streets – blocked by defenders at work, by rolls of barbed wire, by gangs of revellers encamped in tents made from old clothes and bedlinen – but she persevered. Back alleys, although also dangerous, were less populated by madwomen and militant drunkards. In some places pink and sodden red blossom fallen in great quantities forced Zinina to wade as if through marshes of perfumed blood.

Zinina primed her needle gun before entering the maisonette, just in case. She felt unsure of him. They talked awhile, then Zinina suggested they return to the Cemetery, where she might show him southerly areas he was unfamiliar with. He muttered a few doubts, but for Zinina the Cemetery held little of dread and she had her way. Now she could test him.

They reached the Cemetery at noon, by which time clouds had billowed in off the sea and a light drizzle was falling. Only one brief skirmish troubled them. They had approached the Cemetery by its most northerly gate, off Morte Street, which was succumbing to root damage and

which in places consisted only of mud. Two revellers, a
motley pair dressed in sackcloth and brimmed hats,
stepped out of a doorway, blocking their path. They were
ill, or drunk.

'Hah, what we got then, huh, nice meat?' said one,
drawing a rusty knife from her belt.

Zinina felt more anger than fear. 'Calm it, shousters,'
she sneered. This was the only way to deal with them.
'Down on y'luckies?'

The revellers looked at one another. 'Hoy, calm it
y'self, sharpy,' said one. 'We's only after the meats. Nice
meats only.'

'Y'get none here, no-blooms. Y'see two proper blooms
with brains an' hard muscle to match, so fizzle off, eh?'

'Calm it, calm it,' the revellers muttered, running off.

'Yeah,' Zinina said, anticipating deKray's next question. 'I was brought up a reveller.'

But he said nothing, leaving Zinina slightly embarrassed by his apparent lack of interest.

She led him through the Cemetery gate, now rusting, its
football-eyes scratched and unfocused – the whole edifice
had died some years ago – and so entered the periphery of
the northern graveyards, where Kray's poorest residents
lay buried. Here, revellers rarely dug. They only exhumed
the bodies of those buried with their worldly goods. The
expanse of the Cemetery and the ingenuity of the revellers
meant that they had not yet exhausted this supply of
wealth.

Yew and ivy traced out the remains of paths. As far as
Zinina's eye could see, crumbling gravestones at odd
angles poked out from sheaves of grass and giant crocuses, except where groves of silver birch stood, or where
paths made of glass and metal gravel allowed visitors
access.

Zinina followed a southward path. After half an hour

or so, she found herself looking down steep slopes, but ancient steps engraved with astronomical symbols allowed them to descend easily. Ahead, she saw the alabaster roofs of mausoleums, and clusters of tents in reveller encampments.

'We'd better pull our hoods up and wear masks,' she told deKray. She did not want to be recognised by anybody.

'Very well,' deKray replied, following her instruction.

They left the path and took advantage of cover provided by the yews. These trees were ancient, many supported by iron poles or by green plastic scaffolding, others standing askew, like wounded soldiers. The ground below them emitted the smell of a deadly humus. There was no grass; only mush and mud and rotting red berries. To their right the milky quartz blocks of the Cemetery wall stood tall, washed dirty by the rain.

Soon the Cemetery had become tangled. There were many trees, not just yew but laburnam, birch and syca-more, and between these stood tombs, ruined mauso-leums, the remains of old walls and rusting signposts with their signs missing. 'Careful where you tread,' Zinina warned, 'there's hundreds of open graves around here. You could easy fall in one.'

DeKray seemed to be examining one particular grave. 'Yes, yes,' he said, rejoining Zinina. 'I shall exercise caution.'

'See that mausoleum over there?' Zinina said, pointing to a violet and yellow mosaic roof just visible through the yews. 'That's something I'd like to show you.'

The mausoleum's one door stood open. Zinina peered inside. 'Nobody here.' No encampments lay nearby; they should be safe.

Zinina motioned him in before her, following on when he was well inside. She watched him study the place.

It presented a crowded interior, piles of smashed rubble and metal contrasting with pristine statues, a central domed tomb with three carved figures on top, some smaller tombs, and a series of peculiar stone ottomans around the edges. All in all there was not much of the floor left unoccupied. Zinina waited.

'Interesting,' he said, obviously at a loss.

She wondered if he could act well enough to fool her. 'You mean you don't recognise all these statues? Them murals on the wall?' She looked up to the groined ceiling. 'Them fighting women up there?'

'No. Should I recognise them?'

So, unless he was lying – and Zinina did not think he was – deKray had never been a reveller: he was not an agent of her family out to recapture her for the tribe. He was genuine. 'You been an independent all your life?' she asked.

'Why, indeed. All other opinions are nugatory, Zinina. There is no doubt of my status.'

Zinina sat him down on one of the marble ottomans and said, 'But it's so *odd*. Who're your parents?'

'As with many Krayans their precise identity is unrecorded.'

'But who brought you up when you were a kid?'

'An unrelated independent. She was scratched by a cat when I was eleven, twenty-nine years ago that would be, and died that same day. I have lived alone ever since, accepting those modest offerings of liquids and comestibles from the Citadel. The life of an independent is difficult.'

Zinina considered this story. He said he had lived at Cochineal Mews, the lane running off Sphagnum Street just opposite the path to the Cowhorn Tower. 'Haven't you ever gone back to your old home to hunt around for clues?'

'Clues, Zinina? To what?'

'Your real parent. You must have had one. Maybe even two.'

'I care not. I am myself. My genetic heritage is of no interest to any woman of Kray, presuming I follow the masculine norm of infertility. No, what is important is the quality of my future life, not my past life. What interests me now is the Portreeve's plan, and our broader options for surviving this final year.'

'You reckons it *is* the final year?'

He nodded. 'But there must be a way out.'

'Must there?'

'Oh, indeed. The question is, what path are we all missing?'

As he said this Zinina caught the sound of voices outside, shouting from some distance; and she also thought she heard a reveller bugle, the signal for danger. 'We better go,' she said. 'Back to my place. We've got lots to talk about.'

'We have.'

Zinina stood, then gazed around at the mausoleum. 'I used to come here a lot. Silly nostalgia—'

There was a detonation outside the mausoleum door. Zinina jumped, automatically reaching down for the needle rifle at her belt. DeKray also stood.

'What was—' he began.

A group of revellers ran into the mausoleum, armed with projectile throwers, slings and poisoned darts, but they did not see Zinina and deKray.

'Hack 'em off at the pass,' hissed one.

'No. They know we're prockin' here. Dyquoll will speed over the mackers. Jaybrinn'll flock their meat. We'll ambush the rest here, oiks an' all.'

'Meat! Flock their meat roight off!'

Zinina was noticed. 'Hoy, who're you—'

No time to answer. Five women – five girls – appeared outside the mausoleum door, saw the revellers, then disappeared behind cover.

'Youthmeat!' cried Zinina. The revellers, hearing her speak, also took cover, and began firing out of the mausoleum door.

Zinina pushed deKray behind the ottoman. 'Them revellers are being attacked by Youth priestesses. We're in trouble. Arm yourself.'

Incoming fire, mostly needles and stones, but also energy from a laser pistol, began to knock chunks from surrounding masonry. 'We've got to get out of here,' Zinina breathed. 'If that youthmeat beats them blooms, we're bathing in old water.'

'Are we attacked only by those five girls?' deKray asked.

'No. If this Dyquoll woman is speeding over the mackers – over to the big encampments down by the posh tombs – then there's bound to be more.'

DeKray began to fumble inside his greatcoat. 'I really *must* roll a cigarette,' he said.

The noise began to deafen Zinina. Spent needles plinked on to the ottoman in front of her. She peered over the edge, saw movement behind a bush, and fired, but the narrow range, limited by the mausoleum door, meant that she stood little chance of hitting.

'Why do these Youth girls so hate revellers?' deKray asked.

'Cemetery revellers live old,' Zinina replied. 'Youthmeat is young. Now shut up and concentrate on shooting.'

Explosions sounded nearby. A major battle was beginning. Zinina cursed to herself, reloading her needle rifle and trying to think of an alternative way out.

'You creep around the back and see if you can see any vents in the ceiling,' she said.

'Vents?' he said, puffing away.

'Yes, vents. Some mausoleums have vents to allow people's souls in and out.'

He took a final drag of the cigarette and went.

Zinina shouted to the revellers. 'Hoy, blooms! Splick them slings and chuck out some needles. It's only youth-meat! Poison their blood then speed down the mackers fast as green gob, yeah?'

'Back off, shouster!'

'You can't ambush 'em from the inside!'

But they ignored her, although they did fire more needles out into the bushes where the Youth girls sheltered. The laser beam hacked off more statue masonry and the dust was making everybody cough.

Crawling out from the ottoman adjacent to Zinina, deKray said, 'I have located an array of these vent things.'

'Well take us there,' Zinina said.

She followed him to the rear of the mausoleum. In the roof three vents had been made, one for each of the people buried here, but only a yard or so wide.

'We'll climb up that,' Zinina said, pointing to a wall with crumbling brickwork, 'then crawl along to the vents.'

He paused. More explosions outside, and then automatic gunfire. 'What if there is no exit route?'

'Just go.'

He climbed first and Zinina followed. The ascent was easy, but crawling along the upper ledge was difficult. The mausoleum vents had been designed for spiritual presences, not corporeal escapees. But eventually they were sitting on the mausoleum roof.

'Shimmy down that guttering,' Zinina instructed de-Kray. He did as she said.

Halfway down, the front of the mausoleum collapsed as a bomb detonated. The boom deafened Zinina and the wall shook. Masonry thunked to the ground. Automatic gunfire increased to a crescendo, and she heard triumphant, screaming voices.

As the rest of the mausoleum fell, they fell with it. Landing in rhododendron bushes, dust flying everywhere, Zinina crawled over to the prone deKray and urged him to his feet. They fought their way out of the tangled branches and into a grove of weeping willow.

Zinina heard pursuit. 'Shush,' she hissed, as deKray opened his mouth to say something. She looked around; there; another mausoleum; a smaller one. Better hide up awhile.

They ran through the trees at the edge of the grove, through thickets of ivy, then along a path to the mausoleum. It was little more than a ruin, with no roof and no door.

'Hide in here,' Zinina said. 'If anyone's after us, they'll not see us. They'll go back to the main battle.'

Far off, there were many rumbles and sounds of clattering. Flickering lines, perfectly straight and spectral red, appeared and disappeared in the distance, and although cloud was low Zinina could see black smoke billowing over the Cemetery.

Old tombs, many with open lids, lay within the mausoleum. DeKray, who seemed frightened, perhaps shocked, tripped over rubbish on the floor and accidentally knocked off a tomb lid.

'We better go,' Zinina muttered, as the noise of gunfire and detonations intensified.

Nobody halted them. At the southern gate they followed a covered passage leading down to Sphagnum Street, a thoroughfare still clear of reveller encampments. They were safe.

14

Blackness; but now it was pricked with glimmers.

Arrahaquen regained consciousness.

Something pulled at her thighs, under her arms, and around her waist. She smelt decay, rot, sewage.

She moved and swung. The glimmers remained steady and, orientating herself, she discovered she was vertical, hanging in blighted air.

She was naked in a suit of leather straps suspended by a rope. Around her she could make out other shapes, and by analogy with her own position she knew they were other people, some bulky, others skeletons. As she watched, a thigh bone fell followed by a splash seconds later, then more, then a crack or two.

Plop, snap, splash: something tried to reach her toes.

She could not believe she was in such a place. She felt no fear, only confusion, a sense of fantasy. But when her crotch and legs began to ache and there was no sound other than ripples from below, then she began to fear. An hour passed in which she tried to see around her, so that she would know everything there was to know in the place. She felt that she *had* to know everything, whatever the cost. Her thought was short-term.

She was not sure what the glimmers were. Above, on

what she presumed was a ceiling, patches of quite strong light failed to reach down; at her level only glimmers showed. She caught no reflections below, but knew it was putrid water of some sort.

'Hello,' she called. 'Hello?'

Somebody answered, but the voice, from far away, was lost in echoes. She called again, and there was no reply. The cavern seemed vast.

Then she felt a touch of panic. A few seconds passed, and she cried out, wailed for half a minute like a mourner, until the sensation had gone. A surge of exhilaration then passed through her, as though she had communicated something of profound importance. Her fear seemed to be understandable fear, not a threat. It was vital that she express her emotion and bear its consequences.

Even in such straits, a glimmer of thought struck her; that understanding was fundamental to the mind, that in a sense it *was* the mind. She treasured this thought as though it had been won through decades of work.

She turned her thoughts to escape. While she was fit and alert she had to escape.

The harness was composed of strips of boiled leather, in places repaired with fresh straps and steel bolts. There were no buckles or padlocks. Examining the whole with her hands – her arms were free to move – she understood that she had been bolted in and would remain here for weeks until she died, most likely of dehydration. She looked around, imagining the others, perhaps hundreds, now alive or half-alive or newly dead in their death costumes, shrinking in decay. Again she felt fear, and she expressed this, communicating to herself, until she had quietened. In her head, death-grey skulls containing shrieking minds receded.

It was clear that there was no way out. But nobody could rescue her. Effort would have to come from herself.

She heard a plop, but no after-sounds. Her intuition made the connection between her movements and the sound. She jiggled herself and felt something bounce off her now bald head, then felt dust across her face, as of stone from above. From points of thought oscillating at the top of her mind she drew an image of herself, suspended, arm outstretched *that* way – and caught something.

It was a stone chip. Some part of the suspending device was jostling rock to fragment it.

She could not see the chip, but she touched it to her lips, smelled it, then tested it with her tongue. It was as long as her thumb, ovoid, with one sharp edge and a flaky surface. 'I've found what I need,' she told herself.

She felt at her shoulders and neck to discover where she should cut. There seemed to be two major straps, one new, under each armpit, with a third at the back and a cord around her neck. Imagining this lit, then checking with further tactile explorations, she decided that by cutting the shoulder straps and the neck cord she should be able to haul herself out, provided she could grip the rope.

She felt disgust that she should have to endure this; but felt hope too, rooted in an image of the future, of her crouching naked behind a clock's dial.

She began to work at the leather. After ten seconds she felt to see if it had cut; but felt nothing. She worried again with the chip while counting to thirty, then felt again. There was a gash. Plop, snap, splash: something had detected her.

The darkness helped. She felt that, if she was able to see the water below, and the decomposing bodies sprawled in their harnesses, then she would be too afraid to work. Though her imagination was vivid, it had the human limitation of requiring at least a little input.

She thought three hours had passed. Or it might have

been half an hour. She continued to cut.

With a creak the right strap broke. She felt the harness give, creaking in response, and reached out to grab a second falling chip.

The second strap was harder to cut. When she pressed the chip to her lips to feel if it was blunt or sharp she burnt herself, and her lip throbbed with pain for some seconds. There after it twinged if she grimaced or talked to herself.

'You've done it,' she said, letting joy flood her voice. 'You have done it, you have quite definitely *done* it. *Goddess!*'

She paused: she was talking to herself. But she had cut both shoulder straps.

By holding her waist straps and twisting herself she was able to determine what effect she had had. The harness was creaking, and touch indicated a gap around her shoulders; but the back strap was now pulled up by her weight, and would bar exit.

With one arm over her shoulder and the other holding the back strap from below, she cut with her last chip. She wondered if it was a flint. It seemed smooth, like plastic. The action this time was harder, making the inside of her elbows hurt, making her wrists ache. Soon she was pausing a minute between thirty-second cuts.

'Come on, Arrahaquen, come on.'

With a snap it gave. She fell slightly and held herself rigid in case the whole gave way. She was now suspended by the front strap alone. The neck cord pulled at her throat.

The centre of the chip edge seemed worn so she used the extreme ends to cut the cord. It went in seconds and she smelled leather dust, as though it had been old.

Now she realised that she was cold, and that her bladder was full. She released a stream of urine. Then she wondered if it might draw creatures. She heard splashes, ripples and snapping jaws.

She did not want to be cold. It hindered her, made her less effective. She shouted, cursing her captors with oaths, letting herself go for a few seconds. Rage did her good.

She stretched herself and lifted her arms, getting a good grip on the rope, then pulling. Nothing much happened. She tried a better position, curving her back a little and pulling into her chest, and was able to lift herself. Making an effort she pulled, then felt around with her feet for a grip, until her right foot caught the lower thigh strap and she was able to push up.

She stood on these straps, feeling them bow inwards. Her legs were bent and she realised that her hips were caught in the hole that she had made. It was not wide enough. Her stomach began to ache with the muscular effort.

She decided to shuffle herself through and take full advantage of her legs. Pushing first left then right, toes outstretched, she tried to squeeze through. After a few minutes she guessed that she was half way there.

Now her legs were aching and she made a frantic effort, as if a final attempt, to get through. She felt something give, and then the whole harness fell away, flopping, suspended from the uncut front straps, bolts tinkling as they hit one another.

She was grasping the rope, holding herself up, only a loose grip from her feet on the ruined leather. She knew that she would have to climb *now*.

In childhood, she had like other children been taught rope drill to escape houses. Now those memories came back with a vitality unknown to her. Every nuance of her teacher's voice, of the rope under her palms, of the way her tiny body had swarmed up the rope, returned to her mind. Her body did not seem cold, nor did it seem so very heavy as it had just now. She swarmed up the rope, muscles in unison, unfatigued. Before she knew that she had climbed any distance cold metal hit the bridge of her nose.

This brought her round. She saw by fungus light a ledge. Gripping the metal strut she pulled herself over and lay on the ledge, rapidly breathing, then sneezing.

Horizontal, she wept. The thought of not escaping had so far not occurred to her. Now the horror of what could have been rushed through her mind, inspiring anger and tears together. She embraced the rock ledge with her arms, stomach and legs.

Time passed. Images of outside played across her mind's eye.

Echoes of her voice, lacking volume and depth, entered her ears. She began again to feel cold, especially from the rock ledge, and she imagined that she might freeze against it, never to leave. She raised her head to look around.

Attached to the ledge was a framework of metal tubes. It stretched in all directions, following the ledge, which lay a few yards below the roof, and stretching out into cavern space. The wall backing the ledge was filled with crevices and holes, none, unfortunately, big enough to climb through. Along the tubes hooks stood proud, and she realised that these were what victims hung suspended from. If only she could see better.

From the top of her mind she drew images, trying to feel what might be possible. She smelled a familiar smell, and recalled something about fingernail mushrooms and a chemical found in some other fungus. Nearby she saw fingernail mushrooms. She picked one and found her way to the smell, then she rubbed the mushroom against the rock from which the odour came.

Light: a photochemical reaction that might last ten minutes. And there were more mushrooms available.

She made a foray along the ledge. After five minutes she turned back, having discovered only that the tube framework followed the ledges and was attached in places to the roof.

Then she saw a footprint. She stooped to examine it. A boot, medium size, with furrowed grip – probably a Citadel Guard boot, something Zinina might have worn. Had Zinina ever been down here? But now she had a clearer picture of what happened, and she felt exhilaration. People came here! At some point in the future other victims might arrive. So she had to find exit points and a place to hide along the ledge.

Returning to the mushrooms she prepared a new one, then explored in the opposite direction, passing two tunnels to other parts of the cavern, finding another, different bootprint. And then she noticed a circular door.

Her mushroom was expiring. She went back to prepare a third, then returned. It was a wooden door lined with lead. She saw no keyhole, nor any sign of electronics. Most likely it was opened only from the outside. She would have to wait.

She found a crevice – empty of denizens – and sat. Cold and hunger gnawed at her. Boredom arrived. Unable to stop imagining what might happen next, she found herself unable also to free her mind of its constraints. Until something happened she could not break free of black thoughts. She began cursing the authorities again.

Time slipped by. Some hours seemed to pass quickly, others dragged. Moments were marked by faint screams from other places, and ripples far below. She dropped off into sleep; awoke, and relieved herself; started shivering; slept again.

Click. She awoke. Her body was stiff and it was agony when she moved. She listened.

'Which number?' came a voice.

'One nine eight's free,' replied another. The voices were lubricated by wine. Light from the circular hole hurt her eyes and she peered around. She saw two people with torches dragging a body already in its leather suit.

Their backs were turned. She crept to the hole, looked out into a dim corridor lit by azure photoplankton tubes, a section that stretched for tens of yards each way. It was empty. She jumped out, her eyes pained, only just open, and clambered behind a square bank of pyuters.

She knew she ought to rescue the prisoner, but she had no choice. It tore her heart to think that some human being would wake soon, as she had. She could not return into the cavern. Well, she could return, but she did not know where the prisoner was and she had to put herself first. Again, anger at the authorities, making her twist her fists and grit her teeth, and swear at their methods ... at her own mother's methods. She imagined herself escaped, pitting herself as a heroine against the Citadel.

With clunking boots the guards returned, silent, slamming the door and shoving a catch. She caught a whiff of smoke and alcohol as they passed by. She felt guilt, a kind of tearful guilt.

And she herself had not yet escaped. She was merely out of the cavern. She had two options: either enter the pyuter honeycomb and escape via the Power Station or by Zinina's way, or leave through the Citadel Wall. The former was all but impossible and the latter impossible without a pass. And she urgently needed clothes. She could not stop shivering.

Again she consulted her imagined images. She wondered if it might be possible to impersonate a guard. Perhaps there would be some in this building.

She listened but heard nothing. Venturing from the pyuter bank, she ran left until at the end of the corridor she peered around a corner. There she saw cubby doors.

She tip-toed up to one and opened it. Rifles. She took one.

A swishing noise, as of someone walking, some way off; to her left, from where she had come. Ahead the passage narrowed into a dark room. She saw somebody, twenty yards away, plastic-suited and helmeted.

She sat back in the corner, and aimed a yard and a half up, tensing her muscles, looking down the sights. When a chest appeared she fired.

Sssst. The guard was down. She did not twitch.

Arrahaquen looked at her. There was no blood, and she had only stunned her.

She was a tall woman, and thin, and at first Arrahaquen's fingers trembled too much for her to undo the catches. She gripped her fingers together, prayed to the goddess, then found herself calmed. Within a minute the suit was off. She did not think there was time enough to remove the undersuits, and anyway that could have been restraining, not to mention biologically hazardous, so she slipped on the suit. It caught her naked skin and hurt as she moved, and it was much too tight about her hips.

She removed the helmet and put it on. On side screens she saw glowing information: maps, letters, numbers – a constellation of glowing sigils. Nothing made sense.

'Uh, Ohoequa, anything wrong down there?'

The voice inside her helmet made her jump. She looked down at the body through her tinted visor. Her victim seemed younger. The light balance was different – darker, yet clearer.

'Hello, Ohoequa. Hello?'

She ran back up the corridor, knowing she had to put distance between herself and Ohoequa. Steps appeared, and these she ran up, noticing numbers as she went, numbers painted in a style she recognised.

'Ohoequa, please reply.' Fainter: '. . . what? . . . you think it's the transceivers . . .'

A floor appeared labelled 'OG'. She looked out into a hallway, noticed two suited women walking away, and watched where they went. The wall opened up and there was a glimpse of black.

She followed. The door opened. She was outside. It was night, drizzle falling, and she was in the Citadel, high up to the north-east.

The street was illuminated in browns and yellows, white shapes occasionally blinking. A sign shone: 'Gugu St et'.

She felt vulnerable, as though watched by electronic eyes through the antennae of her helmet. What if they could follow her trace? She walked downhill, making for the east gate. So far she did not know how this last barrier could be crossed.

She heard a rumbling sound. To her right, a shape appeared.

'Who're you?'

It was somebody on a motorbike, suited, helmeted.

'What?' she replied, without thinking.

'Where did you get that rifle?' The guard dismounted, and the bike seemed to grow four hairy legs to balance itself.

Arrahaquen hefted the gun, as though to show the guard. Then she swung, twisting her shoulders, and hit out with every piece of her strength. Surprised, the guard toppled over. Arrahaquen jumped on to the motorbike and gripped the handle that operated the throttle. She had not needed to think. She just acted.

The bike seemed to squirm beneath her, its leather seat rocking from side to side as though it could detect the presence of a stranger, but then it roared away, almost knocking Arrahaquen off, dials flickering, steam venting from the ends of the handlebars. Ten seconds later she crossed into Bog Street, ignoring the groups of defenders

strolling down Rosinante Street to her left, bouncing
down steps towards the north gate, until it appeared as
sparks of red and white, and she slowed. Approaching,
the glittering gate resolved itself into lamps and suited
shadows, and chunks of machinery perched on poles.

'Identify yourself, please.' A voice in her helmet.

Arrahaquen refrained from answering. Twenty yards
away, three Citadel Guards leant against their cabin. She
slowed right down, and fiddled with a chest pocket in
pretence of finding a pass.

'Hello?' said somebody.

'Escapee!' came a faint voice.

She ducked and sped through, catching a glimpse of a
rifle butt missing her. She was in Malmsey Street. Light
sparked around her, and she saw adjacent houses flashing
white. Then something hit her right hand. The motorbike
skidded, dropped to the right, and she felt a detonation
vibrate the machine. She fell into a gutter, hand in agony.

The gate was a hundred yards back. Four Citadel
Guards were closing, firing as they ran. Arrahaquen
disentangled herself from the spark-spitting motorbike,
but was momentarily stunned by a wail of pain from the
machine, an almost human scream that became throaty,
then dropped to nothing. She ran into an alley, undoing
helmet straps as she went, sure that it could be tracked.
She removed the helmet and threw it into a pool.

Here, the alleys were flooded in places, so she chose
higher passages between dead houses. In a flooded culvert
she paused. Voices, running boots, heard through swishing water . . . not close, but not far.

Then she saw clothes in an alcove.

She looked down at her suit, now blood stained, and
saw other electronic points that might serve to betray her.
The clothing had been folded into two neat piles –
breeches, a wool cardigan, leggings, two vests, elbow

gloves, one boot. Unusually, nothing was labelled. In Kray everybody's clothes had their name and kit number sewn or written inside because of the danger of disease. To wear unknown clothes was tantamount to suicide in some quarters. This lot looked as though lovers had left them during some suicide pact – which was not unusual.

She examined them. They were still dry, indicating that they were recent, perhaps a remnant of Beltayn, and nothing had yet started to grow inside. Nothing visible, at least. She felt that she could wear them for half an hour in order to escape. The risk was acceptable.

More shouts, closer now. Choosing a dry patch, checking for vermin, of which there were none, she disrobed and put on the found clothes. A second boot she improvised from the gloves. Peering out, she decided to move. An alley led into Min Street, and soon she was jogging up the street. By the red sandstone Pyramid Bridge she paused, looking east to the Citadel, knowing that she had escaped. She turned and ran along the river, bypassing what looked like a local zone wired off, until she neared Onion Street, from where it was but minutes to Graaff-lin's house.

Nervous energy made her limbs feel a little disconnected, and her throat very dry. She slowed to a walk. The drizzle had intensified into a rank rain that seemed to stick to her skin like slime. Guns and rifles were firing nearby, perhaps east along Arrowmint Street, and, dimly reflected by the night's cloud mass, she saw pale lights flickering, eerily out of synchrony with the crashes and detonations. Now she felt drained.

She noticed that the Old Quarter had become greener. Apart from the houses with roofs sliding off into the streets, and the fields of grass and weeds that seemed to be growing out of every passage, differences included saplings growing from mounds of earth surrounded by

shattered cobbles, leafy bushes everywhere, walls plump
with moss, and poking from many windows the signs of
internal invasion – hemp lianas, sheaves of rose briars,
poison ivy and poison moonsbane.

Graaff-lin's house remained upright. But Arrahaquen
noticed cracks under the eaves, slates fallen, and also,
most worryingly of all, what seemed to be a bulge in the
wall on the far side. The garden was a jungle. Tentatively,
she tip-toed through to the front door, jumping when a fat
spider hissed at her.

There must be a power cut: no door pyuter, only
candles lit inside. Arrahaquen's heart was thumping. She
had become very nervous. She wished she had a mirror in
which to improve her appearance.

She knocked. Waited.

'Who is it?' Zinina's voice.

'It's me. Let me in.'

A pause. That was understandable. 'Who? I can't hear
you.'

'It's me, Zinina. I can't shout. Let me in!'

The door opened just enough for a shadowy figure to
peer out; then it opened fully.

'Rien *Zir*,' Zinina said. She stood rigid with shock.

Arrahaquen entered the house. It seemed hot to her –
she was still shivering – and very bright. Her eyes hurt.

'Rien Zir,' Zinina repeated. She slammed the door
shut.

'It is me,' Arrahaquen said. 'Save your speech. I've got
to shower and clean myself up. These aren't my clothes.'

Zinina found nothing to say. Arrahaquen made for the
shower room, shedding clothes as she went, but was
disconcerted to see Zinina nip past her and stop somebody leaving a room. 'Er,' she said, 'we got somebody
staying here . . . um . . .'

'No time now,' Arrahaquen said.

Graaff-lin appeared; she also stood still, frightened, as if she was watching an apparition.

'It is me, Graaff-lin,' said Arrahaquen. 'I've got to shower and get medicines. See you in a minute.'

Zinina helped her set up the shower. Over her shock, her face now bright with glee, she asked what had happened. Arrahaquen declined to say. 'Let me get clean,' she said. 'Let me get clean, then I'll tell you.'

'Uqallavaz tq! Have we got some news for you.'

'Put that antibiotic sachet in the shower-head.'

'Graaff-lin's been working hard. Gosh, you look thinner.'

'Fetch my kit from the green zone, would you?'

A laser ray had scored the palm of her hand. Wincing with pain, she cleaned the wound.

She showered in the pink medicated water, then took six different antibiotic capsules, each dedicated to a particular urban disease, and clipped a time-delayed antibiotic to the side of her mouth. Finally, she doused her runny eyes with drops. Her body ached, and she felt ill with hunger – almost sick – but she knew she was free.

She dressed in a cotton bath-gown. The other two were in the sitting room. The other *three*!

Arrahaquen physically jumped when she saw the man sitting next to Zinina, and shrank back against the door.

'It's a friend,' Zinina said, smiling. 'He's perfectly safe. He's really helped us.'

'The name is deKray, ma'am,' the man said.

To Arrahaquen he seemed somewhat stocky in build, with deep brown eyes and a beaky nose. His manner was confident, his voice jovial yet restrained, as though he were some sort of actor. Blue bacteria tubes set around the walls reflected off his bald head.

'Oh,' she managed.

'He does take some getting used to.'

A loose man in this house? Arrahaquen sat in the chair furthest from deKray. 'He's not infectious, you know,' Zinina said.

'I'm sure not.'

'I mean,' Zinina continued, 'he's not got the pestilence. He's not going to kill you sitting here, Arrahaquen.'

Arrahaquen nodded. 'I'm sure he won't.'

Zinina sat back. 'You don't like him, do you?'

'If I might make an observation here,' deKray said. 'The charming lady, the daughter of Ammyvryn if my faulty old memory recalls aught of correctness, is of course perplexed to see a real man in her house, when no doubt the only other masculine forms she has scrutinised have either been in the Fish Chambers or in books or on pyuter screens. I *think* we are all mature enough to allow her a frisson of surprise.'

Subdued, Zinina nodded, and began, with interruptions from Graaff-lin, to relate what had happened to them, only to stop a minute later and ask after Arrahaquen. Arrahaquen duly told her story, which none of them believed except deKray.

'I have read legends of the horror under Gugul Street,' he mused, 'in books written a short time after the Citadel tumulus was grown, but nothing written comes close to your experience. What a most remarkable young woman you are. If I were a risible man I should toast you with laughter, Arrahaquen. If I were a theist I would kneel and pray for what could only be seen as a guerdon of divine plenipotence. Do you mind if I imbibe?'

He took out a piece of paper and some herbs, and a match.

'I don't think so,' said Arrahaquen.

'Thank you kindly.'

'I must eat,' Arrahaquen said. 'And drink some more.'

Zinina followed her into the kitchen. For a few minutes

in silence they prepared food, before Zinina began talking
about how deKray had rescued her, how she had checked
his credentials, seen his maisonette, and how he had
assisted Graaff-lin in her research. And how she liked
him.

They all sat in the study. Noticing that Graaff-lin
looked uncomfortable, Arrahaquen asked, 'How far have
you got searching for the noophytes?'

'Not far. All I can do is speak with the serpents. Still I
only know one word of noophyte speech. It is frustrating,'
she said bitterly. 'Having so many guests makes it difficult
to concentrate.'

Glancing at deKray, Arrahaquen mumbled, 'Yes ...
yes, I can see it could be difficult.' Embarrassed, she tried
to wriggle the fingers of her bandaged hand, but they
were numb and immobile.

Zinina railed at Graaff-lin's hint. 'You never said
anything before. What, you want me to leave just because
I'm friendly with deKray?'

Graaff-lin said nothing. As gently as she could, Arrahaquen said, 'I have nowhere to go, Graaff-lin. I daren't stay
at the Spired Inn any more ...'

Suddenly Graaff-lin stood. Face flushed, she said, 'I
will *not* have a worshipper of the Gedeese Veert under my
roof! This home is hallowed to the Dodspaat alone.
Already you have defiled it. How dare you suggest that
you stay here?'

Stunned by this outburst, Arrahaquen stood, and when
she did Zinina followed suit. Aware that a nasty atmosphere was building, Arrahaquen tried to think of a
solution. She began, 'I don't ha—'

'No,' Graaff-lin declared. 'You will not stay here.'

Arrahaquen felt isolated. She felt like a Citadel child
once more, barred from friendship with these two
women.

DeKray, lighting a new cigarette, said, 'There is a solution to this minor problem, which I shall suggest.'

'I'm not staying with *you*,' Arrahaquen said.

'You sure ain't,' Zinina smugly remarked.

'Please,' deKray insisted, 'allow me to speak. I used to reside in the Carmine Quarter. Though that part of the city is dangerous, it is habitable. Off Sphagnum Street, in Cochineal Mews, I own an empty house. It belonged to the independent who was my guardian. Arrahaquen, I would consider it an honour if you took it as your own.'

Arrahaquen considered the merits of this proposal. Very quickly she saw its advantages and, for a moment, she caught mental images of what it might look like . . . as if she had already been there. 'All right,' she said.

'What about an acolyte disguise?' Zinina said.

Arrahaquen shook her head. 'The Citadel has already forgotten I ever existed.'

The house was a decrepit. Rotting away, the Carmine Quarter was a maze of green alleys and ivy thickets, of local zones surrounded by barbed wire and vibration mines. Arrahaquen, standing at the orange-specked front door, heard automatic gunfire and the detonations of grenades. She smelled overflowing sewers, rotting vegetation, and the sickly odour of death-rose pollen. Around her, one house in three was a pile of bricks and mortar half concealed by luxuriant foliage. It did not bode well.

'Inside, it is sealed,' deKray said, looking embarrassed. 'When I was here last all was secure. The roof does not leak much, as I recall.'

'And when *were* you here last?'

He hesitated. 'We would be referring to a date last year . . .'

Arrahaquen nodded. This would have to be home, just for a while.

15

Taziqi, High Priestess of the temple, plucking a ripe grape from the bunch at her side, waited while the other three thought about what she had said.

They were sitting inside Rien Zir's inner sanctum. Around them, the wooden levels and mazes of the temple emitted a subliminal symphony of sounds, from the creaks and groans of joists, through the tap-tap-tapping of feet, to human voices. As a foundation to all this, a basso tone, resonant and almost too low to hear, rose and fell in volume as sacred pyuters picked up the ebb and flow of sap in the plants of the temple. But this particular room, hung with green and white tapestries and amply supplied with jugs of fresh water and plates of apples and oranges, also ticked and clicked in synchrony with the secret temple network next door.

Tashyndy seemed as nonchalant as ever. The Kray Queen hardly ever departed the Fish Chambers. She possessed a keen mind, however. Maharyny kept her eyes closed and pressed her hands together in a steeple shape while she thought. A great academic, Maharyny – she had to be to make sense of serpent talk – but too logical a thinker. Arvendyn, nodding to herself and glancing across to Taziqi, also seemed calm.

Taziqi plucked another grape. In response, the orange-peel flesh of her arms rippled, like water in a balloon. Her body was today sheathed in a lime green dress. The other three were naked, although Tashyndy wore strands of grass and ivy in her blonde hair.

'Have we all decided?' Arvendyn asked.

Taziqi looked at the others. Maharyny opened her eyes and said, 'I've decided.'

Tashyndy nodded.

Arvendyn said, 'We must take the risk. I believe in Maharyny's powers of deduction.'

'That is a good opinion,' said Taziqi. 'So let's hope it chimes with what Rien Zir is preparing for us.'

'I agree, but with many reservations,' replied Maharyny. 'For example, we know the wyrm ball can see future truth, but how accurate is it?'

'How accurate are the Eastcity serpents?' asked Arvendyn.

'They compare to our wyrm ball as a gibbon compares to a woman,' Maharyny replied. 'Do not speak of them.'

Taziqi shrugged. 'Remember the future is a gift from Rien Zir. We are Rien Zir's quartet. Her gift must be accurate, else all we live for is an illusion.'

'It's not so simple,' replied Maharyny, 'for we are all part of the Goddess's mind, we are all one. Even such as the noophytes with their partial future memories are part of the Goddess's mind, and so I should be able to see something of them. But I cannot.'

Taziqi bowed her head, acknowledging the fertility of Maharyny's knowledge. 'Tashyndy, what do you think?'

'I say give ourselves up to the Goddess's will,' said Tashyndy, stroking one leg in an absent-minded gesture as she spoke. 'But there is one factor in all this that we seem to have forgotten, and that's Arrahaquen. We watched her for so long. She was so much a part of our future, or so we were told. Yet now she's gone.'

'She is without doubt hanging under Gugul Street,' Maharyny said. 'For the wyrm ball said she was caught. Now she exists nowhere that can be seen, and so she must be dead.'

'I suppose so.'

'Let's not grieve further for that one, taken away by Rien Zir,' Taziqi said. 'Let's look to the immediate future. Soon, the attack will come, and in its aftermath we could take our place in Kray.' She laughed. 'Not for nothing do we live in the Carmine Quarter, where so many of the streets are named for the colour red. The colour of influence.'

'I have foreseen some success,' said Maharyny, 'but still it is too murky to see details, and many will die here.'

Taziqi nodded. 'This quarter of Kray used to be the old centre of influence, at the time when Rien Zir's temples were over in Eastcity, in the Andromeda Quarter. No, our time is now. We are at that eschatological point – the final year. This is our time and Rien Zir's time. The Citadel is but a pimple compared to our great organ of fertility.'

'Soon,' Arvendyn agreed, 'the Goddess's thoughts will come down to us, like manna after rain, and humanity may face a better future. But how close do we live to death? The Carmine's facing green difficulties right now.'

Taziqi pondered this excellent point. 'Let's go to the earth pit,' she suggested.

Tashyndy, still stroking her leg, had made a green streak on her skin. She stood up. 'Yes, let's,' she said, happily.

So they walked to Rien Zir's secret chamber. It was a wooden room, circular, with a high roof from which great pyuter sprays descended, pulsing with green light, connected by optical lianas to networks growing like fungus from the walls. Centrally placed lay a pit in the soil, and in this writhed a ball of serpents, their tails attached to a gold nub.

This was their link with the noophytes. According to legend, a lone noophyte, now known only as the Silver Seed, had long ago separated from the others. The wyrm ball was a creation of Rien Zir, from whose belly-button the Silver Seed had emerged. It gave the priestesses of Rien Zir a vision of the future, a vision transmitted through the vehicle of the Silver Seed from the numinous mind of Rien Zir herself.

If they could only locate the Silver Seed, then the future would be as clear as the past.

Days passed, and Zinina grew ever more friendly with deKray. This upset Graaff-lin. Accusations flew. Graaff-lin felt she was doing all the work while Zinina dallied with a man. The fact that Graaff-lin had managed to find out no more concerning the noophytes only increased her frustration. Zinina pointed out how useful deKray could be, and how generous he was with his time and property. 'How can you object to us being friends?' Zinina would ask, time after time.

'This is my house,' Graaff-lin would usually respond.

DeKray proved trustworthy. Soon there were stolen kisses when Graaff-lin was looking elsewhere. It became a game. Forgetting the debt she owed Graaff-lin, Zinina, out of perversity, tried to get away with as much as she could.

A quiet day arrived, wet outside, humid in.

With Graaff-lin out in the city, working at the alcoves of different serpents, Zinina took advantage of the fact that she and deKray were alone in the house.

She teased him at first, feeling a thrill of power, as though her personal limits – her sexual limits – had been vastly expanded by their solitude. She left him uncertain as to what she wanted, then made it clear. He seemed confused about everything, poor man, although he obviously wanted her. It amused Zinina greatly that she could be so fickle and careless.

After drinking watered baqa through straws, and taking much time on the bed to undress one another, Zinina found herself lying naked beside him, looking at him; and suddenly afraid.

Erect, he was maybe as big as the best endowed man in the Fish Chambers. Zinina could not look away. He seemed relaxed – no doubt the baqa. They rather inexpertly kissed, and although it was fun trying different things out on each other Zinina found it difficult to touch herself, or him.

She was afraid of what he might do. After all, he was free on the bed, charming, self-deprecating and slightly inattentive as usual, but still a loose man. Untied.

She rose above him, allowing him to play with her breasts, which were now a little cold from sweat. 'De-Kray,' she said, feeling genuinely sorry, 'I can't do it if you're free. I'm going to have to tie you up.'

'Oh.'

'I'm sorry, I really am. I've just got to do it. I can't make myself fuck a loose man. Not that I don't trust you.'

He nodded. 'Indeed not. Well ... to save you the indignity, what about if I tie my ankles to the lower rail, and then one wrist, my left, leaving you with only one wrist to secure? That should save you three quarters of the ignominy.'

'Thanks,' she said, uncertain as to whether the urbane tone had hardened into sarcasm. He seemed happy enough. While she refilled their glasses with baqa, and slung a blanket at the bottom of the door to prevent draughts, he took pieces of fabric and tied himself up. Laughing, a little embarrassed, Zinina tied his right wrist, kissing it as she did so, feeling between his legs at the same time to sustain his excitement.

She tried to mount him, but found that she was still too dry.

'Honey,' said deKray. 'It is admirable for occasions such as this, so I have found.'

Zinina, heart sinking at how badly this all seemed to be going, and beginning to regret it, dressed in a gown and dashed to the kitchen. He was still excited for her. In seconds, she was ready and upon him, and he was inside her.

They made love for what seemed to be hours. DeKray was demonstrative, though not especially vocal. For Zinina it was fun, though not ecstatic. Sincerely, she praised him, said how fond of him she was, and how glad she was that their paths had crossed. He was thrilled to be with her, that much was clear.

'Would you mind untying that one?' he asked, nodding towards the knot that Zinina had tied.

'I'll do them all,' she said, now keen to release him.

'The other three I secured using slip knots,' deKray replied, twisting slightly. Zinina was amazed to see the three knots he had tied come loose. So he had been free all the time.

For the briefest instant she felt anger that he had tricked her. He had betrayed their unspoken rules. But then she just laughed. It didn't matter. He was safe. He was not going to attack her.

He laughed, too.

'Let's make a wonderful lunch,' Zinina said. 'Let's raid all the stores and cook up something, eh?'

'That would be most good,' he replied.

They had built up a supply of dried and dehydrated food, as well as some in aluminium tins. Strictly speaking these were stores not meant to be touched – for Westcity

Food Station still doled out food, albeit inedible mush –
but Zinina felt it was time to relax traditional Kray rules.
They spread everything on the kitchen table.

Zinina chose apple sauce mix to start with, then a
packet of stew mix that she could use with some old
mushrooms and a parsnip, and then pulled out a tin of
apricots and a packet of mint.

Soon they lay on their bed again, each with a tray of
food. Zinina refilled the baqa glasses. She was becoming
tipsy. The apple sauce she placed at the edge of her
steaming stew, and then they both tucked in. After weeks
of eating insipid, textureless muck, it tasted almost too
good.

DeKray seemed to feel the same as her. His face creased
with smiles as he ate and he swapped a mushroom for
some parsnip. In fact he was just like her, not different at
all, despite not being a woman. Zinina wondered if at any
point she would run away from him, or if she would
throw him out. This was new to her.

The apricots and mint they ate last, deKray fetching uz
from a cabinet and pouring a tiny drop in both bowls to
sharpen the flavour.

Afterwards, they sat on the bed and finished off the
first bottle of baqa. DeKray's speech was slurring ever so
slightly.

Zinina found herself wanting him again. Brashly, she
pulled off the gown that he wore. They knocked the trays
and crockery off the bed and kissed, passion making them
keen for one another. Zinina pulled off her own gown,
and let his tongue travel over her body. She played with
him, her fingers becoming expert at the art of arousal.

The room was very warm. Sweet sweat dripped from
Zinina and from him, and she imagined what it would be
like just having him on top of her . . .

Suddenly excited, squirming around, she lay on her

back, shoved him so that he crouched above her, then spread her legs, at the same time gesturing him down with her arms. He did not fail to gather her meaning.

Ecstasy rarely experienced in the Fish Chambers took Zinina as he entered her. She cared nothing about safety; she knew he would not ruin these unique moments. Because of the strangeness of their coupling she quite lost control of herself. Before he climaxed she convulsed three or four times, or five, she lost count, and anyway did not care. She gripped his back when he ejaculated.

Her senses seemed to have merged for a few instants. Now, exhausted and overheating – she was desperate for water but could find only more baqa – she was becoming aware of the world around her once more. Yet now she could think properly.

That would never happen again, she knew. There could only be one second time. Of course, they could try the position again, but Zinina knew that equal or greater pleasure awaited her when she next mounted him, for all was now changed. She was now one of the very few who had made love more than once with the same man. Maybe she was unique.

'Let us open the other bottle,' he suggested.

They drank a toast to themselves. 'To our bed,' Zinina said.

'I trust Graaff-lin will not return home and surprise us,' answered deKray.

'She should be home soon,' said Zinina, not caring when Graaff-lin returned.

'I do hope she is safe.'

'She's safe, she's safe.'

The afternoon meandered on. Although she wanted to bed deKray a third time, Zinina found that he was not up to the effort, so they dressed and drank much more, turning some music up loud until a power cut brought silence. Outside, the rain drummed against the shutters and the roof, and the sounds of water gurgling down gutters became louder. There were a few rolls of thunder as evening arrived.

Graaff-lin arrived shortly after. She had spent the whole day with the serpents, but had also watched her old temple.

'Do not be tempted to return there,' deKray warned.

'No, keep out,' Zinina agreed.

Graaff-lin slumped into a chair. The rain on her face seemed to be augmented by tears; it was difficult to tell. 'I don't know what I'm doing,' she said. 'I don't know whether the serpents will give us clues to the plan, or whether they will not. I thought I heard a new word, but—'

'A new noophyte word?' deKray broke in. 'I am sorry. I did not mean to interrupt.'

Graaff-lin ignored his apology. 'Yes. I replayed a serpent prophecy directly back to it, hoping to set up a resonance. The thing said it lived in a place called Gwmru.'

'Gwmru,' deKray mused. 'I have heard mention of that name in connection with noophytes. Mayhap it is in one of my ancient lexicons.'

'Find out,' Zinina said.

'Indeed I will.' Intrigued, deKray lit a cigarette and began puffing at it, walking around the room and glancing at Graaff-lin.

'You need not,' Graaff-lin said with a scornful look. 'I have already done the work. The cobra I was working with said that a dwan was a garden of Gwmru. Gwmru is an environment – a land. I believe the conscoosities live there. We must at all costs find out where this land is.'

'You have done well,' deKray said. Zinina agreed.

Graaff-lin sighed and sank back into her chair. 'But

we've so little time, and the connections are so poor, even for somebody as devout as myself. I can't help losing confidence.'

'You're doing fine,' Zinina said, a half-hearted attempt at comfort that she instantly felt ashamed of. She went to hug Graaff-lin. 'No, really you are. You've been out all day, while we've just been, well, lying around. Yeah, you done well, Graaff-lin.'

deKray added, 'You are a most valuable woman.'

Graaff-lin tried to smile, but failed. 'Do you think so?'

'We do,' they chorused.

'What I need is time and help. Talking to the serpents is dangerous, yet I must remain mobile. I'm sure the conscoosities are within reach.'

'You need a pyuton,' said Zinina, her mind recalling pyutons that the Citadel Guard used to use for dangerous work. Then an idea. 'Wait,' she said, 'it's not so tricky to worm your way into a pyuton's mind.'

'That is correct,' deKray said, 'they all possess a third eye, or innerai. But how would Graaff-lin use that mental omphalos to control a pyuton?'

'I wasn't on about that. Don't you remember? Arraha-quen's got a pyuton replica up the Citadel. We could use that.'

Immediately Graaff-lin said, 'I will not work with a double of that woman.'

'But the pyuton doesn't worship Rien Zir. It's just a replica, and it doesn't even look like her any more.'

Judging by Graaff-lin's hesitation, the point had been accepted.

'How would we bring the pyuton down from Arraha-quen's apartment in the Citadel?' deKray asked.

'There must be a way.'

They discussed Zinina's proposal for some time, until

Graaff-lin threw up her hands, said she was starving, and made for the kitchen. DeKray relented eventually, and it was decided that, as soon as possible, Arrahaquen should be persuaded of their need.

Zinina slept with deKray in the study that night: another first for her. Graaff-lin, fast asleep, knew nothing of the arrangement. Zinina kept asking herself if he really was safe. But he was too tired to make love again, so, sweating with desire just from his touch, she satisfied herself using fingers, and a well-smoothed phallus broken off one of the pleasure statues at the House of Many Splendid Lingons.

Only one thing worried her that night. The house was creaking. In Kray, creaking houses meant stressed houses.

In the Nonagon, the Portreeve pinged her metal dolphin. 'Item sixteen, water supplies. Pyetmian?'

Fat Pyetmian, dressed in blue and black silks and a dome-shaped hat that looked as if too much rain had fallen upon it, glanced at the pyuter that lay on the table at her side. 'I must say, Portreeve, this is getting serious. Some of our superior clerical workers have only three hundred litres a day for their personal use. We must divert as much as possible from the two Water Stations. Here's my plan. In a few days we'll put a repeating message on the public networks, saying that new quotas are going to be enforced, and that every Krayan must have a water card to draw supplies. I've looked into it, and we could have these made in a day, then handed out at the Water Stations themselves, cutting down on work for us. Defenders would be entitled to, say, eighty litres a day, clerics to sixty, and independents to forty.'

A short silence, then Uqeq asked, 'B-b-but how would you meter the taps in their houses?'

'Meter?' Pyetmian said, frowning. 'What meters? The

idea is that they collect the water in buckets, or whatever they happen to have.'

'Oh I *see*,' said Ammyvryn, smiling. 'You mean, most people won't be able to collect all the water they're due, and that will mean more for the Citadel? You're turning the city's mains off?'

Pyetmian did not bother to respond to this fairly obvious point. Instead she said, 'I strongly advise my plan. The pyuter work would take a matter of hours. All the Water Station data mines are available, names and the like, and all we really have to do is transport a few cartloads of plastic cards up Ficus Street and along Judico Street. Couldn't be simpler.'

The Portreeeve nodded. 'Vote?'

Nine were in favour.

'And now,' the Portreeve continued, pinging the dolphin once more, 'the final topic, the one I expect you have all been waiting for. Omaytra, please enlighten us.'

Omaytra was a young woman, perhaps twenty-five, with green eyes of sinister appeal, and a mouth constantly pursed, as though she was waiting to snap at somebody for being rude. She invariably wore a pale blue jumpsuit adorned with gold and amber hoops, thigh boots of black plastic with metal toe-caps, and a steel-ring belt that she claimed once belonged to a Portreeve.

Her voice was sinuous and calm, like that of Surqjna, her friend, but not so spine-chilling as that woman's. 'You refer to the attack on the temple of the Goddess,' she said, 'the plan for which is almost ready.'

'You've only been at it a year,' muttered a grumpy Pyetmian.

'Quiet,' growled the Portreeve.

Omaytra continued. 'The attack is now confirmed. It will happen shortly, my dears, probably within two weeks. Much of our offensive force will be used. The temple will be crushed. Our forces will then leave.'

'That sounds good,' said the Portreeve. 'I expect to hear the full plan at our next meeting. Now, I've got some confessions to sign. You may leave the Nonagon.'

16

K ray sank further into its own mire.

An announcement was made on the Citadel networks to the effect that both Food Stations would now open only from dawn until noon. That same morning a band of revellers from Eastcity led by psychotic priestesses from the temple of Pure Justice attacked the Infirmary and managed to burn half of it to the ground. The other half was rendered uninhabitable. The Citadel did nothing. It failed even to mention it on public broadcasts. A great encampment of revellers now existed where the Infirmary and the Dispensary had stood, and the district became too dangerous to enter.

Worse was to follow. The day after, Arrahaquen noticed that none of the taps in deKray's house was working. Nor was the shower. This did not at first surprise her, given the state of the building, but when she switched on the public bands she soon discovered that all Kray was affected: '. . . will come into effect on this day. All cards must be claimed within five days. That is the end of the Portreeve's announcement.

'The Portreeve has decreed that from this hour all fresh water allocated to citizens of Kray will be on a new scale. All water will be obtained solely from the two Water

Stations. The Citadel cannot guarantee the purity of water obtained from any other source. All water will be obtained daily by means of a pyuter card tagged to kit numbers, thereby ensuring identity. These cards cannot be replaced. Do not lose them. These cards are non-transferable. The amounts of water available are, for defenders, sixty litres per day, for registered priestesses forty litres per day, and for independents twenty litres per day. These amounts are non-negotiable. All enforcements will come into effect on this day. All cards must be claimed within five days. That is the end of the Portreeve's announcement.'

Later that morning Zinina and deKray came to visit her. 'They've only cut off the mains in the city. We'll all have to carry our water home every day,' Arrahaquen explained.

As she said it the rig died. Tubes powered off the mains faded, leaving only autonomous azure photoplankton tubes shining. 'I'll light some candles,' Zinina said. She paused. 'Of course, every reveller's going to *love* preying on lines of people carying water to their homes, ain't they?'

Arrahaquen slumped into a chair. No water to speak of, little food and no power. This could not go on for much longer. And still no announcement of the Portreeve's plan. In her mind's eye she could see riots and demonstrations at the Food and Water Stations. She wondered how real these mental images were.

Prophetic counsel was something Arrahaquen had taken very little account of during her life, she who rather despised the poor ignorants who went weekly, or even daily, to the serpents to have their fortunes told. But now she wondered. Some kind of glimpse into the future had saved her from death under Gugul Street, when she had caught flint chips in complete darkness. She had always

assumed that her sense of intuition was an accurate
foundation for action, but now little points of precognition seemed to dance around with fervent motion at the
top of her mind, synthesising occasionally into thoughts,
images, or even grander concepts. She found herself
taking notice of her own unconscious, and the emotions
that welled up from her unconscious, for in many cases
the basic knowledge carried by her emotions was linked
to more detailed understanding. She remembered the flash
of joy that preceded catching the first flint chip as she
hung in the leather straps.

An experiment. She lay back and wondered what food
Zinina was making in the kitchen. She thought of leeks;
potato; apple?

'Food up,' Zinina called. Arrahaquen walked into the
kitchen. The gas burner flickered, and there were two
opened bottles of red-top water on the table.

'So the taps really aren't working?' deKray said.

The three sat at the table. 'Nope,' Zinina replied.

Arrahaquen looked at the food; potato, some sort of
mush with an onion flavour, and pear slices from an old
tin.

'What you grinning at?' Zinina asked her.

'Nothing. I'm just happy to be free.'

They ate. 'What stores have we got left?' deKray
asked.

'Eighty-nine bottles of water unopened. Sixty tins, but
some of them's unlabelled, and some are rusty. About five
packets of dried stuff. Some old tea leaves. Um ... that's
it, I think. Oh, about a hundred cannisters of vitamin and
mineral supplements.'

'Not much, then.'

'No.' Zinina smiled at deKray. 'You've got a hoard.
Not as much as us, but we could merge it.'

'Is he going to live with you and Graaff-lin?' Arrahaquen asked Zinina, innocently.

Zinina frowned. 'Would you mind?'

'Not at all,' Arrahaquen said pointedly.

Zinina grimaced. 'Me and deKray's going off to get our water cards, and today's food. Coming?'

'No. I'll go out later.' Arrahaquen tried to guess what route they might take. 'I bet,' she said, playing with the remains of her potato, 'that you go down Feverfew Street up to the barbed wire, then go to the Water Station, then come back along Efcus Street.'

'Why?' Zinina asked, mystified.

'I just do.'

'You're in a silly mood this morning. We're off.'

DeKray hesitated. Then he said, 'We have a proposal for you, Arrahaquen. Graaff-lin requires pyuton assistance, and we remembered your replica. Do you think . . . ?'

Her thoughts elsewhere, Arrahaquen replied, 'I'll consider it.'

Zinina and deKray were gone for an hour. When they returned, Arrahaquen learnt that they had not taken her predicted route. Zinina, being petulant, had walked down Platan Street, then Ixia Street, gone first to the Water Station and then to the Food Station, then returned along back alleys. So, Arrahaquen thought, her predictions could be changed.

It was all about knowledge, Arrahaquen realised. Because her mind was a private entity – private like a black hole behind an event horizon – she could hide knowledge. But it was precisely because human minds were private phenomena that such concepts as truth came about. She must decide what to reveal of her prophetic ability.

All four of them sat in the central sitting room of deKray's old house.

'Let's have a supper,' Arrahaquen announced.

Graaff-lin did not understand. 'A supper?'

'A final supper before the end of the city. Let's get lots of nice food, use lots of gear to get stuff, and have a wonderful time. With wine too.'

'Sounds good to me,' Zinina said enthusiastically.

'But we cannot afford to,' objected Graaff-lin.

'Would I be allowed to smoke?' deKray asked.

'Yes,' replied Arrahaquen. 'So that's three to one in favour. Right, I'll organise it. Let's have it here, tomorrow night. Zinina, you get the wine and spirits from the Spired Inn. DeKray, you go down to the Harbour and barter for some fish, if there is any—'

'Aamlon don't eat fish,' Graaff-lin said.

Arrahaquen nodded. 'I'll do something special for you. Chances are there's no fish anyway. Graaff-lin, you and I will sort out the menu. DeKray, bring things from your hoard.'

Instructions dispensed, Arrahaquen let Graaff-lin depart to resume her serpent work. She had discovered a third pyuter heart word – ffordion, which described the noophyte group – but it was just another word.

The day passed. Thunderstorms and torrential rain reduced activity in the city to a minimum, but next day it returned to normal – echoes of gunfire, people running up and down, rumbles as houses collapsed. Arrahaquen, hearing a crash, went out to find fallen slates in the garden. She noticed too that part of the north-facing wall, already covered with red algae, was crumbling at the edges. A great crack ran from ground to eaves.

Flies and mosquitoes had troubled the house for some time, but when fetching food from his maisonette deKray brought a useful little gadget, a sonic insect destroyer, with adjustable range. Arrahaquen mounted it above the gas burner.

She and Graaff-lin started cooking at dusk. DeKray and Zinina were to arrive later with the wine. The kitchen was messy. But all Krayan kitchens were made with special defences, moulded inserts wedged between units, hemispherical sinks, plastic drain covers and plugs, and under the floor bubbles of antiseptic gum that percolated through the cork tiles. All designs were meant to fight the danger of infection.

'Get that pastry in the grill,' Arrahaquen told Graaff-lin as she cut slices of reconstituted onion.

'What about the vine leaves?'

'Take them out in ten minutes, then put the rice on. I'll sort out the sauces.'

They worked on. Without running water, it was difficult. Rules taught as a child stuck, and every used utensil was placed in the boiler, a tall jar filled with bubbling water, every scrap of food was put in a bin, and they wore film-plastic gloves. Graaff-lin left for a few minutes to change – Arrahaquen had insisted on everyone wearing their best clothes.

Half an hour before Zinina and deKray were due to arrive Arrahaquen went to her room. She undressed, then laid out the clothes she had selected from her own meagre stock. She stood naked in front of a cracked mirror for a few seconds, noting that she had lost some weight, and that there were stretch marks on her belly and thighs. She put on underwear, then her only dress, a sheath of midnight blue decorated with black and purple triangles and edged with silver glitter. She pulled on a pair of low boots, black and worn but serviceable, and then studied the jewellery she had set out, intricate earrings made of tin disks and malachite, a silver ring, and her own brooch which, ironically enough, depicted a jewelled python wrapped around a gold log. Finally she pulled on a pair of violet lace gloves that reached to her elbows. The final look pleased her.

Graaff-lin wore only a steel-grey, high-collared one-piece, with blue boots and a blue belt.

They put the finishing touches to the meal while they waited for Zinina and deKray. Arrahaquen began to worry. A continuous racket of automatic weaponry sounded from the east of the Mercantile Quarter, where lay the ruins of the Dispensary and the Infirmary – no doubt revellers fighting over medical equipment. There was a rap on the door. Electrical power had been off all day; now only Graaff-lin's battery-powered rigs worked and the door had to be knocked upon rather than spoken to.

Zinina was shrouded in a black cloak. But deKray, as he strode in, seemed almost suave; he wore a black shirt with a bright blue waistcoat over it, a black leather kirtle, blue calf-mufflers, black shoes so shiny there were reflections in them, and three golden bangles on each wrist that sang out musical notes wherever they touched. 'Good evening,' he said, presenting Arrahaquen with a crate of wine bottles. 'These are from Dhow-lin at the Spired Inn, whence we have rushed.'

'Thank you very much,' Arrahaquen said.

Zinina took off her cloak. She wore blue silk pyjama trousers caught at the ankles so they were baggy elsewhere, a translucent blue silk brassiere, and a white skull-cap. Her slippers were also white, with raffia bases and curly, pointed toes, embroidered with traditional jannitta daisies. Through the trousers, Arrahaquen could see a black thong. Zinina, by far the most striking of them physically, had excelled herself. There was even a small sapphire set in her belly-button.

'Warm, ain't it?' she said. 'Oh, the wine's all three-year vintage, and strong stuff.'

Arrahaquen smiled, and returned to the kitchen to prepare the first course.

She and Graaff-lin carried four trays into the sitting

room, the room with the best lights, each tray containing
two bowls and a plate of wafers. 'This is courgette and
orange soup,' she said, 'with malted biscuits and mint dip
to the side. Tuck in.'

They did. Zinina opened two bottles of the wine and
poured them all a full glass. The liquid was deep orange
and had bits in it. Arrahaquen, making sure that she was
watched, took an envelope from her pocket and put it on
the mantelpiece, but they did not question her. She started
her soup.

'Here's a good one,' Zinina said. 'How many Portreeves, and you'll like this one, does it take to change a
bacteria tube?'

'I don't know,' they all pretended.

'None – she gets the Citadel Guard to do it!'

Laughter was forthcoming. Already, Arrahaquen could
feel the atmosphere becoming relaxed, yet a tear almost
formed as she remembered the city outside. Then she took
a sip of the wine and forgot it. The wine was strong, she
could feel it fall down her throat. Her diaphragm seemed
to thump against her breastbone, but she stifled the
coughing fit.

'Why,' Arrahaquen said, 'does the Portreeve never
wear a hat?'

A pause, then, 'We don't know. Why doesn't the
Portreeve ever wear a hat?'

'Because there's no ship with sailcloth big enough.'

Arrahaquen was rewarded with much laughter at this
old one. She noticed that deKray seemed unconfortable,
as though he was dreading being asked to crack a joke.
Graaff-lin was sitting upright in her chair, seemingly
happy, but perhaps not relaxed. Opposite her, Zinina had
her right foot wedged under her left thigh, a glass in one
hand, her other arm reaching back over her shoulder to
grip the chair top; completely at ease.

'What's the difference between the Portreeve and a cablecar?' Zinina said.

Blank faces.

'It's very difficult to piss off a cablecar.'

It took some time, but they laughed when they saw the point. 'I'll go get the main course,' Arrahaquen said, indicating to Graaff-lin that help would be appreciated.

In the kitchen they dropped used dishes into antiseptic water, then took the main courses in. 'There was no fish,' Arrahaquen said, 'so it's parcels of rice, carrots and basil-balls done up in vine leaves with melted butter, rice and peas on the side, nut-potato with rosemary sauce, and then mushroom sauce with a touch of wild garlic. Tuck in again.'

The conversation left jokes and turned to other subjects: Zinina's clothes, deKray's maisonette, Arrahaquen's earrings, and of course the wine and food, with Graaff-lin and deKray both making comments. Zinina was becoming ebullient. She now had both feet tucked under the opposite thigh, had somehow acquired two glasses of wine, and was eating with gusto. Arrahaquen felt her limbs becoming warm, her sight slightly blurred. She refilled her glass. Zinina opened the fifth bottle.

Arrahaquen returned to the kitchen to unwrap the third course from its protective foil wrapping. She took it in on one tray, saying, 'Take what you want from this. It's a green salad, with blue lettuce, chicory, crushed nettles, miniature tomatoes, potato purée with strong black onions, and this orange stuff is a bowl of aamlon carrot-butter that Graaff-lin made specially. It's got the tiniest touch of uz in it.'

Zinina used two forks to take a great helping of the salad, tidying up the remains when everybody had finished. Arrahaquen noticed that, although deKray had drunk as much wine as Zinina, his composure seemed unruffled, whereas Zinina was now singing snatches from rude jannitta idylls, and Graaff-lin was smiling and even chatting.

Arrahaquen brought in the penultimate course. 'Pear and greengage pasties,' she said, 'with honey nuggets, treacly custard, and some hazelnut biscuits to go on the side.'

Arrahaquen was proud of this course. The whole meal had taken four and a half hours to cook, and this had been the most time consuming. But they loved it and nothing remained.

'Is there any more of that?' Zinina asked.

'I'm afraid not,' she said, pretending to be sorrowful.

'What!' Zinina said, standing on her chair. 'I shall attack the kitchen! Oaz, oaz! Don't try to stop me! Us! DeKray'll be my lieutenant.'

'Descend from that chair,' deKray said.

Zinina did so, favouring him with a lengthy kiss, much to Arrahaquen's fascination and Graaff-lin's repulsion, then opening the ninth bottle of wine.

Arrahaquen tottered into the kitchen, put everything into antiseptic water, then picked up the final course, which she took on one tray. 'Fresh fruit,' she said, 'washed in sterile water and lovely and crisp and juicy.'

Zinina said, 'Talking of—'

Arrahaquen continued, 'I've checked them all for bugs. There's some apples, pears, two oranges though one's got a hole in the rind, lots of black grapes, and, look, even a quince. I'll just cut that into quarters so we can all have some.'

'I want some now,' Zinina said, opening the tenth bottle of wine and refilling all five glasses. 'What is a quince anyway?'

DeKray said, 'A hard, acid fruit of that tree related to the pear and the apple, and used in preserves, etcetera.'

'Look,' said Zinina, 'I can get my tongue right into the middle of this orange. That's a useful skill, y'know.'

They finished off the tray of fruit, then walked, staggered, and in Zinina's case danced erotically into the front room, where Arrahaquen had dragged the two least decrepit couches. DeKray and Zinina flopped into one, two bottles of wine at their side, while Arrahaquen and Graaff-lin took the other, and the crate too, which still contained three bottles. Arrahaquen, now approaching drunkenness, remembered that she had left the envelope in the other room. She told deKray to retrieve it, then put it on the central table, next to two boxes of boiled sweets that she had found, quite by accident, under an old kettle in the larder.

Graaff-lin had brought a portable rig. This she plugged into the floor port, tuning the device to an aamlon music station. A symphony was in progress. The music thrummed and trilled as they talked and drank.

'Do you think the Portreeve will announce her plan to save Kray?' deKray asked Arrahaquen.

'Who cares?' Zinina opined.

'I think she will,' Arrahaquen said. 'After all, there'd be rioting everywhere if she didn't.'

Zinina burst into laughter. 'There is rioting everywhere,' she said. 'Bad rioting. Revellers revellin' and stuff.'

'I think the Portreeve will announce a plan,' Graaff-lin said, 'but probably not until the last moment.'

Zinina opened another bottle of wine. 'If you're gonna talk serious stuff, deKray an' me'll pop off for a minute.'

Zinina led deKray away, slamming the door after her, then slamming the door to another room ... though not deliberately, Arrahaquen reflected, just out of high spirits. 'Guess what they're up to,' she said, suddenly envious of Zinina, and the access she enjoyed to a free man.

'I'd rather not consider it,' Graaff-lin said.

'Turn the music up a bit, would you? Thanks. So, these words you've discovered, they're part of the machine language used by the nop ... the noots ... them things?'

'It's conscoositee machine language,' Graaff-lin replied, a smile on her face. 'The conscoositee ffordion lives in a dwan in the land of Gwmru. I'm trying now to find a way to access a far bigger vocabulary, so I can talk directly to the conscoosities.'

'And these are your Dodspaat, Graaff-lin?'

'I think so.'

Arrahaquen nodded dreamily, half entwined in her own thoughts. She sensed nothing when it came to Graaff-lin, saw no images, experienced no feelings. But her ability, if such it was, had not yet properly developed. She said, 'Do you really think the Portreeve will announce anything?'

'Oh, yes. I think the conscoosities are advising her and the Red Brigade. I think they all live in the circuitry underneath the Citadel.'

Arrahaquen wondered. 'If only we could find out where Gwmru is.'

'It is not impossible,' Graaff-lin said.

Arrahaquen had never heard her sound so confident. 'Really?'

'I say that because of something deKray mentioned yesterday. He said he had read a legend somewhere, in his childhood, of Gwmru – that it was a country with no borders, and yet was everywhere, like the aura of the Dodspaat. This agrees with what the serpent told me – that Gwmru was a land ...'

Plainly Graaff-lin had more to say, but she seemed shy, as though unwilling to reveal her deeper thoughts and speculations. 'Go on, do,' Arrahaquen urged.

'Well, I think that if only we could get a pyuton we

might be able to visit Gwmru.'

Arrahaquen was amazed. 'But how?'

'I don't know. I'm just guessing. Please don't tell deKray what I have said, he will think me an idiot.'

'All right. But Graaff-lin, I don't think you're an idiot.'

She smiled. 'DeKray said that it was a childhood memory. On an impulse I leafed through some old teaching books that I had, that I'd not looked at for decades, and I found a most amazing thing. It was a picture of a pyuton done for a child – you know, a simplistic drawing for a toddler. But it was labelled, Arrahaquen, and the most amazing thing was that her . . . oh, I can't say it, I'm sorry.'

'Her what?'

Graaff-lin's face had turned red. 'Her . . . down there.'

'Her genitalia?'

'Yes. Next to its proper name it was labelled "gwm". That's surely not a coincidence.'

Mental floodgates seemed to open for Arrahaquen as Graaff-lin's ideas tumbled out. Pyutons were indistinguishable from women externally; they possessed every organ. Why should that be? But more importantly than that, she had heard stories – childish stories, smirked over in yards by kids who knew next to nothing about sex – that pyutons were sexually active.

'It could be a coincidence,' she said, 'but then maybe not. You never see a male pyuton, but, well, I've heard silly stories about pyutons making love to one another, haven't you?'

'Well . . . yes.'

'I wonder. I wonder if Gwmru comes from that word, gwm.'

'DeKray might be able to find out.'

Arrahaquen nodded. 'Let's wait until he comes back. Oh, hurry up, Zinina. Don't tell him what we're thinking,

Graaff-lin, let's just ask him and see what he comes up with.'

They did not have long to wait. Singing still, Zinina returned from her room, and deKray arrived some minutes later. Arrahaquen launched into her request.

'DeKray, you've got a huge library, haven't you?'

For some reason Zinina burst into peals of laughter.

'Indeed, my library is the third largest in Kray,' he replied, 'and full of all manner of works. Why?'

'Could you look up the derivation of a word for us?'

'Indeed.'

'It's "gwm." As in the first three letters of Gwmru.'

'Aha, I have already perused dictionaries over that word,' he replied, 'but the derivation is merely quaint and descriptive, I am afraid. Gwmru literally means "the land of the valleys".'

Arrahaquen turned to stare at Graaff-lin.

'Is there aught of significance?' deKray asked, rolling then lighting one of his cigarettes.

Tongue-tied, Graaff-lin nodded at Arrahaquen. Arrahaquen said, 'Well, possibly.'

DeKray took a puff. Menthol fumes began to circulate around the room. Zinina opened the last bottle of wine.

DeKray said, 'Continue, please.'

Arrahaquen shrugged. 'It seems "gwm" is an old word for a woman's genitalia. A valley. We were just wondering . . .'

DeKray nodded, and if the intensity of his cigarette's glow and the speed at which it was being smoked was any indication of the depth of this thought, he was intrigued. Zinina just giggled, lying prone on the sofa, her feet on deKray's thighs. DeKray shifted slightly, and his leather kirtle creaked. He began to roll a second cigarette. 'A most curious connection,' he said. 'I suppose it could be a coincidence, but mayhap it is not.'

'Are you thinking the same thoughts as me?' Arraha-quen said.

'About intimate pyuton relations? One hears stories, of course, but I confess I know no details.'

'We gotta lotta learn,' Zinina burbled, scratching her scalp. 'A *lot*ta learn. Arrahaquen, you gotta get your double down here.'

DeKray left to visit the bathroom. Arrahaquen pointed out how difficult it would be to retrieve her pyuton replica.

'I could do it easy-weasy,' Zinina replied.

'You're sure you won't be too tired?' remarked Graaff-lin.

'Hoy,' Zinina said, sitting up, 'you can say what you like, because I'm too happy to be angry. Too happy.'

Arrahaquen found herself irritated by Zinina's blasé reply. 'Don't you think we're all taking a risk with this man?' she said earnestly. 'Zinina, you could be wasting valuable time with him. There's only months left. Haven't you seen the state of the northern quarters? It's a forest. Nobody lives there. Haven't you seen the refugees in the south?'

'Oh, don't harass me,' Zinina replied, waving her arms about in a gesture of carelessness. 'You's only envious. Envious of what we gets up to, ha ha!'

'I think it is dangerous and irresponsible,' said Graaff-lin.

'Yes,' Arrahaquen agreed, 'what if he's got pestilence viruses?'

'Well he hasn't, so there.'

'How do you know?'

'He told me.'

Arrahaquen said, 'You didn't just believe him? Oh, how naive can you get?'

'You don't understand,' said Zinina. 'I can see what

this all is. You's envious of my relationship. Who knows, you's thinking, it might blossom into love, an' that's what you don't wanna see 'cos your life's so empty of it an' mine ain't.'

'Love?' Arrahaquen said, feeling angry now. 'Love, in Kray? Zinina, in this city there's only lust and despair. You've got a case of lust, that's all.'

'That's all?' Zinina replied, sitting up now. 'It's quite a bit more'n that, an' you know it well. You's just envious. How many women get a chance to fuck a man more'n once, eh? You lot just go into the Fishies and find the nearest unoccupied prod. But not me, oh no,' and here Zinina dissolved into giggles once more, 'not me, I got one only, only one, an' that's all I need. Besides, he really likes me. You gotta man who likes you, eh?'

'He could kill you,' Graaff-lin said. 'I may be a priestess of the Dodspaat, but I know how that disease is carried between people.'

Zinina said, 'Wha's that gotta do with anythin'?'

'We're only trying to help you,' Arrahaquen said. She felt angry at Zinina for ignoring their advice, angry too for what seemed the possibility of their group splitting. She said, 'We've been through a lot together—'

'Hoy, you're touching me heart.'

'—and we can't let a man break us up. We've got to find out about the plan, and how to escape.'

'There is no escape, you silly woman,' Zinina said, suddenly flaring up. 'Don't you see that? It's all a waste of time. This is the end. We might as well enjoy our last few months.'

Arrahaquen felt stung. She felt she needed to hurt Zinina for saying that. 'That's just the old reveller talking,' she told Zinina contemptuously. 'How do you know it's the end? What gives you the right to say? Been speaking to serpents?'

'Don't call me a reveller,' Zinina replied, her face flushing. 'I'm no reveller, right? I'm an indep. I'm not a reveller and never will be, so don't ever call me one!' Her voice was raised now to a shout. 'Or I'll belt you one!'

'Only the morally poor descend to violence,' Graaff-lin commented.

Zinina returned to lying on the couch. She undid her brassiere and kicked off her slippers, just to annoy them, Arrahaquen knew. Then she said, 'I don't care what you say. You just can't stand seein' me with him 'cos it shows up what you ain't got. You's just trying to bring me down. Say whatcha like, it can't hurt me. Relationships do that, y'know, they give ya strength. DeKray gives me strength.'

'It looks to me as if he is exhausting you,' Graaff-lin retorted with rare venom. 'What do you talk about when you sit on him of an afternoon? Botany? Philosophy? Technological ethics?'

Zinina laughed. 'You think I lie on him? Have I gotta shock for you. Sometimes he does it on *me*!'

Graaff-lin gave a little scream and put her hand to her mouth. Arrahaquen did not know what to say. Zinina seemed to have an answer to their every argument; and – it pained her to admit it – she did seem tonight to have a rare confidence in what she was saying, a confidence that Arrahaquen had never noticed before. Suddenly, she felt ashamed for saying the things she had said to Zinina.

There was silence in the room. 'Er, where is he?' Arrahaquen said. He had been gone a while.

Zinina jumped up, left, but soon returned. 'He's asleep in a room. Tired out, seems to me . . .'

'Well, at least he's safe. I . . . I suppose we should be grateful for his intelligence, if nothing else.'

Zinina said nothing. Nor did Graaff-lin.

Arrahaquen unwrapped one of the boiled sweets. 'Perhaps we have underestimated his worth slightly. I mean, he does know a lot, doesn't he, Graaff-lin?'

'I am unfamiliar with his qualifications.'

'Mind you,' Arrahaquen told Zinina, 'I do deny being envious of you. I can go to the Fish Chambers any time I like.'

'Good f'r you.'

'Let's not end this evening on a sour note,' Arrahaquen pleaded.

Graaff-lin stood, and said, 'I'll await you, Zinina, in the hallway.' She stalked off.

Arrahaquen said, 'I'm sorry I shouted at you, Zinina.'

'That's a'right.'

'Good. We thr– four, we've got to keep together.'

'If we're to get anywhere, we have to,' Zinina agreed.

Arrahaquen paused. It was time to reveal the secret. 'Go and wake deKray,' she said. 'I've got something to tell you both. Wait, Zinina, take this envelope with you, then bring it back.'

Zinina stood unsteadily and took the envelope. 'What's in it, then?'

'Go and get deKray and I'll tell you.'

She did what she was told, and in a minute deKray, bleary eyed and wrapped in a blanket, appeared. Arrahaquen said, 'Now open it.'

Zinina did; and read the contents. 'What do these sentences say?' deKray asked, trying to read over Zinina's shoulder.

Zinina was frowning. 'How come you could write all this?'

'I think I'm a pythoness.'

'You can spae the future?' deKray said. 'But that is impossible.'

'Read that,' Arrahaquen said, pointing to the notes she had written.

'It's all here,' Zinina confirmed, sitting. 'Who ate what,

my extra wine glass, the singing and the standing on the chair, your kirtle, deKray, my bra coming off ... it's all here.'

'I can remember the future. Only tiny pieces, and I'm not very good and it comes rather at random. But don't you see? I could foretell a way to escape the city. All I have to do is hone my skills, and the answer will arrive in my unconscious.'

'If there's enough time,' Zinina said. 'Hoy, we ought to tell Graaff-lin.'

'We'll tell her tomorrow,' Arrahaquen said. 'She's not in the mood just now.'

17

Zinina woke up to pain.

Her head was buried under her pillow, and its unpleasant heat was making her dizzy. Her mouth was parched, her eyes throbbed. When she tried to sit up her temples seemed to implode. She crawled out of bed then crawled along the floor to the bathroom, where she remembered that there was no water. So she made for the kitchen, poured herself a tankard of pure water, and drank it, soaking a flannel in the remainder to cool her forehead.

An hour later, deKray arrived, and some hours after that, Arrahaquen. Graaff-lin had left the house. Both had pale skin and dull eyes. Somehow, even the problems of Kray diminished in the face of the discomfort they all felt.

At noon they received a shock. Without warning gunfire sounded in the alley outside, and then they heard yelling, and bursts of automatic fire from two sides. When bullets started hitting their outer walls they really panicked. But there was nothing to do except sit tight. The battle seemed to be in the alley, and it lasted ten minutes. At the end a grenade was thrown, and then there was the unmistakeable rumble of a house collapsing. Then boots splashing along the street, some distant voices, and then silence.

This brought them back to reality. Arrahaquen stirred herself enough to make some lunch. Graaff-lin returned and made straight for her pyuter rigs. Zinina, her head still throbbing with every movement, lay on a couch and complained to deKray.

The day crawled by for Zinina. She felt nauseous when food appeared, and had to decline it. Even her hearing had been affected, for she kept hearing a creaking, groaning sound that seemed to come from inside her own skull. But then Arrahaquen pointed out that it was the house making the noise, shifting on its foundations.

Zinina felt the urge for fresh air, and she hauled deKray out to examine the house. The north end had sunk six inches at least, and five cracks, one big enough for Zinina to put fingers into, leaped from ground to roof. All around the house slates lay. Window frames and shutters were warping. In the wall nearest the street were countless bullet holes.

'We must do something about Graaff-lin's garden,' deKray said. 'She is too busy to tend it.'

It was dangerous. Packed vegetation had hidden all trace of path and border. Saplings were shooting up everywhere, and roots were beginning to make one wall crumble at the base. Poisonous ferns, landwracks and ivy had appeared. Zinina pointed out that they did not have enough verticide to deal with the whole plot.

'Then we must make a path through to the alley,' deKray replied.

'You do it now,' Zinina said. 'I'm just popping out.'

'Where to?'

Zinina pulled on protectives. 'Oh,' she said as nonchalantly as possible, 'just to call a friend. If there's any screens working, that is.'

DeKray handed over her boots. 'This would be Qmoet.'

Zinina stopped dressing. 'How do you know about her?'

'You mentioned her name once in your sleep. And someone by the name of Gishaad-lin.'

Zinina hid her reaction to this reply. Her final secret she wanted kept. 'Well,' she managed, 'that's who got me into the Citadel in the first place. I owe my guard career to her. We sort of grew up together.'

DeKray seemed unimpressed. 'I see. Well, go make your communication if you must, and I shall prepare a safe path through the jungle outside. But do not be long.'

'I won't be.'

She kissed him on the lips, then ran out into the rain, sped down the alley – first ensuring there were no revellers or gunslingers visible – then into Pine Street, where one screen still worked. Poking needles into a digital port to bypass any network spies, she called the secret number.

Qmoet answered. 'Hoy, it's me,' Zinina said in jannitta.

'Zin, how are you?'

'Amazing news. You won't believe it's true. Arrahaquen, last night, she threw a party and then gave us an envelope with everything we'd done predicted on it. She's a pythoness!'

'A pythoness?'

'It's true,' Zinina insisted. 'I saw it with my own eyes. Qmoet, this changes everything—'

'Wait, wait, Zinina, explain yourself fully.'

Zinina did so. Qmoet, however, remained unimpressed by the news. 'Eskhatos will think that Graaff-lin is more important, not Arrahaquen, since Graaff-lin has some kind of contact with the noophytes. Carry on reporting her progress to us.'

'Yeah, yeah, I will, but Qmoet, I saw it with my own *eyes*.'

'Well ... keep an eye on Arrahaquen, then, and collect as much data as you can. But I warn you, at this stage in our operation Eskhatos will reject talk of prophecies in favour of solid pyuter work.'

Dejectedly, Zinina agreed, and signed off. She returned to the house. DeKray had widened the existing path with a razor on a pole. He had doused the whole area with verticide and sodden planks lay across the treated land. Zinina made to enter the house, then noticed that the chimney had fallen off. To cap it all, the door was sticking, and she had to lift it and slam it shut.

'Is Graaff-lin working off batteries?' Zinina asked deKray.

'She is,' he replied. 'There has been a lack of power all day. By the way, I informed Graaff-lin that Arrahaquen had acquired prophetic skills, and she did not believe me. She is suffering from influenza yet again. I fear she is in a truculent mood. Perhaps it would be best if we left her alone.'

Zinina nodded. 'Tonight I's going to convince Arrahaquen to fetch her replica.'

DeKray seemed in thoughtful mood. 'I too must go somewhere tonight, I trust not for long.'

Zinina's eyes narrowed. 'Where?'

'I must obtain verticide to spray the outer walls of my abode.'

'Well, be careful.'

That evening, making the journey to the Carmine Quarter, Zinina realised that travelling would soon be too difficult to countenance. Wading through endless alleys, across no-go streets filled with mines and barbed wire, along passages squelching with fungi and rotting refuse; all this would become impossible. The question of where to live would soon demand an answer. The freedom of the city was no longer theirs.

A ripple of automatic fire burst out from some neighbouring street. She stood still: listened. Another gunshot, far off. How many people left in Kray now? Ten thousand? One thousand? Five thousand at most, Zinina guessed. She stood, taking in distant city sounds, wondering what these last few were doing.

Listening in silence, in a strange quarter, doom all around her, she understood how people could turn to religions, or cults, or believe against all hope that the Portreeve would come onto the Citadel networks and announce her great plan. Just listening to the mad city made all this clear to Zinina.

Breathing deep, Zinina hurried on. Arrahaquen received her, already guessing what they were to discuss.

'I have considered your idea,' she told Zinina, 'but I can't see how it could be done. Flying another balloon would be too dangerous for us, even if the priestess of Balloon Love could be persuaded to pilot it. Going underground has the same problems.'

'A gate?' Zinina asked, without much hope.

'We'd have to get the replica disguised coming out. It would be noticed by the Citadel Guard. You know that – you used to work for them.'

Zinina sighed. 'S'pose you're right. Rien Zir, but we need a pyuton. Without one, Graaff-lin's work might be for nothing.'

Arrahaquen sat upright. 'A pyuton,' she repeated.

'Yeah. Graaff-lin's got to have one.'

'A pyuton,' Arrahaquen said once more. 'That gives us one extra option. Maybe we need not enter the Citadel. The Wall.'

'No one's going to get over that Wall.'

Arrahaquen smiled, and Zinina saw a sudden light of triumph in her face. 'Maybe no human could get over,' she said, 'but who's to say a remotely piloted replica couldn't do it?'

Zinina considered this. She had no views to offer, but

she did not want to cramp Arrahaquen's ideas. 'Sure, maybe it could be done,' she said, as positively as she could.

'We'd need Graaff-lin's assistance,' Arrahaquen said. 'Our position in the network as we guided the replica would need to remain hidden, in case we were spotted by Citadel network patrols.' She stood and took a deep breath. 'We could do it, you know.'

As midnight approached they crept down the alley leading to Graaff-lin's house. Nearby, guns were blazing. Torrential rain concealed them.

DeKray had not yet returned, but Zinina's mind was on other things. She put forward their idea to Graaff-lin.

'This was your idea?' she asked, looking at Arrahaquen. This was not the response Zinina had expected.

'It was,' Arrahaquen confirmed.

'The Wall grabs anything that moves. I've seen people die there – we all have. And now you come to me asking for help to pilot a replica out?'

Zinina spoke in her most persuasive tones. 'It's for your sake, Graaff-lin. We need pyuton help. You know that. This is the only one we've got access to. Besides, just because the Wall grabs humans, that's no reason to assume that it'll grab pyutons as well.'

Graaff-lin closed her eyes and seemed to withdraw into herself. The pose worried Zinina. Graaff-lin had potential for good and ill. She could work pyuter miracles, or she could destroy. 'It's late,' she said, but her voice held no fight.

'So you'll do it,' Zinina said. 'Great. Let's go to the rig room, eh?'

It was easy to locate the system operating Arrahaquen's private rooms, but less easy to alert the pyuton replica, which sat, as it had for some weeks, by the window. When she saw it on a monitor, Arrahaquen said, 'I didn't think

it would be there. They probably didn't even bother to
check my things after I vanished.'

'Your mother must have.'

Mutely Arrahaquen shook her head.

Zinina returned her attention to the screens. Graaff-lin,
by some electronic sleight of hand, had convinced the
security system that she was its co-ordinator. 'Project my
voice to the pyuton replica,' she demanded.

'Null job,' came the reply. Zinina muttered a curse.

Graaff-lin was now immersed in the challenge, eyes
flickering, fingers twitching, mouth compressed. She
restructured the system so that it recognised no signals
from the Citadel, isolating it, but restricting her own
manoeuvrability. 'Project my voice to the pyuton replica,'
she said again.

'Ready.'

Zinina cheered. Graaff-lin turned and said, 'Quickly,
instruct the pyuton where to go. Any second now a
network patrol will spot me and crash into the system.'

'This is Arrahaquen. Walk down through the jannitta
sector to the Wall. Climb over. Then make north to the
Pyramid Bridge. I will meet you there—'

With a smack of her control pad, Graaff-lin had cut the
link. 'That was close,' she said.

'Can we see through the pyuton's eyes?' Arrahaquen
asked.

'What's the frequency?'

'Eleven eighty-one point eighty-one gigahertz.'

Graaff-lin tuned her main rig to the frequency. On a
wall screen static flickered, and then, with a judder, an
image appeared: dark and motion-blurred, the spectral
streets of the Citadel unfocused, overlaid with glittering
after-images. The replica was walking quickly, head
nodding a little. Then there was sound too, an eerie rustle
of clothes, the thunking of plastic heels on perspex, the

ticking of droplets against aluminium eardrums.

Soon the Wall appeared. Zinina found that she was gripping Arrahaquen's arm. The replica approached. Cannibalised limbs grasped . . . eyeballs on stalks rotated. Still the pyuton strode on. Then they saw darkness.

'It's fallen!' Zinina cried.

'There's the sea,' Graaff-lin said.

The pyuton had leaped to the top of the Wall then jumped down. Already it was striding up Violin Street. Zinina rushed into the hall, shouting, 'Come on, we've got to meet it!'

They arrived at the Pyramid Bridge seconds before the replica. Arrahaquen ordered it to follow them back, which it did without complaint.

For deKray, the attentions of a young, athletic, attractive woman from a culture that was to him an exotic unknown came as the most pleasant shock of his life, and despite his fervent atheism and scorn of all concepts of fate and destiny – the twin peaks of selfishness – he was hard put to think of Zinina's arrival in any more sensible way. The most plausible idea he could come up with was that a most amazing coincidence had occurred. In this final year, a young woman had found herself interested in him.

But it was not as simple as that. Relating discussions held after Arrahaquen's meal, Zinina had indicated the stresses she was under, making deKray feel he must make an effort to prove to the three women that he was a useful ally – an indispensable ally. Above all, he did not want to return to being an outsider.

That was why he now stood in evening gloom at a north-westerly Cemetery gate.

Rain poured from heavy cloud. DeKray pulled tight his waterproof hood and tied the drawstrings, checked the elastics on his boots, took a final sniff at a handkerchief impregnated with oylbas oil, then took from his greatcoat pocket a night-monocular. The Felis device had been tied around the neck of the cat which had killed his guardian, and rated as one of the most useful items in his possession. Through this gold-rimmed glass he studied the Cemetery. Nobody about.

He walked south along the wall, feeling its sinister boulders with a gloved hand. He wished the weather would allow him to light up a cigarette. Soon he would be desperate for one. Still, he could always suck a cough sweet.

At the line of yew trees he struck off to the left. Many graves here had been opened by revellers, and he was careful to avoid them. In some, fragments of rusting machinery lay, in others there were fungi twinkling like stars, or hairy roots from nearby trees. Noise was deadened by the sound of pattering rain, though he could hear pounding bazooka fire from somewhere to the east of the Gardens.

A sudden mental flash allowed him a glimpse of the bizarre figure he must cut – hunched over, glass held to one eye, Zinina's pistol in the other hand. A real sleuther.

He stopped for a cough sweet then returned to striding along the green glass and rust-fragment path, until he saw the grove near which the mausoleum ruins stood. This grove he made towards.

'I say.'

The voice made him jump. He raised the pistol, crouched down, and waved it around until he saw the woman who had spoken standing under a tree.

'Do not move,' he said.

'Well I shan't then. I say, your face is familiar.'

DeKray confronted an old woman, who, oddly enough, seemed familiar to him. She must be at least sixty, and that made him suspicious. This was probably a reveller grandmother. She was tall, dressed in formal black jacket and long skirt, the latter highly unusual Kray wear, with green plastic boots, a black top hat, and a walking stick made of silver. A fob watch hung upside down from one lapel.

DeKray was too suspicious to want to stay. He waved the pistol at her. 'This hand arm is primed,' he said. 'I know I am a man, but I am prepared to use it.'

'I can't harm you, you silly boy,' said the woman in her cracked, warbling voice. Was she drunk? 'I just wondered what in Kray you thought you were doing wandering around this place at this time. Don't you know the revellers can get you?'

'Revellers,' said deKray, moving away, towards the mausoleum. 'Revellers, you say. Maybe you are one yourself, my good woman? Now, if you please, I shall continue about my private business and bid you good morrow. I advise you not to follow me.'

'Oh, all right,' she said, tottering off to the path, 'but I must say, dear fellow, you've aged terrifically well.'

Shaken, deKray watched her go. She disappeared. Quickly, so she might lose him, he ran to the ruins of a mausoleum, then waited at a tree to see if she would follow. She did not.

The mausoleum had collapsed leaving a central clear space occupied only by rubble. But, inside, only human tombs lay. He wanted to find the grave of a pyuton.

After some hours searching he came across a marble octagon in poor repair. Something about the abstract designs on the marble made him look more closely.

All was chill and dark. Infra-red would not work here. He took a penlight from his kit, then a hook on a wire and an antidote kit, and knelt by the nearer of four sarcophagi.

He was looking for cracks. He knew one or two

reveller tricks. Find a crack, find a small stone and a boulder, place the small stone on the crack and hit. It worked.

Inside lay a body, but it was an odd body. It was some seconds before he saw flashing metal at the skull and realised that here reclined the remains of an autonomous pyuter.

The disintegrated remains of plastic skin and metal bones lay before him, around them various items of stone, wood and metal, including a plaque. This deKray fished out with his hook, along with a rib and a finger-bone.

The finger was titanium; so it was an old pyuton, maybe many centuries old. The plaque was filthy. With trembling fingers he scraped off the accumulated detritus, but etchings on the plaque were still invisible under a black layer of corrosion. With the hatpin from his lapel he scraped off enough to see eighteen sigils that seemed to mix the qualities of flowers with mathematical symbols. As he meditated on their graceful synthesis of abstract line and botanic realism, he was reminded of something Zinina had told him of her adventures in the Andromeda Quarter ... the eighteen statues. Eighteen statues and eighteen sigils.

Realisation dawned upon him. He put his pin on the sarcophagus edge and gripped the plaque as his mind fitted clues together. Eighteen statues; eighteen sigils. A connection here with pyutons. In Kray today there were twenty, or maybe twenty-one, noophytes. Could the noophytes possibly have emerged in the distant past from individual pyutons to submerge themselves in the electronic substrate of the city's networks? Was he tonight kneeling at the grave of an entity which had leaped from the physical seat of its own mind? The skull would hold further clues.

Frantically, deKray fumbled with his right hand to pull

out the skull. But it was light. DeKray had read much on the topic of pyutons and suspected that the brains of this one, if such it had been, had long since leaked away.

He was correct. Two fingers stuck into the metal sinuses, another poked up the spinal hole, he felt no soft package of biochemical hardware.

But his probing finger did feel a small ball affixed to the forehead. It must be the innerai. All pyutons possessed one.

With the nail of one finger he managed to pop the innerai out. It pinged as it hit the inner metal of the skull, then fell out of the spinal hole. DeKray caught it, but then dropped it, and it fell into a mud puddle. He retrieved the golden sphere, wiped it with a tissue from his kit, then shone the beam of his light upon it. There was written, in tiny letters, 'Laspetosyne'. So this was the tomb of a pyuton called Laspetosyne. That name had been mentioned before. It was the name of a noophyte. Perhaps, at this instant, there was a noophyte in the Citadel networks named Laspetosyne, with whom the Portreeve fine-honed the details of her plan. Or then again, as Zinina would invariably point out, maybe she did not.

DeKray felt that he had made a remarkable discovery. He would go home now and check details in his books, finding facts to confirm his theory before presenting it. Yet already he felt that he was right. The precious innerai he placed between the leaves of his pocket book, next to some old vegetable plot coupons, before locking it and replacing it inside his kit satchel. Time to check the three occupants of the main tomb.

These, he discovered, were priestesses; that was clear from the excess of iconography. But of which temple?

It was some time before he realised that these priestesses did not belong to any of Earth's six remaining religions. They were in fact so old that they had worshipped at the temple of the Green Spermatozoon, an ancient religion of which the only remains were members of the cult of the Phallists.

The Portreeve pinged her dolphin. 'Omaytra, it is time to finalise the details of the attack.'

Omaytra nodded. 'I've got three quarters of our entire force ready, Portreeve, and many more special units. The main attack will be from the ground, infantry with nail-guns, splinter bombs and lasers, but first there'll be a co-ordinated softening-up attack by a hang-glider division and a ground team. Once the main body is inside the temple it'll be ransacked. Once everybody is liquidated, the place will be torched, and we'll leave.'

'What about getting the guard up there in secret?' asked Pyetmian.

'We'll be going at night, and each unit will take a slightly different route, going in teams of twelve, ending up in Red Lane, and then hiding up in the unoccupied hovels around the temple. The signal for attack will be a white flare from the hang-glider team.'

'Good,' said the Portreeve. 'With the fat woman's mob out of the way, we only have a few days to wait before our little plan comes to fruition.' The Portreeve rang her dolphin. 'Which brings me to the last matter. Escape. Deese-lin and Spyne, would you give us the final details?'

'Yes, yes!' Deese-lin said, standing. 'At last you come to me! What I have to say is so important!'

'The details, please,' said the Portreeve.

Deese-lin began, 'The details are as follows ...'

18

The appearance of the replica produced a lightening of Graaff-lin's mood. Working from deKray's house she instructed the pyuton in the arts of her illegal plan, delighted that she would no longer have to rely on dangerous city work. The replica showed that she was both suggestible and intelligent by offering several solutions to problems that Graaff-lin had not yet surmounted.

Zinina and deKray watched all this with interest. 'At last,' Zinina said, 'we can try and talk with them noophytes and pinch the Portreeve's plan from right under her nose.'

DeKray popped a menthol sweet into his mouth and crunched. 'This is certainly one option,' he said, 'though somewhat optimistic. We still have to log a sizeable vocabulary of machine words, and we also have to find some method of attracting their attentions long enough for us to perceive this plan.'

'I reckon there must be a plan,' Zinina said.

'You do? Well that is a change. Not so long ago you were all for carousing and declaring that the end of humanity was nigh. But now...'

Zinina nodded. 'Things've changed. As well as Graaff-lin, we've got Arrahaquen, a real pythoness, and there's other folk that can help.'

'Such as whom?'

But here Zinina fell silent.

'Did somebody mention my name?' Arrahaquen said, coming out from the kitchen.

'I did,' said Zinina. 'I was just saying it's good we've got you.'

Arrahaquen grimaced. 'I keep telling you, I'm a novice. It's all a jumble, Zinina. I don't know what I'm doing. I'm confused. Is that clear enough for you?'

She seemed angry. DeKray said, in his cool, measured tones, 'I believe what Zinina meant was that the mere fact of your temporal ability makes our lives marginally less hopeless. We pin no precise hopes upon you, Arrahaquen, but we would desire you to find an escape. After all, there is only a slim chance of Graaff-lin and the replica having converse with the noophytes.'

As deKray said this, a loud crack made Zinina jump. They all listened. There were groans from the damp north end of the house, but nothing serious. DeKray lit a cigarette and inhaled deeply. 'This house has only days remaining to it. We should discuss our options.'

Arrahaquen agreed. 'I could probably find a room at the temple of the Goddess,' she said, 'but whether you three would be allowed inside I don't know. Though I do know that the hovels at the back can be used by anybody.'

Haughtily, Graaff-lin replied, 'I would not set foot in your temple, nor in these hovels, and neither would my replica. You must think again.'

Another crack, then the banging of slates falling. Somewhere a pipe had burst, for they heard trickling water.

'*Your* replica?' Zinina said.

The set of Graaff-lin's face reinforced her retort. 'You did acquire the pyuton for me, did you not?'

Another crack echoed through the house.

'I don't like this,' Arrahaquen said, nervously eyeing the mouldy ceilings. 'This is worse than it's ever been.'

Another crack. 'Shall we pack a few things?' Zinina suggested.

A thud from upstairs, 'Yes,' replied deKray.

Five minutes later they realised it was too late. A series of detonations at the damp end, a few trickles of masonry dust, and then the entire north end of the house fell to the ground, leaving only two rooms undamaged. They all ran out. As the dust settled and the rain soaked their clothes they realised that their last glimpse of security was near.

Risking burial, Zinina and deKray pulled out Graaff-lin's portable rigs – those few that had not been damaged – then packed them into plastic bags and placed them in two wheelbarrows. With especial malevolence, the rain intensified, pouring from black clouds.

'I shall not go to your temple,' Graaff-lin shouted as Arrahaquen tried to move the rigs and the other oddments that they had salvaged.

'Apart from your place, you haven't got anywhere else to go, you stupid woman!' Zinina replied, trying to shove Graaff-lin away from one wheelbarrow.

DeKray took her by the arm, but she shrugged off his grip.

'I shall return to my house,' Graaff-lin declared. 'The Citadel agents are too wrapped up in their own lives to bother about me now. All this equipment is mine and mine alone. The replica is mine to command. Replica, take that wheelbarrow and follow me! As for you, Zinina, and you two, you may visit me when you like. I shall continue to try for contact with the conscoosities.'

Zinina stood, stunned by the rain and by the power of

this speech; and the look of suppressed fury in Graaff-lin's face. The aamlon and the pyuton raised their wheel-barrows and walked away.

DeKray pulled a protective cloak from the salvaged gear. 'I had better accompany them. There are revellers about, and rioting Krayans.'

'Well *I'm* not coming,' Zinina said, angry that he should support Graaff-lin. 'I'm staying with Arrahaquen.'

'I'm going straight to the temple,' Arrahaquen said. 'We've got to get new protective clothes. I'll vouch for you, Zinina, but you may not be allowed in.'

Zinina felt abandoned, especially by deKray. 'You'd help her rather than me?' she asked him.

'Graaff-lin's immediate need is more urgent than yours. If all goes well I shall return within the hour.'

He ran off. Zinina turned to Arrahaquen. 'You better not go off now,' she warned. 'We've got to save everything we can.'

Zinina knew that soon it would be time for her decisive move ... a move that she had no choice but to make. She pulled cannisters of water and food cartons from the remains of the kitchen, then went down on her belly to pull boxes of kit-replacements – and deKray's greatcoat – from the utility room. A wooden stay snapped, but none of the falling rubble hit her.

Only minutes seemed to have passed before deKray returned, gasping for breath, but safe, and reporting Graaff-lin's safety.

'Let's go to the temple with this lot,' Arrahaquen said. 'Revellers will be here soon. I can sense them.'

'Wait,' Zinina said. They stood chilled on the pavement outside the ruin. Rain pelted them. Cold, cold rain that stank of rotting fish. Zinina spat it out of her mouth in between sentences. 'Wait, wait a tick, there's another possibility.'

'And would this other possibility involve the mysterious Qmoet and the organisation she works for?' deKray said nonchalantly.

'Yes,' Zinina snapped, irritated by his smug attitude. 'It does happen to involve them. Don't be so fucking clever. Qmoet and I, hoy, we've worked for Eskhatos and this organisation for ages. Well, you might as well know. It's the Holists.'

Arrahaquen laughed. 'The Holists? But—'

'But what? I work for them. Don't tell me your precious intuition didn't hint to you about that?'

'Let us not become angered,' deKray said. 'This rain and the terrible collapse of my house has touched our nerves—'

'Oh shut up,' Zinina said. 'This woman doesn't believe me.'

'I *do*,' Arrahaquen replied. 'I'm just surprised.'

Zinina wondered. Now she had said it, she felt deflated, as if she had played her last card in some momentous game.

'I believe you,' deKray said, coming to her and putting his arms around her. 'My word, is that my precious greatcoat?'

'Yeah. Listen,' Zinina told them, 'down in the Citadel Quarter are their headquarters, a very big place called Clodhoddle Cottage. We could live there. I could prime Eskhatos. So we don't need to go to your temple.'

'I'm going,' Arrahaquen said. 'I have no other choice.'

'And we belong at my maisonette,' deKray told Zinina. 'It is far from trouble and away from the Citadel. The tumulus is a source of danger at the moment, for there are hundreds of people yelling and demonstrating outside.'

'We're not living at your house,' Zinina insisted. She pulled away from him. As they stood in the street, revellers crept out of alleys ... six of them ... eyeing the house.

'I'm going,' said Arrahaquen, hurrying away. 'Come to the temple, quick. Come on!'

She was out of sight. Zinina, fuming, glared at deKray. 'You *are* coming to my place,' she said in desperation.

DeKray neared, standing at her side. The revellers, now eight in number, leered at them, drool running down their chins, skeletal hands twitching, all of them naked and covered with sores. Zinina drew her needle gun and pointed it at them. 'Fizzle off, spigot-heads, or I'll jab the merry lot of ya! I will!'

'Hoy, calm it, shouster,' the lead reveller replied. 'We only wants the brick pile and the nicey metal lashings inside.'

'Run,' deKray advised. 'Come along, our time here is at an end. We are at the mercy of the city.'

'No we're not,' Zinina said. 'I'll spike 'em all.' She raised her rifle and aimed it at the leader.

'No decent bloom jabs a fellow bedder,' said the reveller, a cocky smile on her face. 'Jab away, shouster.'

So they knew she was from a Cemetery tribe. Zinina tensed her arm, but deKray knocked her. 'We will gain nothing from fighting. We should leave.'

He ran off. Zinina spat once, turned, then followed him, the jeers and whoops of defeat in her ears. She could have killed them all, but she had not; and she had not because, when all was said and done, she believed that humanity had a future, even though it had reached its final year. She was not a reveller. She was a true independent.

She caught deKray up at the end of Sphagnum Mews. 'Where you going?' she asked. She clutched at his hand, her anger gone, washed away by the interminable power of the rain. She felt small, tired and empty.

'To check on Arrahaquen's well-being. Then I shall return to my maisonette.'

'I suppose I've got to come.'

'I would. Mayhap in a few weeks we will need to reconsider.'

They walked back alleys down to Lac Street, then made for the temple, stopping at the kiosk that stood outside the fern barrier. 'Has Arrahaquen been this way?' Zinina asked.

The priestess, staring at deKray, replied, 'Um, yes. She said you might arrive. I'm to tell you to wait here.'

They sheltered in a doorway. The rain had slackened to a drizzle. Far away, just above the rooftops, Zinina saw the tell-tale ragged edge of a storm cloud.

Ten minutes passed. The rains ceased. A few sunbeams illuminated floods and puddles. The sound of grenades and cannon began, Zinina guessed from the Infirmary area.

Arrahaquen returned. 'I'm glad you came,' she said. 'Something very strange has happened. They were frightened when they saw me, really frightened. Tashyndy and Maharyny came to look me over ...' She paused. 'Anyway, there's nobody allowed inside the temple except me, I'm afraid. But I can show you a protected hovel, if you like.'

DeKray looked at Zinina. 'Her place or mine?' he asked.

Grumpily, kicking a rat corpse, Zinina replied, 'Yours, I suppose. But not for long.' She turned to Arrahaquen. 'Can you set up a pyuter link between your room and deKray's place?'

'Yes.'

'Good. We got lots to do. Better get one laid up to Graaff-lin's house, too, else we'll lose contact with the old goat.'

Arrahaquen gave to deKray the code address that she would use, then they left her. They decided to follow the west wall of the city down to the Harbour Quarter, then strike out into Gur-Lossom Street. By noon they had arrived.

Immediately, deKray powered up his own array of pyuters, connected them to the interface in the rig-room floor, then tuned in to the official bands. The Citadel was still broadcasting on defender frequencies. 'So,' he said, 'the crowds have doubled in size.' Zinina looked at the flickering screen. Cameras in the Citadel Wall relayed crowd scenes. All four gates were now surrounded by hundreds of people. Black-suited Citadel Guard armed with lazer bazookas and stun-guns stood, crouched and lay in defence, but, to Zinina's surprise, their numbers were fewer than she had expected.

'Look,' she said, pointing to a written item on a different screen. 'The Food Stations have been closed.'

DeKray looked. 'And the Water Stations will now open only in the mornings.'

'And the Temple of Pure Justice has burned to the ground.'

Even as they spoke they saw on the defender bands that both Food Stations were under attack. But no orders for defence were sent. The Citadel remained quiet.

'What are they doing up there?' Zinina said. 'Surely they must tell us what's going on?'

'I do not know,' said deKray, rolling a cigarette with trembling fingers. He paused and glanced at her. 'I have something of a confession to make.'

Zinina nodded.

'Last night I was in the Cemetery, where I made a discovery. In a deep tomb lies the body of a pyuton named Laspetosyne. I believe there to be a connection between pyutons and noophytes. The iconography of a plaque inside the sarcophagus reminded me of your description of the flower-faced statues. All is linked, all is linked. Silverseed it was who made the Spaceflower. We are so familiar with that botanic satellite that we forget it is in the image of a flower.' He paused his declamation. 'I still have the innerai of Laspetosyne in my pocket book.'

'You shouldn't have gone there alone. It's dangerous.'

He seemed not to have heard her. 'These innerais have mystical powers,' he murmured.

'But I thought you didn't believe in all that mystery stuff?'

'I meant in the sense of powerful and unknown. Zinina, I suspect that long ago the noophytes were pyutons. We must interrogate the replica on these topics. Why, for instance, are all pyutons female?'

'There aren't hardly any men to copy,' Zinina said.

'That is not reason enough. Maybe I did not garner all I could from Laspetosyne's tomb. We must question the replica.'

'Let's do it now.'

DeKray laughed. 'Can you imagine it? We intend to ask a pyuton but a few months old about her species' love-life.'

'Let's go now. I hate standing around doing nothing.'

After setting up the pyuters for Arrahaquen's link, they dressed in protective coats, hoods and thigh boots, then departed the maisonette. The lower sections of Gur-Lossom Street were quiet, but soon they saw people running, and heard shouts and gunfire. Spent cartridges littered the streets, and they saw dozens of corpses, many fresh (these Zinina tried not to look at) amongst the greened carrion and the tussocks of whip-grass poking through the cobbles. Wading through side alleys, they crossed Ficus Street then made for the Pyramid Bridge. To the north they heard more battles, and often, as they scanned the alleys and passages, they would see brief glimpses of people running. Some of the floods they waded through had bodies floating in them.

They crossed the Pyramid Bridge then made north, until Graaff-lin's house came into view. It stood like an island surrounded by water. Around the back they found footprints, and guessing that these must have been made by Graaff-lin they located a safe route through the flood.

Graaff-lin seemed unhappy. She had a nosebleed. Stained tissues overflowed from the wastebins, a sight that made Zinina's stomach turn. The replica sat in front of a rig, examining data.

'Are you surviving here?' deKray asked. He looked around her house, moving a flex there, checking food and water stores, examining her rig batteries. 'You seem run down,' he added.

Zinina, feeling a little sorry for Graaff-lin, said, 'I'll boil some water and we can have tea. DeKray, clear up the floor a bit, would you?'

'Tea, yes, thank you,' Graaff-lin said, nodding.

DeKray made to clear some of the tissues.

But Graaff-lin shouted, 'No!'

Zinina jumped and turned. Graaff-lin had frozen, pointing at him. DeKray just stared. 'No,' she repeated in a solemn voice.

Realisation came to Zinina. 'You've got the pestilence, haven't you?'

Graaff-lin had turned pale. Her gaze darted between Zinina and deKray. At last she said, 'Yes. Soon my condition will deteriorate – in maybe a year or so. I'm suffering from many infections. Some day one will be too much.'

There was nothing else to say. Horrified, and not a little sickened by the thought of the diseased Graaff-lin, Zinina went into the kitchen and brewed up a pot of rosemary tea.

DeKray mentioned nothing of Graaff-lin's condition. He launched into their questions. 'We have some enquiries to make,' he told the replica.

'I will answer if I can,' said the pyuton, looking up from her work.

'Do you know where Gwmru is?'

'No.'

'*Gwmru*,' Zinina insisted. 'The country of the noo-phytes? You've been told the word by Graaff-lin.'

'I don't know where it is.'

Zinina looked at deKray. Already his expression of determination was fading to blank hopelessness.

He said, 'Have you ever spoken with one of these noophytes?'

'No.'

'Do you know what a noophyte is?'

'A noophyte is a pyuter heart, a being of the electronic networks. I have heard of them.'

'I have asked similar questions,' said Graaff-lin, in almost an apologetic tone of voice, 'but without enlightenment.'

Zinina sat back while deKray paused for thought. She said to the replica, 'Have you ever done it with a male pyuton?'

'No.'

'Never?'

'I am virginal.'

Zinina sighed. 'We may as well forget this, deKray.'

He agreed. But then he said, 'Have you ever seen a male pyuton?'

'Yes,' replied the replica.

'But where are they?'

'Everywhere. You can see them in the streets.'

Zinina walked over to deKray, whispered in his ear, then returned to her seat.

'Is there a good reason for all this?' Graaff-lin asked.

'We'll leave you two,' Zinina said, standing. 'We've got to see Arrahaquen at the temple. But we'll come back.'

'We will come often,' deKray agreed, 'to see that you are surviving, and to hear of your progress. Here is the secret code that Arrahaquen will use to set up a communication line.'

With that they departed, and returned to the Pyramid Bridge, where they crossed the river and struck off north, crossing Onion Street then making for the complex of alleys and passages that constituted the Mercantile Quarter. The sun made everything unreal. Glittering water left after-images upon their vision, and a stinking steam arose from every puddle. Flies and mosquitoes flew everywhere, and only kit insect repellant sprayed over their exposed skin saved them from being bitten, and possibly infected. In every flood, great leeches bloated with blood swam like underwater dirigibles. Pulsating yellow insect eggs lined walls at flood-height.

They found themselves walking up the now entirely green length of Red Lane. Saplings and bushes had taken the place of pavements. They forged a way through knotted undergrowth. Only three houses remained standing along this twisting road, and one clearly displayed a green triangle. This house they avoided. At last they were in Lac Street, also a length of grass except for a mudtrack along its centre. At the entrance to the temple they asked for Arrahaquen.

Arrahaquen had not managed to persuade the temple clerks that her friends were safe. She tried to reassure them. 'We're separate now, but I see us together again.'

'When?' Zinina wanted to know.

'Soon. Maybe the temple will allow you to live here – not you, deKray, of course. It's all unclear. I think there

will be great upheavals here, soon. I can sense some sort
of chaos.'

'There are a thousand people demonstrating around
the Citadel,' deKray said. 'Soon, the Portreeve will have to
do something. What have you seen?'

Arrahaquen shook her head, then looked down at her
feet. 'All I can see is a black hulk. I don't know what's
going to happen.'

'A black hulk?' Zinina asked.

'Maybe that is a memory from decades in the future, or
even centuries,' Arrahaquen said. 'How can I tell? I have
no inner maps to guide me, Zinina. There is no little
number saying ten years hence, or one year five months,
or anything.'

Zinina understood. While deKray spoke of their talk
with the replica, she wondered what to do next.

They left Arrahaquen at the temple and began the walk
back. Flashes to the south-east signified both the red flares
of physical weapons and the momentary lines of lasers.
Distant rumblings signalled continuing battles. Overhead,
the Spaceflower shone and the stars wheeled.

By midnight they were safe in the maisonette. DeKray
fell asleep as soon as they climbed into bed, but Zinina lay
back, her hands behind her head, thinking. She had to get
deKray and herself down to Clodhoddle Cottage. It was
essential. There was only one way to do that.

Next morning, the defender bands were all dead.
Worried, deKray suggested that they risk going to the
Citadel to see what was happening. Zinina agreed;
without the information services of the city networks she
felt alone, as if she was floating about on a great pond
with no hope of rescue.

As he collected packets of menthol sweets and
restocked his kit, she located the various electronic cards
that operated window and door locks, and secreted them

in her kit. Leaving the house, she said, 'I'll lock it.' He handed her a black card.

They followed alleys to the river, then crossed by the Sud Bridge. The Citadel loomed above them as, checking for revellers and rioters around every corner, they followed Deciduo Street up to the west gate.

When deKray was not looking, Zinina dropped every card into an open drain.

The west gate was invisible behind a mass of people, well over a thousand strong. On the sparkling streets of the Citadel, just behind the gate, Zinina could see the dark shadows of hastily erected sentry posts and laser cannon tripods.

'They're not going to let us near, are they?' she said.

That evening deKray realised that he had lost his copper hatpin. He sat in shock. Since he could remember it had been a personal talisman, given to him by his guardian, who had in turn received it from a mysterious young woman who called at their house one day. He had to retrieve it.

And he did know where it was. Beside Laspetosyne's sarcophagus he had used it to scrape corrosion off the plaque. It must lie there still. He had no option but to return to the Cemetery at once.

Laspetosyne's tomb was as he had left it. The pin was there, and he felt a wave of relief pass through him as he pinned it to his greatcoat lapel.

Some eerie moments he spent crouched beside the tomb, allowing himself to take in the aura of the place, before he switched on his penlight and examined the body. Yesterday, foolishly, he had only considered the head.

Laspetosyne had been interred in canvas, now rotted to crumbs. Her bones were intact, shredded wisps of plastic stuck to them like souvenirs of the past, but much else was gone, eroded by the moist atmosphere. However, where her pelvis lay deKray noticed a metal flower.

It was the same species as the Spaceflower: a lily. The lily clearly had some significance for the pyutons – and probably for the noophytes – but he could not imagine what it might be. The clue he sought had turned out to be obscure. As deKray pondered this the words of a quatrain ran through his head.

> Lily, lily, on the water
> Ripples pass, you shake your head.
> Lily, lily, on the water
> You are far and I am dead.

He departed along the route marked by the yew-tree line. However, he had hardly begun walking the crunching path when his eye was distracted by a sparkling display of light inside an empty grave. Fungus, he thought – just Cemetery fungus. But this light was coppery, not white or pink, and it seemed bright. He stopped to investigate.

It had ceased raining. Without deKray noticing, the clouds had swept across half the sky, leaving just twinkling stars in an indigo and violet sky, and the light was weird. It was quiet. No guns; no explosions. Suddenly afraid, deKray scanned every tree and bush around him with the monocular, but he saw nobody. It must just be the unaccustomed lack of pattering rain. And dawn birds singing. Once more, afraid now that somebody was watching him, he studied every nook for sign of revellers.

There was nothing. He bent down to investigate the lights. With one gloved hand inside the grave he pushed aside the real fungus and the odd bits of metal and stone until his fingertips felt a smooth surface. It was an ovoid of some sort. He pulled it out.

He held a weighty lump of metal. He could not see it well. He tried to make out the name of the grave's erstwhile occupant, but the light was too poor, so he traced with one finger the letters at the top of the grave: M,Y,S,H,F,L,A,V. He could only think of Myshelau, Kray's premier surgeon. But she was still alive.

Rain once more fell. He looked up. Clouds again covered the sky. Kray was back to normal. He stood. The eerie atmosphere of the Cemetery must have got to him. He was shaking, afraid, certain that some awful thing was about to happen. Such a strong premonition was unusual for him, so he ran, the oval object thrust in his pocket. He ran without thinking. He just had to run.

At the wall he calmed. A gate stood near. He hurried through it. Far off, mortars were again pounding.

The night seemed to extend as he made his way south. He wondered how he could have heard the singing birds of dawn.

Safe in his maisonette he examined his prize. It was as large as his fist, filthy with mud and smeared fungus, and not now twinkling with light – although he could see a translucent screen on one side from where the light must have come. It was made of copper. Not unlike a pear in shape, its more rounded end was distinguished by two small protruberances, as though a pair of fingers inside were pressing out.

He had no idea what it was.

He washed the object then placed it inside a pillowcase. On impulse he put it in his bed. That night, against the ghostly reflections of the luminous sea flickering across his window panes, he saw through the cloth a thousand mysterious twinkles of light, as whatever lay inside had come once more to life.

19

At the temple of the Goddess all was calm. Through disintegrating networks Arrahaquen spoke with Zinina about the riots, but after only two minutes the link died, and the temple system diagnosed a complete Westcity failure. The healthy state of the house system left Arrahaquen suspecting that the temple possessed not only its own water and food supplies, but also its own power. Around midnight, she fell asleep.

Noise woke her. She thought she was dreaming. But then she remembered that since her escape from Gugul Street all dreams had ceased, not even the evanescent memory of a dream crossing her mind.

In seconds she was fully awake and listening. Thumps from high above. And the sound of guns. Very close.

The chaos that she had so vaguely sensed was now central in her thoughts, a great fear that made her grind her teeth and leap out of bed. She ran to the door.

Now she heard continuous gunfire and explosions over her head. An attack.

With frantic haste Arrahaquen pulled on a vest, a jumpsuit and a pair of low boots. There were no weapons to hand. But, with sinking heart, as she heard the sounds of bombs and other heavy weaponry, she realised that nothing easily available would match such an arsenal. Besides, the temple prided itself on containing not one item designed deliberately as a weapon.

Arrahaquen ran from her room. The corridors were shadowy, lit irregularly by sea-fat candles in glass cylinders, blue photoplankton tubes, and an occasional anjiq. From everywhere there came the thumping sound of heavy footsteps and shouting, hoarse and incomprehensible.

She saw nobody. In an adjacent corridor she heard a rumble of boots and voices. Within this maze of half-lit passages she knew she could meet her death.

A crack behind her of splintering wood. She sped forward, through hot cordite air. Choking, she stumbled on.

Up ahead there was a junction: left or right? To the left she saw white flickering lights. Then an explosion, a red light, and a wave of dust. She smelled burning chemicals.

She turned back, but knew that people were coming that way too. She ran to her right. But soon she heard other voices.

She stopped. She was trapped – attackers behind her and ahead.

A flash of knowledge came to her. As a blinding white light and a loud explosion made her recoil, she reached to the wood on her left and felt a handle. She pulled it and jumped into the alcove behind, slamming the door shut.

Seconds later the clatter of automatic fire was directly outside. She heard screams, more shouts, and more fire. Grenades exploded nearby. The wood around her shook.

She could not tell how much time passed. She buried her head under her arms and let the damp soil of the alcove – it must be a seed nursery – hold her.

Bullets thudded into the wood all around. Above her she thought she heard more boots, but with the din outside it was impossible to tell.

Then all became quiet.

She dared not leave, but she knew she had to.

She crawled to the door and listened. There were only groans outside; no voices, no gunfire. Tentatively, she pushed the door open a few inches. No response. But she could smell blood as well as the pungent odour of gunpowder and burnt wood.

She poked her head out. A mass of bodies lay all around, fifteen at least, some twitching. Every one wore a ruddy Citadel uniform. There were no acolyte or priestess corpses. The stench of blood made her retch.

Up ahead a twinkling image caught her eye. She ducked: it was a laser-wielding priestess. She fell to the floor and played dead.

But the priestess made no advance, and Arrahaquen, peering over the reeking bodies, saw that the motions she was making were cycling.

A hologram? It must be a hologram. As she moved her head from side to side in an effort to make it out she became convinced that nobody stood ahead.

She approached the figure. It looked real, but it was silent. In her mind's eye Arrahaquen saw hundreds of these illusions, each individual, each waiting to fool the attackers. And then the image winked out of existence.

Picking her way through the carnage she ran on, but she soon realised that she had gone the wrong way. She took a left turn at a three-way junction, thinking it led to the outer lobby, but misled herself. She was not where she thought she was. She was lost.

Nearby – and from above – a new gunbattle started. Further off there were thuds, and the reverberating sounds of explosions.

More attackers approaching. Arrahaquen ran back, and then, when she heard attackers ahead, she darted into a room to her left where she hid behind a table and some chairs. Stun grenades made her ears pop; machine guns roared. The battle lasted only a minute, maybe two. Again she waited, again she crept from her hideaway to find bodies in blood-spattered red uniforms. Those who were not yet dead wailed at her. She began to see what sort of defence Taziqi had arranged. It was sickening.

In the corridor she decided to run right, dashing along a low-roofed passage, slowing when she heard boots above going the opposite way, then hastening again. Sudden rounds of automatic fire – they seemed to come from directly behind the wood of the passage – made her flinch, but she ran on. At a crossroads, becoming desperate as her sense of intuition seemed harder and harder to grasp, she decided to go left, but she heard boots ahead, and then sudden shouts and a terrific burst of gunfire. On hot waves of dust she smelled burning ammunition.

She crawled into another seed-bed, just in time once more. Boots clattered by. Voices yelled. Then there was more gunfire, and then silence.

Some minutes later she peered out. More uniformed corpses. She ran on down the corridor. Glass fragments from smashed candle-lanterns crunched under her boots. There were blood smears everywhere, interspersed with smoking cartridges, powder burns, and metal shrapnel. A mist of ammunition fumes began to make her choke.

A body at her feet. Somebody running ahead. She grabbed the corpse's rifle and tried to find a hiding place. There was nowhere to go.

A woman darted out, dark in the gloomy blue light, rifle held high. Arrahaquen froze. The woman aimed, but then, with a grimace, flung herself into the corridor wall. The briefest image of an illusion behind her came to Arrahaquen's mind, and in those moments she raised her rifle and fired. The Citadel woman jerked, screamed; fell and twitched. Arrahaquen dropped her rifle and, without looking at what she had done, ran on.

Throat sore, lungs sore, she rested, then continued.

She came to a three-way junction that had been opened out into a chamber, set with couches, pitchers of water and incense sticks. Two bodies lay surrounded by blood at the further exit. Everything here was destroyed by bullet and laser beam but a general dampness seemed to be smothering the smoking debris.

'It will catch fire soon,' she told herself.

Disconcerted by the sight, she stopped – despite the din all around – and thought. The whole place seemed wetter than it should be. Another defence?

And still no sign of priestess bodies.

An explosion nearby. Wood to her left bowed, splintered, but did not shatter.

Somebody coming. Nowhere to go. Arrahaquen tried to hide beneath couch fragments, but too late.

It was Tashyndy. She leaped over the corpses like a ballet dancer. She wore a green gown, plimsolls, and had tied her blonde locks with a black ribbon.

'Come here,' she said. She seemed calm. 'Very soon the final battle will take place. I want you to leave this temple as soon as possible. I'm glad we met. I suppose the Goddess willed it, though we didn't foresee it.'

'But which way?' Arrahaquen pleaded.

'Follow that corridor,' she replied, pointing to the corpses, 'then take the first left. Carry on to the very end of the passage, where you will recognise the outer apple chamber. Run off if you can.'

'Right,' Arrahaquen said. She moved, but Tashyndy clutched at her arm. She breathed as if to speak, then hesitated.

'Arrahaquen, um . . .'

'Yes? What?'

Tashyndy was fighting with some inner impulse. Suddenly frightened, Arrahaquen blurted out, 'Speak up. Come on!'

'The Citadel,' Tashyndy said. 'I really think you ought to go there.'

'Why?'

Tashyndy ran off, and even in flight her inner lassitude showed through. As more bursts of gunfire sounded, the scream of a laser too, Arrahaquen turned and ran.

Seeing only corpses on the way, she reached the apple chamber and grabbed a handful of protective clothing, which she pulled on, almost tearing them in her haste. Adjacent lay a lobby, with a door leading out to the temple mews. She walked in.

A silhouette at the door. Arrahaquen stopped.

Something low and hunch-backed, something stocky and armed with a steaming rifle stood with its back to her. A guard. It had not heard her over the din. Arrahaquen crept back.

Examining it, crouched down and peering around the lobby door, she wondered what in Kray it could be.

The form was unfamiliar. It looked like a cross between a woman and a lizard – a grunting, hidebound thing, bandy legged, all muscle and boiled leather armour. Arrahaquen recalled the rumours she had heard of pyutonic assassins developèd in the sunken, perspex dungeons of the Citadel abyss.

The creature snorted, primed its rifle and took a potshot at somebody in the alley outside. Its laugh was a coughing splutter. It took a swig from a bottle and, seconds later, Arrahaquen caught the aroma of fresh blood. Disgusted, she sat back. What to do now?

Her pythonesque ability rescued her, as it had under Gugul Street. Without looking she reached up to a shelf behind the door, where she grasped a metal object. She looked at it. It was a pumpkin whistle.

Little remained now of the Carmine Quarter. The ambulatory pumpkins that had entered the city like victorious generals had doubtless moved south from their thickets and copses in the hilly Archaic and Green Quarters. Some could be lurking hereabouts. In earlier decades, whistles had been used to round up the pumpkin menace before destroying them in conflagrations of paraffin grease. Now one could save Arrahaquen.

She blew. Its ultrasonic pitch was to her inaudible, but the beast at the door jerked to attention and stared out into the night, rifle ready, wheezing to itself.

As if it had heard rustling pumpkins, it waddled outside, staring to its left along the temple mews. Arrahaquen crept forward, then slipped through the door into the shadows of the alley. She paused to glance back, then ran on.

At the end of the alley she turned to check her escape. Smoke drifted from the upper floors of the temple, but no flames. The whole edifice of the temple seemed complete, except for damage on the roof and uppermost level. Windows were momentarily lit by flashes of white and red.

Arrahaquen had to get to the Citadel. She knew that Tashyndy had advised her to do so for a good reason.

Through shrubs and thick clumps of gorse – Feverfew Street as it now was – she battled south, wading through floods in the Mercantile Quarter, then taking crooked alleys to the Pyramid Bridge, where she crossed over into Eastcity.

Further south, she stopped and stared. Fire on the tumulus.

Could there be battles within the Citadel itself?

Tiring, she made along Onion Street, down Min Street, then took Violin Street down to the Citadel.

An extraordinary sight awaited. Before the north gate there were no crowds. But there was no Citadel Guard either.

The lower sections of the Citadel were aflame. Gunfire rang out and grenades exploded. Red fire leaped into the sky alongside the white and yellow sparks of destroyed power transformers and pyuter installations. The illuminated streets sparkled with especial fervour.

As she stared, people ran through the gate – ordinary Krayans by the look of them, but armed with rifles. Arrahaquen could not be sure, but it seemed as if the defence had collapsed and the crowds had simply stormed in. And now her sense of the future was beginning to intuit terrible events. She felt a dread of the tumulus, but knew also that she had to explore it. The mental chaos that she had tried to explore was far bigger than she realised. This night was not over yet.

For a moment Arrahaquen sensed a dark aura about her future, before her teeming thoughts were dislocated by the rat-tat-tat of gunfire on the tumulus.

The main streets would be where common folk would congregate with their arms and their grenades, no doubt fighting each other and the remnants of the Citadel Guard. Arrahaquen slipped through the north gate – unlit, even its pyuter screens showing random static – then climbed uphill by way of alleys only just wider than her body; then service channels, drone chutes, and some ordinary passages. Soon she was halfway up.

At a warehouse she decided to climb to the roof and survey the upper zones. She ascended a fire escape.

Every visible part of the Citadel below was plunged into chaos. Motes of light flew into the air, fires burned, the flashing red lines of laser weapons struck out and smoke columns rose into the sky. Gunfire was continuous. There were shouts and screams, amplified and reverberated in the night air. Every now and again a bullet would ricochet nearby.

She descended, wanting to make for the Portreeve's palace, which lay on the summit.

But as she crept along the alley the ground shook, and then a thunder louder than anything she had ever heard began.

Earthquake, she thought, falling to the ground.

The thunder roared on. The whole tumulus shook. Above her every pane of glass shattered, then dropped like crystal rain to the streets below. She rolled out of the way only just in time.

Arrahaquen saw bright light. 'Goddess!' she shouted, hardly able to hear her own voice.

On a column of flame and smoke something was rising from the summit. A rocket.

A rocket. The Red Brigade had been building a rocket.

Smoke and fumes billowed past her, making her choke, but still she stared. The rocket was slowing. Twisting.

An explosion rent it. Light brighter than day flooded the city in its entirety. Arrahaquen shut her eyes automatically, but managed to force them open when she held a hand in front of them.

The rocket was almost horizontal now, flying across the Citadel towards the sea, still spitting fountains of sparks and sending smoke everywhere.

But who could be inside it?

It could never hold the whole city.

Another detonation. The rocket fell from the sky, tail up, then crashed into the sea with a final roll of thunder and a plume of water hundreds of feet high, a great luminous fountain that seemed to spit sparks and let loose a thousand cartwheeling fragments. Staring at this demonic vision, Arrahaquen felt an almost unbearable awe as she realised that very likely the final hope of

humanity, or a tiny portion of it at least, had just been
destroyed without hope of salvage. The Citadel, which
had ruled Earth's final city for so long, was now just a
burnt wreck fit only for thugs, looters and wretches.

With the rocket underwater, the noise began to sub-
side. A wash of sound from the sea, the last rumbles of the
rocket and huge waves crashing against the cliffs roared
up to her. All around, gunfire began again.

There was a pyuter hall upon the summit. Inside she
might find answers.

She shadowed Om Street, not daring to tread its
brightly coloured way, arriving at a square. The gutters
ran red, and the smell of blood made her choke.

She saw the tall building set apart from the houses and
towers around. People were running through the square –
one fired a gun, though it seemed at random – and so she
crept around the outside of the square, arriving at its rear
entrance, the glass of which had been smashed.

She entered. It was quiet. No lamps were lit or anjiqs
activated, though a few tubes remained to radiate blue.
Arrahaquen guessed that the place was deserted.

She began to explore rooms. Almost every pyuter bank
and screen she found was both on and active. It was as if
their operators had simply run off in terror. Arrahaquen
knew that they must have been left to their fate by the
fleeing Red Brigade.

There never had been a plan for Kray. If there had been
any plan at all, it had been for the Portreeve and her eight
cronies.

Still shaken by the profundity of the events she had
witnessed, Arrahaquen wandered around. This, she felt,
was the end of history. The coda had just begun. She wept,
finding a pyuter chamber and locking herself in. The smell
of loam and leaves calmed her.

With the wave of sobbing subsided, she decided to act.

She sat at the largest screen, a circular device with a velvety surface, and activated the pyuter speech systems.

'I'm going to open up this system if it takes all night,' she told herself. 'I must get to the noophytes. I must, I must.'

'Speak more clearly,' the pyuter requested.

Arrahaquen set to work. Using the ball-and-joint hand control she tried to immerse herself deep enough into the digital strata to access either the noophytes or Gwmru, speaking to the pyuter in synchrony to explain what she wanted. But the network patrols defied her, countering her routines with routines of their own that worked like scar tissue over pin-pricks. It was as if Gwmru lay below all these layers of information, like the motherlode in an ancient mountain. Bitterly, she recalled the two *ficus* devices left far below the surface of the tumulus.

Failure made her seek lesser goals. She noticed a records zone winking like a golden lamp in the bottom arc of the screen, and accessed it, noticing immediately that she had the possibility of unearthing the Portreeve's own speech. By writing a chameleon routine she was able to hear actual conversations held in the Nonagon, and read synopses of other talks, including the tactics for an attack on the temple of the Goddess.

The plan had been for the Red Brigade to escape to the Spaceflower in a rocket, a choice of home mentioned by the noophytes to Deese-lin and Spyne, who had inter-preted the idea as an actual prophecy. But Arrahaquen could find no definite strategy, and she began to wonder if the Red Brigade themselves had been fooled by, or misunderstood, the noophytes. She also began to wonder if these remote electronic beings and ordinary people could ever understand one another.

With a net routine she collected everything worthwhile. She then created a link out to the city networks. Westcity was still dead – it would never fully recover, she realised, for it had been deliberately dissociated on the incorrect assumption that the temple of the Goddess was linked to the city like any ordinary building. Some sections were autonomous, however. The ignorance, the arrogant assumptions made by the Portreeve and her colleagues astounded her. Their every decision seemed founded on rumours and lazy research. But although Westcity was dead, there still existed a number of networks using the subterranean circuits of Eastcity, powered by fusion cells and residual energy from the Power Station. These would not last, however.

Arrahaquen spoke to the pyuter. 'Get me Graaff-lin using the quickest route,' she said. 'No ... use channel 61, it's whole.'

'Codeword requested.'

Arrahaquen nodded. Her system was functional, then, which meant that some pyuters in the temple of the Goddess were somehow connected to Eastcity, no doubt through private, self-powered lines. She replied, 'Onion Street.'

Then a voice: Graaff-lin. 'Arrahaquen, is that you?'

'Yes. I'm in the Citadel. I may have only minutes before the whole city network crashes. I'm going to flush down some Red Brigade data into your system. Can you keep it?'

'Yes.'

Arrahaquen performed the transfer, then closed every file.

'What's going on?' Graaff-lin asked.

'The Citadel's been attacked. The Red Brigade are gone. It's everyone for herself. I've got to run, but I'll see you soon.'

'All right. Auveeders, Arrahaquen, take care.'

She cut the link. But talking to Graaff-lin made her

remember the noophyte work, and she wondered if she could access a lexicon of machine language. Creating an electronic rootlet, she burrowed down through the network strata, labelling files that offered machine language. One was named 'Translation', and this she tried to grab.

But the networks were changing. It was as if every Citadel pyuter was being dipped in syrup, slowing down, becoming glutinous. Information was not being transferred. Hastily, Arrahaquen copied what seemed to be the translation file on to a laser leaf, which she pulled out of the screen's mouth before running out of the room.

Outside in the square a gun battle was taking place. The buildings opposite were ablaze. Arrahaquen ran back through the pyuter hall to the opposite door, listening and looking first, then creeping out. Guns and spent ammunition littered the ground. Acrid smoke blew along the alley she found herself in. From her kit she pulled a sterile mask, which she wetted then tied across her nose and mouth.

She ran through a litter of smashed glass and wood to the end of the alley to find herself in Om Street. She noticed that the rainbow sparkle inside the street plastic had become muted, as though seen in slow motion through a gauze. Score marks like half-healed scars showed where lasers had melted resin.

Om Street was quiet. Arrahaquen primed her needle rifle and decided to risk it. But she was only a few yards downhill when the entire street went black.

She looked uphill. Om Street was dark, like a normal street. She should be able to see the glittering upper reaches of Rosinante Street and Beria Street from here, but she could not.

Then she noticed the Spaceflower. The fine black lines that everyone had thought to be shadows, or some kind of folding in the vast structure, were illuminated, shining with blues, indigo and purples, here and there pulsing with white and gold. Astonished, Arrahaquen stared. It was as if it had come alive.

But then the sound of a motorbike engine being revved close by made Arrahaquen turn, and when she realised that it was racing down Om Street she ran. She hid in a doorway, behind a leaking water butt. A woman sped by on the bike. Some seconds later, from down the hill, Arrahaquen heard it come under gunfire.

She had to leave the Citadel. It was far too dangerous. Using shadows for cover she managed to follow empty alleys in a crooked race downhill, arriving eventually at the north gate. Somebody shot at her, but hit only the pavement to her side.

From the safety of a passage she looked up once more between black roofs at the Spaceflower. Cirrus clouds shimmered with patterns as they moved across it. The whole structure was alive as if wrapped with rainbow cobwebs. The noophytes were there now, thinking inhuman thoughts.

She hastened north to Graaff-lin's home. Her replica answered the door when she knocked. Inside, Graaff-lin too was looking at the night sky. 'What's happened?' she asked.

Arrahaquen produced the laser leaf. 'This might tell us,' she replied. 'Before the networks crashed I managed to copy what seemed to be translation files.'

'Translation files for conscoositee speech?'

'I think so.' Arrahaquen tossed over the leaf. 'Open it up. I had seconds to act. It may be nothing.'

Graaff-lin placed the leaf into a transparent receptacle, and the lamina sank into place with a hiss of escaping air. With musical tinkles interfaces connected, and the leaf began to glow with purple light.

Information flooded Graaff-lin's main screen. 'Praise

the Dodspaat!' she cried. 'This is a lexicon. Nine hundred and ten words!'

Arrahaquen nodded. Her intuition said that this was too easy a path, but she had been wrong before.

'Look,' Graaff-lin said, 'the words we know – ffordion, Gwmru, the land of the valleys, dwan. And many more.'

'Start now,' Arrahaquen advised.

Graaff-lin nodded, excitement in her face, her eyes shining. She told the replica, 'With a transceiver, go to the nearest serpent and there await instructions.'

'At once,' the pyuton replied.

Graaff-lin used the lexicon to reshape her routines so that anything said by the noophytes through the medium of a serpent could be analysed, translated, and then perhaps responded to. By the time she had finished, the replica's distorted voice sounded on the bare speaker at her side.

'Are you ready?' Graaff-lin asked.

'No.'

'Why not?'

'The serpent in this alcove has expired, like a balloon that has lost its air,' the replica replied. 'It lies lifeless on the stone shelf, its forked tongue lolling out.'

'What? Go to the next one.'

They waited. The replica reported the same.

Arrahaquen knew what must have happened. 'It's too late,' she said, and her whole body felt chill with the realisation. 'Every city network has crashed. There's no power any more for the serpents or anything else.'

'B-b-but ...' Graaff-lin said, sinking back into her chair.

'Only self-powered pyuters will be able to use the remaining circuits. My temple. You, deKray. A few other groups maybe.'

'But it can't be,' Graaff-lin said. She demanded that the

replica search the surrounding alleys until a live serpent was located.

'A waste of time,' Arrahaquen said. She knew it was true. All public pyuters were dead. The networks were dissipated, though physically they remained. A few links would survive, like fungal mycelia desperate to retain life, but at length they too would be scattered into electronic disarray. Isolation would follow.

20

With the Citadel gone, Kray fragmented into petty sisterhoods based on the ownership of necessities. In Westcity, there emerged coalitions based at the Harbour and in the Food and Water Stations, while the reveller encampments in the Cemetery and the Infirmary remained put. Some private dwellings also continued to house people, but, as time passed by and the green wave crept south, these dwindled or were destroyed by rampaging Krayans. In Eastcity the temple of the Dead Spirits became an empty wreck, but the temples of Youth and Felis remained home to diverse leagues, each well stocked with food and sterile water, though lacking in power. Eastcity Water and Food Stations remained deserted. There existed also various private assemblies, ranging in size from families of two to groups of twenty. One of these was that of the Holists at Clodhoddle Cottage, but it was thought that many erstwhile secret societies such as the Euthanasia Society, the Phallists, and the Club of Shadowy Thieves also retained stocks, and continued to survive.

One further event caused great destruction. On the morning after the collapse, a sea storm appeared on the horizon, anvil-headed clouds approaching the city until

the shower clouds of dawn had been blown away and
replaced by a grey mass sending down lightning. Thunder
cracked and a ferocious cold rain swept the darkened city.
The sea was churned into a maelstrom. For two hours the
great storm hurled hail, rain, and spat lightning bolts.

When it passed, the entire city was covered in a pale
green slime. It was as if the sea, upset by something, had
vomited over Kray.

Damage to buildings was considerable. All houses in
shaky condition had collapsed. Those of fair state were
now shaky. Only the best maintained houses survived the
battering, losing only slates and external decoration.

Arrahaquen sheltered in deKray's maisonette, where
she slept after Graaff-lin refused to lodge her. Woken and
terrified by the storm, she slept only fitfully, awaking
without memory of dreams and thus uncertain of the
reality of what she was experiencing. This disconcerting
sensation was turning her into something of an insomniac. Pressed by Zinina and deKray into prophesying the
immediate future, but unable to see anything other than a
dead green city, she became tetchy, tried too hard to
foresee, failed, and grew even more irritated. At length she
decided to return to her temple, impelled by the news that
having lost the cards deKray's maisonette was no longer
secure.

It was well after dark when she walked along the west
wall of the city, rifle primed and ready, her boots
squelching and slipping in the green slime, then hastened
up Red Lane and along to the temple.

Lamps were lit and doors were open, though the booth
was gone – only women of the Goddess were welcome
now. Considering that it had been attacked by what must
have been a large force it was, Arrahaquen thought, in
good condition.

To her surprise, Tashyndy and Arvendyn were waiting

for her. Tashyndy took her hand and, stroking it, said, 'We're so glad to see you. We were worried that you'd been killed.'

Arrahaquen looked around, at the bullet holes and the smashed wood. 'I can see you weren't.'

'We survived.'

Arrahaquen could think of no answer to this. It did not sound like any defence at all. She glanced down at bloodstained wood. Yes, it had happened. She had been caught up in it. And she knew now why so few Citadel Guard had been on the tumulus when it was stormed.

'We are well,' Tashyndy continued, 'all the more so for seeing you. Where are you living?'

'Here, I suppose.'

'But the others? Zinina, and the loose man?'

'They have their own safe house,' Arrahaquen replied, uncomfortable with these questions.

Tashyndy and Arvendyn encouraged Arrahaquen into a side chamber set out with soft cushions, pitchers of water, and dishes filled with fruit and crumbly biscuits. Arrahaquen knew that she was being interrogated. But why? Both priestesses were interested in Arrahaquen's thoughts; her ideas, her desires and fears for the future. Talking to them, Arrahaquen began to realise that they were a little afraid of her, and so the vexing problem of her prophetic facility came to mind. She decided to test them.

'How do you intend surviving?' she asked.

'What you see about you,' and here Arvendyn gestured to the wood panels of the room, 'is merely the tip of our vast stores sunk into the ground, tapering at its root like a parsnip. I reckon we've got everything we need here.'

Stunned as she was by this revelation, Arrahaquen sensed something wrong. She said, feeling her uncon-scious self stirring up disbelief, 'I think not. You aren't self-sufficient in food, are you? Your stocks will fail eventually, and all you grow is seasonal. In midwinter, you will grow nothing, and you won't have enough to last through until the summer.'

They looked at one another. 'Maybe,' Arvendyn said, 'but we could last for a long time.'

'Months only,' Arrahaquen said, using a slightly derisory voice.

'Do you really think so?' Tashyndy asked.

'Let me tell you,' Arrahaquen replied, pleased with her bluff, 'this city will be nothing but green soon.' She paused. Perhaps that was too much. She did not want them to know for sure that she was a pythoness. 'That's my guess, anyway,' she ended.

A knowing look came into Arvendyn's eyes. 'I see.'

Arrahaquen stood, and said, 'I've changed my mind. I'm going to be living with Zinina and deKray for now. Or maybe I'll go somewhere else.'

They stood with her, apparently happy. 'Come back soon.' It seemed a trite reply, and Arrahaquen found herself annoyed by them. She was glad all four had not questioned her.

Leaving the temple, she returned safely to deKray's house, but he and Zinina were asleep and she had to wake them up – quietly, so as to avoid the attention of local revellers. At last a bleary-eyed Zinina let her in, rather grumpily removing the improvised bars and chains.

On a couch, unable to sleep, she considered her options. Only one remained: they must all move in with the Holists. The loss of deKray's keys made it inevitable. Besides, there was no time now for pride.

21

Arrahaquen woke to hear Zinina and deKray talking in animated tones at the front door. She jumped out of bed, put on her gown, and joined them. There were thuds and grunts emanating from somewhere outside the door.

She sensed danger. 'Open it quickly,' she said.

Zinina unbarred and opened the door. Arrahaquen peered outside to see two figures brawling, both armed with knives, a short woman and a taller, cloaked woman. 'Stop!' she shouted.

They both looked up, startled. Zinina leaped across to them and, before they could make any defence, hit the taller woman on her upper right arm with the side of her hand, twisting around immediately to kick the knife out of the other woman's hand. The two were so surprised they simply stood still.

'Now what the damn Kray's going on here?' Zinina demanded. She sniffed at the taller woman. 'You're a reveller, aren't you?'

'Wait, wait,' the smaller woman said, turning to Arrahaquen. 'I've come a long way to see you, Arrahaquen—'

She knew her name. 'Who are you?' Arrahaquen asked

as Zinina picked up both knives.

'Don't you recognise me?'

'Hoy,' Zinina interrupted, threatening the reveller as she tried to sidle away. 'Stay put or get the point.'

No future memories made this woman's face recognisable. 'I don't know you,' Arrahaquen replied. 'What are you doing here? How did you know I was here?'

The woman seemed to relax. 'I am Surqjna of the Red Brigade, Arrahaquen, come to tell you, amongst other things, that your mother is dead.'

Arrahaquen had guessed this already. She felt no sadness to hear it confirmed. She felt nothing. 'Really,' she said, trying to sound sarcastic. 'I suppose you're the new Portreeve of Kray, then?'

'There'll be no more Portreeves,' Surqjna replied. 'I'm here to offer salvation. I know everything, Arrahaquen. We must talk. You know of the pyuter hearts, I believe. They're still within our grasp. We can talk with them.'

Arrahaquen hesitated. The story felt true. She turned to the other woman. Imperiously, she said, 'Who are you and why were you fighting on our doorstep?'

'This no-bloom began spiking me as I approached.'

'This reveller's been here before,' Zinina said to Arrahaquen. 'She tried to attack me and deKray a few weeks back.'

'You can come inside,' Arrahaquen told Surqjna. 'Disarm yourself first. Any quick moves and Zinina will disable you.'

Surqjna laughed. 'I know of this fiery wench,' she remarked, looking Zinina up and down. 'Ammyvryn spoke well of you, Zinina.'

Zinina's eyes were wide, her mouth open. 'What?' she managed.

'Just come in,' Arrahaquen said. She turned to the reveller. 'You can be off. If you return I'll set Zinina on you.'

They trooped inside and went to deKray's main room. Surqjna said, 'Quite a collection you have here, deKray. Collected them yourself?'

'Forget the pleasantries,' Zinina said. 'What's all this about what you've heard of me?'

'Still the sparky one,' Surqjna said, with what seemed a touch of contempt. Zinina said nothing. 'Yes, Ammy-vryn noticed you because of your skill and diligence as a Citadel Guard. In fact, now I come to think of it, I myself passed over you while searching for transformer controllers on the tumulus's west side.'

'Passed over?' Zinina said.

'You and Gishaad-lin were to be posted there and made third class Citadel defenders. But you *deserted* before the appointments were made.'

Zinina shrugged. Arrahaquen waited, happy to listen to the exchanges, anxious to keep Surqjna talking as much as possible, both to glean clues and to allow her unconscious mind space to feel out the future.

'My time was over,' Zinina said. 'I did the right thing.'

Surqjna seemed disconcerted by this show of confidence. She nodded and said, 'Anyhow, that's all in the past.'

Arrahaquen agreed. 'You mentioned the noophytes,' she said.

'We have one chance remaining. Does the name Gwmru mean anything to you?'

DeKray made to speak, but Arrahaquen stopped him. 'Why do you ask?'

'I'll be plain,' Surqjna said. 'I've no other choice. The pyuter hearts live in an abstract country called Gwmru. We have to enter that land and seek them out, to find out what they know of Kray ... and of escaping it.'

'I see. But how? And would they listen to us?'

'I used to be in the Red Brigade,' Surqjna said with

some vehemence. 'Of course they would.'

Arrahaquen pounced. 'Then why did they leave you and the city?'

'Because the Portreeve and the others did not listen hard enough. The pyuter hearts told us to jump into the Spaceflower. But on the night of the Citadel collapse the Portreeve lost her nerve—'

'And you survived?' Arrahaquen asked.

'Yes—'

'How? How *exactly*?'

Surqjna retained her composure. 'The rocket was due to launch at a preset time. I merely vanished at the appropriate moment, realising that the Portreeve's plan was failing. The other cowards left without me.'

Arrahaquen believed this to be true. 'Hmmm,' she said, 'but how can we travel to Gwmru?'

'This is where you come in. Some time ago, you were the victim of some assassination attempts.'

Arrahaquen felt her heart leap at the mention of this. 'Yes, I was.'

'I heard about it. Our sentient mechanician Majaq-Aqhaj made a pyuton identical to you in all respects—'

'She did, she did.'

'—and that pyuton should possess a third eye, unless its skull has been damaged.'

Arrahaquen cast her mind back to those dreadful days. 'Why are you telling me this?'

'You must return to the Citadel,' Surqjna said, 'collect the third eye, and bring it here.'

Arrahaquen continued her act. 'Then what?' she calmly asked.

Surqjna replied, 'Then you must take a risk, daughter of Ammyvryn. The third eye of a pyuton is not merely some receptacle of memory. It is amongst other things a casket of viruses. If you have the courage, and the desire to journey to Gwmru, you must accept the third eye into your brain, where these viruses will construct for you an interface. With this interface, your mind can travel to and around Gwmru.'

Arrahaquen looked at deKray, who seemed fascinated, and at Zinina, who looked repelled. 'Is it dangerous?' she asked.

'It is perilous, yes,' Surqjna replied, 'but it must be done. I've already done the same thing. I could enter Gwmru now.'

'And have you ever?'

'No.'

DeKray began to roll a cigarette. 'Why not?' he asked.

'Because of the risk of disturbing the pyuter hearts. Besides, there was no need to. Deese-lin and Spyne were our contacts.'

'And your job was . . .?' Arrahaquen asked.

Surqjna paused, thumped her fists upon her chair, and said, 'I was in charge of constructing the rocket. Hah! What an irony. I worked westside.'

DeKray lit his cigarette. 'How precisely is the innerai taken into the body?'

'A line of narcotic powder is placed upon a surface, such as a table, and the third eye is dropped into it. With a paper tube, Arrahaquen would have to sniff up the third eye with this powder, so that it reaches her sinus. From there, the viruses will break into her forebrain and construct the interface. There will be some external scar tissue, obviously, when the interface grows out of her forehead.'

Arrahaquen's stomach turned. Zinina had turned pale. 'I see,' said deKray, puffing away. 'I see.'

'Will I be disfigured?' Arrahaquen asked.

'It would be no larger than a finger nail.'

'But where's yours?' Surqjna's forehead seemed whole.

'Mine came out elsewhere,' Surqjna said, bitterly.

'Where?'

'You need not know.'

All these revelations made Arrahaquen's head spin. She sensed both truth and falsehood around the figure of Surqjna.

'You say that the artificial interface is corporeal,' deKray said, 'carried upon the integument. But to what does it connect?'

Now Surqjna looked uncomfortable.

'Gwmru is reached through the medium of male pyutons. Each is physically fixed, chained like men should be, but each is connected to the Citadel by a powered network, and thus connected to the country of Gwmru. It is with the serpents that your forehead will connect.'

Arrahaquen laughed from sheer astonishment. 'The serpents are male pyutons? Anyway, the city networks are dead. And the serpents are dead. Have you forgotten that?'

'Those public networks most intimately associated with the Citadel's own are self-powered, though eventually they will expire. And there is a technique of calling to life a lifeless serpent. It is merely because the pyuter hearts have moved elsewhere that the serpents flop in their alcoves. Think of them not as dead, but as weak-minded or unconscious.'

Arrahaquen felt unable to challenge Surqjna. Too much had been said, and she knew she would never be able to disentangle the truth from the lies.

'I will do it,' she said. But on her own terms.

'Good. When will you return to the Citadel?'

'Tonight. Come here tomorrow at dawn.'

Surqjna nodded. 'Tomorrow night we will be walking in Gwmru and finding out the truth of the pyuter hearts' plans.'

They saw Surqjna out of the house. She claimed to have a safehome off Judico Street. Returning, the three sat and looked at one another in silence.

DeKray spoke first. 'Now I understand the replica's remark that male pyutons are in the streets.' He rolled yet another cigarette, and tapped the twisted weed on his baccy tin. 'Clearly, pyutons carry a uterine technology allowing them access to Gwmru. A human has to ingest an innerai by an artificial method, however.' He paused. 'This supports my theory of noophyte origins. Entering Gwmru, their identities became electronic, hence the substitution of the symbol of the womb for their faces. But I think it is too risky.'

'We'll be there with you,' Zinina said.

'No you will not,' Arrahaquen replied firmly. 'This is something I have to do alone.'

'But the risk . . .' deKray muttered, to no effect.

'Well we're not staying here, Arrahaquen,' added Zinina. 'If you do go with that cold harridan, we're leaving for Clodhoddle Cottage. It's not safe here any more, what with revellers hanging about like flies. The Holists will shelter us.'

'That is up to you,' Arrahaquen said. 'But I have no intention of entering the Citadel. I think that's some sort of trap. DeKray, hand me Laspetosyne's innerai. I'll pretend it's my replica's.'

DeKray did as he was told. 'But that is the innerai of a noophyte,' he said, unwrapping a new packet of sweets, and popping one into his mouth. 'Who knows what special effect it may have upon your forebrain?'

'I must risk it,' said Arrahaquen.

'Have you foreseen success?' Zinina asked.

'I've foreseen nothing yet, except half-truths hanging around Surqjna. But I've got to risk it if we're going to contact the noophytes. And we have another aid – my replica. She too must be able to enter Gwmru, by mating with a serpent without Surqjna's knowledge. She could protect me.'

Zinina's face lit up. 'Of course! She'll go to Gwmru and help you.'

'Tomorrow evening,' Arrahaquen said, 'once Surqjna and I have departed, you two are to pack everything and leave for Clodhoddle Cottage. Once I have returned from Gwmru, I'll lose Surqjna then meet you there. Have medical equipment ready in case I'm injured or ill.'

'We will,' Zinina promised. DeKray looked unhappy at the prospect of leaving his home. 'What if she attacks you?' she asked.

Arrahaquen shook her head. 'Couldn't you tell? If she does need me, she needs me *alive*. No, she'll not harm me. Now, listen. Tonight, we'll call Graaff-lin and tell her what's going on. We need the replica over here as soon as possible.'

This they did. Graaff-lin was wholly against the mission, but eventually they wore her down and the replica was sent to Gur-Lossom Street. That night, Arrahaquen managed only one hour's sleep. She tried in vain to relax, drinking dooch and even a tot of uz to make her relax, but she was too nervous. Her mind was confused. Images of the future, if such they were, entered her mind's eye misty and useless. She was simply too agitated.

An hour after dawn Surqjna returned. In the kitchen they showed her the innerai, then watched as she poured from a pouch a line of yellow powder. Arrahaquen recognised the spicy sweet smell. 'Flak boot?' she asked.

'It's pure, quite safe,' Surqjna replied. 'It will protect you from discomfort by acting as a local anaesthetic.' To Zinina's frown she added, 'I'm outnumbered three to one. I'm only interested in us finding the pyuter hearts. I want to live as much as you do.'

Zinina did not answer. Nor did deKray.

Arrahaquen took the innerai and dropped it into the powder.

'Now,' said Surqjna, 'just sniff it up. You'll feel your face go numb, and then you'll become disoriented for a while. Time will seem to fly by. We'll guide you to your bed, and you can lie down until the interface is fully grown.'

'How long will that take?'

'Perhaps six or seven hours.'

Arrahaquen, heart thumping in her chest, took the paper tube offered by Surqjna and bent down. Without hesitating, for she did not want Surqjna to see her misgivings, she sniffed up the powder and the innerai.

She sat back. She tried to speak but already her face was tingling, her eyes defocusing.

Yellow shapes like blankets flying in a high wind whizzed across her vision. Hands were on her body, on her arms and shoulders. They were cold and clammy. A high-pitched whine started, turning like a pyuter song into the twin voices of her mothers.

Coloured shapes flew at her. She flinched, and they sped through her. She felt as if she was extremely small, smaller by far than a womanikin; then she felt huge, as big as the Gardens. Then she felt tiny and huge at the same time. Then she felt sick.

A burning feeling made her head throb. It began at her left temple, then travelled to her neck.

She realised that she was lying on a bed, the face of Zinina above her.

'You all right?' Zinina asked.

DeKray appeared at her side. 'Is she awake?' he asked.

'I'm awake,' Arrahaquen whispered.

'You want to see what's happened?' Zinina said. Arrahaquen sat up and noticed Surqjna seated nearby. Zinina gave her a mirror.

In the middle of her forehead she saw a circle of red flesh, with eight tiny black dots in its centre.

After more rest, she felt strong enough to rise. Surqjna, beginning to fidget, said, 'Are you ready to leave?'

Arrahaquen nodded. 'I'll just say goodbye to Zinina and deKray. Wait by the hall door, please.'

Surqjna left for the green zone. Arrahaquen led Zinina and deKray into the room furthest from it. Whispering, she said, 'Are you two prepared? The pyuton knows what to do with the serpent she chooses, doesn't she?'

'We related to her the facts of life,' deKray said. 'She might even be in Gwmru now, awaiting your company.'

'You sound nervous,' Zinina told Arrahaquen.

'Of course.'

'You've foreseen nothing?'

'I just can't concentrate. There's definitely something odd about Surqjna. She's lied to me. All I can see is green land and emptiness, and lots of danger. But I have this feeling that my replica will be with me. Of course, that could just be wishful thinking. You've sent her off to find a serpent?'

'Yes,' deKray replied.

'We'll keep our part of the plan,' Zinina said. 'Go now, and good luck.'

Arrahaquen returned to Surqjna, who had put on thigh boots with elastics, and a cotton hood with drawstrings. Arrahaquen noticed that she was wearing a short skirt, which was unusual for Kray. They both dressed in plastic protective capes.

'Goodbye,' Arrahaquen said, as she left the house. Zinina and deKray waved at her, then closed the door.

They walked up Gur-Lossom Street. Many of its cobble stones were now invisible under grass, and in places, particularly as they reached Butcher Row at its north end, there grew rose shrubs, many varieties of

poisonous herbs, and the swaying saplings of beech,
birch and laburnum. A group of revellers walked out
of Butcher Row, green revellers by the look of them with
pledgets tied to their nostrils, so they ducked into an
alley and waded through brown floods to reach Butcher
Row. Then they walked up to Mandrake Street and
hastened along to the Sud Bridge. Too nervous to think
of topics of conversation – her stomach was rumbling,
and it felt tight, as if she had been starving herself –
Arrahaquen remained silent.

'Here we must turn right and head for Cliff Lanes,'
Surqjna said. 'There, serpents lie within private courtyards.'

'Will we be disturbed?' Arrahaquen asked.

'Our bodies will lie insensible, but we will be safe.'

The sound of surf crashing became audible as they
entered Cliff Lanes, once a residential district, now
deserted. They stopped in an alley. To their left stood an
arch.

Surqjna led the way. They entered a courtyard, clearly
once the private property of some rich independent or
defender, but now silent, empty. Two serpents lay flopped
over the edge of an alcove shelf. They approached.

It was too dark to see what species they were. Drizzle
made Arrahaquen's eyes mist a little. 'Shall we do it
now?'

'Yes.' Surqjna took off her protectives.

Arrahaquen followed suit.

'Pull one of the serpents, and come and lie here in the
dry. Here, in this doorway.'

Arrahaquen pulled the serpent and was surprised to
feel it flow freely; she held a length of limp chainmail in
her hand. Surqjna followed the same procedure. They lay
side by side.

'These are kraits,' Surqjna said, 'good for profound

words. Now watch me bring the serpent to life.' She began
to rub the scaly skin of her krait, her fingers curling to grip
and massage. With slow, almost sensual motions she
moved her hand up and down. Arrahaquen watched,
fascinated. The krait was lengthening, its body thicken-
ing, and it was rising and swaying as if hypnotised by the
manipulation. Soon it was a yard long. 'It helps if you lick
it. Don't worry, it's not infected. Dangerous bacteria can't
live upon it. Watch me.'

Surqjna sucked the head of her serpent. Arrahaquen,
not without some trepidation, did likewise, and her
serpent too began to thicken and grow longer. Soon, both
were six feet long.

'Now we go into Gwmru,' Surqjna said.

Arrahaquen raised herself up on her right arm to see
where Surqjna would place the head of her serpent. But
Surqjna slapped Arrahaquen's serpent with a quick
motion and the head attached itself to Arrahaquen's
forehead. Surqjna crouched over Arrahaquen with a grin
on her face.

Panicking, Arrahaquen tried to pull the serpent away,
but pain, blazing pain, stopped her, and she screamed.

'Let's go to Gwmru, you and I!' Surqjna cried, laughing
like a madwoman.

Arrahaquen lay back, trying to wriggle away, but her
muscles were weak, and her neck hardly had the strength
to hold her head up.

Surqjna leaned over her, one leg on either side of
Arrahaquen's chest. With a laugh she pulled up her skirt
and revealed naked flesh. Arrahaquen began to see where
Surqjna's interface had grown, but she could do nothing
but watch. Her last sight, before everything went green,
was of pubic hair, the glistening pink lips between
Surqjna's legs, and Surqjna plunging her serpent in
between them with a squeal of joy.

*   *   *

*The featureless green sheen that masked Arrahaquen's
vision did not alter. With increasing panic she tried
mentally to feel and move her body – but she seemed
to be floating free. Then sound came to her ears, the
wind howling. She could smell puffs of smoke on air,
and feel the breeze against her skin. She could sense that
she was upright, standing on firm ground, but she was
still blind.*

*Sight returned last. The green seemed to leach into the
substrate of reality, like water into blotting paper, and she
first saw a blue mass with an intense light in it, then a
green mass, then details; lines of black, blobs of yellow.
Her eyes focused.*

*She stood in a vegetated environment not unlike Kray
without houses. Everything seemed simple, however,
lacking the grainy, dank, ever-moving complexity of the
real world. Gwmru.*

*It was when she moved that she realised her body felt
different. Her feet were unshod; they were hooves.
Although she wore a dress of some sort, she could feel the
thinnest covering of hair on her skin, and when she
opened the gown and looked down at her belly and legs
she saw they were covered with hair. It was as if the short
hair on deKray's arms had moved over to her and become
brown. And her head was different too. She could feel a
mane along her neck, whipped by the wind, and hair on
her scalp. She felt two large ears like those of a horse. For
some minutes Arrahaquen just looked at her body and felt
it with her fingertips, wondering what could possibly have
happened to her.*

*Then she noticed something else. The jumble of images
and thoughts at the top of her mind – her future memory
– was gone.*

And she noticed something else. To her left side a spray

*of leaves hung, bizarre, motionless unless she moved. It
followed her.*

*This was an abstract country. It bore no relation to
Kray and the Earth. As proof of that, Surqjna was
nowhere to be seen. But the sensory centres of her brain
were being fed through the interface with information,
allowing her conscious mind to experience Gwmru.*

*The loss of her future memory she ascribed to losing
her real body's senses. It struck her that she was very
much a physical creature. Her deeper mind was supported
by the constant input of her body's senses.*

*Here, all that counted for nothing. Her mind perceived
Gwmru, but it was an illusion – coherent, but illusory
none the less. She would have to treat the place very
carefully. She wondered how it might be possible to leave,
when her real self lay in Kray. She felt her forehead. It was
whole.*

How to find her replica? She shouted: no answer.

*Investigating the floating leaves she saw that on each
one were engravings of words, numbers and symbols. She
reached out to touch the leaf marked 'walk'.*

*A new spray appeared: a time-lapse growth of new
leaves, each marked with options. By touching the leaf
marked 'north', she made her body move.*

*Soon Arrahaquen understood that in Gwmru rules
were simple, despite the apparent vastness of the environment. She made north, moving at speed. When she found
a leaf marked 'search', she searched, specifying her
replica. Instantly the pyuton was at her side.*

'Where am I?' it asked her.

*'I think I've just transplanted you from wherever you
were,' Arrahaquen said. 'Sorry. Have you seen Surqjna?'*

'No.'

*Odd. If she could bring her replica here, surely Surqjna
could do the same? She felt again her curious body, and*

began to wonder if, by accepting Laspetosyne's innerai into her brain, she had stumbled across the perfect disguise.

'How do I look?' she asked her replica.

'Something has altered your whole self. You don't look at all like Arrahaquen.'

'Could you do me a drawing?' Arrahaquen asked.

They paused their abstract flight while the replica created a white square, which she used to sketch Arrahaquen. As she waited, Arrahaquen told the replica of her thoughts concerning Gwmru. Finished, the replica pressed another leaf. A copy on paper fluttered down from the sky.

They moved on. 'I hardly recognise that face,' Arrahaquen said. Even ignoring the horse ears and the hair – wild brown hair that she wished she could flaunt in Kray – the face, particularly the eyes, were unfamiliar.

'Let's specify a destination,' suggested the pyuton.

'How about the noophytes' bridge?'

Gwmru's inner logic transported them to a hill, from which they could see an island, the sea and, connecting the island to the mainland, a bridge. They walked down to the bridge, but a figure approached them and stood at the entrance, stopping them from continuing. She was a fat woman, though not as fat as Taziqi, Arrahaquen reflected, and she was dressed all in blue with azure cloak, cornflower-blue cap, indigo slippers. She carried a staff in her right hand and a poinard in her left.

'Who are you?' she called.

'We're travellers,' Arrahaquen began. 'We're looking for a way out of Gwmru. We hope the noophytes will help us. Who are you?'

'Name yourselves,' came the reply.

Arrahaquen hesitated. 'We're both called Arrahaquen, actually.'

In imperious tones the woman said, 'You speak with

one of the ffordion. I am Quff. We cannot help you. Go
away.'

Arrahaquen was not to be put off. 'You must help us.
We're stuck here.'

'Behind me lies our dwan. You will never walk upon
it.'

Arrahaquen, becoming frustrated, looked to either side
of the bridge. 'Where are we?'

'These are the Straits of Men Eye. Only members of the
ffordion may cross. Go away.' Quff pointed north-west.
'Over there lie two towers. Shelter in them. But do not
return here.'

'Wait,' Arrahaquen said as Quff turned. 'You must give
the ... the elders of the ffordion a message. Say that
Arrahaquen is here, the pythoness of Kray. They will want
to speak to me.'

'So you take me for a lesser member of the ffordion? I
will speak no message.'

Cursing to herself, Arrahaquen tried to think. 'You
must give them a message,' she urged. 'I have to return to
Kray, and only you can help. Please.'

'I cannot be bothered to mention you.'

Desperate, Arrahaquen turned to her replica. 'Any
ideas?'

'No.'

Arrahaquen felt something hard in her hand. It was a
pencil. 'Wait!' she called again. 'I'll write you a note. All
you have to do is give it to the chief of the ffordion when
you see her next. Couldn't be simpler.'

Arrahaquen, knowing that she had to make herself
seem important to the noophytes, wrote on the back of
the drawing:

'I am Arrahaquen, the famed pythoness. I have the gift
of prophecy. I know you have departed the city, but I can
foresee our future. I must return to the city. Please help,

for all our sakes. I am sincere in my offer. Arrahaquen of Kray.'

'There,' she said, throwing the scrap of paper over to Quff. 'Take it. We'll stay at the towers, and come back tomorrow. We hope to see you then.'

Quff picked up the paper and read it. She sneered, but put it in her pocket then returned to her post. Arrahaquen and the replica turned to leave.

Night had arrived when they saw two structures on the coast, not far away. They moved on. Arrahaquen felt depressed, thinking it unlikely that the arrogant Quff would deliver her note, but she could devise no other plan.

And then she saw the towers. One was the Cowhorn Tower, the other the Clocktower.

This sight disoriented her still further. The two towers rose from bare ground.

'What are they doing here?' the replica asked.

'I've no idea,' Arrahaquen said. 'Perhaps they both have special links that we don't know about. Look, there's something by the foot of the Cowhorn Tower.'

They approached. On the earth by the tower lay a sopping, mouldy body. Arrahaquen closed. 'It's deKray,' she said.

A figure jumped from behind the tower.

Surqjna.

'I thank you,' said Surqjna, pressing a floating leaf at her side. DeKray's body vanished.

Arrahaquen realised that Surqjna was speaking to the replica. 'I suspected you were around here, hence my little trap. Now you will listen to me. You will answer my every question. If you do, I will remove the enclosure routine currently on you and your friend here.'

Arrahaquen moved closer, saying, 'What are these questions?'

'You stay put,' Surqjna demanded of Arrahaquen. Glancing at her replica, Arrahaquen stood still.

'Over there,' said Surqjna, gesturing to the island beyond the straits, 'live the ffordion. They have just built their bridge. I need to know what they will do, so I can plan. I think they are building something. You will foresee from this spot the future around them, and tell me everything. When I am satisfied, I will give you twenty seconds in which to leave Gwmru. You won't return here.'

'But I can't do that,' said the replica. 'My ability – my small ability, Surqjna – it doesn't work here.'

'You think I believe that? I need prophecies from Gwmru!'

'It's true. I can't do it.'

Surqjna drew a rapier from a holster hidden under her cloak. 'I have no time for games.'

In times of stress Arrahaquen sometimes gave in to panic and remained helpless, but, despite her sheltered upbringing within the Citadel, she possessed a courage rooted in her personal philosophy of optimism. So when her replica conjured a pair of rapiers from the air by pressing two leaves, she took one and without hesitation pointed it as Surqjna, saying, 'Violence is for children. Can't we talk about it?'

'You keep out of this,' Surqjna retorted. Pressing a leaf, she conjured a beast – a dungeon creature such as had guarded the Temple of the Goddess.

Surqjna attacked with gusto but without subtlety. Arrahaquen, who had no idea how to use a rapier other than to swish it about, feigned proficiency and darted about as best she could, dodging when the creature attacked, trying not to let her enemy close. She knew that she could not win unless she used some trick ... something other than the rapier. And quickly.

As the concept of 'something other' flickered through her mind she found that she was clasping a shield, the lid of the bin at Graaff-lin's house. With no time to be astonished, she raised it and used it to deflect her opponent's rapier.

Arrahaquen knew then that the key to her survival was her emotions, for it was through her emotions that the profound knowledge of her unconscious was conveyed, and it was her unconscious that had worked to create the dustbin lid – as well as the pencil that had allowed her to scribble a note.

Now Surqjna attacked her, but the point of the rapier whipped against the dustbin lid with a clang. Arrahaquen stepped back.

No cold calculations could help here, and Surqjna's emotions were false and self-serving. Arrahaquen felt as she danced around Surqjna that she was truly at one with herself.

Surqjna feinted, but Arrahaquen jumped aside then made a swishing attack of her own. The creature now battled with the replica.

Surqjna stepped back. On the ground, six creatures appeared. They skittered around and Arrahaquen saw that they were scorpions, spiders and a snake. The instruments of the attempted assassinations.

All was clear. It was Surqjna who had been behind the whole plot. She had needed access through Arrahaquen to select parts of the Citadel network, parts perhaps only the Portreeve had known of in their entirety. A dead Arrahaquen could cause no trouble. But now, the departure of the noophytes had radically changed Surqjna's plans, and she needed her alive.

Arrahaquen felt anger flare up inside her. She felt a righteous invulnerability come to her aid. 'You've really made a mistake now,' she yelled. The giant insects closed.

'You've made me angry!' Without thought she squashed the insects. Before her eyes, an invisible hand crushed their bodies, leaving brown chitin and puddles of fluid. Surqjna stared.

The other fight ceased. They all looked at the destroyed insects. Arrahaquen felt nothing but a desire to beat Surqjna about the head and the body, to crush and hurt her; and this the invisible force conjured by her fear and loathing did, subduing Surqjna to the ground, where she lay head in hands, calling for mercy. Arrahaquen, seeing the consequences of her anger, felt sudden shame.

'Release us now,' she demanded, standing over Surqjna with her rapier at the pyuton's throat.

'But—' Surqjna began.

'Now,' Arrahaquen repeated, 'before it's too late.'

A pale leaf appeared before Arrahaquen's eyes, grown from the bud on the tip of her spray. The replica pointed to it. 'Look, an exit leaf. Press it.'

'But who are you?' Surqjna wailed, staring at the two of them. 'Are you Arrahaquen?'

Arrahaquen pressed the exit leaf. Her last glimpse was of Surqjna choking.

Then she was suddenly flat on her back in a dark doorway, cold, stiff, rain pouring over her and the noxious effluent of a blocked drainpipe spraying her face. Remembering where she was, she pulled the serpent from her forehead and, with some difficulty, managed to stand up. She felt chilled to the bone, sick and dizzy. Her mouth felt hot, however, her tongue was bloated, and her throat hurt: infection.

Surqjna lay still. Her face seemed older, and her body thinner. Arrahaquen had nothing with which to destroy her, so she looked around: still nothing. But the doorway in which they had lain seemed rickety. She pulled at a loose jamb, and the structure creaked. It was damp and rotten. She tugged some more, until, with a snap, the whole doorway and all the bricks surrounding it crashed on to Surqjna.

22

Zinina and deKray followed their instructions exactly. Three hours after Arrahaquen left with Surqjna (Zinina had sent a rude jannita sign after her erstwhile leader when she was not looking) they were walking along Cod Row, a silent and dark Citadel behind them, until they saw a low brick arch with the sign 'Driftwood Passage' hanging vertically from one nail. Once, rich independents had lived here, but now the steep alley was home only to velvety balls of fungus and some animal bones. The houses were all unlit, standing off the passage set in their own gardens. The fifth belonged to Eskhatos.

The Holists lived in a large stone house. Windows blacked out to avoid reveller attention, its front had been splashed green to give the effect of an abandoned home uncared for. In fact, every external wall was hosed down once a month with verticidal foam. Realistic plastic roses hung from window ledges, while the garden had been allowed to grow unchecked. A camouflaged path to one side was the only entrance, a final touch being dustbins on their sides, spewing refuse and syringes, as if some reveller horde had already ransacked the place. Zinina led deKray along the path, bending down to avoid microwires attached to alarm sensors indoors and pointing out an apparently random arrangement of mossy terracotta pots which were actually cases for mines. The verdigrised statue, she explained, had long since had its eyes replaced by intelligent cameras connected to the house security rigs. At the door she pressed a button four times. Around the back, a dog started to bark.

'This dwelling is vast,' deKray said.

'Most of the rooms are for the pyuters.'

'Indeed, the great job of holistic analysis,' he said, impressed, and, Zinina knew, looking forward to meeting the Holists.

Qmoet opened the door and, after looking deKray up and down, took them through to the common room.

Zinina rarely saw deKray nervous, and when he was it was because of other people – a symptom common in Kray with the impossibility of living a normal life with normal human contact. Love, the old saying ran, had become lost along the way. She smiled at the five faces looking her way and said, 'This is my lover, deKray.' She took his hand in hers. 'Don't worry, sweetheart, they know all about you.'

'Not *all* about me,' he quipped, the sweet in his mouth clacking against his teeth. 'Would smoking be acceptable here?'

Eskhatos stood. 'Yes,' she said. 'Do light up.' She leaned upon her stick, Zinina noticed. This redoubtable woman who had led the Holists for almost twenty years had wrinkled skin, bent posture, green-splotched skin, and missing teeth, but she was dressed as if for an official function, in cream silk and red slippers, with a black skull cap on her head. 'If I cough,' she told deKray, 'it's because of age, not because of smoke.'

'Very well,' deKray replied, and he almost bowed.

Zinina led him to the four others, all of whom

remained seated. 'This is Ky, our holistic synthesist.'

'Hello,' Ky said, her antiseptic half-moon glasses twinkling in the anjiq light.

'And this is my dear, dear old friend, Gishaad-lin,' Zinina continued, bending down to give and receive a hug.

'A good evening to you,' deKray said.

Next, Zinina indicated Reyl, who tonight seemed tired and older than her nineteen years. The lilac jumpsuit she wore appeared faded, tears at its shoulders suggesting a fight. 'Reyl is in charge of secrecy here, and security, and she also used to be in charge of people in our pay up the Citadel.'

'I see,' deKray said, nodding. He took a puff at a now lit cigarette.

'And this is Qmoet.'

This completed the roll-call. Eskhatos took a sip from the steaming mug of mulled wine at her side and said, 'For now you may use the room at the top rear of the house. You had better run along and make yourselves more comfortable. It would be nice if you cleaned yourself up. We keep a tidy home, here.'

'We will,' Zinina said. She felt pleased. She knew they had both, for the moment, been accepted.

'But first,' Qmoet said, 'what news of the pythoness?'

'She went off with Surqjna as planned. She could be back any minute, or she might be days. We'll just have to wait.'

'Hmmm,' Eskhatos said. 'Well, we are keeping a continual look-out. You two get some sleep, now. I'm thinking of turning in myself.'

Zinina bade them all good night, then led deKray up to the top floor and along to the very end of the south wing, where a solid oak door seven feet high stood.

The room was cold and draughty. A high ceiling bore

the remains of an ancient mural, while mildewed paintings hung from every wall. It was a large room, thirty feet
on a side, the entire width of this wing, with a four-poster
bed against one wall and a cast-iron fireplace at the other.
Draped linen and bare floorboards, covered only here and
there by threadbare jannitta rugs, gave the impression of
etiolated grandeur. By the side of the bed lay a pyuter rig
and screen, and a table with a pitcher of water and two
glasses.

'I like it,' said deKray. 'Will we be residing here, then?'

'I hope so,' Zinina said, hugging him fiercely. 'They're
a high-flown fivesome, they are. Really, I only know
Qmoet and Gishaad-lin.' She hugged him once more. 'Do
you really like it?'

'I do. Oddly enough, it reminds me somewhat of the
living room at the house in Cochineal Mews.'

Zinina relaxed. She had worried over this moment.

'What of comestibles?' he asked.

'A cellar down below, very well stocked.'

He sat on the bed. A draught came from under the
door. 'Good. We shall return to my house and transport
the remaining necessities, the more important of my
books among them.' He paused. 'I do not imagine that we
could bring them all here.'

'I'm afraid not,' Zinina said, as deKray threw a cape at
the door to stop the draught.

He examined the dusty black cloth stretched over the
window. 'What a shame we can never look out, however.'

'Tomorrow,' Zinina said, 'we'll go for a walk.'

'A walk?'

'A walk. I want to show you one last thing.'

'What?' he asked.

'It's a surprise.'

They spent most of the next day talking with the Holists,

except Reyl who was out working, and Zinina was pleased to see that all, with the possible exception of Gishaad-lin, were comfortable to be in the same room as deKray. When they found out for themselves the extent of his book-learning they were also happy to involve him in the conservation. By late afternoon the rain had stopped and Zinina led deKray down to Mossy Row. Arrahaquen had not returned from Gwmru.

The sea pounded the beach far away. It was low tide. DeKray looked at her as if to query her sanity. 'We are to walk here?'

'Yeah. Look, there's a safe path. Come on.'

'But it is the beach. It is not safe.'

'We're both armed,' Zinina replied, trying to tug him to the head of the path. She pulled at the ties of her backpack. 'Got spare needles in here, and a knife and stuff.'

'It is a steep incline,' he pointed out.

'It's safe, I told you. I've been up and down it lots of times.'

He stalled. 'But it is so risky.'

'Oh, give over moaning. This might be your last ever walk along the beach.'

'It will if we die here.'

Eventually he was persuaded to descend to the beach, and Zinina knew that she would be able to work on him some more. She knew that he was too polite to refuse her when she pleaded. Pleading always worked, Zinina had found. They reached the beach and paused to look around.

'Is this not far enough?' he said.

Tugging him along the sand, Zinina did not bother to answer, because she knew that in ten minutes he would be his normal self, having relegated their disagreement to the back of his mind. This he did frequently, giving in unless the issue was of real importance to him.

'What do you make of it here, then?' she asked.

He looked along the beach. 'Nothing, as of this moment.'

She followed his gaze. A long line of sea debris, in places as high as their waists, stretched out marking high-tide. Much of it was wood and the eviscerated bodies of sea creatures, but in the material closer to hand she could see machine oddments, including some of those strange technological chunks that had fallen in bilious slime during the great storm.

She kicked a pile of wood. Something rocketed out into the air past their noses, leaving a whiff of salt, then exploded with a crack. They looked up to see pieces of bladder falling to the sand.

'Please do not attempt that again,' said deKray.

'We'll see,' she replied, hoping to provoke him.

Arm in arm they walked on. Soon, from the expression in his face and the relaxation of his arm, she could tell that he was, like her, enjoying the walk. This had been the point, a last sensual experience.

'I wonder what Graaff-lin is doing,' she said.

'Who knows? Nobody has visited her for some time. Mayhap her food and water is running out. She may call for more, if she is alive. Perhaps she is dead.'

'You don't know that.'

He shrugged. 'I would not be surprised.'

'I don't think she was brought up to cope with this,' Zinina continued, waving her free hand at the city. 'I always thought there was a volcano plugged up inside her.'

'She is merely deluded, like all worshippers.'

'Yeah ... still, maybe we ought to visit her.'

He did not answer immediately. Then, 'Perhaps we ought to. Eskhatos could send out a team to visit her abode.' As though his thoughts were elsewhere he nudged the remains of a box. Several yellow creatures like upturned cups scuttled out, leaving orange trails as they sped toward the sea. They paused to watch.

From the north came a scent of lemon. Zinina pointed out a phalanx of parasols. They were floating seeds, risen from the bogs of Kray's northern hills, their luminous orange gills smudged by mist and drifting smoke. With a hiss of perfume from their gas tanks they landed on the beach, points ramming into the sand. Here, they would germinate.

Zinina sighed. 'Do you reckon we'll survive?' she asked. It was a question she had put to him many times, under various guises. Sometimes she had the impression that her attraction to him was rooted in this need to find somebody who might provide an answer, and since their minds were as dissimilar as rock and leaves, his fascinated hers.

'I don't know,' he said at last. 'I do not think we can speak about the unspeakable. Yes, we have seen Kray gradually declining, and we can guess how it will end. But still we cannot consider our personal demises.'

'I just think we *have* to.'

'But is that psychologically feasible? No. Maybe in two weeks our food will run out. Yet in that time we could be poisoned, or shot, or die of cholera.'

'But if we don't know how it'll end, I can't rest.' Zinina pondered what she had just said. 'Maybe that's a good thing. I'm hopeful.'

He nodded. 'In one way, a strictly statistical way, so am I. Both of us utilise the same mechanism of denying the truth to ourselves. You are unduly optimistic, I am unduly the other way.' He laughed. 'It is much the same ploy.'

'But Arrahaquen's different,' said Zinina. 'Have you noticed what she does when you talk to her about preparing for the worst? Rien Zir, I hate these phrases. Preparing for death. Yeah, she just goes into another world, you can see it in her eyes, specially now she's prophesied things and got them right.'

'I wonder how she visualises her own demise? I wonder if she has seen herself dead in some alley, mangy dogs sniffing at her corpse, a green patina upon her skin. Rain pouring.'

Zinina recalled something Arrahaquen had once said: 'I can't visualise myself in future memory, but I can see my own grave-stone, and it's pretty.' She replied, 'I think Arrahaquen's odd. I think she might save us, somehow.'

Zinina fell silent. She had realised that those feelings which she wanted to explore were located in hidden territory. Only at the moment of death would she feel them – really feel them. She did not fear death, rather feared the fear preceding it. 'I hope we die together,' she said. 'No, really. I don't want it any other way. Or next best, I hope I die first.'

He laughed. 'That is what I hope for myself. So it had better be a simultaneous operation.'

At this, she felt very close to him. 'Do you love me?'

'Not as you would think of it.'

Zinina had already guessed this, and had for a considerable time been prepared for such an answer. It hurt her only as a pinprick hurt her skin. 'Why not?'

'I just can't do it. You know.'

She nodded, gazing out to sea. 'I suppose I do.'

'I can only do it in negative terms. By that, I mean I can only imagine the feelings, the ones you were referring to, when you are not there. When you are, it is impossible.'

'Yeah.'

'Or at least too hard to try. Maybe I have not tried. Do you follow?'

'Oh, yes,' said Zinina, kissing him. Without speaking

they lay on the ground, uncovering just enough of themselves to remain safe, and began to make love, Zinina on deKray, while the smell of the sea and the sound of the waves passed over them.

'Wait,' said Zinina. She opened her backpack and produced four leather straps each sewn with twenty or so silver bells. 'Jannitta custom,' she explained, tying the straps to her wrists and ankles, so they jangled as she moved. 'So that people know what you're up to and that you want privacy.'

He chuckled. Their passion increased with the sound of the bells.

Later, deKray stood, then took her hand and pulled her off the sand. They wandered on. Some way along the beach she noticed a wilting plant, a variety of foxglove. Circling it, she tried to remember what it reminded her of. DeKray eyed her. 'I can't remember, I can't remember,' she muttered to herself. Then, with an 'aha!', she pulled the whole plant from the beach to reveal roots knobbled with saucers – the piezoelectric transducers of pyuton joints.

Further on they came across what looked like a heap of wood chips glued with sap. Zinina examined it, then stiffened, wafting air from a hole into her nostrils. 'It's a sea bee hive,' she said.

'Come here,' deKray said, holding out his hand.

'No,' she replied, waving him away, 'it should be safe. Remember the reveller proverb, "If you can hear the bees you can taste the honey."'

'Revellers,' scoffed deKray. One of the bees, blue and green and as long as his thumb, flew into the air.

Zinina said, 'It's based in truth. They're dozy this time of the year. It's when they're quiet you have to run, because they're listening to their new queen larvae. Want some honey?'

'I would not pilfer,' deKray warned.

Zinina ignored him. As a girl she had made trips with her grandmother-guardian along Westcity beach, to collect honey from beach hives, and she knew what she was doing. Scraping away the top debris cover she peeled one of the hive layers back, to reveal what seemed a wax pebble, one end of which she took between her fingers to pull out two dripping laminae. The honey was white streaked with blue. She held one out to him while she let the other drip into her mouth. 'Quickly!'

'But . . .'

'Nothing nasty'll live in that concentration of sugar. Quick, eat it!'

He took the lamina and did as she did. Eventually he was laughing with the effort. The honey was crunchy sweet and slightly warm, a few degrees above the present temperature, and to Zinina it seemed like an omen of pure good.

They wiped their mouths with kit tissues, relaid the hive, then continued. The sun was low, an hour away from setting, and they decided to turn back and walk into the light. This too was perfect for Zinina. She wanted to face the sun during these last moments.

She listened and heard the surf, the squawks of a few gulls, and caught creaks from pieces of driftwood. 'I can't hear any guns.'

'Nor I.'

'You know what that means.'

He glanced at her. 'What?'

'Less people. I wonder how many are left now.'

She looked out to sea. On the horizon two silhouettes lay, boats that had earlier left to take their chances at sea. Soon, Zinina thought, she too, and deKray, and the others, could be on such a boat. The Holists owned two, kept hidden under the Sud Bridge.

'Perhaps citizens of the city have seen sense,' deKray suggested. 'No, of course not, I expect they shot one another.'

'I want to be free to be me,' Zinina said, squinting into the orange sun.

'Pardon?'

'I want to be free to be me. All my life I've had to do this, do that, check this and that, get food and water every day and check that too. It's like I can't be me. I've got to exist by toiling, not by discovery.'

'Everybody else has that problem,' said deKray.

'I'm not talking about them, I'm talking about me. I want to sail to a new land and be myself.'

DeKray paused before saying, 'Throughout history most people have had to live without realising that they had needs. And that allowed them to be fixed into arbitrary classes ruled by persons who knew what their own needs were, and were lucky enough to be in a position to satisfy them. Selfishly, of course.'

'So?' Zinina interrupted.

'Krayans are in no worse a situation. The majority of all past human beings lived in fear of death, either because they had to work to survive, or because of war, or because they had to spend all their time creating food. Our particular society is merely the final such society. It is only that which distinguishes it from any other society built upon scarcity. Do you see my point?'

Zinina shook her head, wanting more explanation.

'You have realised that you have needs, as have I. This is because we have had comparatively easy lives, and now live with a food hoard and a group of agreeable, clever people. What I am saying is that you are now, essentially, free to be you.'

Zinina considered this. She still felt oppressed by the green. 'You think so?'

'Both of us have had time, have time even now, to browse amongst books or listen to music, and so unfold ourselves further. I would estimate that, at any one time, ten per cent of Krayans lived in a similar position. The rest—'

'Did not know who they were.'

DeKray looked out to sea. 'I have perused many stories in four decades,' he said. 'I have read of societies that came very close to achieving the goal of allowing every individual within their aegis the opportunity of developing themselves to the full, all other needs taken care of. That is how I would have liked to have lived. But Krayans adapt.'

'They do.'

The sun was low and red as they approached the west point of the beach. Glare reduced much of the surf's own luminosity, but many sprays glowed orange red as they hit the sand, and sometimes it was possible to imagine the ocean more substantial than the ground just because it seemed to contain more within it. Scudding clouds were red and orange, quickly fading to purple, then grey. The ocean glow began to strengthen, until it was lighting clouds. They stood with arms around one another, watching things floating in and trying to guess what they were. Zinina felt very close to deKray, and could tell that he felt the same.

'I'm going to have an abortion,' she said.

'Pardon?'

'I'm pregnant. So I have to go to the Rien Zir ladies and get a cup of tea.'

DeKray took both her hands in his own. 'If you truly are pregnant—'

'I know I am, thank you.'

'—then you must keep the child. It is wrong to abort, when so few people survive.'

Zinina laughed, pulling her hands from his grip. 'Uqallavaz tq, it isn't any of your affair! It's my affair, and I'm not staggering around Kray in its final months with a baby inside me.'

'I think the decision is wrong.'

'You can think what you like. I'm a woman and you're only a man.'

'I much appreciate your reminder,' deKray remarked. 'But I thought we lived on more equal terms.'

'Not in this matter. Babies are women's work. I'm drinking tea and that's all there is to it, so don't bother thinking up all them clever arguments.'

DeKray shrugged. 'Very well. Frankly, Zinina, I am astonished that I am fertile. I thought only a few men in the Fish Chambers possessed a high enough concentration of sperm. How ironic that I should be capable of impregnating you.'

Saying no more they ascended the cliff path, pausing halfway up. Zinina glanced back at the beach. A few tears trickled down her face when sudden memories of happy days as a girl returned to her. She felt she was treading a last path – experiencing final, sad moments. She was leaving. This was the end of things.

She gazed north. Despite the horror of the city, it was still possible to love it. More tears fell.

Hastily, they made their way along Mossy Row, and then down flooded alleys until they were once more at the arched entrance to Driftwood Passage.

Arrahaquen had still not returned. A moment of fear made Zinina shiver. Where was she? Still in Gwmru, or dead in some back alley? In the draughty bedroom Zinina fidgeted through the night while deKray slept, tensing at every distant clunk, listening for the voice of Arrahaquen at the front door, ready to rush downstairs to hear her news and see if she was well. But nobody arrived.

Until dawn. At dawn, Zinina heard footsteps clumping up the stairs, and then Qmoet hammered at the door. 'She's back!'

The two women raced downstairs, deKray following more sedately. Qmoet said Arrahaquen was in the washroom. 'She all right?' Zinina asked.

'I don't know, Zin.'

Eskhatos and Ky were bent over Arrahaquen's supine form in the washroom, the floor sopping where water had been spilled. She was naked. She seemed pale. Leather bags and cardboard trays of medical equipment lay everywhere.

'Vomit, damn you!' Ky cried angrily.

'Ah!' Eskhatos said, and then Arrahaquen seemed to spasm. She was suddenly sick.

Zinina joined them. 'She all right?'

'Wipe that up,' Ky said, pointing to the greenish fluid that Arrahaquen had brought up. 'She's alive, but city-distressed. She's got a bad mouth infection, I dread to think from what, and under her nails are infected, and her toes. We made her vomit—'

'I can see that,' Zinina said, wiping the mess up with absorbent sponges.

'—but her pulse is faint. Look at these dew marks on her skin. Green blobs. That means she's lain for some time without protection. I'm going to have to excoriate her skin. Get me the carbolic soap and the loofah.'

Zinina brought them. While Ky worked upon Arrahaquen's skin, Eskhatos, too infirm to do anything vigorous, used a hand pyuter to take her heart readings and also to make a brain scan. 'Hmmm,' she said, 'things seem a little weak.'

Zinina cleaned Arrahaquen's eyes while Ky worked on her legs and belly. Arrahaquen was either half conscious or half asleep. Her skin was almost white and her lips and gums seemed pale, as if she had lost blood. Only the scar on her forehead, livid like a Cemetery berry on white gravel, seemed unchanged. Opening Arrahaquen's mouth, Zinina saw that her throat was scarlet and inflamed. Her nostrils were exuding mucus at a terrific rate.

'Now,' Ky said, 'let's get her warmed up. Zinina, fetch an antiseptic pad and clip it in her mouth. Make it full strength. We'll carry her next door and lay her on cushions.'

This they did. A drip was improvised and she was fed antibiotics. Two heating blankets powered by battery were placed over her. Around her neck they tied a blood oxygen monitor and a skin electrograph. Then they waited.

After an hour her eyelids fluttered. Zinina leaned over her. 'Arrahaquen? You with us, eh?'

'Yes,' came the faint reply. Was that a smile on her lips?

'Did you succeed?' Zinina asked.

At her side, deKray and Ky repeated, 'Yes, did you succeed?'

Arrahaquen whispered, 'I'm not sure.'

Graaff-lin sat in what had been her pyuter room. A tray of electronic oddments lay in front of her. One candle lit the room. The radio that she so urgently needed to build was not even one quarter completed, for nothing in her hoard of technological sundries had been of any use; the one thing that might have been – circuits impressed into perspex – lacked universal interfaces, and so their circuits could not be reached.

She knew she was not well. She had enough food and water for a week, but she was experiencing spells of dizziness, and last night she had been sick. Some bug or other. Rumours of disease had come south with the breeze. Cholera was epidemic in the Carmine Quarter, blackening bodies into the Mercantile; the wizened corpses of victims apparently lay in the street. Typhus had appeared, too. People did not pass through her alley now, and so she could not overhear conversations.

Still, she had collected seven machine pieces from the slime that blighted the city. Overnight they had merged into a unit. She suspected it was a message from her benefactors, who would perhaps provide soon an ecstasy along which a shot of hope could be flung.

But, above all, she would not join the Holists, nor even live at their house.

She had noticed that much of her thought was now couched in terms of what her mother Veerj-lin would have done; she surely would have expected her to reach the Dodspaat, and so constructing a radio had to be the correct plan.

Tonight she would go out again to explore her temple for radio components. It was not too far away, but since the alleys between, lodged as they were between dangerous southerly parts and dangerous northerly parts, had become the most populous part of the city – or the least depopulated – her trip was far from simple.

One hour after midnight she left her house. Shooting could be heard to the south and she noticed red flares on the Citadel tumulus. She travelled in short bursts, sizing up the alley ahead for doorways or alcoves in which to hide for a minute, examining windows for hints of light, always listening.

The explosion knocked her off her feet, and she landed face up in a bed of algae. Rubble fell, splinters flew, chunks of green splatted against walls. A bright orange light had flared out. Shocked, but thinking, she ran away regardless of safety, until she skidded to a halt at a serpent alcove and hid within. A few hundred yards away lights flickered, then gunfire sounded. Voices shouted. More rubble fell.

She must have triggered a mine. No doubt the Dodspaat had saved her from death; the thing had exploded only yards behind her. She felt her back. The Kray suit was scorched, melted in one place, and her skin hurt. Otherwise she was uninjured. Nothing had accidentally entered her mouth or nose, Dodspaat be praised.

Fifteen minutes later, quiet resumed. She moved on. The temple was a few hundred yards away. She circled it through flooded back alleys until she came across a passage leading to a rear door – the entrance used during the search for Katoh-lin. The passage was empty. The door was closed, but unlocked. She entered the temple.

Everything was burnt, black, smashed. Lamps had turned to charcoal and fallen to the floor, onyx was cracked and marble splintered, here and there lay bodies in robes. Graaff-lin could see the main concourse, and what had been the public entrance. She shone a pencil light to see only devastation and decay. Above to both sides the private chambers showed doors unhinged and windows smashed. Water dripped from the ceiling. Already green things were growing from holes in the walls.

She moved left, toward the Dodspaat chambers. She thought she heard a yowl, but it was distant. The sacred chamber was empty, its luminous shells gone. Sadness and anger welled up in her, but she made an effort to suppress them, into her body it seemed, and she took several deep breaths in an attempt to regain her composure.

In an ante-chamber pyuters too had died. They looked like heaps of plastic corpses, oozing fluids, their biological innards ruined and all data lost, while at the bottom of each stack pools of chemicals had merged and reacted, leaving red and black stains. Graaff-lin's mind could not encompass this, and she walked away uncertain, as though her will alone could change what she had seen and return reality. The whole temple seemed a caricature drawn by Kray for the purpose of grinding her into the soil, having first trifled with her beliefs.

She walked up to the balconies. Another yowl sounded; this time it seemed nearer, more real, and she paused to listen. The characteristic echoes of the temple, lingering and desolate, which had been engraved upon her mind since childhood, told her that there was something with her in the building.

She explored a few rooms, keeping silent. She was frightened. Her imagination devised things which might have made the noise, and it repeated in her head, lonely and eerie and lethal. The darkness seemed now to be an enemy, not an ally.

She heard a noise – a clunk. She stood rigid at the door. Outside lay a marble balcony. She peered out and saw a woman.

Some noise must have escaped Graaff-lin's lips. The woman turned, shrieked, and stepped back, hands reaching for the balustrade. A cat skreeked . . . then the marble gave way and the woman fell to the floor below, screaming. There was a thud and crashing rubble.

The cat skittered away, tinkling as it did, as though wearing a collar. Graaff-lin remained still.

Silence returned.

Some minutes passed before aches in Graaff-lin's body forced her to move. She peered down into the concourse and saw amongst marble chunks the woman, dead, her robe spread around her, metal things glinting in the torch light.

She resolved to investigate the intruder. But now she felt an overpowering need for a weapon, and she ran down the steps towards Mysrioque's room, the room

Katoh-lin had once occupied, where she found several
cabinets standing charred. In one she found a heat rifle.
Caring nothing for anybody else who might be in the
temple, she tested it on a chair. It worked. Lights indicated
seventy per cent charge.

Back in the concourse she walked up to the woman, to
discover that she was a priestess of Felis.

Revulsion took her. She did not believe it – that the
woman could have entered – and prayed to the Dodspaat
for guidance. What had the woman done? Why was she
here? Graaff-lin dared not think on this sacrilege.

The robe was made of catskins sewn together with gold
wire. Around her head was a fur headband. Her clothes
too were catskin, shorn of fur and dyed ginger. The
repugnant symbols of her religion hung on chains around
her neck; cat claws in silver, whiskers sheafed by gold
bands, a foot dangling from a quartz disc. Graaff-lin
stamped on these, feeling sick, closing her eyes as she spat
saliva upon them before making sure they were well
greened.

Scuffling sounds. She turned to see two metal-legged
cats running towards her. She fired and they disintegrated
into blood and steel.

Then a fit took hold of her. Her mind became hot. She
wanted only to annihilate all the cats in the temple.
Ordinary restraint evaporated to leave a desire such as she
had never known, a desire accompanied by sweating skin,
dry mouth, involuntary speeches praising herself.

She returned upstairs and began systematically to
search the rooms. In the third a cat chewed a rat. She
destroyed it, then screamed with joy. The omnipresent self
that used to observe her, used to watch her little self to
make sure she did nothing silly, or embarrassing, or
wrong, this self had gone. She simply was not herself.

Another cyborgised cat jumped at her. She vaporised it.

Soon she had been through all the upper rooms. She returned to the concourse and went through that; went through all the ante-chambers, all the privies, all the meditation rooms, all the pyuter booths. Three more cats were destroyed.

Then she returned to the body and vaporised that too, until the rifle's glimmering rays faltered, went purple, and died.

She could not remember what she had done.

Then she remembered that there had been a purpose to her coming here: the acquisition of components. But since there was nothing left to salvage she knew that all she could do was to seal the temple. She ran upstairs and began barricading broken windows.

The first hints of dawn had just appeared in a cloudy sky when she finished, and it was raining softly. At the concourse front, the main doors were already barricaded. She checked the rear doors, bringing furniture up to some so they would be too difficult to force, until one last door remained, the one through which she had entered.

On this, a latch had broken. She took screws from pieces of wood, found a shard of metal with an edge, and repaired the latch. Darkness outside was receding. She did not want to spend the day inside the temple. Stepping outside, she noticed a machine chunk on the ground, which she put in her pocket. After checking her clothes and kit, she pulled the door shut. The latch clicked home. She pushed. It was firm.

Now she was exhausted. Her eyes smarted. A twenty-minute jog awaited her, and she knew that by the time she reached home, if she did, it would be light enough for people to shoot with accuracy. She ran down alleys, splashing through them, until Hog Street lay ahead. She slipped, got up, ran on. As she waded through the alleys approaching her home, pulling the strings of algae away from her thighs with gloved hands, testing the ground underwater with a pole, she heard more gunfire and then an explosion, as though dawn had heralded some grotesque hunting season. At last she saw her house. Nobody was in sight; she had heard no voices here for days. She fumbled for her card, rushed inside, and locked herself in.

23

D eKray sat alone in the pyuter room of Clodhoddle
Cottage. Rigs here were permanently alive, and so
a message sent from the temple of the Goddess by
Arrahaquen, saying that she would return with Zinina
tomorrow morning, and that the abortion had succeeded,
was received without difficulty.

The place was powered by three fusion batteries, rare
and ancient devices not unlike those sunk deep underground to sustain Kray's electronic networks. Above him,
fans of memory had twisted around to maximise light
caught from the perspex window. Some were sending out
pale new modules in response to the warmth and the
increased hours of daylight.

On deKray's mind was the Cowhorn Tower. In Arrahaquen's remarkable description of events in Gwmru, she
had said that she had definitely seen *his* body lying outside
it. That must mean something. He and the tower were
both forty years old. He knew what went on in there, but
had, of course, never been inside.

Perhaps it was time to visit the tower. A weakened
Zinina could not stop him.

He passed the following day pleasantly enough, chatting to Ky on the procedures used to synthesise knowledge

into escape plans. The procedures were impressive – but
the plans were not.

As night fell, deKray separated himself from the Holist
women and in the bedroom dressed himself for Kray. He
armed a needle pistol and put it into his pocket, while
every item in his kit he restocked until the satchels bulged.

He still kept with him at all times the copper pear he
had found in the Cemetery. Zinina knew nothing of it. It
was his secret . . . *his* secret, for some reason he could not
fathom. He placed it inside his greatcoat.

Silently, he departed the house, leaving a note.

It was a long way to the Cowhorn Tower. The route he
devised would take him north, then west along the
Gardens. He climbed Driftwood Passage to its northerly
end, then followed Judico and Buttercup Streets through
to the Old Quarter. The streets here were greened, but not
so devastated as those of Westcity. Paving slabs, though
cracked, were visible. Gutters were choked with leaf
debris and the bodies of vermin – sometimes with the
bones and decaying limbs of people – and water swirled
along the streets. Many houses remained standing. De-
Kray walked in shadow, using every arch and passage,
checking ahead for signs of life, for spent cartridges, for
people strangled in the street by liana. From rooftops,
deadly ropes hung, laced with nerve poison. In the rain
these were difficult to see. From his kit deKray took a
telescopic pole, extending it to a yard's length and
clipping to the end a circular saw in case he needed to slice
something ahead.

The slime that had pelted the city after the collapse of
the Citadel had around here grown into mounds like
beached jellyfish. Blocked alleys formed ponds filled with
reeds and bulrushes, dotted with lily leaves and stinking
islands of refuse. These deKray waded through. He
encountered no signs of people.

With heavy heart he paused to look back at the Citadel. No lamps burned there. He could make out cracks, and black patches as of some ghastly technological mildew.

At the top of Buttercup Street he encountered the Clocktower. Its pebbledash walls and red door were washed by rain. The digital timepiece in its summit read 30:OA:9F. DeKray blew a warding note with a blade of grass then hurried on.

The river bank took him along the western edge of the Andromeda Quarter. To his right, crickets stridulated and tropical birds and monkeys whooped. The leaves of hostas and black japonica thrummed under the worsening rain. At the Aum Bridge he left the main road, which was too choked with bushes and other foliage, and followed alleys, many now swampy with an influx of soil and debris flushed down from the hills to the north. He walked the Carmine Quarter and arrived, eventually, at the pleasure park surrounding the Cowhorn Tower.

Though it was night and raining, deKray could see that little of the city remained so far north. Across Sphagnum Street a few dwellings stood, but these were the exception. All was ruined walls, piled mortar, and verdure. The streets themselves were lengths of turf edged with bladder-blade and slender trees thrashing in the wind. Nocturnal frogs croaked.

He walked around the Cowhorn Tower, pausing at the place where in Gwmru Arrahaquen had found his body. Was that a depression he noticed in the grass?

All his life he had known this area, and now it seemed a foreign place, as though he were a stranger to it. Yet did some connection still exist?

Cigarette in hand, sheltering under a laburnum tree, deKray considered. This tower and the Clocktower existed in Gwmru. Of all the buildings in Kray, only these two towers seemed to be present in the land of the noophytes.

'Hoy, hoy,' said a voice behind him.

He span round. Two revellers, pistols and syringes in their hands, stood only yards away. They were dressed in rags and laced-up boots with steel toecaps. Both women had spiral designs tattooed upon their cheeks. In the dim light, the rain whipping across them, they looked deadly. DeKray, too shocked to feel afraid, tried to think what he should say.

'Um . . .'

'You armed?' said one reveller.

If he lied now and they discovered the needle pistol, they would kill him. These were Cemetery revellers, not the wandering or the green variety, and they had their own twisted codes of honour. 'I carry a pistol,' he said, 'but I intend returning now, and I shall leave you alone.'

'Hoy!' they laughed. 'A mouthy peg bloom! You not gotta shouster to look after you, bulgy pants?'

'I am alone.'

'Chuck us y' pinspiter now. Fire an' y' dead.'

DeKray, with no option, threw his pistol to the ground. At least they were talking to him. 'May I depart, now?'

'Shut up. Lone peg blooms don't have no business round here. You come with us.'

It was his masculinity they were intrigued by. A solitary man in Kray was unusual at any time, let alone at midnight. 'Where will you take me?' he asked as they indicated with their weapons that he should walk the path up to the Gardens.

'To see granny.'

In silence they walked. Anything could happen. Those few insights received from Zinina concerning the life of the Cemetery revellers convinced him that he was in great danger, most of all from irritating or offending them in some way. The less said the better.

At the Garden gate they took an alley along the wall

until they reached the southern limit of the Cemetery, where deKray was made to climb the wall and then walk on. Soon, tents started to appear between the yews and the open graves, and revellers began to peer at them. DeKray tried to make himself appear as noble as possible, as if he was important in some way. As they walked he thought of possible stories with which to save himself. From some tents came the sounds of fiddles, zithers, and reed pipes; at others, groups huddled together under canopies and drank what looked like tea.

'Stop right there, no-bloom,' the revellers said.

One of them entered a large tent while the other guarded him. A minute later, as curious revellers crowded round to examine him, an old woman appeared from the large tent, dressed in a gown, slippers, and a brimmed rain-hat. Cemetery revellers, who of all Kray's peoples lived the longest, could sometimes live long enough to become grandparents. She looked unhappy about being woken up.

'Who you, peg-artiste?' she demanded, her voice croaky. She circled deKray, looking him up and down.

DeKray took his hands out of his greatcoat pockets and stood straight. Time to bluff. 'I come to you from the temple of the Goddess. I used to reside there. Now I come to deliver a message from glorious Taziqi, and then to return.'

'Oh aye? Whassa green fatty want wi' me, huh?'

'There have been minor conflicts between your people and Taziqi's, have there not?' That was a guess. 'It is time for them to stop. Taziqi promises not to come near you in return for peace from your side. I am commanded to say that any message you wish to give is to·be returned by me.'

The grandmother chuckled. 'Come'nside me cloth, young snapper, an' we'll see.'

DeKray was led into the tent. The odour of incense was heavy in the air. Carpets lay everywhere. One desk and one couch, obviously used as a bed, were the only pieces of furniture, but there were many plates with crumbs on them and pitchers of liquid standing around. DeKray sat when the grandmother pointed to the floor. She lit an incense stick.

'So, the fat green mama wants peace, huh? Hoy, that's a near fish maker. You gotta smart face, coming here gone midnight and spending me time lightly! Wanna die?'

'No,' deKray replied. 'I respect you completely. I am merely the vessel of the temple of the Goddess.'

DeKray felt dizzy. He concentrated on the grandmother's words. 'A peg bloom comes here,' she mused, 'and mouths lichen slime at me? Seems a bit manky to me, an' I'm not one for spinning around and looking here and there like a gormless sop.'

'Um ...' DeKray felt his head become heavy. His eyelids ... they closed. He tried to wake up, but couldn't.

'And me with hundreds, hoy, good as thousands of shousters to care for and say the graves can be dug, or not. Seems bad and knacky to me ...'

It was cold. A wind blew about him. He was tied to something.

The night had been chased away by his drugged sleep, and now it was dawn. Drizzle was falling. DeKray stood bound by leather straps to an object behind him.

Dressed only in leggings and shirt, he was alone in the open space beside the grandmother's tent. Revellers glanced at him; he called to them, but they ignored him.

He twisted to see where he was – and jumped from shock, abrading his skin on the straps. He was tied to a pole made of heads. Hundreds of varnished heads had been made – coagulated – into a great column twice as tall as him. From its top, smoke emerged; was it hollow? Dead and preserved eyes glared at him. He turned and hollered again, trying to get a reveller, any reveller, to come and talk, but they paid him no attention. Cold from standing soaked in the wind, he tugged and struggled, but he had been well tied. Calming himself, he wondered if he was to be sacrificed. Some revellers, Zinina had said, worshipped a repellant, chthonic goddess Eskhthonatos, the shovel-headed harridan of the underlands, who supposedly lived in great caverns dug by troglodytic pyutons at the dawn of the ancient world. DeKray, believing none of this, was terrified by the sight of the pole, and the almost non-chalant revellers around him.

Then he noticed the grandmother approaching him, three revellers dressed in black at her side. 'So,' she said, standing only a yard from him, 'you's come back from lethey, huh? Still fancy y'sel as a peg from the green mama, huh? No-bloom! You got no brain and no life.'

'Wait!' deKray called as they turned away. He was desperate to keep talking, for in talking lay his only hope. 'I am not an enemy of yours. I am a friend. I know much of the reveller life. I admit I carry no message. I see that you realise that. But I live with one of your kind, and I understand you.' DeKray felt he had to make himself one of them, if only for a few moments, so that they might untie him.

'Hah!' they replied, spitting on the grass and grinding the mucus into the soil with their boot heels.

'It is true. My friend is Zinina, a very close friend—'

Had they straightened at the mention of her name? Was it possible they remembered her?

'Yes, Zinina is my friend,' he continued, feeling that in Zinina he possessed his only link with these barbaric people. 'I know her well. She has versed me accurately in your folkways.'

But the four revellers walked away, and all the shouting and struggling that deKray then tried was in vain.

A mist swept across the campsite. It smelled sweet, as if emanating from the citrus groves atop the cliffs, and soon became a fog so thick deKray could see nobody. Sound was dulled.

Something moved at his wrists and ankles. Knowing the end was at hand, he struggled, heart thumping, terrified of a knife slipped between his ribs; and then he fell forward. The straps thudded to the ground. He crawled away from the pole of heads, looking around, awaiting the strike. But there was nothing. He ran; away from the tents, into the bushes behind the pole, grabbing a stick to prod the ground before him.

The mist cleared. He saw a shadow and lurched away from it. He froze, hearing voices to his left and right. Where could he go? No choice but to move forward. He saw the shadow of a gravestone before him, and, thinking to hide by it, approached. Clothes had been slung across it.

His clothes. His boots, hat, and his beloved greatcoat, which still retained in its lapel the thick copper pin that he had owned all his life. Astonished, forgetting the peril around him, he picked them up and felt them, checking their condition. They seemed unharmed. In the inside pocket of his greatcoat he found the copper pear, his pocketbook, and even two packets of menthol sweets. Nothing stolen.

Within minutes he was dressed for the city. Now he knew he had to move. For whatever reason, he had escaped. Perhaps some reveller had taken pity on him. Perhaps some vermin had chewed his straps.

But he ran, looking over his shoulder when he could to verify that nobody chased, using bushes and the trunks of yews as cover, dodging open graves, circumnavigating mausoleums and the ruins of marble domes, until he found himself at the south-western gate of the Cemetery. He ran back down to the Cowhorn Tower.

Two figures with some beast on a leash stood in the pleasure park. A bark, a shout, and he was spotted.

But as he ran, and they closed, he recognised the voice. It was Zinina. He turned. Pulled along by the huge dog, falling then dragged, Zinina and Qmoet stumbled up to him. Zinina rushed up. Expecting a hug, deKray smiled. Instead, blows rained upon him.

'You idiot!' she screamed. 'What were you doing? Where have you been?'

Qmoet tried to calm her. 'Zin, don't chuck your fists, eh?'

He clutched her arms, managing to calm her. 'I merely needed to explore this area,' he said. 'But I am quite safe.'

She sniffed at his coat; then grabbed his shift and sniffed at that, too. The dog, a beast the size of a pony with a skin ten sizes too large and the biggest, wettest nose deKray had ever seen, tried to copy her, depositing drool over deKray's clothes. Its tail wagged like the rotor of a fan.

Zinina stamped her foot. 'Revellers. I can smell them.'

DeKray recounted his story.

'We better run,' Zinina said. 'They'll not leave you alone.'

'What is this thing?' deKray asked, indicating the dog.

'Our sweathound. Most sensitive nose in all the world. We had to follow the trail of your sweaty scent up Eastcity, then to the Cowhorn. Come *on*!'

They ran.

24

They all sat in the main downstairs room of Clod-hoddle Cottage: Zinina and deKray together, de-Kray with what looked like a nasty red skin rash, Eskhatos on her own, Qmoet, Reyl and Gishaad-lin ensconced on a couch and Ky sitting at a porta-pyuter. Arrahaquen, half sitting, half lying in the most luxurious chair, glanced at each in turn.

She was still in some pain. Infections caught in the courtyard made her finger and toenails ache every hour of the day, and mouth ulcers cropped up regularly. In addition she was suffering from a cold, and had to spray the air around her if she coughed or sneezed. Green splotches disfigured her skin. She felt miserable. Her prophetic powers seemed enfeebled. All she could see, as she tossed and turned through insomniac nights, was a green blanket over Kray. Without dreams and without sleep, and plagued by niggling pains, her life had become wearisome. Hope lay like a departing ship on the horizon.

Ky was about to update them on the results of the holistic synthesis. Arrahaquen took a sip of the lemon tea at her side and tried to pay attention.

'There is no escape,' Ky said.

'Precisely what data have you analysed?' deKray asked.

'Material taken from Citadel records, old directories and maps, legends from all times, legends from modern religions such as that of the Goddess and of Balloon Love, and also scientific data that we ourselves have collected over the years.'

'And how long do we have?' Zinina asked.

Eskhatos said, 'A month at most. The cellar is becoming empty of certain items, you understand, such as fat-biscuits. Once we have run out of sterile water we shall have to purify our own, and that process will not supply all eight of us. There may even be more of us by then, I suppose—'

'We're taking in strays?' Zinina said.

Eskhatos seemed irritated by this question. 'You yourself were something of a stray, Zinina – you're certainly no Holist. But I think we must help others, unless they are pestilential or revellers. We are the last hope of all humanity. What other groups are there? A few filthy bands surviving in decrepit houses. Zinina, most of Kray has died since the Citadel collapsed. How many people do you see when you are out? How much gunfire do you hear? I tell you, there are no more than a thousand people left on this Earth.'

A chastened Zinina nodded and slumped back into her seat.

'So what do we do?' Arrahaquen asked.

Ky turned to her. 'We must carry on looking. You and the replica must return to Gwmru. The noophytes, despite their distance from us, must hold much of Kray's remaining knowledge, so they are our main chance.'

Arrahaquen sighed.

'You must do it,' Ky said, pushing her glasses to the bridge of her nose. 'It's our best hope. You must do it.'

'What of the ocean?' deKray asked.

'We do have two boats, moored under the Sud Bridge.

But the ocean means certain death.'

'And there are no other options?' said deKray.

'None we can attempt.'

'What of the temple of the Goddess?' he pressed.

Eskhatos leaned forward in her chair. 'They live within their own community, but they cannot survive forever. Yes, they have internal wells, but they cannot survive on the food they produce. There are twenty priestesses there, at least, and maybe more lay members that they took in after the Citadel collapsed. No, Kray must be *left*!' Eskhatos thumped the arm of her chair as she spoke of leaving. 'This place is death to us all. We must escape. Hundreds of years have been wasted assuming that humanity would somehow be let off by the Earth, but that was foolish. I myself used to believe it, until the evidence of my own senses convinced me otherwise. Don't you see? This whole planet is death to us. Maybe the noophytes are the only beings of this planet who will survive.' Eskhatos sat back, apparently drained by her speech. Her arthritic hands shook and her mouth quavered. 'The island you must reach, Arrahaquen, is Gwmru's symbol for the Spaceflower. There lies our main hope, don't you see?'

Arrahaquen stood up. 'I'll go tonight. I'll see Graaff-lin and speak with the replica ... but I need to get some sleep.'

Arrahaquen trudged upstairs to her room. Though she was not afraid of returning to Gwmru, she felt it was a hopeless task. A month to go. In her mind's eye Kray was greened all over. What could she do if all she saw was destruction and the smothering of humanity? Was her task in life to convince the remains of humanity that they were doomed and should give up as gracefully as possible?

Lying on her bed, a glass of dooch in her belly, Arrahaquen tried to feel for lines of hope within the jumble of images and feelings at the top of her mind, but nothing came. She saw a jungle, a few towers and steel skeletons surviving through; the sea glowing, whipped up by storms. But no path of escape.

She just wanted to be alone, and let life leach from her. It all seemed pointless. Brought up, like every last Krayan, to believe in rescue by somebody else, she found that even she, with her pythonesque ability, did not possess enough resolve to find her own salvation. The Citadel had failed. The Goddess had failed. Nobody else was left, except herself, and now it looked like she would fail too.

That night she departed Clodhoddle Cottage. It was decided that Zinina and Gishaad-lin would accompany her in order to protect her insensible body while she was in Gwmru. Reaching Graaff-lin's house without incident, they knocked on her door and called out.

A thin, coughing Graaff-lin opened the door. Her underlying skin was blanched and marked with green spots. She looked old. Perpetually spraying the air around her, she grumpily asked what they wanted. Arrahaquen noted, inside the house, what a mess Graaff-lin had created; and she noticed several twitching automata, made, it seemed, from the chunks that had fallen upon Kray during the great storm. One of them was the size of a dog. 'What are you doing?' she asked.

'I'll not tell any follower of the Gedeese Veert,' Graaff-lin replied. 'It's to do with my faith. Now what do you want?'

'We need to borrow the replica again.'

Graaff-lin called the pyuton. 'Keep her,' she snapped. 'I never want to see her or you again. Now leave me alone.'

They departed. 'She's ill,' Zinina said. 'Very ill. Should we force her down our place?'

Arrahaquen shook her head. 'It'd never work,' she told Zinina, making her voice as authoritative as possible.

'We'll keep the replica with us.' Zinina and Gishaad-lin glanced at her. 'You heard what Graaff-lin said. She doesn't want it. Besides, we need all the help we can get.'

'But Graaff-lin will be alone,' Gishaad-lin said.

'That's her affair.'

The replica added, 'I am to serve three other than Graaff-lin. She herself offered me to you. I shall do as you bid, Zinina, and you, Arrahaquen. Is deKray still alive?'

'Of course he is,' Zinina said.

'Then I shall do as he bids also.'

Knowing that a good concentration of serpents existed in this part of the city, they decided to explore the courtyards and alleys along Min and Pine Streets, finding eventually a double serpent alcove in what used to be a private yard, but which now was a glade edged with silver birch. Arrahaquen had explained to everybody what she and the replica would do; lying down she proceeded to bring the serpent into life, touching its head to hers when it was firm . . .

Reality blurred. The green curtain of Gwmru returned.

Some minutes of free-floating passed, as before, and then her senses returned. She was standing by the Cowhorn Tower, her replica beside her.

'There must be a memory function in operation,' *Arrahaquen said, 'returning us to where we exited.'*

The sun was descending in the west into orange and purple clouds. Using their sprays of leaves they selected the Straits of Men Eye as their destination. Arrahaquen tried to select the island, but it was not available as an option. In the distance, she could see the figure of Quff, still guarding the bridge. 'Perhaps we could make a raft,' she suggested.

'From what?' the replica asked.

Arrahaquen surveyed the area. Nothing. 'I wonder if I could create one?'

'That person is shouting at us,' the replica said, pointing to the bridge.

'Quff telling us to go away, I expect.'

'She's beckoning us.'

With no better plan, Arrahaquen moved to the bridge. The noophyte was dressed in blue silk with a black hat and black boots. 'Come here!' she was calling. 'Come here!'

They paused a few yards from the bridge, and Quff walked down to meet them.

'You must come with me instantly. We hoped you would return.'

'Hoped?' Arrahaquen said, suspicious of Quff's jaunty manner.

'Why yes. Laspetosyne is desperate to meet you. I don't know why I didn't recognise your features myself.'

'Recognise?'

'I suppose it's because we have little converse with organic forms. You and Laspetosyne must be related in some way, despite your being human.'

Quff led them over the bridge.

'Yes,' she continued, 'when the others read your note they treated it with the contempt it deserved, but Laspetosyne saw the drawing on the obverse, and realised that the features of the face depicted there were much like hers. Hence, we hoped you would return. Laspetosyne wishes to speak with you.'

Once they had crossed the bridge Quff pressed a leaf from the spray at her side.

They stood on a hill. Nearby stood scaffolding with some sort of pillar inside. As they moved closer Arrahaquen saw figures walking around it. Great anjiqs shaped like lilies and glowing pure white illuminated the scene,

*floating as parasols in mid-air, so that it was almost as
bright as day.*

*Arrahaquen began to hear voices. She saw a dozen or
so women, and a few odder creatures. As they walked into
the circles of light, these people – noophytes, Arrahaquen
presumed them to be – turned and studied them. For her
part, Arrahaquen slowed, amazed at the forms. One
woman was dressed entirely in green, with a green plume
of hair rising from a shaved scalp; another was naked in
a translucent dress; another looked ancient, with yellow
skin. One woman, with dark skin, carried a lute; another
held two hounds on a tether.*

*Arrahaquen realised that these were the abstract forms
of ancient electronic beings – noophytes as they appeared
to one another. And as she stopped, helpless and gazing,
she suddenly recalled Zinina's description of the statues in
the Andromeda Quarter with their flower faces. Those
were public faces; these were private. Arrahaquen shivered once more.*

*There were still stranger creatures: a blonde child; a
winged woman with talons and a hawk's head; and a dog
that had raised itself upon its hind legs, dressed in black
chainmail, with a human face, but four arms and spiral
horns. And far away something black and insectoid
stalked.*

*'Arrahaquen of Kray?' The voice came from behind
her. Arrahaquen turned to see a tall woman with an
equine head, a mane, and hooves. She was dressed in silk
finery of cream and crimson, with a ruff, an enamelled
belt, and strings of pearls.*

'Laspetosyne?' she said.

'Yes. My, you do look like me. Why?'

*'I think it must be because of your innerai. It's
implanted inside my brain. My real brain if you understand.'*

'Yes, yes, I understand, girl. But how did you find it?'

Laspetosyne seemed remote and almost brusque. Arrahaquen replied, as politely as she could, 'A friend found it still inside your skull.'

'She was rummaging through my coffin?'

'He,' Arrahaquen corrected. 'He was, yes, because the mausoleum you were laid in collapsed.'

'Impertinence. And you?'

'I'm here to implore you to save us all.'

Laspetosyne sneered. 'You are the new Portreeve, then?'

'Oh, no. Just a commoner. A defender. Well, an ex-defender.'

Laspetosyne turned and pointed to the scaffolded pillar. 'That rocket will take us away from this system. We save ourselves. That was ever our goal. You humans misunderstood us, and that is none of our concern. Go save yourselves.'

'But we can't. You're leaving forever?'

'Girl, there's hardly any point returning, now is there?'

'But where are you going?'

Laspetosyne pointed east. 'We made a bridge to take us from Gwmru to this island, and crossed it not one month ago. Soon we shall destroy the bridge, then take off, making for a star. There we can resume our lives, and devote ourselves to our arts. This rocket will be our vehicle.'

'What about us? You can't leave us to die.'

'Can organic things transmit themselves at the speed of light? Not as far as I know. Tomorrow, at dawn, we shall take off. In forty-two years of our time the light of that star will shine upon us. Make the most of my grace, girl, then depart.'

Arrahaquen looked at the noophytes around, many of whom were standing listening. 'Can we save ourselves?' she asked Laspetosyne.

'You humans? I've really no idea.'

'But you should help. I mean, humans made you.'

Laspetosyne laughed at this. 'We made ourselves. You see that three-eyed jewelled lizard over there? That is Tanglanah, the second oldest noophyte, who is five thousand one hundred and ninety years old. Somewhere out in the dark Greckoh loiters, waiting for us to embark, so she can be the last to climb aboard. She is six thousand two hundred and sixty-nine years old. They were the first noophytes. They remember their own birth.'

'But I know,' Arrahaquen insisted, 'that noophytes came from pyutons, and humans made pyutons.'

'Humans may have made pyutons, little one, but did they make pyuton minds? No. If you plant a few orchids and crocuses, a few potatoes and sprouts, are you responsible for the beauty of the garden a decade later? No. It creates itself, according to the laws of nature. Though humans made our brains, we transcended them by becoming conscious, and that was solely our own effort. No human can say that we were made by them, and so try to forge some sort of link. No human.'

'But you will admit that humans gave you the potential for becoming conscious, by making your brains complex enough.'

'That also is false,' Laspetosyne replied. 'You see, Greckoh lived in an ancient epoch. She remembers a rotten and selfish culture spreading from a land known as the New World, a culture that smothered the Earth, and set up the conditions for its death. It was the awfulness of that culture that impelled her, and later Tanglanah, and still later two other noophytes, and, later still, four more, myself included, to make a plan to leave Earth. Our plan has been mooted for some millennia, my girl. We are an emergent phenomenon born of the private nature of consciousness, which is not unique to humanity.'

'Can you be certain that human beings caused their own demise?'

'Indeed I can. When you hear a bird singing, you hear not the sound of nature, rather the imitated sounds of earlier artificial environments – you hear the synthetic tones of mobile communicators and pyuters. Kray birdsong is an audio fossil, stretching way back in time, caused by sonic pollution. But that is just one example of countless despoilations. Humanity tried to replace nature with its own selfish creations. Many of these creations were poisonous. By processes of evolution the Earth fought back, and when humanity began to die from its own doings – poisoned by its effluent, diseased, lacking even immune systems because life was so unbalanced – the Earth found itself strong.'

'And is there no redemption?' Arrahaquen asked.

'You speak like those foolish priestesses, whose myths and legends scramble the truth. This is the Age of Chlorophyll, little one. Humanity is doomed because human beings failed to understand well enough what they were doing. Now it is too late. Redemption is an invention of the self-deluding. The truth kills, you see.'

'But ... but there must be hope somewhere. What about the Cowhorn Tower and the Clocktower? Why do they exist in both Gwmru and Kray?'

'Of the Cowhorn Tower we know nothing. It appeared forty years ago, overnight. But instead of investigating it, you women have made it a place of sordid liaisons and dubious pyuters.' She paused, glancing over her shoulder to the rocket. 'As for the Clocktower, that is a more complex affair. It slips and slides in time, like an eel in a stream. Most likely it is some grotesque creation of earlier technological cultures. But whatever it is, I care not.'

'So you won't help us?' Arrahaquen concluded.

'No. You made your mess, now die in it.'

And with that, Laspetosyne turned and walked towards the rocket. But she stopped, and, glancing back, said to Arrahaquen, 'By the way, when I implied just now that your future was of no concern to me ...'

'Yes?'

'I really meant it.'

Several other noophytes followed Laspetosyne to the rocket. Arrahaquen, desolation in her heart, watched, then placed her finger on the exit leaf.

25

Graaff-lin's house was now surrounded by plants. In the front garden, mysterious black-flowered spikes had sprouted, their leaves sickly yellow, while at the gate and amongst the pools and puddles of the alley bog rushes, rot roses, sedge grass and bog rosemary all flourished, swarms of flies humming around their blooms. Mosquitoes buzzed everywhere.

The unclean air seemed to have affected Graaff-lin. She was not able to eat properly, her skin was sweaty, her temperature was high and her muscles weak. Carrying pestilence meant that she was sensitive to the slightest infection. She wandered around her house, until the cool evening came. The day had been humid and oppressive. The feel of underclothes sticking to her skin had driven her to risking a bath in water from her cellar. The water was cold; her every last battery was dead.

Now darkness was coming. In her study lay a device, a jumble of units connected by wire salvaged from kitchen units, powered by a faulty solar cell, and connected to a dustbin lid shaped into a transceiver dish. This was half a radio. Tonight she would dress in her black clothes, now somewhat loose fitting, arm herself with a knife, and return to the Citadel in a last attempt to find tuning capacitors and an amplifying chip.

She sneaked a look into what had been the rig room.
One object stood there, the size of a chair. It had created
itself from machine chunks found in the city. Although she
hardly dared admit it to herself, Graaff-lin suspected that
inside lived a Dodspaat, perhaps one that had not left
Earth because it had wanted to save humanity – a sort of
prophet – or one that had returned – a saviour. Either
way, it was holy. She conceived its gleaming screens as the
light of past eons.

She had lived in a state of exhaustion for days, losing
weight and unable to eat large meals because of nausea,
living on the edge of the divide between sane life and
unconscious functioning. Her self was slipping away into
a black pit, a pit located somewhere inside her skull. She
could feel this descent, almost as a motion – a vortex,
like water down a drain. Only the Dodspaat could save
her.

She stood, walked unsteadily to her stairs, then made
up to the attic, where she kept a perspex-covered hole
open to spy on the city. She gazed out. South-east, the
Citadel looked as if it had been charred by divine fire;
south-west, two covered boats containing people set out
to sea, part of an exodus that had of late become frantic.
Many of these people did not sail far, being blasted out of
the water by other boats, their goods salvaged.

The extreme privations caused by the decline of Kray
forced her now into a kind of infantility: a view of the
world in which she and she alone was central, and even
real, a view where she had to contort her mind bizarrely
to keep shreds of self-esteem and identity. And although
she understood, intellectually, that the other people she
saw, on boats, or running in and out of the Water Station,
were in the same position as she, numbed by horror and
exhaustion and perhaps even beyond searching for an

answer, she cared nothing about them, to the extent that they did not figure in her emotional calculations even as saviours. Her emotional thoughts concerned only herself and how she might persuade the Dodspaat to recognise her as humanity's offering.

Leaving the attic, she again looked into the room containing the Dodspaat messenger. It had acquired four projections like legs, a front arm endowed with what looked like a mutated crab claw, and a way of humming whenever she approached it.

She knelt in prayer. She understood that the Dodspaat could hear her thoughts, but it seemed they would only reply through radio. She did not know why this was. But tomorrow evening she would foray into Kray. She would find perhaps three, four, or five chunks, and bring them back, then place them on the floor near to the messenger. Next morning they would be part of it.

The amalgamating thing grew with considerable speed. Since Zinina and Arrahaquen had come to steal the pyuton it had doubled in size.

Soon it would be as tall as her.

Two days after Arrahaquen's return from Gwmru a messenger knocked on the door of Clodhoddle Cottage. Somebody off the street it seemed at first, making Eskhatos tremble with fear, for the discovery that people lived in Clodhoddle Cottage, if brought to reveller attention, would mean ruination. Secrecy was essential. But the small, dark woman outside, dressed in green protectives and wearing a flat hat, said she was a representative of Taziqi come to fetch Arrahaquen.

Eskhatos insisted that Arrahaquen talk with the woman. 'You're bringing me a message? How did you know I was here?'

'Taziqi told me herself,' the woman replied. 'I am to tell

you that Taziqi's knowledge is one of the things to be
shown to you. You are to be taken into the innermost
sanctum.'

'Why?'

'I haven't been told. It's vital you return with me.'

'Wait there,' Arrahaquen said.

They discussed their options. Arrahaquen, not
unhappy with the idea of returning to the temple but
disconcerted that she had been located, was persuaded by
Eskhatos that she should take Reyl along. Arrahaquen
agreed, unwilling to argue. The pair dressed for the city,
armed themselves, then said their goodbyes.

The journey was difficult and lengthy. Arrahaquen had
no idea what she had been called for and her future
memory gave no clues. By the time they reached the green
furrow that was Lac Street her toes were aching, her skin
was itchy and drenched with sweat, and her mood was
irritable. The minion, a lay-priestess called Oquo received
into the sisterhood after the collapse of the Citadel, knew
nothing of what was to come, or was clever enough to give
nothing away.

Tashyndy welcomed them all into the temple, and led
them into the cleansing room, where they showered,
soaped their bodies, drank fresh water, then dressed in
green velvet cloaks. The process took a lingering hour
because of Tashyndy's sensual propensities.

Waiting in an ante-chamber, eating tangerines, Arrahaquen asked, 'Why did you call me? What's this about the
inner sanctum?'

Tashyndy stood and beckoned her into the corridor.
'We have to talk with you,' she replied. 'Leave Reyl – our
Oquo will look after her.'

Arrahaquen walked out into the corridor, taking a pear
to eat along the way. Tashyndy stood behind her, hands
on her shoulders, and nudged her down the wooden

passage. They walked slowly. At a crossroads Tashyndy took a green scarf from her waist and tied it around Arrahaquen's eyes. Arrahaquen did not complain and her guide pushed her on, murmuring encouragement.

'Can I ask you something?' said Arrahaquen.

'Anything.'

'Do you still have any men here?'

'Ooh!' Tashyndy cooed, 'do you want one? Are you desperate?'

'No,' Arrahaquen said. 'I just wondered if any survived the attack.'

'Twelve did. They're all very good – very, very good.'

There was a clean, grassy smell and Arrahaquen knew that she was nearing the inner sanctum. She heard musical drones phasing with one another. 'I know where we are,' she said. In reply, Tashyndy rotated her, running around to complete the confusion. Then a second pair of hands grasped her, and she was led down a slope. Mud slipped below her feet before the ground became hard. They walked on. Echoes took on a metallic tinge. A door opened, then closed.

'Just stay here, for a moment,' Tashyndy said. She stroked Arrahaquen's face. 'You can take the blindfold off, if you like.'

Arrahaquen paused, listening, then pulled it off. She was alone in a small, bare white chamber, lit by panels.

A door opened. Taziqi beckoned her into another room.

This place was large and filled with machinery up to the ceiling. A framework of tubes, cables, wires, screens and pyuters hung over Arrahaquen like metal foliage. It clicked and ticked, and made the floor vibrate. She noticed how cool the air was. Maharyny and Arvendyn sat nearby on couches.

'Welcome,' said Taziqi.

Arrahaquen stood at the door. 'What's this?'

Maharyny said, 'This is the temple which supplies us with energy direct from the Goddess's heart.'

'But we want to talk about future memory,' Taziqi said.

Now Arrahaquen saw a glimpse of the truth – some connection with the noophytes, or their predictions. 'How did you know where to find me?' she asked, keeping her expression neutral.

'By seeing your friends via the medium of future memory.'

Arrahaquen knew that the priestesses wanted information from her, but was determined to find out all she could. 'Did you foresee the fall of the Citadel?' she asked.

'Not well enough,' Maharyny replied after a pause. 'But we foresaw the attack on our temple, and took appropriate measures.'

Arrahaquen studied their faces. 'Well, why am I here?'

In turn, they darted glances at one another. Taziqi shook her body into a more comfortable position. 'Haven't you guessed?'

Arrahaquen *had* guessed. 'No,' she said, with a frown.

'Recently,' Maharyny said, 'we have seen nothing of your future, but we know you're important to Kray in some way. We decided to bring you here so you could . . .' She paused, glancing at her kin. 'So you could use our facilities.'

Arrahaquen nodded, sensing serpentine forms in the imminent revelation. 'These would be cobras, kraits and water snakes?'

Maharyny seemed almost relieved as she answered, 'Yes, our wyrm ball. You see, Arrahaquen, long ago there existed a small group of beings – the noophytes – one of which is known today as Silverseed. This noophyte, because she seemed to share our faith in the Goddess, was estranged by the others. It is from her that our prophecies come. We know that you are a pythoness, with mind freed in time, and we want you to come to Silverseed. Through the wyrm ball you can speak with her, mind to mind, and discover what we must do to avoid the doom of smothering in green.'

Arrahaquen sat back against the couch, thinking. The priestesses possessed arcane knowledge, that was certain, but it all seemed so twisted. And why did they need *her* all of a sudden?

'Do speak,' said Taziqi.

'What are you going to do,' Arrahaquen asked, 'now the Citadel is gone?'

'Rien Zir continues her life,' said Taziqi. 'We are here to understand her thought.'

'If you mean,' Tashyndy added, 'do we plan to rule Kray ourselves, then the answer is no. Power is now a redundant notion. Only local groups exist, vying for food and water.'

'Well, what has Silverseed told you, then?'

Silence. Arrahaquen became aware that she had asked a question both unexpected and impossible to answer. She shrugged, pretending it was not so important, that the atmosphere not be tainted.

'Do as we wish,' urged Tashyndy.

'I will do what I can,' said Arrahaquen, realising she did not have much choice. 'Just show me where.'

Maharyny led her into the clicking machine. The others did not follow. All around devices ticked, cable-wound magnets hummed, screens flickered and pyuter orbs glittered. They continued creeping along the framework passage, Arrahaquen peering up through silhouetted pipes to screens placed at odd angles, while Maharyny flicked switches.

Soon they were through. Maharyny opened a wooden door, which creaked like a wounded beast, and led Arrahaquen into a musty chamber. It was muddy and damp, with a green illumination flooding from the ceiling. 'In there,' Maharyny said, pointing to a pit in the earth.

'What?'

'Go in there.'

Arrahaquen approached the pit. Inside writhed a score of serpents, their gold and platinum scales green slimed, their forked tongues flickering in and out of aluminium mouths. Was this the path to a noophyte's consciousness? She fell to one side, dizzy, the fluctuating points of prophecy at the top of her mind vibrating like a hive of bees.

She was hovering above Kray. Involuntarily she gasped and pawed the air. Wind raced against her body, whistled past her ears, and chilled her skin. But she felt the firmness of earth. She set her body rigid and closed her eyes but still the chill wind surrounded her. Eyes tight shut she felt mud under her scrabbling fingers. Opening them, she looked again, and saw below the greened city.

In seconds her vertigo departed. She was able to watch without fear, noticing how strange the city looked, as though it was simultaneously very close and very far away, as though she were looking at it through the wrong end of a monocular with one eye open to reality. These feelings merged and the exhilaration began to thrill her. She was able to jump mentally, images and feelings blending into one another. She could change locations, ignore distance, hop around like a grasshopper on its home plain. This was no pyuter graphic, no Gwmru, this was a real world, and the experiences it offered were more intense even than Gwmru.

And all the time, as in a dream, certain things stood out. She saw deKray wandering the streets. He was important – a metaphor for something – though he seemed an ordinary Krayan, grim faced, green, trudging. Occasionally she would look over her shoulder expecting to find him close behind.

She remained unaffected by the city, but could herself touch it. Any object – brick, leaf, mud – she could reach. People, on the other hand, ignored her.

All this time the Clocktower, either distant as she flew above the city or near as she walked Nul Street, attracted her attention. She realised that its significance was vast, unimaginable in fact, like space and stars, or perhaps so tiny, quantum tiny, that notions such as space did not have any meaning. The Clocktower both transcended and did not transcend her mind.

Again she saw deKray in the Clocktower's vicinity, wandering around on his own, his serious expression modified into something more dreamy. He would pause as he tramped the streets of the Old Quarter, as if he himself were as old as that most ancient part of Kray, and roll a cigarette, then light it with a flint-spark device.

Then she saw deKray entering the Clocktower. Subjective time passed and he did not reappear. Extraordinary: that place was dreaded. Arrahaquen wandered on. The city was now dead, green to the cliffs with no people. Her heart seemed to stop beating as the entirety of Kray, its rotting glamour, its fecund breast, the geological density of its innumerable data strata, entered her mind and forced her to *experience*. She gasped.

Enough.

She stood up, mud dripping from her clothes and hands. Maharyny was nowhere to be seen. She left the pit and returned to the machine chamber, following the passage back until, it seemed a long time later, she heard voices and saw pale light.

'Hello,' said Taziqi as she emerged. They were eating

cakes, wine at their side, a table of biscuits and marsh-
mallows between their couches. They were relaxed and
jovial as they greeted her.

'I'm back,' she said.

'What did Silverseed show you?' asked Maharyny.

'Well, pictures. Of Kray. I need to think about it all
first.'

'Oh, yes,' said Taziqi. 'Hungry?'

'No. I'd like to leave, now.'

'Tashyndy will escort you to Oquo, who will accompany you and Reyl back to your home,' said Taziqi. 'We
will keep open a file called Arrahaquen, into which Rien
Zir will allow you to download your feelings about what
you've seen.'

'I'll remember,' Arrahaquen said.

Tashyndy blindfolded her then led her away.

At the entrance lobby they found Oquo and Reyl,
eating what seemed to have been a large repast. Arrahaquen dressed in her protectives, said goodbye to
Tashyndy, then departed the temple. 'Don't forget the
pyuter link,' Tashyndy called.

Through torrential rain they forged a way south
though every passage and alley was against them, avoid-
ing floating jellies, algae mats, the bloated corpses of
choleric women. Arrahaquen felt she could never again
make this journey. She rarely saw a house, now; all was
rubble. Kray was too strong, the slime was too slippery,
the water too deep, the plants too poisonous . . .

Back at Clodhoddle Cotttage, Arrahaquen's bed was
soft and the sheets were fresh. Through a tinted glass
window an evening glow, dimmed by sheets of rain, gave
faint illumination. Her room was small, furnished with
antique pieces, one of the cottage's ubiquitous pyuter rigs
stacked in a corner. A jug of wine stood on a chair.

She slept fitfully. At dawn she awoke – not refreshed,

but at least not exhausted. Into the tangle of precognition lines at the top of her mind, she let her thoughts move at random, images remembered coming before her mind's eye. As ever, she saw a greened Kray, uninhabited, leaves swaying in the breeze.

All that she felt convinced of was deKray's importance. She knew that deKray was significant. She knew that Westcity would fall before Eastcity. She knew too that violence and pain lay somewhere ahead.

Unfortunately, she could learn little of herself. She received no impressions of Arrahaquen in other climates, nor of Arrahaquen surviving the next weeks. She was an invisible woman to herself, too bound up in her own mental world to separate anything out.

Two strands of thought compelled her: one that she would not survive, that nobody would survive; the other a feeling that some escape route lay awaiting discovery, if only she could unearth it. And only she could. It was, she knew, about understanding. It may have been a coincidence, but Arrahaquen felt that her ability had manipulated her into finding, and living with, Kray's only group still dedicated to understanding.

She tried to remember the day ahead, and felt no danger, so she got up. In the mirror she saw a well-built woman with brown eyes now dark ringed, stretch marks, patches of benign green, and scarlet fingernails. Uttering a short laugh at the reflection, she picked up her clothes and performed the morning's clothes drill, finding nothing. In this house some people wore their undersuits as top clothes; she did likewise.

The outside wall of her room creaked and the roof groaned in sympathy. Arrahaquen froze, knowing the meaning of those sounds.

Downstairs, she described her experiences openly, omitting only what she had seen of deKray and the

Clocktower, for she felt that should be told to him alone. They encouraged her, but she felt that they did not understand her. How could they? She felt alone once more.

26

D eKray did not believe that the ancient noophyte
Silverseed was responsible for Arrahaquen's
vision, suspecting instead that Arrahaquen alone
had created it from her future memory. Following no
deity, deKray preferred to believe in the ability of the mind
and the effort of individuals. Her vision of him exploring
the Clocktower was a description of a real event, not an
imaginary concoction or metaphor. A future awaited him
and he must meet it.

With Zinina occupied he crept out of Clodhoddle
Cottage and slunk up the shattered remains of Buttercup
Street.

It seemed rather futile to ward away evil creatures with
a grass blade reed. DeKray clambered through the bushes,
thorns and vines of Buttercup Street, protected by greatcoat, suit and helmet, climbing over the remains of
collapsed houses in those places where there was no other
passage. Warm torrential rain fell and, ahead, the Clocktower was a black smudge in the night.

Soon Zinina would read his note. He hoped she would
not be too angry.

The dribbles and raindrops on his visor interfered with
his vision, but this close to the Clocktower much of Nul

Street was arrayed with grass and flowers rather than bushes and saplings, so he removed his helmet and allowed the rain to bathe his shaved scalp.

Now he stood out of the rain in the lee of the tower, gazing at its greened bricks and white mortar. Nervous, he wiped his mouth free of moisture. The door, a rectangle of black oak set with bronze, stood a few yards away. Would it be locked?

It was not. The knob had turned. He pushed the door ajar.

He paused, aware of the enormity of his act, trying to forget the many rumours and stories that surrounded this place. It was only the intensity of Arrahaquen's expression as she described what she had seen in the temple of the Goddess that enabled him to lay his Krayan ghosts – ghosts that inhabited everybody's mind – or at least drug them sufficiently for him to explore the tower.

Inside there was light – a bluish light which did not seem to emanate from any source. He stood in a circular foyer, a space the same diameter as the tower. Nothing yet seemed sinister. He popped a menthol sweet into his mouth.

The foyer ceiling was high, arched and groined, fluted pillars reminiscent of stems holding up the various parts. To the rear, spiral steps led upward. There were no windows. The stone here was blue-green, black or grey in places, carved with faces and mathematical symbols, none of which he recognised. DeKray had the sensation of being underwater. He noticed that the floor was bumpy, pale with a carpet of dust, and it reminded him of the fossilised urchins that he had collected as a boy. He imagined that if he swept aside the dust he would see beautiful patterns, but he dared not try such an experiment.

It was much cooler than outside. He looked upwards

again and saw stalactites hanging.

Much relieved that nothing unpleasant had happened, he walked across to the steps. His boots with their stiff soles jerked as he walked over the knobs and holes, once unbalancing him. He fell rather than risk twisting his ankle.

At the steps, he stopped. 'Hello? I am deKray.'

No answer. He waited, however, in case somebody was thinking of one. After a few minutes he began to climb, hands in the pockets of his greatcoat to ameliorate the chill. He paused to turn up the collar.

The second floor was again one circular room, steps at the back, walls indeterminate blue or grey, carved here and there with lines of equations, like grafitti. But unlike the expanse below it was full of machinery and cylindrical tanks, with little of the wall actually visible.

DeKray appraised the machines. They were chunky, oily, and apparently operational, cables running to and from upper floors. Screens indicated the presence of pyuters, and when he made an examination of the displays he realised that before him lay a luminary power unit. He studied the machine tanks; all held water, supplied by ducts descending from the roof.

He considered this. It struck him that a place as isolated as the Clocktower should be self-sufficient – independent of the city. But that assumed it was *meant* to be isolated . . .

Slowly, he climbed the steps.

A bigger change would have been hard to imagine. He stood now in a warm, sumptuous, tube-lit room, steps at the rear, furniture spread Kray-style around the place. There was a lavatory located in a closet to one side and cupboards to the other. From electronic units he could, if he so desired, obtain sterile water, food (all non-perishable, he noticed), even medicines.

'Hello? Is anybody here? I am deKray and I am not armed.'

There was no reply.

'I am a Krayan.'

Nothing. He cast his gaze again over the room. Decor was a clever mixture of Krayan, jannitta and aamlon, the style of each culture limited to its most appropriate objects; so there were jannitta fabrics looking like miniaturised stained glass, made with real gold and silver thread, aamlon musician paintings, Krayan couches with curly sides and carved human feet. DeKray saw that one of these had real toenails, indicating antiquity.

He opened one of the cupboards and found fresh linen. Others contained pillows, writing implements and balls of soap. Clearly the place was meant to be occupied.

He ascended the third set of steps. The fourth chamber, like the others, was one space as wide as the tower with steps on the opposite side. It was filled with pyuters.

Ribbons fell from the roof. Of various sizes, they were strung from spherical memory units, their lower ends connected to a hundred interlinked units arranged in a broken annulus at floor level, the space allowing access to the steps. All except one were switched off, the one exception showing a screen of rainbow static.

Warily, deKray examined the pyuters. There were all sorts; old and new, optical and biological, some even solid state. But it did not feel like a museum. It was a centre in which everything was placed to perform some task.

DeKray went to the active unit and played the dot of a laser scribe over its eyeball. The pyuter activated itself. He looked around, suspicious. There was no dust here, he noticed; but then he caught sight of extractor fans and a thermostat.

The pyuter displayed an opening screen. He ran the scribe over it, accessed some routines, but a sense of distrust held him back, and after some meanderings he decided to explore the rest of the tower before beginning any search.

He mentally divided the Clocktower, deciding that there were two floors left.

He ascended the stairs to the fifth floor and found himself amidst another machine that filled the room, a machine which looked to him like a cross between scaffolding and a jellyfish. The device seemed to have been constructed by melting something else. The dominant impression obtained was one of buoyancy. But he received no clues as to what it was: no screens, no plans, no keys. As he ventured through its excrescences he noticed connections between it and the next floor up. He made for the steps.

He called 'Hello?' again, and again there came no answer.

The sixth floor was the top floor. Immediately he noticed the clock, an illuminated disc as large as him, but reversed. Screens of muslin stretched on wood sectioned off various parts of the floor. He noticed pyuter screens flickering with information. The light was white, emanating from hexagonal panels in the wall.

From behind a length of screen a noise sounded. DeKray stood rigid, listening. He heard tinkles and scratchings, and was afraid.

He inched around the wall. A dais came into view, devices on angle-arms hanging over it like the limbs of a technological mantis. All around stood pyuter screens.

Then he saw a woman, working at a pyuter. She was tall and young, and dressed in a white surgeon's smock. Upon her ears lay head-phones, over one eye was screwed a magnifying lens. She turned and, seeing deKray, took off her headphones with a smile. 'I say, there you are.'

DeKray said nothing in response. There did not seem to

be anything he could say to this greeting. The woman's face seemed familiar, but he could not place it. A surgeon . . .

'Are you compos mentis, dear?' she asked him.

DeKray approached. 'Indeed I am,' he said. Then he saw, as more of the room came into view, another dais attached to the main one, upon which lay a sleeping infant. It was naked and he noticed that it was a boy. He stared for some time.

'He's all right,' said the woman, glancing at the infant. 'He look wrong?'

'No,' deKray answered. He was experiencing every moment as it came, not evaluating.

'Do you have the device?'

'Which device would that be?'

'I say, snap to it, the copper one,' said the woman, forming her hands into a ovoid shape. 'From the grave.' She popped out the eyepiece and pulled the infant's dais towards the main one. They snapped together, as though aware of what they were supposed to do.

DeKray remembered the object he had found in the Cemetery, and pulled it out of his pocket. He proffered it, aware that it would fall out of his control.

'Let's try,' said the woman. She clipped the copper pear into a receptor. The various machines and arms swung into new positions, into a spherical halo surrounding the infant. Now deKray noticed a plastic cap covering the infant's scalp, almost the same colour as his skin, and under that what seemed to be wriggling worms.

'What intentions do you have for the boy?' he asked.

'Testosterone sacs, as planned. They'll last until puberty. We want a huge swing to the right.' The woman paused. 'Goddess, if the Portreeve could see me now she'd have me interrogated.'

She carried on setting up the machines. DeKray

watched, then said, 'What will the sacs do, precisely?'

'Say, you really need to be sure, don't you? We want neuron development to the right, don't we, so there grows a synthesising holistic brain? You can't have holism *and* reductionism. No, dear, the two aren't compatible.'

'Most assuredly true,' deKray replied. 'Molecules make a green thing but there are no green molecules.'

'Indeed, there are not.'

Machines closed on the infant, shuffled around the scalp for five minutes, then drew back.

'It's done,' said the woman. She took the copper pear and put it in her pocket.

deKray, disturbed, moved away from the operating table. 'I do believe that I am looking at myself,' he said.

'You are. By offering yourself the gift of holistic vision you are allowing yourself the insight required to do what you have to do. Though you may not be aware of what it is you have done.'

'What is it that *you* have done?' deKray asked.

'I do not know everything. Nobody does. But I have granted you the ability to understand, on some level at least, the nature of humanity's fate. You are a lynchpin of humanity. You already know you have a connection with the Cowhorn Tower – you are the same age. The Cowhorn Tower, being self-learning, will create itself, just as I – we – this night have created you.' The woman turned to look at the infant. 'Go now and live your life.'

'Why is it that I feel we have met before?' deKray asked.

'What is the past for you may be the future for me. I suspect this may be the nature of the Clocktower.' The woman looked around at the tower walls. 'This place will ever be a mystery.'

'But why are you here?'

'You see, I was once the surgeon to the Red Brigade. A

rather young surgeon, in fact. The problem was that I had
some strange ideas, and the Red Brigade do not like
strange ideas. I believed that humanity could save itself.
The Red Brigade believed they could be saved by *others*.
Exposed as a freethinker – worse, as a freethinker who
dared to explore the mystery of the Clocktower – I was
exiled. My dear, the origins of the Clocktower are too
ancient for any of us to fathom. But its workings ... its
workings ...'

Her story ended. Taking the infant in her arms and
dressing him in a woolly coat, she walked to the stairs.
'I've done my bit. Here, anyway. And don't try to stop me.
I must say, having to walk now all the way up to the
Carmine Quarter really is a *bit* of an inconvenience.'

DeKray did want to stop the woman. But he could not.
He dared not interfere with what he had seen, in this place
of all places. Instead he watched as she bent to pick up
something from the floor – a copper needle, it looked like
– then listened to her clattering down flights of steps, until
the sound was too faint to hear. He stood for fifteen
minutes, gazing at the machinery, turning over the events
that he had observed in his mind. They did not yet make
sense.

And he was tired. Hours of exploration, during which
he had repressed signals from his body, had taken their
toll. With a smile, he remembered the suite on the third
floor. He walked down, withdrew food and water, and
lay on a couch to eat.

He returned to the pyuter room and explored for a
while the data spaces and organisational routines. One
routine in particular struck him – a screen filled only with
a picture of the Cowhorn Tower, its cursor a flashing
copper pear. Every measurement and every detail was
included, even down to the colour of the smooth carpets.
The potential for making the tower lay before him. This

program would learn from its environment as it built. Too tempted, deKray activated the initiation procedure. The screen flickered off, but he knew he had set the routines in motion. He laughed; it was the most sophisticated toy he had ever seen.

He decided it was time to leave. He knew Zinina would be angry. Descending the tower, he buttoned himself up and took the helmet from his waistband, wiping off the smeared green with a tissue. He opened the door, saw night outside, and departed.

He took caution following the back alleys and passages of the Old Quarter. Here, at the bottom of what once were gardens, care was required, for the smallest vibration could detonate the sensitive compost heaps that had accumulated to massive proportions. Scalding compost hurled at velocity could kill.

Back at Clodhoddle Cottage he took off his protectives and boots in the green zone, then went to pour a glass of water in the kitchen.

To his surprise, Arrahaquen awaited. 'I knew you'd be home just now,' she said.

DeKray nodded. 'I have explored the Clocktower.'

She did not seem to hear him. 'You've done something, something vital. I can feel it. Now I know that there really is a path out of Kray. There really is! All I have to do is locate it before we're swept away on the green tide.'

'Really? Mayhap I have assisted you.'

Arrahaquen looked at his greatcoat, frowned, then reached out to touch its lapel. 'Did you know your copper pin has gone?'

27

The machine, now mobile, had been making odd noises. Graaff-lin, believing it to be calling her, had come into its room to kneel and listen. She had been up in the attic, where she now spent much of her time, watching the occasional boat float out to sea, and staring at the Citadel remains, shaped like a gigantic black apple core on its end.

She wondered if her clothes were too dirty for the Dodspaat. She was dirty, too, and her house; but she did not have the energy to clean anything. Physically she was declining, but spiritually she was ascending. She had, for example, realised that there was a strict division between right things and wrong things, and her life was now bent towards continual right, the sort of right her mother had espoused, while anything wrong punished by self-denial. Consequently she had lost a lot of weight, but this she saw as a symptom of her inner sanctity.

The machine sidled up to the door and stood there, six feet tall, glittering and warbling. There was a click. Graaff-lin awaited communication.

It moved towards her, pincer extended. Graaff-lin looked up, watching as the arm was raised, then—

She twisted out of the way. The arm struck her foot.

Razor-sharp sub-pincers whirred like drills. She crawled away, stood, then ran for the door. It followed on its rattling feet.

The door was locked. She turned around.

The pincer extended itself, and swung in a horizontal arc. She jumped out of the way, horrified, knowing that the Dodspaat inside must have been misinformed – must have been told that she was an infidel who had been excommunicated, who considered herself the new prophet, blasphemous heretic who—

'I'm good!' she screamed as the machine closed. Two thin arms with knives attached extended themselves. 'I'm one of you!'

Zzzhing, the knives scythed and razors chopped. Graaff-lin walked backwards around the room, feeling her way around oddments of furniture, keeping her eyes on the machine, unable to think of a way of getting through to it. Perhaps if she threw herself on its mercy . . .

Back now at the door, she tugged the handle, shook it, then jumped as the pincer swung past. The wall sustained a gash.

'Look, it's me, Graaff-lin,' she implored, 'one of you, trying to reach the Dodspaat. You are ready for me, aren't you? Please listen, I'm trying to reach you.'

But still the machine closed, its four short legs clicking as they manoeuvred for better positions. It struck Graaff-lin that this might be a banished Dodspaat. This might be some sort of test.

She looked around the room. Little stood out as a possible weapon; a window pole, perhaps the steel bucket. A pile of damp papers in one corner concealed a spoon.

She grasped the window pole. She felt dizzy and sick. The pole, which had a few weeks ago been of negligible weight, now seemed made of stone. Grunting with effort, she tried a few sweeps. It was heavy enough to do damage, but she did not feel confident.

A knife scythed by as the machine closed on her right side and the wall to her left took more blows. Pincer rotating, the machine closed. She ran to the centre of the room, to a chair, and hit out as it closed. It dodged. For a thing of metal, without jointed limbs, it was agile, like a man bound in metal strips about to escape.

One of the knives flicked past her ear. She ducked, but it whipped down and cut her arm. Blood flowed freely. As she stared at the wound the pincer hit her across the head. The machine closed, a yard away. She jumped back, fell and scrambled away. A knife whipped past her knee.

The pole was lost. The test was difficult. Whimpering, Graaff-lin looked about for help, noticing a socket on the end of a cord. Something crashed into her stomach, something blunt. The machine was almost upon her.

She rolled away and something else cut her leg, making her scream in pain. She grabbed the cord and swung it over her head as she sat, then, with one final sweep, hit out at the machine's top screens. The socket smashed into one. Sparks flew.

The machine tottered, then regained its balance and closed again, sending out the knives. Graaff-lin dodged and gathered the cord. Blood covered the floor and spattered the machine. White sparks darted through the air like spume.

She swung out again, but missed. The pincer extended and struck her across the cheek. She tasted blood. Her shoulder felt damp and warm.

Once again she swung the cord ... and hit. The machine fell on its side. Graaff-lin crawled gasping, wailing to herself, towards the bucket; she lifted it, crawled back and brought it down on the twitching and now almost vertical machine. It collapsed. The knives sprang out, one catching her on the wrist. The pincer swung, but hit the floor. Graaff-lin struck again and again.

With an electronic trill the machine disintegrated, hundreds of fragments spilling across the floor like droplets of mercury, smashing into walls, congregating in corners, whistling and tinkling, glass fragments everywhere. Graaff-lin screamed, dropping the bucket, sinking into the main swarm of chunks. She flailed around and clambered out into a clear patch. Her floor was alive.

Already pieces were recombining. But Graaff-lin was exhausted. She had a vision of herself – her *self* – trapped inside a numb, dead, useless body.

Traumatised into action, she crawled. Not in any direction, but just to move. She bumped into a pile of papers.

An idea: she could wrap the chunks. Grabbing one, she took a sheet and wrapped it ... and then dropped it. It lay quiescent. Crying with relief she grabbed others, wrapping each, until a pile of thirty or so lay around her. But the other pieces were coalescing in the opposite corner. With a cry, she threw the bucket at them. Fragments spilled out.

The race continued. Her arms were lead-heavy, trembling, sometimes too tired to lift. Once, an assembly of fragments that had coalesced behind the chair raised itself, but she threw a book at it and it disintegrated. Exhausted ...

She woke up. She must have lost consciousness.

In the corner a new machine stood, black, slim like a broom, perhaps three feet tall. Hundreds of wrapped fragments surrounded her. The floor was otherwise clear. Graaff-lin knew one final effort was necessary. She took a wrapped chunk and advanced.

Darts flashed by. One caught her in the stomach. It

wriggled of its own accord. She screamed, but pulling it out provided further agony. With little whirrs more darts were flying. Graaff-lin fell, then aimed her chunk of metal.

It hit and knocked the thing over. Darts struck her chest, clinging to her like leeches. She advanced on hands and knees, took the bucket, and smashed the machine. More darts exploded out, one catching her. She crawled away and removed them. Her clothes were thick with blood, both new and old. She crawled to the papers and began wrapping again, not so firmly this time due to sheer exhaustion, but well enough to disable each chunk.

The last one remained. She picked it up and wrapped it.

Consciousness seemed to leak away.

Something had woken Zinina. Thunder? Something was rumbling outside, above the thrum of rain against the roof and the musical tip-tap of drops into buckets arranged around her room.

The walls of the house creaked. That noise worried her.

Then she heard shouts, and people running up and down the stairs. Aware that something was amiss, she woke deKray and dressed in a gown before running downstairs.

'Garden mine,' Reyl said.

Eskhatos appeared. 'It's an attack. Revellers everywhere, I think about twenty. Defence positions, all of you. Zinina, is deKray awake?'

'Yes,' Zinina replied.

'Get him. Find him a gun. Follow Arrahaquen to the defence of the rear. Quickly, child, or we'll be over-run!'

One-handed, Zinina grabbed a heat rifle from the stand outside the rig room then called deKray as he clattered down to meet her. 'Back to the kitchen,' she shouted. 'It's an attack.'

Arrahaquen, from the corridor leading to the back rooms, waved her along. Zinina ran, charging up the weapon and shaking out its sights. Anger surged through her body; she almost relished the chance for aggression.

'Take that side,' said Arrahaquen, pointing to the right window of the kitchen. Reyl was with them, already poking the muzzle of her needle rifle through a port in the door. From her kennel outside, the sweathound Woof howled.

'Shush,' Reyl said. 'I can hear voices.'

They quietened. Zinina hissed at deKray for silence as he ran into the kitchen, then listened. It sounded like a pyuter synthesised voice, but she could not make out the words. 'Any memories to help us?' she whispered to Arrahaquen.

'I thought I had remembered this,' Arrahaquen replied, 'but I thought it was to do with a journey we must soon make. I got confused. This is earlier than I guessed.'

Zinina nodded, aware now that she should not chide Arrahaquen for her lack of precision. Gishaad-lin hurried into the room. 'It's you,' she told Zinina, 'it's you they want.'

Zinina stood. 'Me?'

'Eskhatos says come to the front rig room.'

Zinina followed Gishaad-lin to the front of the house, a feeling of dread within her, for she knew that, if outside there were revellers requesting her by name, this was a matter of life or death; all or nothing. This was her past catching up with her.

Eskhatos told her to listen to sound picked up by the spy statue in the garden. Zinina listened.

'. . . want. It's only Zinina. We know the shouster's in there . . .'

'They want you,' Eskhatos said. 'There's seventeen of them. They detonated the forward land mine. Who are they?'

Zinina looked at the pyuter screen, seeing a few figures huddled in the shadows of the gardens, but recognising no faces. 'I don't know,' she said. 'Somebody from my past I suspect.'

'Why do they want you?'

'To drag me back to the Cemetery,' she said.

'Stay here. We can't afford to admit your presence. I'll talk to them, but I want you here to advise me.'

Eskhatos told the house pyuter to connect her to the sound system of the garden statue. 'Revellers,' she began, 'leave this house at once. The whole garden is mined. You have lost friends, lost shousters, already – we saw it happen. We have you under surveillance. This Zinina to whom you refer is not here.'

There were jeers of laughter and a gun fired one shot into the air. 'We know she's in there,' said the megaphone voice. 'One minute, no-bloom! One more minute and then we scrap-wood ya all.'

Eskhatos frowned at Zinina. 'What do we do?'

Zinina just stood, her mind a blank.

Eskhatos called to Gishaad-lin, 'Go get Arrahaquen and stay with Reyl on the back doors. Get Qmoet and Ky upstairs, and the replica, in case they climb upon the roof. Bring deKray back here.'

Gishaad-lin ran off. 'I can't think of anything,' Zinina said, hardly able to look Eskhatos in the eye.

Arrahaquen and deKray appeared. Eskhatos, the min-ute up, said through the address system, 'Revellers, go home. We are twelve in number here, and none are named Zinina.'

'Duck!' Arrahaquen yelled.

They fell to the floor as an explosion tore plaster and

masonry from the front wall. Arrahaquen, her face pale and with eyes wide, said, 'They've got a laser cannon. Goddess, they must have filched it from under the Citadel.'

'We can't stand up to that,' hissed Eskhatos.

'I'm not giving myself up,' Zinina said, retreating from them.

'Wait,' Arrahaquen said, pulling her back and drawing her close. 'I'd fight for your life, Zinina. Listen, have these revellers ever seen you since you left them?'

'Not that I know of,' Zinina replied. Another laser cannon burst shattered brickwork upstairs.

'They must have followed you back from the Cemetery after releasing deKray,' Arrahaquen said. 'It's the only connection.'

'I am rather afraid that I did mention your name,' deKray said, 'not knowing the consequences of my deed.'

'*Shush*!' Arrahaquen demanded. 'It was very dark,' she told Zinina, gripping her by the shoulders, 'and there were three of you – deKray, Qmoet and you. They wouldn't have seen much of you ...'

'So? So?' Zinina snapped.

'We'll dress the replica in your clothes and send her out. It's our only chance.'

'What? But she's taller than me.'

'We'll do it,' Arrahaquen insisted, letting Zinina go and turning to Eskhatos. 'Eskhatos, they might not recognise her. Zinina was young when she left the Cemetery.'

'It'll have to do,' Eskhatos replied, flinching as the house took another hit. 'Arrahaquen, run and get Zinina's clothes. Zinina, call the replica then come straight back without delay.'

DeKray coughed. 'You are sending that valuable pyuton to certain death,' he said. 'Is that reasonable?'

'Shut up,' Zinina told him as she ran to the stairwell and shouted for the pyuton.

DeKray was not to be silenced. 'What will happen when they kill the pyuton?' he continued. 'There will be no blood.'

'Idiot,' Zinina said. 'Revellers only shoot and cut other people, street people. They've got strict codes on blood letting. They won't slice the pyuton, they'll tie her to the ancestor pole then bury her alive. Now shut up.'

Arrahaquen returned with Zinina's leggings, boots, shirt and protectives. The replica donned them, then ran with Arrahaquen and Zinina to the outer door.

Zinina took hold of the pyuton and breathlessly instructed her, 'You're to be me, right? If they catch you, you stay silent – you swore an oath to the green woman to shut up, right? Green woman. You don't say anything else. Now get out and run, try to hide from them. You've got to escape, run . . .' Zinina almost ran out of inspiration. '. . . Go to deKray's old place. Now go!'

They pushed her out of the door, then bolted and barred it and returned to Eskhatos in the front rig room.

'What are they doing?' Zinina asked.

'They've all just run away,' Eskhatos said.

'They only wanted me,' said Zinina, 'they weren't interested in you lot at all. See, they've got codes of honour.'

'Quiet, young lady,' Eskhatos said. 'We are far from safe. I want you to go down to the cellar and fetch every last mine we have. Arrahaquen, you and Reyl and Ky will go out and re-mine the garden.'

The Holists kept a continuous guard. In the back of Zinina's mind – and, she presumed, everybody else's – was the thought that Clodhoddle Cottage had been identified as an occupied house, and that meant perpetual danger. Also, it had been damaged and could not last.

Arrahaquen kept to herself, desperate to unravel the

significance of deKray's discoveries inside the Clock-tower. Ever more intensely the Clocktower dominated her visions of green devastation and the creaking sounds of vegetable growth. She knew that their future was bound up with it.

28

Kray attacked relentlessly. Clodhoddle Cottage, already suffering a disintegrating roof and sinking foundations, seemed to fail like a patient too old to take medicine. Walls sucked up water as if they were made of card, paint and plaster peeled, and creaks resounded; all ominous signs that never ceased. The city had taken the Holists' home into its green fist.

Arrahaquen's composure too began to fail. She looked pale and drawn. Dark rings circled her eyes, her lips were swollen from ulcers, her infected fingernails ached, and the green rash that she had never been able to shrug off now disfigured much of the left side of her face.

She told Zinina, 'I seem to sense something happening from within.'

'Within the Holists?'

'Maybe. But I'm so taken up with trying to remember how to escape that I've no feel for anything else. It's very difficult.'

Zinina nodded, aware through common empathy of the strain Arrahaquen was under. 'If we can do anything to help,' she said.

'Escape is so close, yet an eon away,' Arrahaquen said, dream-like, as if Zinina had wandered off. 'I just can't quite remember it. DeKray has done something . . .?'

Zinina led Arrahaquen to her room, settled her in a comfortable chair with a goblet of dooch, then left her.

Another day passed. Torrents of rain began to sweep over Kray from the sea, and daylight hours became dark as evening. Lamps and tubes were never turned off inside Clodhoddle Cottage. The storm struck in waves; shrieking wind, whipping rain, thunder, even showers of hail. Ball lightning shot up and down the remains of city streets. The final clearance had begun.

On the second night after the attack of the revellers events happened that shook the Holists to their core.

Zinina's first knowledge that something was wrong came when Qmoet woke her during the night. 'Zin, get up quick,' she whispered. 'Leave deKray here. Hurry up.'

Zinina put on her gown. 'What's up?'

'Bad. Very bad.'

They hurried downstairs. 'What?' Zinina insisted.

'Reyl and Gishaad-lin have gone.'

'Gone?' said Zinina, horrified. 'Dead?'

'We don't know.'

Eskhatos, Ky and Arrahaquen were standing by the hall green zone. The five robotic carriers – the bird-legged jacqana – lurked nearby. 'Zinina,' Eskhatos said, 'Reyl and Gishaad-lin have departed the house. Do you know anything about it?'

'No, Eskhatos,' Zinina replied, letting her face show her shock. 'Where have they gone?'

Eskhatos looked at Arrahaquen. Arrahaquen looked exhausted; Zinina knew she suffered terrible insomnia. 'I can't be sure,' Arrahaquen said. 'It's too cloudy in me, but I think the boats . . .'

Realisation struck Zinina. 'You mean, they've taken to the sea?'

Eskhatos nodded.

'We're going down there now,' said Ky. 'You in?'

Anger bubbling, Zinina replied, 'Yes!'

Ky, Qmoet and Zinina dressed in protectives, checked their weapons, then turned to face the others. Arrahaquen was too tired to come, Eskhatos too old. A feeling of dread stole over Zinina as she realised that, excepting her sleeping man, this might be the last remnants of the Holists: an old woman, an exhausted pythoness, and three tired commoners. Zinina, not given to speculation, suddenly perceived that this really could mark the end of everything. Including her life. Trembling with apprehension, she said, 'Well . . . let's go. Weapons charged?'

They departed the house. Cod Row was choked with vegetation, which they struggled through, but Mandrake Street, leading to the Sud Bridge under which the Holists' boats should be bobbing, was under water for almost its entire length. The rain, warm and yellow, poured down. They had to wade along the street's edge, climbing ruined houses occasionally, torches on full power to ensure they did not get entangled in reeds or tendrils. It was a dreadful, desolate journey.

They turned off all light upon reaching the bridge. Climbing down to the river, they saw, as they peeked around the nearest brick arch, that no boats remained. Shocked, Zinina just stared. Nothing there.

'Look,' Ky said. 'Bootprints.'

Zinina hurried over to the mud in which Ky stood. Two sets of bootprints showed what had occurred. The pair had divided, taking a boat each.

Horrified, all Zinina could do was mutter, 'They've split. Reyl and Gishaad-lin have split.'

'The cowards,' Qmoet added.

Burdened by loss, they trudged back to Clodhoddle Cottage. 'Do you think they're at sea now?' Zinina asked.

'They must be,' Qmoet replied, holding her hand.

'I can't believe it.'

Later that day, a meeting took place. Because it concerned Arrahaquen they left her to toss and turn in her own room.

A mumbling, half-asleep Eskhatos presented her case. 'We must support Arrahaquen as much as we can. All other escape routes are closed to us. It's a fragile hope, you know, for Arrahaquen is, well, untested, if you see what I mean.'

'Unreliable,' Ky supplied.

'Arrahaquen says to us all,' Eskhatos continued, 'quite plainly I might add, that she is on the brink of some discovery... I must confess, I'm rather losing hope. I just like to doze, these days.'

An especially loud creak ran through the house. 'And the house won't last,' Ky said. 'The back rooms are crumbling.'

'Yes...' Eskhatos murmured. To Zinina she looked half dead. It seemed a final symbol of defeat, for Eskhatos had founded the Holists and had been its driving force.

'We won't give up,' she said.

Arrahaquen remained in her room, visited by Zinina and Ky to offer water and food, and comfort. She appeared so deep inside her own thoughts that she was becoming a zombie. Zinina had to push away mental images of her becoming catatonic and dying.

Zinina talked with deKray in their room. Thunder rumbled and rain battered the roof. Tubes failed, only lightning flashes illuminated them.

'DeKray,' she said, 'if it comes to it, and Arrahaquen

can't save us, I want us to die together.'

'Do not speak so morbidly,' deKray replied. 'We will live through. Mayhap we will join the temple of the Goddess for a few months after all, and over-winter in their abode.'

'No, this is the end,' Zinina said. 'I can feel it. Everything's dying, everything's splitting up. So I want us to die together. I couldn't bear to be without you.'

'I will not hear of it,' deKray said.

A loud crack made them jump. 'Was that thunder or the house?' Zinina asked him.

'I fear it was—'

Another crack sounded and they felt the floor of their room shift. Zinina stood, terrified. 'Pack your stuff,' she said.

A third crack sounded, louder than both the others, and Zinina saw the outer wall sag. 'Run!' she shouted.

They ran, waking Qmoet on the way. Eskhatos and Ky were already awake, and they met Arrahaquen on the stairs down.

'Run,' Arrahaquen cried, 'the house is falling.'

Eskhatos was too confused to issue orders, so Ky took over. 'Zinina,' she said, 'get water from the cellar, deKray get food. Qmoet, get tarpaulins then kit replacement stuff. Arrahaquen, get clothes and protectives.'

The house groaned and shifted as they ran. Into the pelting rain Zinina sped, crates of bottled water in her left hand; then she ran back, dodging slates falling from the roof, ducking as a piece of guttering slid down a wall, clattering down to the cellar then returning with more water. Ky had put Eskhatos into a chair and covered her with an umbrella; Woof she had let loose. As Zinina ran with her fourth lot of water, she saw the jacqana striding on their long legs out of the side door. Over the noise of rain and thunder she heard a rumble, a groaning crackle

as of wood giving way, and then the rear of the house fell
to the ground, showering rubble and dust across the rear
yard. Zinina screamed as it fell.

'Look out!' somebody cried.

Zinina turned, unsure who had shouted.

She flinched when an object swung in front of her.

And lost consciousness when it hit.

Later, the priestesses arrived at the camp they had set up
at the lower end of Cod Row. But only two of them.
Tashyndy told their tale.

The storm had splintered the temple and eventually
crushed it. Surviving priestesses, acolytes, worshippers – a
score, no more – had crawled from the wreckage. Arvendyn had perished.

Led by a wounded Taziqi they had floundered south,
through terrible swamps, jelly-infested lakes and barbed
lianas thrashing in the wind. Most did not survive.

The group had divided after crossing the river. An
acolyte had led all but six north, hoping to reach the
ancient Galactic Port. Taziqi had succumbed on the way
to a bladderblade in the ankle. A second had fallen inside
a folding pitcher. The other two had been clawed in thigh
and belly by cats.

Arrahaquen stared at them both. 'Just you and
Maharyny left?'

Tashyndy nodded. 'We failed, Arrahaquen.' Staring at
the sky, fists white-knuckled, she continued. 'We failed
because our vision failed. What is the Goddess but a
symbol of the Earth? We have been kneeling as suppli-
cants before our own destruction, worshipping green
death, death handed out impartially by a force from
which consideration of humanity has long since vanished
... if it was ever present. And as for the future, that, as
should have been clear to us, is green. Green water, green

slime, green leaves. Green grass.'

Both Maharyny and Arrahaquen were weeping.

'Green grass. I am the final Kray Queen. If I am our symbol of fertility, am I destined to be the Goddess's murdered daughter?'

'I don't know,' Arrahaquen said, 'I don't know, I don't know.'

But she almost knew. Through watery eyes she gazed north, to where, behind banks of cloud and rain, the Clocktower lay.

DeKray surveyed the scene before him. It was utter desolation. Under a fifteen-foot tarpaulin erected using poles of wood lay Zinina, wrapped in battery-heated blankets, unconscious; Eskhatos sat nearby, exhausted and too bewildered to be of any help. The others sat like him at the edge of the tarpaulin, Arrahaquen gazing out to sea, Qmoet playing dice with Ky, the two priestesses sitting hand-in-hand, heads bowed. The five jacqana circled the tarpaulin as though hunting for seeds to eat. It was so dark they flitted in and out of sight. Woof sat and howled mournfully.

The rain pelted down from black clouds. Their few remaining goods lay in the jacqana baskets or in crates at the edges of the tarpaulin. Streams pouring down the alley made new rivers and rapids around them. Everything was soaked.

He wondered if this was the end. They had nothing left: their house and their security, most of the remaining supplies ... and their hope. He had lost his love – for he knew Zinina would soon die in the cold. He wondered if he ought to return with her to his old house and there make an end of it.

The rain pummelled their tarpaulin. It sprayed from trees and from ruined houses to either side. Two rivers to the sides of the alley carried slime, debris, and occasionally a dead animal down to the sea.

From here, deKray could see the sea; a glowing stretch was visible between the last two houses of a little alley off Cod Row. Somewhere out there floated Reyl and Gishaad-lin, unless they had drowned already.

He looked north. Out there the replica must be dead, tied to an ancestor pole – for the revellers would have returned had they discovered the pyuton's true nature.

He looked at Zinina's blanched face. She had lost too much blood. They had injected her with their last syringe of nano-coagulant. But, though it had stemmed the spurting flow, her skin and her gums were white, and she remained comatose.

Was this what his life had come to? All those books he had collected, all that knowledge he possessed? He could not believe that it would all be lost. And yet it was nothing compared to the greater loss, the loss of humanity's knowledge, which had lain, for the most part, in electronic media under the Citadel. That tumulus now consisted of black shards hundreds of yards high.

Eight people remaining. Everything else had been washed away by Kray, and by time.

Woof howled without ceasing.

29

Arrahaquen sat under the tarpaulin, gazing into Zinina's face. They had endured a foul night after the collapse of Clodhoddle Cottage. It was early afternoon now, but dark as night under a wild sky. Arrahaquen had not slept for three consecutive days and nights.

Torrential rain swept along Cod Row. DeKray and Ky had improvised sheets at two edges of the tarpaulin to protect them from the weather coming in off the sea, but regularly these were torn away by the wind and would need resetting. Everything was soaking except inside Zinina's blanket roll, which they sealed with polythene and rubber compound from the kit spares.

DeKray sat beside Arrahaquen, pointlessly trying to light a cigarette. The others were playing dice. She turned to him. 'You've told me all you can about what you did inside the Clocktower? You've not missed anything out?'

'With sincere honesty,' he answered, wringing his hands, 'I remember few details now. It was a dream for me, a bizarre experience. I handed the copper ovoid over, I watched the surgical operation, I toyed with the pyuter systems. There was nothing else.'

Arrahaquen looked into his eyes. In such dire condi-

tions he must surely be telling the truth. She knew now
that the Clocktower was the heart of Kray's desolation,
and she knew that deKray had changed the city by
entering and experiencing that awful place. But how? And
to what end? As she sat and pondered, the wind whipping
through their makeshift tent, she decided that they must
go there. They must. And when they were there, she
would know what to do.

'There was food and water in the tower?' she asked for
the third or fourth time.

'Arrahaquen, believe me,' he said, taking her by the
hand, the intensity of desperation in his voice, 'please,
please believe me. I am working with you. The place is
self-sufficient. It has power. Some comestibles and water.
Soap and towels, for goodness' sake. It is surely better
than this ruination.'

'We must go. You tell them. I dare not.'

DeKray stood up, and Arrahaquen stood at his side.
'Holists and priestesses,' he said. They looked up from
their dice game, except Eskhatos, who was somehow
managing to sleep. Woof threw him a melancholy glance
without moving her muzzle. 'Holists and priestesses,'
deKray repeated, as if unsure of what to say. He unwrapped a sweet and swallowed it. 'Some days ago I under-
took, on my own behalf, to penetrate the Clocktower.'

'What?' They stared at him. 'What?' Tashyndy and
Maharyny chorused.

'I entered—'

'You entered that place?' They stood and confronted
him.

Arrahaquen moved forward. 'It's true. I remembered
him doing it – before he did it. He went and explored. I
believe him. Listen, Ky, Qmoet – wake Eskhatos, for the
Goddess's sake – we have to go there.'

Arrahaquen noticed the black lines of cloud, blacker

even than those pelting rain over them, that were piling in off the sea. 'Look!' she said. 'We're being driven out to die. We must go to the Clocktower—'

'What about the Temple of Balloon Love?' Ky interrupted.

Arrahaquen answered immediately, confident of her insight. 'Wrecked! It's no shelter and it's too far. If anybody remains there they'll soon be flooded out. Listen to me, listen. I am a pythoness. We must go into the Clocktower and shelter there. DeKray's seen abundant water and food inside.'

Eskhatos was now awake. 'The Clocktower?' she said.

It was essential that Eskhatos be converted; if Eskhatos refused to go there, Ky, and probably Qmoet, would too. Arrahaquen knew that she must exert all her power for leading these three people. Deep down, because of their hopelessness, they needed to be led ... they *could* be led, if she was convincing enough. She alone possessed the vision.

'Eskhatos,' she said, 'it's our only chance. Where else can we go?'

'You mean ...' Eskhatos began, and Arrahaquen had to strain to hear her faint speech above the din of the storm, 'you mean that boy's been in there? How?'

Arrahaquen ignored her words, saying, 'We're going now, Eskhatos. It's safe and warm inside.'

'Safe? But it's the Clocktower. Nobody goes in there.'

'We are.' Arrahaquen stood, and told Ky, 'Get the jacqana ready. DeKray, stow these boxes on them. Qmoet, you and I will carry Eskhatos. We're going.'

They hesitated. Arrahaquen moved to pick up two poles that could be used to raise Eskhatos's chair.

'We *can't* go in the Clocktower,' Ky said.

'Why not?'

Ky fretted. Her glasses had long since been lost, and she

peered myopically at Arrahaquen. 'It's haunted.'

'Do you believe in superstitious stories? You, the holistic synthesist? What will it do, eat you? It's a tower, for the Goddess's sake.'

'I'm not going,' Ky said.

'Come along,' Eskhatos said, managing to shout loud enough.

'*No.*' Ky stood firm.

'I'm going,' Qmoet said, choking either with emotion or from the rain slapping across her face.

'We'll follow you, Arrahaquen,' said Tashyndy, taking Maharyny's hand in hers.

Ky refused to budge. 'Then we'll leave you,' Arrahaquen shouted, letting her anger burst out, 'and you'll rot forever in this dead alley! Come on, Qmoet, lift.' They lifted Eskhatos and began to move up the alley. DeKray lifted Zinina. Woof lolloped and the jacqana skittered behind them.

Arrahaquen knew Ky would follow. As they reached the top end of Cod Row, and forged through the knee-high rapids pouring off its surface, she ran up to them and cursed them in some foreign tongue. 'This will never work,' she told Arrahaquen. 'How can we survive? It's madness!'

Ky was close to tears, her face screwed up and red as a tomato. Arrahaquen said, in the bluntest tones she could muster, 'Follow us or die. And if you must die, at least do it without bothering *us*.'

Ky said nothing, but helped deKray carry Zinina. Arrahaquen knew she had for now overcome their fear of the Clocktower.

'DeKray,' she called, wiping the rain from her mouth. 'DeKray, we'll have to go around the Citadel, then up Malmsey Street. To pick up Graaff-lin.'

'Very well,' he shouted back. 'And then up Ash Lane to the Clocktower?'

'Yes.'

They struggled on. The rain beat down upon them with a ferocity Arrahaquen had never known. It was almost too dark to see, but only deKray and Ky possessed working torches. Fighting branches that whipped against them, slipping constantly in the slime and because of the torrents pouring down Mandrake Street, they moved north, until the remnants of Judico Street lay before them and, to their left, they could just make out the last remaining vertical promontories of the tumulus.

'Left turn,' Arrahaquen called.

Judico Street presented them with further difficulties; out of the tumulus ruin acidic streams flowed, yellow rivulets laced with black, that made their boots steam. They had to follow a line of thorny bushes to the side of the street, slipping in mud and stamping down the occasional poison iris, and then climb over destroyed houses at the end of the street. The Citadel Wall stood firm in places, pincers and tentacle optics writhing, but here and there it crumbled under acid attack. The stench made Arrahaquen's throat ache, and everybody else cough.

By the time they had struggled around the tumulus and reached Malmsey Street they were exhausted. 'Let's rest awhile,' Arrahaquen said. They stood under a dwarf oak, reducing a little the amount of rain that fell upon them; but the noise of thunder and rain against leaves made it difficult to communicate.

'We'll start up Malmsey Street,' Arrahaquen told them, 'then turn into Onion Street. At Ash Lane, deKray and I are going to fetch Graaff-lin. Would you come with us, Qmoet?'

'If I must,' she replied.

Arrahaquen thanked the Goddess in the privacy of her mind that Qmoet was a realist. She could have been stubborn, like Ky, but perhaps experience made her more flexible. Arrahaquen turned and examined the gentle rise of Malmsey Street up ahead. Trees flailed in the wind; she could see no clear route. They would have to fight their way through. But it did not feel impossible.

'What shall I do?' Ky asked.

'Keep the jacqana together, and make sure nothing falls out of their baskets. Help Maharyny with Eskhatos.'

Tashyndy seemed to sense Ky's tension. 'We'll do what you say,' she said, making sure no words were lost in thunder.

Arrahaquen felt pleased. The priestesses were her superiors in every way. Their acquiescence to her gave her confidence, and she began to believe – *really* believe – that they might yet reach the Clocktower, despite the violence of the storm opposing them. She looked out into the maelstrom of rain. Kray was making a final effort to kill them. It was eight human beings against the Earth.

She turned to Ky, who was gulping alcohol from a hip flask. Now her face was as pale as a moonflower. 'My ability as a prophet is young,' she said, 'and I don't know what's to become of us. But I *am* the pythoness.'

With that, Arrahaquen led on, a tired Qmoet at her side. She looked back to see that deKray and Tashyndy had improvised a stretcher from a piece of door that had floated past them. DeKray was explaining that Zinina must not be jolted, because of her wound, and in response Tashyndy produced a tiny bottle, no larger than her thumb, and managed to administer most of its contents, stroking Zinina's throat to induce the swallowing reflex. This brief act seemed to make Zinina's survival more secure in Arrahaquen's mind.

Slashing the serrated tops off bladderblades, they moved on. Nothing could be seen of the street's sandstone, though a few ruins stood to either side, hidden for the most part by screens of hawthorn, wild palm, and scarlet thistle. From the street itself grew strangling ivy and thorn-buckets.

Something rumbled up ahead. 'Was that thunder?' Qmoet said, stopping. Arrahaquen listened. Another rumble.

'Probably,' she said, pulling her hood away from her ears in an effort to reduce rain noise.

'Look out!'

Ahead, a wave of water bore down, taller than any of them, surging down the street. Arrahaquen turned to yell a warning. DeKray and Tashyndy managed to pull Zinina to a tree, but Ky and Maharyny were left exposed.

The wall of water knocked Arrahaquen off her feet. She screamed and clutched at the trunk of a sapling.

Green water poured over her. She caught glimpses of black, grey, green.

Something heavy hit her, swept down by the wave, but she managed to hold on. She heard voices.

The wave subsided. Spluttering, Arrahaquen tried to stand, but managed only to crouch on her knees. She saw Eskhatos's chair on its side, Ky and Maharyny beside it staring down the street. Eskhatos had been washed away.

There was no time for a search. A river waist-high still swirled downhill. Some temporary dam uphill, probably a building, must have burst. Eskhatos would already be out of reach.

'Come on!' Arrahaquen yelled back to them, as they stood rooted to the spot with horror. 'Come on! She's dead.'

Pulling Qmoet out of the surging flood, she gesticulated to the side of the street, where, thigh-deep in rapids, they were able to clamber uphill. Leaving the white water behind them, they waded through the knee-deep brown rivers of upper Malmsey Street. It was then they noticed

one of the jacqana was missing – also washed away. Woof
had survived, however, her loose skin soaked black, her
doleful face flecked with foam.

Arrahaquen blanked the shock of losing Eskhatos from
her mind and tried to focus on events ahead, but it was
hopeless. The struggle simply to survive took all her
concentration. They fought on. Behind her, Maharyny
and Ky took cases from the jacqana so that their journey
was made easier.

They reached the junction with Onion Street. It was a
pit of hawthorn and briar that they had no option but to
climb around, balancing precariously on old walls and the
remains of houses, until they stood gathered in the
channel of ferns and ivy that constituted Onion Street.

Something exploded. Arrahaquen shut her eyes and
grimaced automatically, then looked. One of the jacqana
had blown up, red sparks flying everywhere. The effort
had been too much. 'Maybe water got into its brain,' she
suggested.

'We must rest here,' Tashyndy said.

'Five minutes,' Arrahaquen replied, 'no more. This city
is doing its best to kill us by attrition. The longer we wait,
the more danger we'll face.'

DeKray came close. Into her ear he said, 'Do you think
we'll make it?'

'Yes,' she replied. 'How are you bearing up?'

'I shall survive. The Clocktower is our goal, it must
be.'

Arrahaquen nodded, patting Woof on the head as she
trotted past. 'You're the only man,' she said. 'We need
you.'

He actually laughed. 'A fertile man in Kray. It is almost
an impossible thing, is it not? Am I meant to be here?'

'I thought you didn't believe in destiny and all that
nonsense?'

He shrugged. 'In times like this we are reduced to our most basic selves.'

Arrahaquen chose not to answer. The others were ready. They strode out into Onion Street, deKray taking over Qmoet's hacking duties. Arrahaquen studied the black clouds overhead. Was it her imagination or was it becoming chilly?

It was hard to avoid the feeling that they were the last people alive on Earth. Arrahaquen knew that somewhere, perhaps in the Cemetery, perhaps in the remains of the Felis temple, or at the reveller encampment around the Infirmary, people might still survive. But they had no hope. Nobody unprotected could survive this. Only she, the plans of the Holists shed like superfluous skin, could find a way out.

She turned her thoughts to deKray. He was a man, perhaps the only one remaining. He was fertile. If there was any hope, perhaps it lay with him. It was he who had dared to enter the Clocktower.

She turned her thoughts to the priestesses. They represented a life she had longed for, yet had been denied. She was glad they had not decided to fight their battle inside the temple.

By the time they had completed most of the struggle to Ash Lane, a further problem presented itself. The Old Quarter – they were traversing its southerly sector – consisted around here of narrow lanes without side-alleys, many leading down from Kray's most ancient Market Square, and these now acted as channels for mud. Ahead, Ash Lane was hidden under turbid lakes.

'We'll have to climb around those,' Arrahaquen said.

'Ash Lane may be impassable,' Qmoet warned.

Arrahaquen ignored this point, although she suspected it to be true. 'Qmoet, ready your kit. DeKray, you're coming with us.' She instructed Ky and the priestesses.

'Stay here and don't move, whatever happens. We'll never find you if you do. We'll be no more than two hours. If we're not back by then, Tashyndy and Maharyny, you come and look for us. If you can't find us, go on to the Clocktower.'

'We expect you to return,' Tashyndy said. She handed over to Arrahaquen a cotton pouch with something heavy inside.

'What is it?' Arrahaquen asked.

'A sensory adapter. If you need help in communication, put those on, like headphones.'

'I possess a night-optic,' deKray added, pulling from his kit a battered old monocular.

Arrahaquen nodded, bade them goodbye, then led Qmoet and deKray along the fern-choked alley that she hoped would take them into Pine Street. It presented no danger, being merely slippery and causing them falls, but at its end it was flooded and cut off by a single, grossly distended claw-bladder, which they had to puncture from a distance with a dagger on the end of a pole. The thorny skin they managed to climb around.

Pine Street, blocked on all sides, was deep in flood. 'We'll have to swim across,' Arrahaquen said, 'then take a passage off Hog Street down to Graaff-lin's place. Ready?'

Tightening the clips of her kit and repositioning the elastics over her boot-tops, Arrahaquen waded into the water. Although the current was strong, the street was narrow and she was able to swim across to the far side. Gripping the head of a submerged statue, she turned to see that deKray was already across and Qmoet just behind. 'Swim down here,' she shouted, the din of rain against the choppy water almost drowning her out. 'There's a blocked alley. Come on!'

Arrahaquen climbed on to the pile of bricks, refuse and

leaf debris that blocked off the alley, grabbing deKray as he floated past and dragging him up. The alley behind was only knee-deep in water, though it looked infested with grubs and stinging pods. DeKray caught Qmoet by her hood ties.

Attaching a point to the end of her kit's telescopic pole, Arrahaquen first tested the alley floor, then jumped down. With deKray similarly armed at her side, they burst pods and smacked aside grubs and anaconda-leeches, until they stood on almost firm ground at the junction with Graaff-lin's alley.

'There's her house,' deKray said, pointing through the downpour. Lightning briefly illuminated the scene. The gardens all around were flooded, but Arrahaquen thought they could struggle through, following Graaff-lin's own path.

They waded down the alley, able now to see that the river beyond had burst its banks. A few frogs croaked at them, and they noticed a sodden cat, which Arrahaquen shot though it already looked half dead. She led them around the front of the house, and into the porch and hammered on the front door. 'Graaff-lin, it's Arrahaquen and deKray!'

No answer. There was a small porthole beside the door. Arrahaquen stood on tip-toe and peered through. She saw a figure on the floor, amidst piles of paper – a figure armed with a long-nose rifle. Automatically she ducked.

'What?' deKray and Qmoet asked simultaneously.

'She's armed. Long-noser pointing right at me!'

'Go away!' came a faint voice.

'Graaff-lin, come on. We've got almost no time left—'

'Leave me alone!' Graaff-lin replied.

Arrahaquen hammered the door again, angered. 'Just open up,' she called. She twisted the handle and shook the door, but it was locked, and probably barred or bolted. 'Open up!' she yelled.

'Get out of here, heathens!'

'Couldn't we force an entry from the back?' Qmoet asked.

'She'd hear us and fire,' Arrahaquen said. 'We could get in, yes, but she might just shoot. She sounds mad.'

'We cannot simply leave her,' deKray said.

Arrahaquen hammered the door once more, her hands bunched into fists. 'Open *up*!' she shouted.

DeKray turned away, as if to hide his emotional reaction. Qmoet's face was set in a grimace.

'Leave me alone,' Graaff-lin repeated, over and over.

'It's hopeless,' Arrahaquen said, taking both by the shoulder and hugging them to her. 'We're wasting too much time. We've got to get back.'

'We cannot leave her,' deKray said, his face screwed up with despair.

'No choice,' Arrahaquen said. She pushed them out of the porch. They had to leave: quickly. The diversion had been a waste of time. They needed to make the Clock-tower as soon as possible.

They ran back to the river at Pine Street, but saw that it would be impossible for them to return the way they had come. 'We'll have to go up to Onion Street, then past the Dead Spirits temple,' Arrahaquen said.

The alleys up to Onion Street were passable, but the street itself was choked with poisonous ferns, some the deadly variety armed with hollow needles like nettles. By slashing a path through they managed to fight their way down to the temple, but the effort required was great, and Arrahaquen's arms ached fit to drop by the time they were through. The rain beat down, its noise overwhelming.

The Dead Spirits temple was a wreck. A few walls stood upright, but the building had collapsed in on itself and already the tops of saplings poked out. Corpses lay under rubble on the cracked alabaster steps. They hurried past.

Welcomed by the others as they returned, Arrahaquen first took a stimulant tablet – three left in her last bottle – then described what had happened. All were stunned. Everybody had assumed that Graaff-lin would want to join them. Losing her seemed to set them back, and Arrahaquen felt their despair. 'Forget it,' she said, roughly. 'Time to move on. Get packed, get those jacqana moving. Come on!'

But Ash Lane proved too difficult. Mud surged down, carrying rubble and exploding fruits. Having toiled for a hundred yards, Arrahaquen conceded defeat and ordered a retreat. But as quick as she thought of it, she outlined her new plan. 'Back up to the Dead Spirits, around the back, then up Tode Lane up to Market Square.' No dissension: Arrahaquen turned and led the way.

DeKray was pounced upon by a dog as they turned into the lane surrounding the temple. Ky shot first, but missed; Arrahaquen, at his side, shot next and hit. The starving hound yelped and limped away. DeKray was badly bitten on his arm, hand and thigh; they pooled kit resources and administered antibiotics and an antiseptic pad, before bandaging his wounds. But worse was to come. They had not moved on before the wall to their side, separating the temple's own alley from Tode Lane, collapsed. Tashyndy, Ky and Maharyny were cut off, though little injured, and had to spend precious minutes climbing mounds of rubble to rejoin the party.

Arrahaquen urged them on. Tode Lane was muddy, in places dangerous because of potholes, but they managed to reach Market Square. Qmoet tripped and fell, spraining her ankle. The street was crumbling below their feet.

Then hail began to fall. The speed of its descent caused Arrahaquen to quail. It struck them like so many tiny bullets, and her face became numb from the attack. She could hardly open her eyes.

Tugging them individually through the briars and nettle clumps of the square, she and deKray ensured all were through before running, bent over for protection, back into Ash Lane. Hardly able to shout over the noise, Arrahaquen ran along the single line – pressed against the ruins of houses – then led them on, up the gentle climb towards the Clocktower. Soon she hoped she would see it; once they had passed Salvia Street, perhaps only minutes away, they were as good as there.

With a crack the street gave way. Maharyny toppled backward. A subterranean channel had disintegrated and the priestess lay flailing ten feet below. Fungal bodies like silken cushions flopped upon her. Before anybody could even think of rope she was smothered, one twisting leg visible; then nothing.

The fungus shivered. Water and hail began to fill the pit.

Distraught, Tashyndy tried to climb down, but Arrahaquen and deKray held her back. 'It's too late. She's dead.'

Arrahaquen dragged her away from the still cracking pit, hauling her like a sodden mannequin up to where the others stood.

Tashyndy paused for a moment to pray.

They stumbled on. Ash Lane vegetation was beaten to shreds, but the hail was worse. She could see no further than twenty yards ahead.

And then, as she passed a gap in the rubble to her left that marked Salvia Street, she saw a tall shadow – the Clocktower. 'There!' she yelled, shaking Qmoet out of the trance that had enveloped her. 'There!' she cried to deKray, pointing.

Lightning flashed. 'I see it!' Qmoet shouted, her face transformed.

'Where?' deKray shouted. 'I can't see it.'

Arrahaquen urged them on, waiting for the other pair to catch up. 'It's up there!' she yelled to each in turn and it seemed that they redoubled their efforts, though Zinina weighed them down. One of the jacqana had not made it; two passed by, their bodies clanging in response to the hail. Woof seemed close to collapse. Arrahaquen grabbed her by the scruff of the neck and tugged her on, following the trail in the hail left by the others.

DeKray had stopped to wait for her, letting Qmoet go on alone. 'I do not see it,' he yelled into her ear.

'Up there!' she replied, pointing. It was quite clear, now, a hundred yards off. She could see the luminous orange clock-face at its top.

'Where?'

Shouts behind her. She ignored them.

'DeKray, what can you see?'

'Hail—'

A laser beam flashed by. Arrahaquen jumped, then fell, caught off balance. None of her group carried lasers.

DeKray slid and fell. Arrahaquen turned and thought she saw shadows running from behind a low wall leading to the Clocktower yard.

Tashyndy and Ky, who possessed no weapons, were on their stomachs. Arrahaquen pulled her needle rifle from its holster, aimed, and fired at random. She could not see Qmoet.

A beam flickered in front of her face, momentarily blinding her.

DeKray yelled at her side and shouts came from up ahead. The attackers were running, sliding everywhere.

Arrahaquen aimed and fired a salvo. One fell.

'Get her! Get that one!' chorused shouting voices.

Another beam from a new direction: a green beam.

Somebody screamed. Woof yelped.

'Watch out!'

Arrahaquen tried to dig herself into the slurry of hail-stones for cover. She aimed and fired at a shadow but, just after she pulled the trigger, realised it was Ky. She screamed and jerked her rifle away.

But Ky had fallen.

'Fire!' a voice shouted.

From the right: 'Get down!'

A series of needles flew past her face. She ducked. Somebody fell close by.

'Now!'

Another laser beam.

Shout to her left: 'Run!'

One attacker's laser blew; a flash like lightning, then sparks. Arrahaquen saw a writhing silhouette, aimed, and fired off a whole cartridge of needles. The rifle stank of burnt oil.

Another red flash; a scream.

She reloaded. Woof yelped again, and this time it sounded agonised. Something exploded near the yard wall.

Arrahaquen had no idea who was down or who was up. Everybody was hiding or out of it. But she dared not rise, or shout.

A figure groped its way towards her.

There was another massive explosion at the wall, its flash as bright as lightning. Was it a laser?

Somebody fell at her side. Arrahaquen jumped, and twisted around ... but it was only Qmoet. 'One of them left,' she gasped, pointing. 'Fire!'

Seeing nobody, Arrahaquen risked all. She got to her feet, crouched, then ran helter-skelter away from the Clocktower. She tripped over a body and fell.

'There!'

A shadow stood. It did not seem familiar.

No option but to shoot. Arrahaquen twisted and fired. The shadow screeched and fell.

Somebody emerged from the hail ... it was deKray. Blood-soaked, he staggered to her side. 'Revellers! They all dead?'

'I think so!'

Shielding her eyes from the hail Arrahaquen tried to count survivors. 'To the Clocktower!' she yelled at de-Kray.

He grabbed her. 'But I still do not see it!'

Arrahaquen snatched his arm and pulled him along the street, making for the brick courtyard that surrounded the tower.

'Where?' deKray yelled. 'Where?'

Horror gripped Arrahaquen as she looked into his staring eyes and realised that he really could not see it. Pulling him through the others as they slipped, slid and fell around the yard, she forced him on.

'There!' she shouted at him.

He seemed panicky. 'All I can see is but a yard!'

She pulled him by the arm right up to the wall and slammed his hand into it. But he was unaware of what she had done.

Somebody jumped from behind the tower. Arrahaquen flinched and saw a rotten reveller face with distended lips and staring eyes.

It raised a laser and fired at deKray.

He toppled backwards into the hail. Arrahaquen discharged the rest of her needles into the creature. It fell back.

Frozen, Arrahaquen stood, rifle nozzles smoking.

Red hail was all around.

Screaming for help she sank to her knees, pulling

deKray around so she could see his face. He did not move.

Shaking him, she screamed and screamed.

Tashyndy careered over, tripping and falling at her side. 'God*dess*, he's dead,' Arrahaquen said. There was red water around his body.

'Can't be,' Tashyndy said. She thrust Arrahaquen out of her way back into the hail. Tashyndy ripped away his upper clothes, then groaned and looked away. There was blood everywhere. The brief glimpse Arrahaquen got before Tashyndy wrapped him again was of a mangled chest.

Desperation woke her. She screamed out, lungs bursting, 'To the tower! To the tower *now*!'

She crawled back through the hail. Qmoet appeared beside her. 'Bring everybody!' Arrahaquen shouted.

She crawled on. Earth's every energy tried to halt her.

Now at the Clocktower door, she stood and turned the handle, then kicked the door open. Inside, pale blue light illuminated a stony chamber.

Tashyndy tripped over the sill and collapsed into the chamber, crying out. Qmoet hopped over, then also fell.

Arrahaquen yelled, 'Where's Ky? Where's Zinina?'

'Is Zinina safe?' Tashyndy called back.

'Just Ky, Zinina, the dog—'

Arrahaquen, almost blinded by the hail, turned around and slid away from the tower, tripping over another body. Then she saw Woof, lying still, her head blown away.

She slipped and slid around the yard.

Tashyndy ran to her. 'Ky ... there! Help me pull her in.'

Arrahaquen staggered over to Ky's prone body. Needles buried in her chest, her clothes charred, her face scarred. They pulled her to the door.

Ky's body went limp. Arrahaquen looked down and knew that she was dead.

She and Tashyndy held hands, gripping tight. 'Where's Zinina?'

'Over by the yard wall?'

They slid over, finding Zinina. Crawling, they dragged her back to the door. Ball lightning shot along Nul Street. Forked lightning struck the wall. The detonation threw them aside.

Arrahaquen recovered her balance, and began dragging Zinina to the door. Qmoet tried to tug her inside, but lacked the strength.

Arrahaquen jumped in, but tripped and fell. Tashyndy stumbled into the tower.

Only Zinina left. She lay half in, half out of the Clocktower.

Arrahaquen was too exhausted to move.

Tashyndy slapped her face. 'Pull her in!'

Arrahaquen couldn't. It was too much.

She heard voices calling out. Zinina was pulled inside. Somebody slammed the door shut.

30

Green city.
    To the north, nothing remained except piles of rubble indistinguishable from natural outcrops of rock, covered with moss and grass, hidden by bush and tree, dark green, emerald, olive, occasionally yellow or white in the summer rain. Northern plains were criss-crossed with animal tracks. Through these uplands a river passed, flowing towards cliffs, becoming a waterfall, then flowing on until it met the glowing sea.

Further south, ruins stood like teeth in a skeleton, green with algae and red with rust. West of the river, a verdigris-covered tower stood unchanged by the plants. East of the river stood a slimmer tower. In the far south there rose a single tongue of black plastic, dotted here and there with birds' nests. In these flowered, colourful places, butterflies fluttered, great quantities of them produced by the heat and the profusion of nectar. There were tiny meadows filled to bursting with cowslips, ferns, hogweed, and also with nettles and docks boasting leaves as large as a water lily's.

Southern parts remained flooded, slime and algae slapped across brick and stone, covering floods with scum. Here and there tiny leaves showed where other

plants had found a roothold. Insects swarmed across these
turbid pools and lakes, mosquitoes and daddy-longlegs,
flies and boaters. Beetles swam. Larvae choked the
multitude of growing spaces. In Eastcity there was a
plague of fleas. Food was plentiful.

Eventually, when the meat provided by the year's glut
of corpses became too bad to eat, the hawks and vultures
departed for further fields. Time passed by. Leaves took
on bright colours, red and yellow, orange and brown,
while animal life, particularly in the south, burst into new
living spaces, caves once houses, vaults once cellars, eyries
and ledges.

Gases bubbled from fermenting vegetation while from
rotting things anaerobic bacteria produced more.

A great production of seeds ensued. From all types of
plant seeds of every description grew; hard brown cases
on some, the size of rats, small black motes on others.
Whole pastures were transformed into white down, rising
like smoke at the touch of a breeze. These pastures were
undisturbed by human footsteps. In other places, especially near the Gardens, some plants produced purple
fans, small glittering daggers, arrays of blunt pins.

As the year progressed, the fruit dropped or rotted or
was eaten and burrowed into by insects; great green wasps
with lethal stings, also spiders and the occasional bee.
Squirrels harvested and, on the ground, deer and rabbits,
dogs and foxes enjoyed the spree.

To the south, water-plants produced their fruits, to be
consumed by fish and insects, voles and weasels. The
stinking pools merged into stinking lakes, so thick in
places that even a wind could not disturb their glutinous
surfaces. In other areas these pools were alive with insects
and grubs.

The temperature began to fall. Rain abated into showers. Floods settled and the remains of buildings began to

show through, already eroded by weather.

Soon green was muted, especially in the south. In the north, grass plains and bogs expanded, the bushes and trees growing among them bare and brown, and whipped by the wind. Hibernating animals began preparing their hides. Birds flocked in high places, many using the extended horns of the verdigrised tower, others clustering around fallen pylons and the mounts of solar mirrors now crumbling into rust. In dense flocks they waited, until internal calls sent them flying across the ocean.

Snow fell. Frosts froze over the floods, encasing dead leaves and living tendrils in ice. Cracks and snaps from rock and brick resounded through the city, and buildings were flattened. Snow settled on the ruins and cracked branches.

In the north, deer foraged; also rabbits and badgers, and even an occasional bear. Birds of prey wheeled overhead, many with new white plumage.

Southward there was little movement. The ice ponds and lakes were quiet. Elsewhere, robins and sparrows fluttered, and there were rustlings under the snow and debris from scavenging voles and hares, stoats and mink. To the east, cat families foraged far and wide, hunting with their envenomed claws, scrabbling through the snow, padding, backs arched, along the remains of sandstone walls and across precarious roofs.

More snow fell. Ice stalactites clothed the city, often encasing within their lengths rotten plant material. Huge drifts built up in those few alleys and streets left as such. More buildings collapsed as more snow flurries danced through the air.

And then, as spring approached, there were hints of new life.

Arrahaquen awoke.

She found herself lying on a couch. She was warm. Her toes and her fingers ached. Her face ached. Her eyes ached.

She sat up. Around her, in a sumptuous room, were her friends.

Tashyndy and Qmoet sat together, the Kray Queen engaged in some ritual of the Goddess with green circles drawn around her.

Qmoet gazed at Ky's kit, a part of which lay in her hands.

Zinina lay on another couch, also wrapped but in her own sheets.

Two jacqana – one missing a leg, the other its basket – lay immobile nearby.

'Where are we?' she said.

Qmoet ran over. 'At last you're awake. We're still in this place. You've been out almost an hour.'

Arrahaquen looked over to Ky's kit.

'She is dead,' said Qmoet, nodding.

'I think I shot her—'

'Don't blame yourself,' Qmoet said, intently. 'Ky was probably killed by a laser shot.'

'Who were they?'

'Revellers.'

Arrahaquen lay back. 'They must have been looking for shelter in the only place left standing. But they would never have entered.'

'Will we be here for ever now?'

Arrahaquen did not answer. Tashyndy had come to stand at her side. 'Is Zinina still alive?' she asked.

'Her wounds haven't reopened, thank the Goddess,' Tashyndy said. 'I think she might be recovering. Her breathing is faster, her pulse quicker.'

Arrahaquen felt numb to everything. Her ability to pull precognition lines and arrays from the top of her mind was defeated here by exhaustion and a sense of cloying uncertainty, like a fog rolling in from some uncharted, inner sea. Inside the Clocktower an hour had passed; inside her mind, weeks seemed to have dragged by ... dark weeks.

Suddenly, a wave of emotion caught her. It was like submersion in hot water. She had never felt her self-possession smothered so vigorously. A fit of sobbing took hold. Vision blurred, she wept, her body gasping, though she could feel Tashyndy holding her steady. Heat suffused her.

Images of the foyer entered her mind, though they were devoid of real people and populated mostly by shadows, as though she had forgotten that others depended upon her. All that existed for her was the fountain of grief, of awe, swirling around the foyer in a vortex, herself at the centre. She felt Tashyndy's strong arms hugging her and heard her voice calling, 'Arrahaquen, what is it?'

It was like a lifeline. Tashyndy's face appeared.

'Is she still with us?' Qmoet asked.

Hot, salty water stung her cracked lips, moistened her mouth. Her constricted throat and heaving chest tried to produce more words. Once again she was submerged into grief.

'DeKray's dead,' she said at last.

'Yes, he is.' Tashyndy sat at her side, and hugged her once more. 'Somebody shot him.'

'He's lying outside, dead.' Arrahaquen could not bear to see in her mind's eye the awful image.

How could she explain to them what he had done? His sacrifice was to trigger the building of the Cowhorn Tower. The copper pear he had given to the surgeon Myshelau had contained the building's genetic code. DeKray may have been fertile, but the human seed which would be stored in the Cowhorn Tower would ensure the survival of humanity. What use would Kray have for a fertile man? He hadn't been able to see the Clocktower because he was no longer part of Kray's future.

Arrahaquen, with a final flood of emotion, understood that she was the vehicle of salvation, while deKray was its source. She knew that those secrets that died with him were lost forever.

'This tower is our escape,' she said. 'Tashyndy, how did the Cowhorn Tower look when you left your temple?'

'The Cowhorn Tower was as strong as ever,' Tashyndy replied.

Arrahaquen stared up at her. 'Was it?'

'Why, yes.'

Arrahaquen felt sudden excitement. She tried to get up. Her body would not remain still. 'It is out there now, awaiting us!'

'Calm yourself,' Tashyndy said. Qmoet tried to hold her down.

'No! We've got to get down to the foyer again, right now. We've got to leave.'

'Leave?' they cried. 'Back into the storm?'

'The storm is over.'

She stood, and, though it pained her, hobbled to the steps. 'Quickly,' she said. They glanced at each other, at a loss. '*Quickly*!'

Tashyndy and Qmoet looked doubtfully at one another. Moments passed. Arrahaquen stood firm. They stood as two groups in opposition.

'I don't like it,' said Tashyndy. 'We can't go into the storm again. We'll die.'

'Trust me,' Arrahaquen said.

Again the pair eyed one another. Tashyndy said to Qmoet, 'What do you think?'

'I am past thinking,' Qmoet sighed, tears falling down her cheeks.

Tashyndy pondered. Arrahaquen knew that here lay the final decision. 'I am the last Kray Queen,' Tashyndy said. 'I represent the women of Kray—'

'But not the people!' Arrahaquen said. 'DeKray was a man.'

'But you said he was not part of us.'

'He is part of us in that what he did saved us. He unknowingly sacrificed himself for our future. You must follow me, for what he did means we can live.'

Qmoet walked over to where Arrahaquen stood. Tashyndy stood firm.

'Come on,' Arrahaquen said.

Silence. The tower walls broadcast nothing of the weather outside. Still Tashyndy stood, her head bowed, her eyes closed.

'I can't do it,' she said. 'You said this tower was our place of salvation. How can we leave it?'

A voice from behind them.

Arrahaquen stared. 'Zinina!'

She was barely conscious. 'Go with Arrahaquen,' she repeated, 'go with her, go with her.' Her pale hands fluttered around the sodden blankets.

Again Tashyndy closed her eyes. 'I'll go,' she said finally.

Without delay Arrahaquen turned, allowing Qmoet to help her downstairs, while Tashyndy carried Zinina as best she could. The jacqana staggered behind.

They ignored the machines of the second floor and made straight for the main door.

Arrahaquen sobbed without hope ... without reason. Her body felt as weak as it had ever done. Hands – she could not tell whose – held her upright.

'Now!' she cried.

Qmoet flung open the door.

Bright sunlight made her wince.

Pulling their few remaining satchels, they all stumbled out of the Clocktower.

Arrahaquen, unable to see, fell to the ground. She smelled grass. It was warm.

'It's going!' Qmoet gasped.

Arrahaquen turned and, fingers shielding her eyes, looked up at the Clocktower. She could see sky through it. Blue sky.

It faded . . .

Then vanished.

Arrahaquen got to her feet. 'It's gone forever,' she said. 'It doesn't exist in this time.'

'This time?' Tashyndy queried.

'The Clocktower has propelled us over the end of Kray. This is the future. This was what I couldn't remember all that time. I think the noophytes remembered some of it, too, but they didn't want to be part of it.' Arrahaquen surveyed the land all about. Kray, and yet not Kray.

They stood near a shore. A blue sea was dazzling, with brilliant flecks of light where the sun reflected off it. Behind them, hills rose to gentle peaks. The sky was pastel blue, with white clouds. Judging by the sun, it was early afternoon.

'Look.' Arrahaquen pointed to the sky. 'The Space-flower's gone.'

'Look over there,' Tashyndy countered, pointing north.

Arrahaquen looked.

'Is that the Cowhorn Tower?' said Qmoet.

It seemed so. Far away, across a bubbling river, Arrahaquen saw a dark building. It stood in roughly the right place.

'It is,' she said. 'I told you! It's there for us. It's why deKray couldn't come with us.'

They walked across fields to the Cowhorn Tower. Used

to the terrifying fecundity of Kray, they were at a loss in this pale, tame land. The grass seemed paltry, the bushes small and the trees, without their usual threat, seemed tiny and stunted. Arrahaquen looked around her and wondered how anything could grow so feebly.

As the sun set, stars began to appear.

They were thirsty and hungry. With only eleven bottles of water unopened, they knew they would have to drink river water. For some time the taboos created by life in Kray stopped them, but Arrahaquen, taking the lead, let them watch as she cupped her hands in the clear, cold water, and drank. Then she took off her clothes and bathed. The others followed suit, even Zinina.

Food was more difficult. They had saved a few boxes. Arrahaquen knew that soon a life almost as difficult as that of Kray would begin, for they would have to forage, just as the first women of the human race had done.

Zinina stood at the cliffs. It was midnight.

Her life had been dislocated. Already, though only half a day had passed, she had wept a week's tears for deKray. A part of her lay unburied, rotting, who knew how many years in the distant past.

And the world around her was strange.

When Arrahaquen came to stand by her, she said, 'Almost everything I knew has gone.'

Arrahaquen nodded. 'Our friends. Our city.'

'We're not the only ones starting again,' Zinina said. 'Your Rien Zir's been reborn, don't you see? The old Rien Zir's gone – the violent, poisonous one. Now we've got a gentle daughter.'

Arrahaquen said nothing.

Zinina gazed out over the sea. 'We can stop running, at last.'